continued . . .

Real Vampires Get Lucky

"Let's just say, if you know what's good for you, then you'll check out *Real Vampires Get Lucky*." —*Romance Reviews Today*

"Another humorous chapter in Glory's life that will not disappoint." —*Romance Junkies*

"Gerry Bartlett delivers another winner . . . Ms. Bartlett's gift for humor, the bawdier the better, is evident throughout, and the different story lines are interwoven seamlessly to give the reader a thoroughly entertaining read. Fans rejoice—this one's a keeper!" —*Fresh Fiction*

"Fun, fast moving and introduces some wonderful new characters, along with having plenty of familiar faces." —*Romantic Times*

"A laugh-out-loud series. Ms. Bartlett puts a different spin on the vampire romance. Fast paced with appealing characters you can fall in love with. It's like visiting old friends." —*Night Owl Romance*

Real Vampires Live Large

"The return of ancient vampiress Glory surviving in a modern world is fun to follow as she struggles with her lover, a wannabe lover, vampire killers and Energy Vampires; all want a piece of her in differing ways. Fans of lighthearted paranormal romps will enjoy Gerry Bartlett's fun tale starring a heroine who has never forgiven Blade for biting her when she was bloated." —*Midwest Book Review*

"Outstanding." —*Fresh Fiction*

"A laugh-out-loud book that I couldn't put down. *Real Vampires Live Large* is a winner." —*The Romance Readers Connection*

"Glory gives girl power a whole new meaning, especially in the undead way. What a fun read!" —*All About Romance*

Real Vampires Have Curves

"A sharp, sassy, sexy read. Gerry Bartlett creates a vampire to die for in this sizzling new series."

—Kimberly Raye, *USA Today* bestselling author of
In the Midnight Hour

"Hot and hilarious. Glory is Everywoman with fangs."

—Nina Bangs, *New York Times* bestselling author of
My Wicked Vampire

"Full-figured vampire Glory bursts from the page in this lively, fun and engaging spin on the vampire mythology."

—Julie Kenner, *USA Today* bestselling author of *Turned*

"Hilariously delightful . . . Ms. Bartlett has a winner."

—*Fresh Fiction*

"A sexy, smart and lively contemporary paranormal romance . . . The plot is engaging, the characters are stimulating (not to mention, so is the sex), and the writing is sharp. Glory St. Clair is . . . a breath of fresh air." —*Romance Reader at Heart*

"If you love Betsy from MaryJanice Davidson's Undead series or Sookie from Charlaine Harris's [Sookie Stackhouse novels], you're gonna love *Real Vampires Have Curves*."

—*A Romance Review*

"Nina Bangs, Katie MacAlister, MaryJanice Davidson and Lynsay Sands, make room for the newest member of the vamp sisterhood, because Gerry Bartlett has arrived."

—ParaNormalRomance.org

"A real winner. Bartlett brings a fresh spin to paranormal chick lit with this clever combination of suspense and humor and wonderful style. Hang on to your seats—this book is a wild ride!"

—*Romantic Times*

Real Vampires
Have More to Love

GERRY BARTLETT

BERKLEY BOOKS, NEW YORK

THE BERKLEY PUBLISHING GROUP
Published by the Penguin Group
Penguin Group (USA) Inc.
375 Hudson Street, New York, New York 10014, USA
Penguin Group (Canada), 90 Eglinton Avenue East, Suite 700, Toronto, Ontario M4P 2Y3, Canada
(a division of Pearson Penguin Canada Inc.)
Penguin Books Ltd., 80 Strand, London WC2R 0RL, England
Penguin Group Ireland, 25 St. Stephen's Green, Dublin 2, Ireland (a division of Penguin Books Ltd.)
Penguin Group (Australia), 250 Camberwell Road, Camberwell, Victoria 3124, Australia
(a division of Pearson Australia Group Pty. Ltd.)
Penguin Books India Pvt. Ltd., 11 Community Centre, Panchsheel Park, New Delhi—110 017, India
Penguin Group (NZ), 67 Apollo Drive, Rosedale, North Shore 0632, New Zealand
(a division of Pearson New Zealand Ltd.)
Penguin Books (South Africa) (Pty.) Ltd., 24 Sturdee Avenue, Rosebank, Johannesburg 2196,
South Africa

Penguin Books Ltd., Registered Offices: 80 Strand, London WC2R 0RL, England

This is an original publication of The Berkley Publishing Group.

This is a work of fiction. Names, characters, places, and incidents either are the product of the author's imagination or are used fictitiously, and any resemblance to actual persons, living or dead, business establishments, events, or locales is entirely coincidental. The publisher does not have any control over and does not assume any responsibility for author or third-party websites or their content.

PRINTING HISTORY
Berkley trade paperback edition / December 2010

Library of Congress Cataloging-in-Publication Data

Bartlett, Gerry.
Real vampires have more to love / Gerry Bartlett.—Berkley trade pbk. ed.
p. cm.
ISBN 978-0-425-23697-0
1. Saint Clair, Glory (Fictitious character)—Fiction. 2. Vampires—Fiction. I. Title.
PS3602.A83945R4285 2010
813'.6—dc22 2010037205

PRINTED IN THE UNITED STATES OF AMERICA

10 9 8 7 6 5 4 3 2 1

For Gloria McDowell Rae,
an original Glory with lots of spirit
but definitely without the fangs.

Acknowledgments

It always takes a village to make a book happen, but this one more than usual. I wouldn't have a career without my brilliant agent, Kimberly Whalen. I certainly have to thank the patient and very talented senior editor Kate Seaver for really saving this book, and the amazing staff at Berkley for their support. I especially appreciate my copy editor, Mary Pell, who keeps track of the series and manages to remember EVERYTHING when this author certainly doesn't.

I'd be nowhere without my loyal readers. My amazing fan sites are run by two dedicated ladies—Danielle Garrett and Heather Weygandt. I can't thank you enough. And my Facebook friends keep me smiling. Love the comments.

My first readers are always the talented Nina Bangs and Donna Maloy. I couldn't do it without you guys, and haven't we come a long way?

So you can see my village is more like a small town. Soon I'll have to start paving the streets. So maybe I can get the book in faster next time. If only . . .

One

"Would you quit walking around here naked?" I'd tolerated the smell of coffee and—much, much worse—baking cinnamon rolls, but I'd be damned if I'd watch my new roommate eat and drink wearing nothing more than a damp towel.

"Why, Glory? Is the sight of my bare chest getting to you?" Rafael Valdez licked white icing off one fingertip, and my fangs stabbed through my gums.

"Listen. I've put up with your marathon showers until there's no hot water left for mine. And your cooking smells." Oh, great. Tears. But was it fair? Rafe's a shape-shifter with a shifter's insatiable appetite. He'd spent nearly five years stuck in dog body acting as my bodyguard. Now he was staying in hunky human form and was no longer at my mercy for his menu. Who knew he was a gourmet cook? Maybe popping open a can of sweet rolls wasn't gourmet in some books, but I knew nirvana when I smelled it.

He polished off roll number six—yes, I'd been counting—then stood. I would *not* notice the towel flapping open. He strolled over—flap, flap—to lay a gentle hand on my shoulder. Someone in this apartment was making a trip to the nearest discount store to get jumbo beach towels tonight. Since Rafe obviously didn't care who ogled his family jewels, that someone would have to be me. Serve him right if I bought hot pink Hello Kitty. Let him strut his stuff in that.

"I'm sorry, Glory." He smiled, his dimples showing.

It was still a shock to see Valdez as a human hottie. He'd been a cute dog, usually a Labradoodle with wavy black hair. Still had the thick curly locks, with dark eyes to match, but now there was a whole Latin-lover thing going on, complete with those teasing dimples that were an absolute killer where the ladies were concerned.

Not me, of course. We were friends. That's it. V knew way too much about me. He'd been an up close and personal witness to my love life, a tangled mess at the moment. And he'd listened to me wail ad nauseam about my issues. Which were numerous. I'm even afraid he knows my deepest, darkest secret—the number when I step on a bathroom scale. I'd been through a weight-loss experiment recently and had a feeling he'd peeked. I mean, wouldn't you if your best friend weighed in mere feet away?

"Forget it, V. I'm a mess. Doesn't take much to set me off these days." My voice cracked. Oops. Was another meltdown coming? Personally, I was sick of myself. Made some tough decisions lately, and regretted at least one of them almost instantly.

"No, Glory, I've been an ass. I get it. Vampires can't eat. I know what it's like to crave what you can't have." He pulled me into his arms, and I felt weepy enough to actually lean into him. Damn those cinnamon rolls. Out of a can, but still.

"It's just that they *smell* so good." And he looked so fine. And felt so warm and strong and . . . I sucked it up and pushed back. "We need to get some things straight here." I didn't have to glance down to know that, hello, part of him was already headed in that direction under the stupid skimpy towel. Nice to know Mr. Tall, Dark and Shifty wasn't immune to my dubious charms.

Oh, who was I kidding? I still had on my shapeless Snoopy

nightshirt and hadn't combed my hair since yesterday. It was probably his breakfast Rafe was excited about.

"Yeah, well. It's your place. But I've got to eat." His dimples were showing again as he headed back to sit at the kitchen table. "I'll scarf these down, then spray some air freshener. Will that make you feel better?"

I sighed and collapsed on the couch. "It would make me feel better if you put on some clothes. And, excuse me for noticing, bought some underwear."

"Whoa. Guess I *am* getting to you." He laughed. "Cut me a break. I spent years naked inside a dog body. No wardrobe necessary." He dragged a finger through a puddle of icing and licked it clean. Tormentor. "And I've never been too crazy about underwear. But for you, I'll deal. Shopping's just low on my priorities right now. I've been trying to get this nightclub off the ground."

"Yeah, how's that going?" I picked up my bottle of synthetic blood. Yawn. Not even my favorite type. Because my fave is expensive. And Glory St. Clair is always on a budget.

"Not great. Everything costs more than I thought it would. So today I finally caved and called an old friend. She has plenty of money and likes the club scene. Unfortunately, knowing Nadia, she won't be a silent partner." Rafe picked up his empty plate, rinsed it off and set it in the sink.

"Nadia? Is she a shifter too?" Even the name sounded exotic.

"Vampire. I worked for her back in the seventies. She's got bars and nightclubs all over the world. Austin, Texas, in general, will be a new scene for her so she's coming tomorrow to scope it out. If she likes what she sees, we'll strike a deal." Rafe plopped into a chair across from me.

Oh, he did not just flash me. I stood and stalked into the kitchen to rinse out my glass bottle. We recycle.

"Good luck with that. Now I'm going down to the shop. Up here we need some rules. You've got to shower during the day while I'm conked out in my death sleep. The hot water heater here is only good for one shower a night, and I have a feeling you just took it." I strode over to the bathroom door, figuring the cold shower I'd get was what I deserved with these instant replays of leaning on the almost naked Rafe in my brain.

"Sorry. My body clock's still on vamp time. Work all night, sleep all day, but with one eye open. You know?" Rafe got up and sauntered over to face me.

"Right. You went way above and beyond what any paycheck required to protect me." I kept my eyes on his. Otherwise, I'd be checking out that truly great chest just inches from my nose. Didn't help that his scent was as familiar as my own. Hey, Valdez the dog had slept on the foot of my bed for *years*. One inhale and I felt safe and close to the best friend I'd ever had.

"We're even. You saved my furry butt a time or two." He grinned. "Like from a crowd of energy-sucking psychos."

"We'll *never* be even." I couldn't smile about that memory. He'd almost been killed by a group of vampires who'd been trying to get to *me*. "I'll always be grateful to you. But you're off the payroll. And I've got to learn to deal without a bodyguard now. We're friends. Roommates. So sleep with both eyes closed, buddy. You deserve that."

I admit that, while I was determined to be independent for the first time in my life, the concept freaked me out more than a little. But I'd told my overprotective maker and long-time lover, Jeremy Blade, to give me my space. That included no more freebies like the twenty-four-seven security he'd provided for the past, oh, four hundred years. Stupid me had even turned down the chance to stay in Hollywood and play house with the amazing rock star Israel Caine.

Sure I'm insane. But that's me. Now I was out to prove that I could stand on my own two feet. In cute shoes, of course. The fact that I'd cried myself to sleep ever since I'd come back from Hollywood was just me being stupid.

"You deserve to be safe. How I sleep is my business, Glory. Don't stress over it." Rafe put his hands on my shoulders. "And get this, lady." He stared down at me, suddenly serious. No sign of a dimple. "Yeah, I'm your friend, and I'll always protect you if I see the need, with or without a paycheck."

"You shouldn't—" I blinked when he backed me up to a wall.

"I don't take orders from you anymore. Right?"

"Right. Rafe, what's the deal?" Compared to my vamp sub-human temperature, his body was almost hot. I inhaled again, but this time instead of "safe" I got a sizzle of something I hadn't expected.

"The deal is I've watched you with Blade and Caine, and I figure there's a reason you won't commit to either one of them." He moved his hands from my shoulders to my neck, his thumbs doing funny things to the skin behind my ears.

"Uh." I shivered, absolutely speechless for once.

His grin was slow and knowing. "Don't worry, Glory. I'm not going to rush you. But one of these nights I'm going to end up in your bed again, and it's not going to be lying at your feet."

He stepped back and headed down the hall, his towel hitting the floor as he walked into the bedroom and shut the door.

I was left with the image of his perfect taut butt burned into my brain. Dimples there too. Damn.

"Glory, I'm glad you're here. Things have been crazy." Lacy Devereau, my day manager and right-hand girl in the shop, looked me over. "You okay?"

"Fine. Rafe's been torturing me with his cooking again, that's all." I smiled at a customer heading toward a dressing room with a vintage dress over her arm. "Business good, then?"

"Okay, but that's not the crazy part. It's Flo. She's made this place into wedding central. You know I'm one of her bridesmaids." Lacy glanced behind her and lowered her voice. "Stop her, Glory. She's talking about changing the dresses again. I don't care if she is paying. With the wedding only weeks away, they'll never get here on time."

"You're right. I'm on it." I picked up a pile of receipts. The daily take hadn't been too shabby. My vintage clothing and antique store was on trendy Sixth Street, between Mugs and Muffins, a coffee shop owned by a fellow vamp, and a tattoo parlor. The location for Rafe's nightclub was a few blocks down. We weren't far from the University of Texas, and my shop had become a hangout for some of the students. Since I call my place Vintage Vamp's Emporium and my bud Florence Da Vinci, the not-so-blushing bride, had painted a vampire mural on the wall, we were really popular with Goths and vampire wannabes. I'd tried to discourage that at first, then played along, even passing out fake fangs at Halloween.

"Where's Flo now?" I was maid of honor and had finally persuaded my former roomie to go with slimming black and a bodice that would cover a double-D cup. Being a tiny size six herself, Flo really didn't get a full-figured gal's issues with some of the cute little numbers she liked for her bridesmaids.

"I'm right here, *cara*. Come see what I have in the back." Flo had thrown open the door to my storeroom. "You'll love this dress. Purple. Your color. It will look fabulous on you. Jeremiah will take one look at you and—boom!—he's yours again."

Jeremiah. Jeremy Blade. Whatever the hell he chose to call himself this week, we'd parted ways in Los Angeles. He was there, I was here. One of the reasons for my recent crying jags.

"Jerry won't be seeing me." I didn't resist when Flo dragged me into the back room. She slammed the door. I'd told Jerry we needed a break. So we were broken. Sniff.

"I fix everything." Flo hugged me. "He's going to be Ricardo's best man so you two can get back together. *Sì?*"

Ricardo, or Richard Mainwaring, was Flo's husband. They'd been married at a private ceremony, but now Flo a.k.a. Bride-zilla with fangs wanted a big wedding. Her brother Damian was footing the bill, so this promised to be the wedding of several centuries.

"Doubt it'll be that easy, but thanks. I'd have thought Richard would have asked one of his Vatican cronies." Richard is a former priest. Long story.

"Oh, there will be plenty of those guys here. One will be honored to perform the ceremony again, of course." Flo flipped open a magazine and stabbed a picture. "This dress. Cute? No?"

"What's with the manicure?" I couldn't help noticing that each of her nails wore a slightly different color. I lifted her finger to examine the dress under it. It *was* cute. Actually might work on my size-twelve figure, if there was elastic involved. Forget puff sleeves. Made my arms look fat. But Jerry liked me in purple. And loved a low neckline. I had visions of him seeing me walk down the aisle and forgetting all our issues.

"Glory! I said I'm trying out colors for my wedding day." Flo held out her hand. "Which one do you like?"

I focused. Okay. Flo and I compared colors to the fabric swatch from her wedding dress until we settled on "Blush."

"*Es perfecto. Grazi*, Glory." She hugged me again. "I knew you would help me. Now I have another favor. Did you see this?" She pulled a local newspaper out from under her magazine.

"What is it?" I glanced down and recognized the picture. "Ray? He's coming to town too?" Ray a.k.a. Israel Caine. The other man I'd left in L.A. Okay, I admit it. My heart, which barely beats anyway, gave a little jig of happiness. Both my guys, hot vampires who I loved and had decided to give up, were coming to town. Would either of them want to see me again?

Well, Jerry wouldn't have a choice, would he? And Ray? I grabbed the paper. The rock star was singing at a venue at the South by Southwest Music Festival. The festival was held every spring in Austin to give music producers a chance to hear new talent. The article claimed Ray was coming with the owner of his record label, another vampire. Maybe Ray would drop by the shop. I'd been his mentor, and it had only been a few weeks since Ray had claimed he loved me. But then I'd dumped him. Not an action guaranteed to keep his love light burning.

"Glory? Look at me." Flo fiddled with a bottle of nail-polish remover. "That favor?"

"What is it, Flo?" I threw down the paper. How pathetic. I'd been on my own for less than a month, and I was already imagining scenarios where both men were begging for me to come back to them. And then there'd been Rafe's interesting move. Forget it. I'd looked like hell. Surely he'd been playing me, hadn't really meant—

"Glory, quit ignoring me. And blocking your thoughts." Flo frowned and shook my arm. "This is serious, *mia amica*."

I hid my smile. Didn't everything to do with my friend's wedding rank right up there with the desire for world peace and half-price sales? "Okay, Flo, I'm riveted. What's up?"

"Ray, Israel Caine. He'll be in Austin right before my wedding, *sì*?"

"Yes." I didn't like the calculating look on Flo's face. She was blocking her thoughts too. But then she always blocked. Not that I usually tried to pry into them anyway. But this was an emergency. "What do you want, Flo?"

"I want Israel Caine to sing at my wedding, Glory. Please ask him for me. He'll do it for you. You saved his life."

"He's done a lot for me too, Flo. We're even." I frowned down at that purple dress. Six to eight weeks for delivery. But Flo would figure out a way around that minor technicality, probably by throwing money at it.

The major issue? Ray and Jerry at Flo's wedding. The two men hated each other. Because I loved both of them. And Rafe would be there, of course. I'd ask him to be my date. He'd love to jump into a brawl with my name on it. I smiled.

TWO

"**You're** the bride. You want Ray, I'll get him for you." I winced when Flo hugged me a little too enthusiastically. "Easy there, girlfriend. And wait, I have conditions." Gee, I was on a roll laying down the law, now wasn't I? But I'd spent several hundred years being the doormat for everyone else to walk on. Those days were over, thank you very much.

"Conditions?" Flo stepped back and gave me a probing look. I blocked her of course. No way was I letting her stroll through *my* thoughts. Not when she never let me see hers.

"The purple dress. Lose the puffed sleeves. Or go back to the black. And this is the last change. Swear it." I grabbed her shoulders. "Seriously, Flo. I don't know how you're managing to get these dresses anyway, but decide already. Concentrate on the important stuff like—"

"The bachelorette party you'll be giving me!" Flo hugged me again, more gently this time. For someone who'd never been touchy-feely—with women anyway—Flo was being positively mushy.

"You're kidding. Right? What do I know about stuff like that?" I knew enough to not want any part of it. Male strippers. Too much alcohol. I'd seen movies. Watched TV.

"Hah! I see it in your eyes. You know what to do. Get some hunky men to dance for us. Gather all my girlfriends and we'll party all night. It'll be fun." Flo danced around the room. "Maybe you can have it in Rafael's new club."

I bit back a snarky comment. Flo had no girlfriends other than me. She was scraping together *my* friends to get a bridal party. Even the Siren who'd threatened to send me to hell recently was on the list to wear purple. My BFF was all about men and had never bothered to cultivate girlfriends until she and I had bonded over great shoes and designer handbags. I sighed and shook my head.

"Fine, I'll throw something together. At least there won't be alcohol involved. How bad could it be?" I had three weeks. Maybe Rafe's club would be open. Hopefully he'd let me do it after hours and wouldn't charge me. But with a new partner in the picture . . . And male dancers? Maybe a desperate student—

"Glory, not all of my bridesmaids are vampires, you know. Of course you'll serve alcohol. And some of those special treats the EVs make for vampires to eat. Don't worry about cost. I'll pay. I know you can't afford this."

"That's not fair." I realized it was the truth, though. Flo liked everything first-class. I had a coach budget.

"Life isn't fair, *mia amica*. This is my fantasy. So I pay. You be hostess. Send me the bills. We'll have a blast." She grinned and picked up her cell phone. "Now I call and order the dresses. When they arrive, I'll get the seamstress to rip off the sleeves. Yes?"

"Yes. Now I'm running to the store. Rafe doesn't wear underwear. I'm buying him some. And bigger towels." I slung my purse over my shoulder, wishing I'd snagged his credit card.

"Whoa. This is interesting." Flo nabbed me just as I reached the back door. "I get a picture of you and Rafe, that's our Valdez, eh? And him with no underwear. He's a fine-looking human now, isn't he?"

"Sure. You were a better roommate. He cooks, Flo. Tor-

tures me with great smells, then struts around in a tiny towel."
I leaned in. "He's a friend. That's all. But I know how to appreciate a great male body, just like you do."

"Oh, yes. Tell me." Flo licked her lips. "I'm married, not blind."

"He's built. With these cute little dimples . . ." I sighed. "I'm buying him underwear. So he'll quit flashing his butt at me."

Flo arched an eyebrow. "So. A friend who flashes you. Seems he wants you to notice him. And not in just a friendly way. *Sì?*"

"Maybe. But I can't deal with it right now. I've got Blade coming to town, thanks to Richard. And Ray to talk to, thanks to you." I couldn't help it, I grinned. "Now I'm supposed to consider Rafe as a potential more-than-friend? I just can't." Well, I could, but that would make me a megaslut, now wouldn't it? I jerked open the back door. "I've got to go. Tell Lacy I'll be back in an hour."

"Right. And do you know Rafael's size, *mia amica*?"

I grinned. "Thirty-two waist, but otherwise? Extra large, girlfriend, extra large." I heard her laughter as I shut the door. My aging Suburban sat parked in the alley in its usual spot. I had a fifty-fifty chance that it would start. Past time I traded it in and got a more reliable car, but that budget . . .

I was a foot away from it when I realized I wasn't alone. I smelled . . . human. Two humans were nearby. I whipped around, suddenly on high alert. Without a bodyguard I had to be smart. A hell of a lot of bad things had happened in this alley. I stuck my key in the door and jerked it to unlock the old car.

I could hear them breathing as they came closer. Damn this lock. It finally gave, and I wrenched the door open and leaped inside. Overreacting? Maybe, but I slammed it shut and locked myself in anyway. Good thing. The woman dressed in black from head to toe who stepped out of the shadows didn't look friendly. Neither did the large man who stood behind her. In fact, they both had the "Death to all vampires"

glare down pat. I stuck the key in the ignition and turned.
Nothing but clicks. I slapped the steering wheel. Unreliable
hunk of junk.

The woman's fist in a black leather glove hit my side window. I admit it. I cringed.

"What the hell? I'm calling 911. Go away." I pulled my
cell out of my purse and made a show out of dialing. Not that
I would really call the police. Vamps avoid law enforcement.

"I don't think you'd do that, Glory St. Clair." She was pale
with dark hair tucked into her black baseball cap. Her black
leather coat was long and expensive, and I wasted a few seconds calculating the value if I had it in my shop to sell. Nice.
Italian. Small size. Too small for me, that was for sure. She
had black jeans tucked into equally expensive black leather
boots. Okay, so the woman knew how to dress. How did she
know my name, and what the hell did she want with me?
Bonus question: Why did she have a sumo wrestler with her
as backup?

"Who are you? What do you want?" I yelled through the
closed window. "Glory who? Never heard of her."

"I'm Vivien Westwood. And I know you killed my father.
You were dumb enough to leave witnesses alive to tell the
tale. Now I'm here to get revenge." She snarled. Perfect teeth,
of course, but I wasn't exactly shaking in my own Gucci
knockoff brown leather boots.

Come on, vampire versus human in cute outfit? Even
Sumo Guy, who looked like he could bench press my Suburban, would be an easy takedown. I blamed my earlier panic
totally on the men in my life treating me like a helpless female. Naturally I'd fall apart at the first sign of trouble.
Trouble? Yeah, that crossbow Viv had tucked against her
side definitely qualified. So did the stake her buddy pulled
out of his pocket.

Damn. Westwood's daughter. The billionaire techno-
freak had had a thing about vampires. He'd really hated me
and had stalked me until we'd had the last fatal showdown

where I'd killed him with a crossbow a lot like the one his daughter was toting. Self-defense. No jury would have convicted me. Of course a grieving family member wouldn't care about that. I looked her over. Vivien didn't exactly look grief stricken.

"I'm sorry for your loss, but I don't know what the hell you're talking about." No way was I admitting anything.

"You're a freak. My father wanted to wipe out your kind from the face of the earth. I'm taking over where he left off."

"My kind? A shop owner with great taste?" I shook my head. "Get a grip, lady. You've got the wrong freak."

Viv wasn't listening. She nodded at her pal. "Sean, knock out this window."

"No!" I scooted over to the other side as the Hulk reached in his belt for what looked like a sledge hammer. I jerked open the passenger door and put on vamp speed to get out of there. I felt a sting and realized the bitch had shot at me and scored a hit. Damn. I didn't slow down, just leaped over a Dumpster, hearing a clang as Vivien smacked the side of it with what I bet was one of those wooden arrows. I didn't stop, just kept going, grateful for the dark as I ran around the corner and kept going until I found a deserted side street.

My vamp speed paid off, and I'd left my pursuers far behind. To be on the safe side, I jumped up into an old oak tree and straddled a branch. Then I reached back and pulled a wooden arrow from my shoulder. Ouch. Yep, just like her father, Brent Westwood, had used. Rafe had taken one like it in the hip in the same alley. Wooden tip so if it had hit my heart, I'd be history. Nice legacy, Brent. The nut hadn't fallen far from the tree. I took a moment to thank a higher power that Vivien obviously hadn't had target practice lately.

The bark was digging into my backside, and I felt like I was going to hurl if I thought too much about how close I'd come to ending my eternal life. Scoping out the area, I climbed down then took off my jacket, frowning at the hole ripped into the red wool. The sweater underneath was probably ruined too. I could tell I was already healing since wood wounds itch like a son of a bitch. Another Westwood. I could hardly believe it.

Underwear and beach towels would have to wait for another night since strolling into a discount store with blood stains wasn't exactly a low-profile move. I cautiously made my way home, keeping my eyes open for a woman and a not-so-jolly giant, both dressed in black. Geez. Just when I thought my biggest worries were puff sleeves and buff roommates . . .

M**y** blood matched my jacket, but that didn't fool the vampires in the crowd. One whiff and it was fangs down and eyebrows raised for everyone in the back room of my shop.

"You've been bleeding." Richard had arrived while I'd been playing hide-and-seek.

"Yeah, well, I had a run-in in the alley. Still not my favorite place to park." I shrugged out of my jacket, studied the hole, then tossed the thing into the nearest trash can.

"Gloriana, did I hear Richard correctly?" Jeremy Blade, real name Jeremiah Campbell III, stood in the doorway. The storeroom door was ajar, but it took vamp hearing to pick up on our conversation above the oldies station blaring in the shop.

"Hi, Jerry." I was ridiculously glad to see him and realized I was grinning like a kid at Christmas. "The wedding's still weeks away. I'm surprised to see you."

"Don't change the subject. Were you or were you not bleeding?" He frowned, looking strong and handsome in a navy sweater and jeans.

"Yes. Westwood's got a daughter. She was going for the revenge thing with her daddy's crossbow. She got off a lucky shot. No big deal." I tried to scratch the wound that was driving me crazy as it healed, but couldn't quite reach it.

"No big deal?" He marched over to my side and grabbed my shoulders, turning me so he could look at my back. I felt him jerk up my sweater.

"Hey! We have an audience!"

"Don't mind me." Richard sounded amused, until I heard him grunt. I imagined Flo had either stomped on his foot or tested her right hook. "I'm going out to the shop. Florence, darling, wasn't there a piece of jewelry out there you fancied?"

"Yes. And I think you're going to buy it for me." Flo stopped to pat my arm. "Are you all right, Glory?"

"I told you, I'm fine." I winked. "Though I did lose some blood. I feel a little weak. I need to sit down."

"Damn it, Gloriana, this is what comes from going about without a bodyguard." Jerry eased me into a chair as Flo headed out of the room behind Richard and closed the door.

"Relax, Jerry. I handled the Westwood chick. But if you want to help me, please scratch where I was hit. It's itching like crazy." I sighed and closed my eyes when he did just that.

"You said you're feeling weak. Do you need to feed from me?" Jerry pulled up another chair and sat close beside me.

I inhaled and felt my fangs go on Jerry alert. No one did it for me like Jerry did. He'd made me, was part of me. I craved him like plants crave the sun. And of course I loved him too. I leaned against him, refusing to take advantage of his kindness. We hadn't parted on the best of terms. My fault. I wasn't about to step backward a few hundred years into the whole Jerry dependency thing. Though it was so tempting it hurt.

"No, I'm okay. But thanks." I smiled at him. "It's good to see you, Jerry. Why *are* you here? It's too soon for the wedding. And last I knew you had duties in Los Angeles. Family obligations."

"My brother is handling them. I had business to take care of here." Jerry slid his arm around me. "And I didn't like where we left things. I was worried about you."

"I told you I could stand on my own two feet, and I'm doing it. Financially and every other way." Defensive much? Oh, well.

"Tonight's not a very good example of that." He gently scratched my healing wound. "She could have killed you."

My stomach rolled over. It was the truth. And a body-guard would have been a welcome diversion. As a dog, Valdez had always been front and center when I'd been attacked before, throwing himself between me and danger. I swallowed, my mouth dry and my itchy back suddenly much more than a minor annoyance. It was a freakin' warning. That the woman would be out there, waiting for another chance.

"Let me hire another bodyguard for you, Gloriana."

As usual, Jerry had read my mind. And was willing to ride to my rescue.

"No. It's not right. Just because you made me, doesn't mean you have to be stuck with me forever. Other vamps make fledglings and let them go. You've got to do the same."

"Don't be ridiculous. Are you comparing yourself to a mere fledgling? You think you're the only vampire I've created? I can think of a dozen off the top of my head." Jerry stood and walked around the small room. He stopped at the trash can and picked out the red jacket I'd tossed away.

I stared at him with an open mouth. Wasn't he the one for dropping bombshells. "Since when do you create other vampires?"

"When I was young, I thought I was the next best thing to God, giving people immortality." He thrust his hand through the hole in my jacket. "Not guaranteed though, is it?"

"Obviously. Do you keep track of your other fledglings? Provide security like you do for me?"

"Of course not. They wouldn't tolerate it." Jerry realized he'd just talked himself into a corner. "They were men, Gloriana. You were the first and only woman I turned. I did it to you for love, not power. It was totally different."

"Right. Women are helpless creatures in need of guidance. Which sums up our basic problem." I faced off with him.

"Here we go." He grimaced and threw down the jacket. "I swear I—"

"Forget it." I knew he was frustrated. He was who he was,

the sixteenth-century man I'd fallen in love with. I had to admit he'd evolved more than most men from his time would have.

"I'd love to." He shook his head when I moved closer. "Why can't I convince you that I only want to protect you?"

"I get it. And I begged you to turn me, back in the day. For love." I put my hand on his chest. He was and would always be in his prime. I'd fallen for him in 1604 because he was the whole package—a Scot in a kilt with battle scars. I'd loved him so much I'd been incapable of rational thinking, not even scared of the vampire thing. It had just added to his attraction. I'd been mesmerized by his dark hair, dark eyes and masculine body that knew just how to pleasure mine. That he'd wanted me, a lowborn actor's widow, had seemed a miracle. I'd have done anything to keep him. Taking on my own pair of fangs had been a no-brainer.

"I took advantage of your innocence. But I selfishly wanted you with me forever." He smiled and pulled me against him. "I haven't regretted it."

"I was not innocent." I rubbed against him.

"Of the vampire world you were." Jerry growled when I nipped his ear. "Give over, Gloriana. Let me take care of you again. It's always been my pleasure to do so." He met my lips with his, kissing his way into my mouth until I sighed and let my tongue tangle with his.

My Jerry. I grasped his hair and felt the edge of the work-table when he sat me on top of it. He leaned me back until I lay on it, then trailed his fangs along my jugular until I moaned and tried to press them into the vein.

"Drink from me, Jerry."

"No, lass, you're too weak. Take from me." His hands were on my breasts as he angled his neck to within an inch of my mouth. "Please. Let me help you heal properly."

I knew I shouldn't take anything from Jerry. It was opening a door. A slippery slope and all that. What about my independence? But this was my sire. Vamps just can't say no to their sires, or at least that's what I told myself.

So I settled in. He tasted like everything wonderful and familiar and what I needed to be whole again. By the time I came up for air, I could fight a hundred Westwood kids. Which was just as well, because it turns out Vivien wasn't an only child.

Three

"Feel better?" Jerry sat beside me on the table.

"Like new." I jumped off, then pulled off my sweater. "Check out my back. Is it healed?" I turned around, then felt his fingers trace the spot where I'd been hit.

"You seem fine." His finger slid down to the edge of my bra. "But I'd better make a more thorough examination." He deftly opened the clasp.

"I don't think that's necessary." I grabbed my bra to keep it from falling off. "I wasn't hit anywhere else." His arms wrapped around me. "Jerry, stop. I'm not doing this."

"Why not? I can lock the door. This is your shop. No one will bother us." He put his hands over mine, both of us holding my breasts. "I've missed you, Gloriana. Missed touching you." His breath was warm against my neck. "Tasting you." His fangs slid lightly along my throat.

"Jerry." I sighed, almost admitting how much I'd missed *him*. I closed my eyes and leaned back. I hated being so weak with him. All my resolutions, all my vows of independence were so much talk when it came to actually saying no to Jerry. He slipped one of his hands inside the waistband of my jeans to stroke my stomach. Oh, give me strength. When he eased his fingers into the Promised Land, I gasped and clutched his arms. My panties had been damp since I'd seen him come through the door.

"Shall I lock the door?" His voice was deep, his breath tickling my ear.

"Mmm." His arousal pressed against me. He wanted me, had always wanted me. And wasn't that an ego boost to a woman who had too much junk in her personal trunk? I wiggled against him and he groaned.

"I'll take that as a yes." He locked it with a glance, then plunged his fingers into me and bit my earlobe. The combo was enough to make me shudder and reach back to grab his ass. I held him tight, wild for him.

"Yes." I let go and opened my jeans, sliding them and my panties down. I heard his zipper as I leaned over so he could spread my legs. My jeans were stuck down near my calves because I still had on those damned boots.

"Yes." Jerry held my breast with one hand while he surged into me from behind. He gripped my inner thigh to keep me from toppling over.

The pressure was exquisite torture as he found his place and his rhythm. I reached out, grabbed a shelf and held on. The shelf wobbled and sweaters tumbled to the concrete floor. I didn't care. I was too focused on how, um, *wow* this felt to worry about my storeroom.

"Jerry!" I shrieked as I lost my grip on the shelf. Jerry tugged me against him and sat on the table with me on his lap. The new position did it for me, and Jerry clapped his hand over my mouth to keep me from screaming the building down when I came.

At least one of us had remembered there was a roomful of people on the other side of the door. Not that it inhibited us. Still hard and pulsing inside me, Jerry held my hips. I moved and his arms tightened around me. I shivered, savoring the pleasure he'd given me. When his hand fell from my mouth, he leaned on my shoulder, his kiss trailing up to my neck and that pulse point vampires can't resist.

I came back to Earth and heard rock music through the walls and people talking. Flo, Richard, Lacy and a few customers were right outside. I leaned back and realized Jerry had never even taken off his sweater.

"Drink from me, lover." I smiled and felt his answering grin against my cheek.

"You sure you're recovered enough?" He kissed my vein.

"Mmm. I think I just proved that." I tugged on his hair. "Bite me, baby."

He growled and did, drinking with a rhythm that I felt from my throat to my womb. Then he moved inside me again.

Oh, my God, but he was going to give me another orgasm. Surely not. I couldn't—but he reached around and touched me where he knew I was so incredibly sensitive, and I exploded. This time I held my own hands over my mouth and bit my palm. Maybe someday I'd learn self-control. But not tonight.

By the time I slipped off his lap and found another sweater to wear from the pile on the floor, I was so boneless I staggered. Glory the slut grinned at Jerry the satyr.

"You going to let me stay with you today and sleep beside you?" He slung his arm around me, the picture of a sated male who was pretty damned proud of himself. I couldn't fault him for it.

"Afraid not." I smiled to soften what came next. Oops. His arm slid off of me and his face was stony. "Come on, Jerry, you know that shouldn't have happened. I was in shock after my brush with death. We have issues. You know that."

"Issues be damned. You love me, or did I imagine your words when we made love just now?" He didn't smile.

"No, you're right. I love you. So I'm willing to work on our relationship. Are you? Are you back for a while?" I put my hand on his chest and smiled. Cozening. It usually worked.

"Yes." No answering smile. Not good.

"And you still have your house here, don't you?" I grabbed

my purse and put on fresh lipstick, then ran my hands through hair that had to look wild. Flo and the rest had probably heard enough to know what we'd done, but I didn't need to look like it.

My friend wanted Jerry and me together. And since she'd gotten married, she thought everyone should enjoy wedded bliss. I didn't believe an immortal should tie that particular knot. Jerry didn't agree, had even bought me a ring. I wasn't going to fight either of them about it. One battle a night was enough.

"You want to come home with me? I've got great security. Westwood's brat couldn't get to you there." Jerry smiled at last, sure he'd just misunderstood my answer the first time, and squeezed my shoulders. "And we could talk tomorrow."

"Talk." A four-letter word in any man's vocabulary. My, but Jerry was serious about this relationship.

"No. My security's fine." I stroked his cheek. "I'd love to fall asleep in your arms. Really. But I've got phone calls to make. Call me tomorrow night?"

"This sounds like I'm getting the brush-off again." Jerry stepped away from me.

"I'm not brushing you off. It's business, Jer. And important. I'm sure you have things to do too." I glanced at the clock on my phone, which I'd dug out of my purse. "We've got a few hours before dawn, and I need to deal with some wedding stuff, among other things. Okay?"

"See you tomorrow. You'll not get rid of me so easily then." He kissed me long and hard. "I'm going out the back way. If I see that Westwood female, I'm taking care of her."

"Jerry, no! It's too dangerous. She has backup. Don't—"

"I'm shifting first. Besides, she's after you, not all vampires. So I'll have the element of surprise. Right?"

"I don't know that. She recognized me. Guess her father left records, maybe a photo album." Which was a creepy thought. Westwood's most-wanted list. "She knew I'd been the one to take out her father. Maybe one of his bodyguards got away the night I—" I shut up. Didn't want to go there again. Sure I'd been stalked by that lunatic. But it still bothered me that I'd killed a human being, though I'd known at the time I had no choice. It had been kill or be killed. I've gotten used to the immortality thing.

"Glory, quit second-guessing. You did what you had to do." Jerry put his arms around me. "I won't go on a killing rampage. Yet. But she did attack you. I won't let that happen again."

"How? Whammy her into forgetting the whole thing? Maybe tell her that Daddy dear died in a hunting accident?" I said this into Jerry's sweater since dredging up the whole Westwood fiasco had me near tears and he'd pulled me close.

"Sounds like a plan to me." Jerry stepped back and stared into my eyes. "Valdez told me exactly what happened. Westwood brought on his own death. The fool should have known better than to take on a vampire, especially one with your skills. I'm proud of you, Gloriana. And I'm damned glad he's dead. I just wish you'd made him suffer more at the end."

"I know you do, Jerry. Because he killed your best friend and flaunted his kills with his sickening fang trophy necklace." I cupped his cheek. Jerry had taken the loss hard and almost inherited his friend's widow on top of everything else. Mara. No man deserved that woman.

"So you did all vampires a service that night."

"Sure, I'm a freakin' hero." There had been a dozen or more fangs on that necklace. I shuddered, remembering it.

"Yes, *my* hero." He kissed my palm, then stepped back. No sign of the emotions that his own memories must have dredged up. "Now open the door to the alley, Gloriana. Then lock it behind me. Promise you won't go out there without shifting first yourself. It's your best defense." He gave me a searching look. "You're easier with the shifting now, right?"

"Right. Good idea." I'm not crazy about shape-shifting, but I've learned to do it without freezing in fear that I won't get back to Glory as usual after I'm done. For centuries I'd had a phobia about that. "My car's dead anyway."

"I'm sure Westwood's daughter doesn't just use the alley.

Crowds are a great protection. Use them. And—" He shook his head. "Damn it, where's Valdez? I want to hire him again."

"Forget it, Jerry. He's into this nightclub he's opening. He's done with the bodyguard gig." I gave Jerry an "I mean business" look. "Even if I would tolerate it. Which I won't."

"Hardheaded woman." He stared at me until I wanted to kiss his stubborn mouth.

"Exactly. You should be used to it." I gave in to the impulse and pulled his head down to trace his firm mouth with my tongue until he pulled me hard against him.

When he finally lifted his head and licked his lips, I couldn't read his mood. "At least the rest of you is soft."

I laughed up at him. "Yep. And you seem to like me well enough to overlook my faults."

"Unfortunately I'm a man enslaved by his cock." He squeezed my backside then turned toward the door.

"Jerry!" I fumed as he shifted into a blackbird. "Yes, fly the hell away while I'm still speaking to you. And be careful, damn it!" I opened the door and watched him fly into the night. Thank God no arrows hit the door as I closed it and threw home the dead bolts.

Flo would give me knowing looks once I walked into the shop. So what? Jerry and I were two of a kind. If he was a slave to his cock, then I was a slave to my . . . I grinned. Yes, and wasn't I lucky to have a man who could satisfy me so unbelievably well?

I touched the table where we'd just made love. What did they call what we'd just done? A booty call? I straightened my sweater and adjusted my jeans, which had enough spandex to have helped when Jerry had reached inside and . . . I shook my head. Time to get a grip. I had life-and-death issues to deal with. Like planning a trap for Ms. Westwood. Jerry was right. I needed to use some vamp mind control and make her forget she'd ever heard of Glory St. Clair. I headed for the door into the shop.

"Hold it right there, missy." Emmie Lou Nutt, one of my resident ghosts, shimmered between me and the doorknob.

"Not now, Emmie, I've got things to do and people to see out there." I saw her husband, Harvey, shimmer into place beside her. He wore his usual overalls, never wore anything else. Emmie was stuck for eternity in the cowgirl outfit she'd worn the day Harvey had accidentally run over her in his pickup at the Texas State Fair. They lived in my shop because they'd met in this building more years ago than they'd admit.

"Reckon you don't wanta be goin' out there right now, missy. There's a mischief maker wantin' a piece of your hide waitin'." Harvey had a toothpick in his mouth, and he shifted it from the left to the right as he looked at his wife. "Tell her, hon."

"He's right, Glory. Hidin' a stake in his pocket. Good thing he's not wearin' them vampire-detectin' glasses, or he'd of had him a field day with your friends out there. Instead he's got a picture of you in his pocket right next to that durn stake." Emmie Lou swished her skirt. "Harvey tossed a purse at his head." She giggled. "Made him jump. Right, Harvey?"

"Sure did." Harvey sidled up close to me. "Call your vampire buddies in here and have a confab. You know, send 'em one of them there mental messages like ya do. Get Flo to read that fella's mind. Find out who he is."

"What is this? Stake Glory week? I wonder if he works for Vivien Westwood?" I realized Harvey had the right idea. I unlocked the storeroom door and sent a mental message to Flo. "What did this guy look like?" I listened while Harvey described him. Not exactly rock-star material. In fact, he sounded cute but ordinary. A lot like—

The storeroom door opened, and Flo and Richard rushed inside, then slammed and locked it.

"He's David Westwood, another heir to the Westwood billions. He's trying to kill you." Flo hugged me close. "Don't worry, we'll rip out his throat as soon as he's outside and away from your shop. I know how you are about bad publicity."

I breathed in Flo's expensive perfume. What was this—a vamp-hunting contest? I pulled back. Yes, got it in one. And how like Brent Westwood to arrange something creepy from the grave.

"Killing Westwood's son would be a little more than bad publicity, darling." Richard leaned against the door. No sign of my ghosts. Apparently they were back in the shop, ready to toss more purses if necessary. I hoped they stuck to non-breakables.

"He's right, Flo. As much as I'd love an easy solution, I have a feeling that if both a son and a daughter are after me, then there's probably some kind of paper trail that would make a cover-up difficult." I sat on the table where I'd had such fun just minutes ago. "And how many kids did this billionaire have anyway?" I wished for my laptop, which was in the shop.

"Easy to find out." Richard opened the door a crack. "I'm also going to discover how many men he brought in with him. I thought it was busy for eleven o'clock on a Tuesday night."

"Anybody buying anything?" I jumped off the table. At least if business was good that would be some consolation.

"Zilch. Except for this." Flo held out her wrist. "I love my new bracelet. Vintage costume jewelry is very in right now. And this was a signed piece. Lacy gave Richard a discount."

"It's perfect on you." I knew it was one of my more expensive items too. I smiled at Richard. "Bring my laptop in here. We can research the Westwood family, and I've got to check on stuff for Flo's party if I live long enough to throw it. You did register, didn't you?"

Richard grimaced. "Of course we went through that nonsense. Can you imagine vampires picking china and sterling flatware? The crystal goblets? Fine. Bed linens? Sure." He glanced at Flo. "But my beloved is enjoying this, so I do what

I must." He smiled at me. "Don't worry, Gloriana, you'll live to endure every one of these wedding festivities. Now, Florence, lock this door behind me." He slipped into the shop and closed the door.

"Pah! He loved picking out everything. You should have seen him feeling the towels and comparing thread counts on the sheets." Flo locked the door. "He's right. We'll take care of these Westwoods. Nothing is going to spoil my wedding."

"I hope you're right." I forced a smile. Now Flo frowned. "What?"

"It's Aggie. She says she's giving me a shower. Do you think she means one of those parties with gifts? Or . . ." She paced around the workroom.

"Well, Flo, she *is* a Siren. Weather is her specialty. I've seen her drum up a typhoon when she's unhappy. I'll check with her." I hugged my former roomie. "Of course you should have a bridal shower. Wish I'd thought of it. Tell me where you're registered, and I'll make sure she puts it on the invitations." I'd put the screws to Aggie a.k.a. Aglaophonos. The Siren *owed* me. If a bridal shower would make Flo happy, then Aggie would deliver. And no one would end up wet.

We both looked up when there was a knock on the door.

"It's Richard." Flo unlocked the door and eased it open.

"They're gone. I planted the idea that you'd had a run-in with his sister and had fled town. Wouldn't be back for months." Richard laid the laptop on the table. "That should hold them off for a while. But we can't count on that to last. He's bound to have his own investigators." He opened the laptop and booted it up. "Now let's see just how many little Westwoods are running around praying for a Glory sighting."

"But Richard, what's the deal? Why are they all after me?" I looked over his shoulder. Google had a lot of sites about the billionaire, but Richard had become a pro at picking out the best one. Soon we could see a family portrait. I sagged with relief. Two kids. Vivien and David. Okay.

"Seems Westwood's determined to get you even from the

grave, Glory. I read young David's mind. The will says that if Dad's taken down by a vampire, the kid who gets the vamp 'assassin' gets the gold. All of it."

"What?" I sank down on the table.

"Yep. Billions, made from the tech industry. And, trust me, Westwood sold out long before any problems with the economy. So it's a huge pile." Richard was on a page now that showed a bio for each child. Neither Vivien nor David seemed to work for a living, obviously sponging off Daddy. One lived in Hollywood and the other in Paris. Both had expensive tastes judging by the homes they kept.

"David was really ramped up about it. He didn't even know Dad was missing until his allowance check didn't come on time. Seems they weren't close. Anyway, he and his sister jetted here to see what's what and met two bodyguards who told this wild tale about how Dad bit the big one at the hands of this female vampire. Had a cell phone video to prove it." Richard put his hand on my shoulder.

"You're kidding. They took video?" I looked at Flo. "I'm cooked."

"Maybe, maybe not." Richard still looked very serious. "It was poor quality. Made at night, from a distance. The guards knew your name because Westwood had talked about you so much. You know he was pretty obsessed."

"Oh, yeah. He stalked me." I was mad now. Haunting me from the grave. How sick was that? "But what are his kids doing here? I mean, revenge? Surely a will that mentioned vampires wouldn't hold up in court."

"Of course it wouldn't." Richard smiled. "And I think when David and his sister calm down, they'll realize that. They got into his papers without consulting a lawyer. One look at the terms and sibling rivalry kicked in. Unfortunately, Westwood set up a timeline in his will. If he's not avenged within a certain time frame, the bulk of his estate goes to some charity—the Save the World from Vampires Fund. A crock, of course. Run by one of his hunting buddies." Richard was on the fund's Web site.

"Listen to this: 'Our mission is to hunt down and exterminate the fanged monsters who prey on innocent victims for their blood. Membership in our organization is free to any who share our core values. For information on special vampire-hunting equipment, click on the following links.' Then there's a list of places where you can buy things like stakes, holy water and crosses, the usual foolishness."

"Not Westwood's special goggles, I hope." I hated those things. He'd developed goggles with lenses that could identify a vampire by the lack of a mortal's normal body heat. The worst was that he'd had a pair that looked like regular sunglasses. It made my usual blending into crowds impossible.

"No, I don't see them here." Richard glanced at me. "Guess he didn't want to share all his trade secrets. But his crossbow and olive wood arrows are here. Expensive as hell."

I shuddered and scratched my back. "Thanks a lot."

"Glory, *mia amica*. We will take them out. Set a trap and make these Westwoods vanish. *Sì?*" Flo put her arm around me.

"No, like Richard said, we need for them to see this will is bogus. No court would let it stand. And so far Westwood is just missing, unless they found his body. David have any thoughts about that, Richard?" I swallowed, thinking about it.

"He hired a private firm to search the area the bodyguards told him about. Didn't want to involve the police because Dad was always low-profile and it wasn't unusual for him to go off on hunts for months at a time without communicating. He did always arrange to sign important financial documents though. That's what got the kids' attention this time. Bottom line, David didn't want his father's vampire obsession made public."

"If he doesn't want the vamp stuff public, he should get that Web site you're looking at taken down." I felt like I wore a target on my itchy back.

Richard suddenly swore, using words I'd never heard from the former priest.

"What is it?" Flo and I ran to stand behind him.

He started to slam the laptop shut, then shook his head. "You're right. This site has to come down. But not to protect Westwood. No one should see these pictures. They're sickening."

"Ricardo?" Flo put her arms around him. "*Caro*, you're scaring us."

"It's Westwood's 'Kills.'" Richard stared at me. "You should never regret ending that worthless sod's life, Gloriana. Look." He lifted the screen and clicked the mouse. There was a gallery of photos. He double clicked, and we could see Westwood standing with his crossbow, his foot on the body of a man who'd been shot in the chest, the arrow still in his heart.

"Oh, my God!" I felt sick as Richard enlarged the photo. In Westwood's bloody palm were two fangs. Tears filled my eyes. "Do you think . . . could Jerry's friend MacTavish be there?"

"Look away, Glory. Ricardo, shut that damned computer right now!" Flo led me from Richard's side as she muttered Italian curses under her breath. "He's there, *cara*. I saw him. But you don't need to. Eight men, four women. *Bastardo!* I recognized . . ." Her voice caught. "I knew at least six of them, maybe more if I had time to study." More bitter Italian.

I turned, and we held each other as we cried. I'd never seen Flo cry. Richard wrapped his arms around both of us. We stood there, a sad, sad trio for several moments. Then Richard stepped back and grabbed a roll of paper towels out of the bathroom.

"Dry up, ladies. Thanks to Gloriana, the man will never kill another vampire or take another pair of fangs." Richard handed us each enough paper towels to dry every window in my shop.

"*Sì, mia amica.*" Flo sniffed and dabbed at her eyes. "Never forget that you did a wonderful thing, putting down that monster. We will make sure his children do not go on with their vendetta. Am I right?"

"It'll be tricky, but I swear it." Richard sat in front of the computer again. "There's this damned Web site, and he owned a tech company. I don't see how we can crash the site." Richard shut down the computer. "But, Glory, we're in this all the way. Whatever needs doing, we're here to help."

"*Sì.*" Flo smiled at Richard. "And pray for a miracle too, eh, Ricardo?"

"Couldn't hurt." He smiled at his wife and pulled her into his arms.

I wished for Blade's strong arms then. But I was glad he hadn't seen Mac posed as a trophy. I'd swear Flo and Richard to secrecy on that point. They had good intentions, and I appreciated that. But that's all they were. Intentions. Right now what we needed was a solid plan of action. And right now we had zilch.

Four

"I love purple. Not as slimming as black, but not all of us have figure issues." Aggie and Flo had their heads together over the magazine picture of the new bridesmaid dresses. Flo had agreed to pay an extravagant amount to rush the order, and we were good to go. Unless I killed Aggie before the wedding.

"When you were a disgusting scaly sea monster, you didn't even have a figure, Aggie, so I wouldn't go there, if I were you." I'd called Aggie to come over to discuss the shower she'd proposed, not sure a Siren knew squat about wedding customs. That was the sixth dig since she'd arrived. We weren't buds.

"You'll both look beautiful in this dress." Flo ignored the tension. "This is my wedding. All eyes will be on me anyway."

"Right. They will be. We're just the warm-up for the main event when we walk down the aisle in front of you." Even I had to admit Aggie looked sexy and stylish now, but as a sea monster, she'd been willing to send me to hell to save her size-six butt.

"You sure you need so many bridesmaids?" I stepped between Flo and Aggie.

"You trying to cut me out?" Aggie pushed me aside. "I'm into this now. Get over it."

"I want both of you. But, Glory, you're my number one, the maid of honor." Flo smiled.

"Exactly. So it's my duty to make sure things are done right." I fake smiled at Aggie. "Now tell us what you've got in mind for Flo's shower." I snatched the magazine.

Aggie grinned, her once slimy green teeth now a gleaming white. "No worries. My boss the Storm God is all over it. There will be an awesome display of thunder and lightning, Flo. Then a water spout over the lake. Your guests will love it. I'm renting out the banquet room at that cute Mexican restaurant overlooking the water. I know you can't eat, but the shifters can, and there will be drinks for them too. Margaritas. Olé." Aggie fluffed her blond hair and gave me a look that said, "Top that."

"Get a clue. A bridal shower isn't about the weather, Aggie. You shower gifts on the bride." I glanced at Flo, sending her a mental message that this sometime mermaid had to go.

"You think I don't know that?" Aggie had her chin up. "Watch your mouth, fang girl. You have no idea what I had to do to get my boss to loosen the purse strings." She smiled at Flo. "But it's all good. Achy likes seeing me make nice with"— she looked me over—"the not-so-little people."

"Why you slimy—" I lunged for her, sick of her attitude.

"Stop!" Flo jumped between us. "If you fight, where's the fun? The celebration?" She glared at Aggie. "Fang girl? Look at me." She pointed at her own impressive pearly whites. "Glory and I are vampires. Never forget it." She turned to me. "And Aggie isn't slimy now. She's *trying* to make nice. Do me a favor? Make nice back." Her mental message was more blunt, but I loved my best bud and bit the bullet.

"Fine. Have at it, Aggie. A shower? Hell, throw a typhoon if you want to." I knew a challenge when I heard one. "I've got the bachelorette party." I smiled, full fang. "Flo, a hot male dancer and exotic synthetic brews. How does that sound? My party will blow Aggie's right out of the water."

"In your dreams, sister. This is a lingerie shower, Flo. New undies and sexy nighties for your man to enjoy." Aggie's face was flushed, and if she'd had her fish tail, I'm sure it would have been whipping back and forth. "I've got a hundred bucks says our gal here goes for that over watching some random guy do a bump and grind while she drinks fake blood."

"You're on." I'd worry about where I'd get an extra hundred later. No, I wouldn't. My party would beat hers all to hell. If I could find a hot guy to dance, that is.

Flo was dancing around the room. "Yay! A party contest and I'm the winner."

Aggie stopped Flo with a hand on her shoulder. "You bet you are. I'll have some kind of imported blood at my deal too. Maybe I can find margarita-flavored stuff for you on the Internet. Or I could bring in some mortals for you to suck dry." She winked at me. "I've been studying human wedding customs, but maybe vamps do things differently. It's my first time as a bridesmaid since I don't count ancient rituals." She smirked. "The sacrificial virgin thing is a blast but doesn't exactly include a happily ever after for the bride."

Hmm. Aggie definitely had a dark side. But Flo sighed.

"No mortals for drinking. The Austin vampires have rules against that, and my brother is on the council. I promised him I would obey their stuffy rules." Flo smiled. "Margaritas for vamps though? Go for it."

"Why's the Storm God involved in Flo's shower? I figured he'd be back in the Mediterranean by now. Doesn't he trust you on your own?" I'd had a run-in with him, and he was freaky scary. Any place where he hung out was a place I didn't want to be.

"Aw, Glory, afraid he'll zap you with another lightning bolt?" Aggie laughed. "Flo, that would make your shower sizzle."

Flo shook her head. "Forget it, Aggie. Last time Glory got hit by lightning, her hair was ugly frizzy for days. I want her to look nice for the wedding."

"Not to mention it hurt like hell." I sat on a stool. "I hope you have some control over Achelous."

"Yeah, right." Aggie sighed and grabbed the magazine again to stare at the bridesmaid dress. "He'll do what he wants." She ran her hand down her perfect figure, which was poured into a green sweater and skinny black jeans. "I have to let him play weather guy at the shower, or it's back to sitting on a rock in the lake with my fish tail, singing for my supper." She wrinkled her nose. "I'm so over that this century."

For a moment I almost felt sorry for her. Then she gave me an evil look and turned to Flo. "Flo, honey, I need a guest list and your sizes. I'll send the invitations out this week. Here's the date I've reserved. Will it work for you? I bet Glory hasn't even started working on her party yet." Aggie whipped out a pocket calendar from her designer handbag.

"You'd be surprised at what I've got going." I glanced at the date and made a note of it. "I'm going upstairs to nail down details right now. Flo, I'll let you know all about it later."

My ex-roomie dabbed at her eyes. "I'm so lucky. Such thoughtful friends doing this for me. I can't believe I never got married before. Glory, marry Jeremiah. We'll throw many parties and a giant wedding. Lots of presents. You'll love it."

I grabbed my purse. "Thanks but no thanks. See you later. I'm sneaking upstairs. Front door. Hopefully no one will try to shoot me this time. Maybe I'll use a customer as a human shield." I heard Aggie bombarding Flo with hopeful questions as I stepped into the shop. Like maybe I'd be killed and she'd win by default? Bitch.

My night clerk had come in to relieve Lacy, and there *were* no human customers. I glanced out the plate glass window, and the sidewalk in front of the store seemed clear. Three in the morning. A dead time of night but staying open twenty-four hours was still a novelty that had served me well. I knew the action would pick up later when shifts changed at a nearby hospital and the downtown hotels.

I'd called him earlier and expected Rafe to be waiting for

me, but once safely upstairs, there was no sign of him. I kicked off my shoes and pulled out my cell phone. Wait a minute. Was that the shower running? Hadn't we just had this conversation? I stomped over to the bathroom door and pounded on it with my fist.

The water turned off immediately, but I felt heat through the door. There wasn't going to be a speck of hot water left. I'd worked up a good mad by the time the door opened a crack.

"What the hell are you doing?" I kicked at the door.

"Taking a shower. Who the hell are you?" The door opened wider, and the woman wearing a towel looked me over from head to toe, then sniffed.

I recognized that look and that sniff. Had endured that treatment for centuries. It was the "I've got what you wish you had, honey, now get out of my way" look. I stood my ground. I mean, it was my apartment, wasn't it?

"I'm Glory St. Clair, the woman who pays the rent on this place and who gets first dibs on the hot water here. Who the hell are you?" I checked her out. Didn't take long. She was tall and slim. Her dripping hair was midnight black and so thick it would probably take her an hour to blow it dry. The towel was knotted between small perky breasts. That same towel barely met around me and had certainly never tied into a firm knot. Damn.

"Nadia Komisky, Rafael's business partner. I'm sorry if I've inconvenienced you." She smiled, showing perfect teeth, shiny white with cute little fangs, and held out a hand.

"Ah, Nadia. So glad you've decided to help Rafe." Against my better judgment, I shook her hand. She didn't do any creepy vamp moves on me, just touched palms and backed up to grab another towel for her wet hair. She was so damned gorgeous with her pale skin, dark eyes and thick lashes, I wanted to hate her. Too bad her smile was friendly and she was actually being nice as she kept apologizing while she wrapped her hair in the towel.

"Rafael didn't warn you, the bad boy. But when I got to

Austin, I found there was no safe place to stay. This town is so primitive!" Nadia laughed. "Well, for vampires anyway. I told Rafe we should open a vampire hotel. But he is hot to do the club thing. Really wanted a cozy bar, but I said that is silly with the college so close. Students like music and dancing, and the space he's leasing is perfect for a nightclub."

I followed her out to the living room. Did she plan to put on clothes? She had long legs and bare feet that were elegant with pretty red-painted toenails. Mine needed a fresh coat of something.

"Students do love a good club. And something new. Sounds great." I noticed a small open suitcase by the door.

Nadia casually dropped her towel and stepped into a black thong then pulled a black T-shirt over her head. Next came a stretchy black skirt, and she was dressed. She sat on the couch and went to work on towel drying her hair. I couldn't imagine being that unself-conscious about my body in front of a stranger. I kept my double-wide hips hidden from everyone but Blade, who had a weird liking for them. No wonder I loved him.

"We have a name for the club now. N-V. What do you think? Can you see it? In bloodred neon? For Nadia and Valdez, of course." Nadia pulled a brush out of a black leather tote and ran it ruthlessly through her hair.

"N-V. Yes, I get it. Like envy. Has a sexy vibe. What does Rafe think?" I turned when the hall door opened.

"Rafe thinks money talks. We're still working out the kinks, but Nadia's an old pro when it comes to the club scene. I see you two have met." Rafe walked in with a grocery bag and set it on the kitchen table. "Sorry about this, Glory, but there was nowhere else for Nadia to stay."

"No problem. Vampires have to stick together. Will you two be sharing your bedroom?" I got that out with a straight face, though I felt my cheeks go warm.

"What do you say, Rafael? Do you want me to sleep on the couch? Glory wants to know if we are lovers." Nadia raised an eyebrow.

Rafe glanced at me. "We're all just friends here. But you can use my bed during the day, Nadia. I'm sure I'll be busy with the club."

"Listen to him, breaking my heart." Nadia sighed. "We used to be lovers. Now he offers me his bed to die in during the day. No hokeypokey, Rafael?"

I hid my grin. Rafe laughed out loud.

"Look out, Nadia, your Russian roots are showing. I think you mean hanky-panky. And we've got a lot to do to get this club up and running. Let's keep us strictly business."

"Too bad. You were a very talented lover, my friend." Nadia smiled and looked me over. "Are you and Glory exclusive?"

"Rafe and I are just good friends. But you can stay here as long as you need to." I got up, my mind full of Rafe's "talents." He just grinned and winked. "Can we talk business? I have a proposition for you. Nadia, I've got synthetics. Not the best, but you're welcome to try one."

"No need, Glory. Rafe went out to get some of my brand. I insist you try it." Nadia gestured, and Rafe pulled a six-pack out of his bag. It was an exotic synthetic I'd never heard of.

"Where'd you get that? I'd love to try something new."

"Damian had some. Nadia wants what she wants, so I called and he agreed to sell her some." Rafe went to work on a sealed cap. "He charged you big bucks for it."

"Of course. Damian and I had a hookup in Belgium once. He and I are both business people, so I didn't expect a discount. You gave him my credit card number?"

"Yes. He'll keep it on file, he said. I guess he's remembering that hookup fondly, because he said just call when you want more. He'll have it delivered next time to wherever you end up staying."

I held out my hand and took the bottle from Rafe. The aroma was incredible and the taste . . . Well, whatever Nadia had paid was well worth it. I'd planned to sip, to make it last, but it was gone way too soon.

"That was delicious." I sighed and put the empty on the

table next to me. I guess I'd known Damian sold high-end synthetics to vamps who could afford them, just never paid attention because I wasn't in his league. I ordered my budget stuff off the Internet.

"It's made in Bulgaria. I suspect there's genuine blood in here. Which makes it extra fine, don't you agree?"

"Oh, yes." I noticed Rafe frowning at me. "What? Surely they use a blood bank."

Nadia laughed. "Whatever you say, Glory."

"It's not that. You can drink whatever you want as long as I'm not your donor." He focused on me. "Glory, why didn't you tell me there's a bounty on your head?"

"Because there's not. Exactly. And how did you find out? Damian?" When Rafe nodded, I sighed. Flo must have called her brother. He wasn't just a member, he was head of Austin's vampire council. I hoped the council didn't decide to get involved in my personal problem. If they thought I was a threat to the vampire community, they could demand I leave the city.

"Glory? What's wrong?" Nadia leaned forward.

"I killed a billionaire. His will leaves everything to the child who takes me out first. Thank God there are only two children."

"A hell of a legacy, sending them after a vampire. My father slapped me around, but at least when he died, we were done." Nadia sipped her drink, which she'd insisted Rafe pour into a goblet. "Kill them and your worries are over."

"That doesn't seem fair." Of course, was it fair to be shot with a crossbow? Rafe straightened from where he'd leaned against the doorway into the kitchen. Oops, forgot to block my thoughts, and Flo must have left out that detail. "Besides, it's not that simple. They die, and the money goes to a vamp-hunting foundation dedicated to staking Glory St. Clair. Then I'll have legions of vamp hunters after me." I grabbed my empty and got up to recycle it.

Nadia smiled at Rafe, who looked like he was about to

explode. "Rafael, give Glory another bottle of Diablo Red.
She obviously needs it. Then tell me how you killed this billionaire. I love a good story that ends with death."

"She took him out to save me." Rafe handed me the bottle, then blocked me from leaving the kitchen. "Where'd you
get hit?" He touched my shoulder, then tugged aside my
sweater to stare at the pale pink scar that would be gone by
tomorrow night. "Shit, Glory. Thank God this Westwood
isn't the shot the father was."

"I had something to do with the miss. I ran like hell." My
skin tingled where Rafe's warm fingers touched me, and I
put my hand over his. "I'm fine. No worries."

"For now. But I'm sure there'll be a next time, and you
might not be so lucky." He stared down at me, his eyes dark
and reeling me in closer.

"Lucky? Maybe I don't need luck. I can take care of myself, Rafe." I put my hand on his chest, feeling wobbly. "Now
that I know I'm a target, I'll be more careful."

He steadied me with his other arm at my waist. "I can see
that. What the hell were you doing that they got off this kind
of shot? Hanging out in that damned alley again? Probably
digging in your purse for keys or a lipstick."

"You're making me sound like an idiot." I shoved back.

"No, just spoiled. Used to someone else watching your
back." He grabbed my arm when I tried to walk away. "Seven
inches, Glory. Seven inches to the left and you'd be gone now."

"Quit trying to freak me out." I looked down until he
released me. "I'm scared enough without you piling on."

"Sparks are flying, you two. You sure there's no hanky-
panky here?" Nadia chuckled. "What's going on?"

"Rafe won't stop playing guard dog." I immediately regretted that. Especially when Rafe's lips firmed and his eyes
narrowed.

"Damn straight." He stomped into the kitchen, coming
out with a cold bottle of beer and twisting off the cap. "Not
every woman is as self-sufficient as you are, Nadia. Some
vampires need keepers."

"And some keepers need a muzzle." I shot him a mental finger and, ignoring the fact that innocent Bulgarians might have been sacrificed in the making of this delicious drink, chugged another bottle. Then I told Nadia all about Brent Westwood. She gasped when I mentioned his vamp-detecting glasses.

"That's horrible. If he sold those to every hunter, it would make us easy targets." Nadia frowned. "How do they work?"

"It's not new technology. It's the same thing they use for night-vision goggles. Westwood just figured out that he could use them to scan a crowd of people, checking for body heat. Any person who isn't giving off normal heat has to be one of us." I sighed. "He made them look like regular sunglasses. So you never know whether a guy is someone who thinks it's cool to wear shades at night or if he's checking you out for fangs."

"Very clever. The man was obviously a twisted genius."

"Yes. Twisted for sure. He collected fangs. He had over a dozen pairs on a necklace he wore around his neck." I shuddered. "One set was from a dear friend. When V's life was on the line, I didn't hesitate to kill the bastard."

"Bravo." Nadia smiled at me. "Rafael, admit it. Your friend here *is* a strong woman. Why did you need to guard her for so many years?"

"Her boyfriend hired me. Blade's very protective." Rafe polished off his beer. "Glory's a little late to the game, but she says she's through letting him interfere in her life. Or has that changed?" He smiled, like maybe he'd smelled Blade on me.

I smiled back. "No, he's back in town, but I told him I'm still going it alone. No more of his hired goons." I faked a wince. "I mean guns."

"Blade is your sire?" Nadia looked from me to Rafe.

"And was my lover. So it wasn't easy for me to refuse his help." I realized that sounded lame, especially when I was talking to a woman like Nadia, who seemed so together. "Anyway, I'm on my own now. I have a business and it's doing well. But these Westwood brats are trying to ruin it for me. I've got to figure out a way to derail the 'Get Glory' train. Without killing anyone," I added, because it was clear Nadia was still on board with taking out the kids and worrying about the consequences later.

"I guess it's out of the question to ask you to skip town, then." Rafe grabbed my empty bottle then stalked to the kitchen.

"I'm not running away. I've got friends here, a business. I won't let them spoil it." I followed him. "That's not fair."

"Run or stay and fight. If it's a fight, I'm in. Sounds like fun." Nadia yawned, reminding me that it was just an hour from dawn. "You had a proposition, Glory. What is it?"

"I know you're not open yet, but I was hoping I could rent your new place. For a bachelorette party. Is that possible?" I glanced at Rafe. We'd been sniping at each other all night, but I figured he'd still do me a favor. Nadia was an unknown quantity. Sure she was friendly, but when it came to business, I had a feeling she was all about the bottom line.

"What do you think, Rafael?" Nadia smiled at him.

"Why the hell not? I don't think we can turn away business at this point, and this is for a friend's wedding." Rafe gave me a nod. "The bride's my friend too. A party for a bunch of women? How much trouble can it be?" Rafe dumped the bottles in the recycle bin and walked back into the living room.

"Are you kidding? A bachelorette party? Listen, Rafael, you have no idea how ugly those things can get. I have experience in these matters." Nadia looked around the apartment, assessing my net worth. "There will be a security deposit of course."

"Sure." I smiled. "The bride's footing the bill. Damian's sister. Maybe you know her too. Florence da Vinci."

"Ah, Florence. Of course. She's good for it, then. And she's getting married?" Nadia's eyebrows were up and her mouth amused. "The man who caught her must be something special."

"Richard Mainwaring. Do you know him?" I saw Nadia

shake her head. "Just as well. Flo's the jealous type. Anyway, Richard knows how to handle her." I grinned at Rafe. "Am I right?"

"No comment. Guys stick together. And any man who thinks he can handle a woman is clueless." Rafe was on his second bottle of beer. "Bachelorette party. You ladies are going all out."

"I want this to be amazing. I've got to find a male dancer. One of those Chippendale types." I figured that was something Aggie couldn't beat with her panty party.

"Look no further." Nadia's eyes gleamed. "Did Rafael ever tell you he's one of the best?"

"What? Rafe, you can dance?" I looked at him slouched against the kitchen table. He certainly had the body for it. I remembered him in a towel. Now if he had the moves . . . I swallowed.

"Oh, yes. He can shake his moneymaker, eh, Rafael?" Nadia laughed and stood. "Why are you frowning? Surely you would do this for your friend. Think how this will make the party a success. When he danced in my club in Charleston, he was called the Fallen Angel, Glory. The wings were the first to go, of course. His G-string was made out of white feathers. Very few white feathers." She laughed again and grabbed her suitcase.

"Thanks for sharing, Nadia." Rafe slammed his empty bottle on the table.

"You said your bedroom is at the end of the hall, Rafael? I'm going to bed. It was a long flight from New Orleans. Thanks for letting me stay, Glory." She stopped next to my CD collection and plucked out a case. "Put this on and let Rafael do his thing. I think you'll like what you see." She winked and headed down the hall.

"The Fallen Angel?" I grinned at Rafe.

"You want to see my moves?" He stalked over to my chair and pulled me to my feet. "Fallen for sure. Nothing angelic about it. The ladies wanted a bad man." His lips parted, and I saw the tip of his tongue. "I could handle that."

I sucked in a breath. I felt his heat, a shifter's heat, an inferno compared to a vampire's temp. Then there was his smell, earthy with a hint of the animal I knew he could be. I'd memorized it in the five years we'd been together and would know it with my eyes closed in a crowd of a thousand men.

Bad? Suddenly he had the vibe down, from the gleam in his dark eyes to the way he leaned into my space, just inches from the tips of my aching breasts. His gaze raked over my body like he was remembering how I looked naked. Oh, yeah, he'd seen me a time or two. Accidentally, but still . . . I wanted to step back, to touch myself, to do something to ease this damp welcome that hit me hard and fast.

Instead I smiled and shook my hair back, pretending I was unfazed by his act. Yeah, that's all it was. A show. He didn't mean any of it. He'd done the same hot-gaze thing hundreds of times with strangers in crowded clubs for tips. Good to know.

"Would you dance for Flo's party?" Yay, Glory. Got that out in a normal voice.

"Not a good idea." His eyes lingered on my lips, then swept over my body again, every spot sizzling where they touched.

"Why not? Nadia says you're very . . . talented." I didn't shift so much as a toenail. God, but I was working my self-control.

"You decide." He abruptly stepped away to pop the CD into the player and turned the music on loud enough so the bass vibrated. I knew the walls were well insulated, but my neighbors wouldn't care that it was close to dawn. They were night creatures too. I did hear a laugh coming from down the hall. Forget the hall. Rafe shoved me onto the couch and pushed the coffee table out of the way.

"What are you doing?" I sat sprawled where I'd landed and watched him unbutton his shirt, his hips moving to the music. His chest was broad, strong, ripped. I knew that. Shouldn't care. But combined with that sexy beat and those moves . . . Oh, my.

"Giving you the full effect. I'd take off my pants, but you know how I feel about underwear."

"Damn." I flushed from my cheeks to my toes. "I mean, for a really good audition I should see the whole act."

"Use your imagination." He moved closer.

No problem. His skimpy towel routine had given me plenty to work with.

Get with the program, Glory. Show him this is no big deal. I jumped up, grabbed my purse and pulled a twenty from my wallet. I waved it in front of me, laughing when Rafe danced closer.

"What does this get me?" I looked to where his jeans hung low on his hips. The arrow of dark hair below his navel made my fingertips itch.

"In a club? Sit back down and I'll give you a lap dance. But you'd need to add another couple of twenties to that." He shoved me onto the couch again. "I'll give you a discount."

Then he was on the couch, his knees on either side of mine. The bulge between his legs brushed against my stomach as he braced his arms on the seat back. He lowered his head with a heavy-lidded stare before he pushed my hair back with his nose, his hot breath teasing my right ear.

"Gloriana."

I was surrounded by his heat, the pulsing of the music echoing the throbbing inside me.

"Rafe, I . . ."

He wasn't actually touching me anywhere. Well, unless you counted the occasional bump of his zipper against my sweater. Trust me, I was counting it. And thinking about reaching for that weight that proved he wasn't unmoved.

The music sped up, and Rafe was off of me again, my twenty between his teeth. What the hell?

He strutted over to the CD player and hit a button. The silence was startling. Worse. You could hear me panting like a teenager after heavy petting.

"So, how do you like my moves?"

"Fine." Had I really squeaked? I cleared my throat. I

tried again. "Great. The ladies will love them. So you'll do it? Dance for Flo's bachelorette party?" Flo would go nuts. Aggie would too. No way could she top this.

"Not a chance. Not for a bunch of vampires. One-on-one or in a regular club, no problem." He picked up his shirt and shrugged into it. Darn. "But get a bunch of female vampires worked up like you were just now, and you're liable to find yourself drained dry in a Dumpster. You think I can't see you have your fangs down?"

"I wasn't all that worked up." Oh, wait. Maybe I did have a little bloodlust thing going along with the other kind of lust. I struggled to my feet and told my fangs to hide again.

"Yes, you were. I know the signs, sweetheart. Even the ones that aren't so obvious." He grinned and laid his hand between my breasts. "For a vampire, this heartbeat is pretty fast, and you didn't drink enough of that Bulgarian brew to have cheeks that pink."

"So I'm not immune. But that's what you were after, wasn't it? To get me stirred up? Mission accomplished. It's a party for Flo. You'll know a lot of us. Don't you think I can control my friends?" I lifted his hand off me, though, truth be told, I'd have welcomed it a little closer to my tight nipples. Instead, I fluttered my eyelashes and put my hand on his chest, on top of his shirt. "Come on, Rafe. I need this."

"Don't take this the wrong way, sweetheart, but have you ever controlled anybody?"

For a moment I was too fascinated by the speed of his heartbeat (Hah! I wasn't the only one turned on, now was I?) to realize what he'd just said. Then it sank in.

"Excuse me? That was unnecessary. So I have a few issues. I've been working on them, haven't I? Didn't I come back to Austin by myself?" I shoved back and headed for the hall.

"Yes, you did." Rafe was by my side in an instant. "But I smelled Blade on you the minute I came into the apartment. He's already back and got you where he wants you. Am I right?"

"Damn it. Maybe I've got *him* where I want him." I blinked

back tears. But Rafe was right and I knew it. "We have this connection. It's in my blood. *He's* in my blood."

"I get it. You can't say no to him. Too bad." He glanced down the hall toward his bedroom. "So you do your thing, I'll do mine. Batting your eyelashes at me to get me to dance at your party is pretty lame, Glory. Instead of worrying about shit like that, you should be taking care of this Westwood threat."

"I can't figure out what to do, so I move on to something I *can* deal with. Won't you help me out, Rafe?" I didn't do the flirting thing this time. Rafe was right. It was a cheap ploy, and we were friends who should be able to be straight with each other. I couldn't play naughty games with Jerry and then lead Rafe on. It wasn't fair. To which one of them, I wasn't sure. My body still throbbed from Rafe's sexy dance moves.

"I'll think about it. Now if you ask me to help with your security, then I'm in. I've got guys I can call. I'm sure Blade will pay the freight again for bodyguards."

"I don't want that." I leaned against the wall next to my bedroom door. "But, Rafe, what am I going to do? I can't kill two mortals who have the misfortune to have had a crazy father. I feel bad enough that I robbed them of a dad."

"Westwood needed taking out. This may play out the same way, and you can't feel guilty about it." Rafe's voice was hard. I understood. He'd felt the sting of one of the hunter's arrows too, after throwing his body in the line of fire.

I shivered and wrapped my arms around myself. That night, when we'd had the "showdown" as Rafe called it, was still way too vivid a memory. I'd managed to wrestle Westwood's crossbow away from him and pull the trigger. Then I'd been hustled away from the scene. My last sight of Westwood had been of him bleeding out with one of his own arrows in his gut.

"You could always run." He pulled me to him, his look of sympathy making me feel weepy.

"It's tempting." I took a breath. "Damn it, Rafe, I don't

want to leave Austin, but if I stay here, I'm risking all my friends. Those vamp-detector glasses will spot every vampire who comes near me. The Westwoods might decide to use them for target practice." I felt overwhelmed and couldn't see a way out.

"I'm here for you, Glory. We'll figure this out together." Rafe gave me a comforting hug, nothing sexual about it, and I relaxed against him.

"Thanks, Rafe. I like your friend Nadia. I know you'll make a success of this club." I pulled back and touched his cheek. "She can stay here as long as she needs to."

"Appreciate that. But I checked with Damian. He's got a secure house she can rent, and I'll set her up there. She likes her own space. And she'll be bringing in other people to work in the club. *Her* people. More vamps and shifters she trusts to watch over her during the day." He glanced in the bathroom. "She use up all the hot water?"

"Yes. But I'll just shower when I get up. 'Night, Rafe." I was sinking fast. Dawn couldn't be very far away. I opened my bedroom door and kicked off my shoes. I hoped Rafe could help me figure out a way to beat these Westwoods. Because right now I felt like waving a white flag and getting it over with.

Five

"**Where** are you going?" Rafe stopped me the next evening as I was stuffing my cell in one pocket of my jeans and my credit card in the other.

"To work. By way of the roof." I reached up and patted his cheek. "No worries, pal. I've got a plan."

"Care to share?" He grabbed my hand and pulled me to the couch. "You know Vivien Westwood's not going to give up after one failed attempt. And her brother will quickly figure out that you're still in town."

I'd filled Rafe in about the night before. No choice. He'd threatened to go to Blade and offer up some bodyguard buddies for hire if I didn't come clean with every excruciating detail, right down to Viv's hair color and where I'd tossed the arrow I'd pulled out of my shoulder after the attack.

"I get it. So I'm going to go up to the roof, shift into bird form and fly down to check out the alley. If I see it's clear, I'll shift back and go into the shop, Glory as usual." I jumped up, grabbed my keys and stuffed them in with my credit card. Didn't like the added inches on the hips, but unavoidable.

"And if it's not clear?" Rafe frowned, obviously trying to

decide if I needed him as backup. But I knew he and Nadia had an appointment in a few minutes to sign papers.

"Then I sneak inside. I know better than to take on the crossbow queen and her hulk by myself again, thank you very much." I smiled. "Relax, Rafe. I can shift now without freaking out. I'll use that to my advantage. Once I'm inside the shop, I'm sure I'll be okay. The Westwoods wouldn't dare do something stupid like attack me in front of witnesses."

"I hope you're right." Rafe put his hands on my shoulders. "I'm coming up on the roof with you. I want to watch how you handle the alley." He shook his head when I started to object. "Old habit. Let me do this. It'll only take a few minutes. Nadia's still working on her makeup. I'll be back before she's got her eyeliner on straight."

"Don't interfere, Rafe. I *am* handling this. But if you want a front-row seat, for purely entertainment value, come ahead." I slipped out of his grasp and headed for the door.

"Cocky, aren't you? I hope that doesn't work against you." Rafe grumbled as he followed me up the stairs. On the roof, the sky was clear and the stars were out. It was a beautiful night. Too bad. A little cloud cover would have helped. But then the lights were out in the alley so that was okay. Not that I needed them to see Vivien and her tough guy crouched behind my Suburban. What? Did they think I'd go back to my car that wouldn't start?

Maybe I *was* feeling a little cocky, but that was way better than the depression and defeatist attitude of the night before. I'd decided to have a little fun at Viv's expense.

"Here goes." I glanced at Rafe. "Payback for that hurt Ms. Westwood put on me."

"Damn it, Glory. Be careful." Rafe was talking to the flutter of my wings, as I'd already shape-shifted into a small brown bird that could land on a wire behind my stalkers without being noticed.

I settled on the wire and got into some mind reading. Interesting. Viv was aggravated that she'd broken a nail on that crossbow the night before. I chirped with pride when she blamed her misses on what she called my supersonic speed. Her sidekick called the whole thing a pain in his ass. But a paycheck. So he'd crouch here all night as long as he was getting the big bucks. Didn't believe in this vampire shit. No way. But something was up with the chick from the night before, standing up to them like that. He could usually intimidate women with his size. I chirped again.

Back to Viv. Now she was worried about the rustling sounds coming from the Dumpster. Didn't blame her. I'd smelled a rat as soon as I'd landed. And roaches. Trust me, I may be a bloodsucker, but I'm as freaked out by insects and rodents as any other sensible person. Phil the exterminator and I were bosom buddies, so to speak. I flashed cleavage and got the shop checked out twice a month at half price. Of course my own phobia didn't mean I couldn't use Viv's to my advantage . . .

"You believe in vampires, Sean?" Viv moved closer to Sean when there was another rustle and a squeak from the Dumpster.

"Seems like that's a question you shoulda asked yourself before you shot at that woman last night, Ms. Westwood. My answer is hell no." Sean just barely kept from laughing. He was thinking that it was a shame rich people were nuts, but maybe he could use it to his advantage.

"Daddy was so sure. You saw his house. It's full of vampire stuff." Viv grabbed Sean's arm. "Did you hear that?"

"What?" Sean pulled out a sidearm.

"I think there are rats out here." Viv was having a hard time concentrating on vampires. Didn't blame her. "Anyway, if the woman wasn't a vampire, why didn't she call the police? I wounded her last night."

"Lots of reasons people don't call the police. Maybe she's running a little something illegal out of her shop here." Sean shrugged and put his gun away. "I don't see anything. You ready to leave?"

"Five more minutes. I'd like to talk to this woman. See what she and Dad had going. Maybe she can tell me where

Daddy is or if"—Viv's voice cracked—"he's alive. Those body-guards swore she killed him. Maybe she was after his money. Wouldn't have to be a vampire to be a greedy bitch."

"True enough." Sean sighed, obviously resigned to waiting.

A roach scuttled out from under my car, and he casually smashed it with his sneaker. Viv and I both jumped and squealed. Luckily mine came out as a chirp.

Greedy bitch? Westwood had come after *me*. I hopped off my perch and landed behind Viv. Another shift and I was ready to show Viv how a real monster worked. Not that Sean would have considered what I had in mind such a freak-out. But Viv would go absolutely nuts. Not even a glance at Sean's lethal size twelves could stop me. Hey, I was pissed.

I eased around beside her really nice boots, gray suede, and crawled up the sole to the edge of her jeans. Inside gave me an interesting perspective and a fragrance in a "the woman used a really expensive body lotion" kind of way. It was almost too much as I headed north. I got to the top of her boot and hit the inside of her knee.

Hey, Viv, you've got a visitor.

"Oh, my God!"

She jumped, and I slid a few inches down a well-waxed and toned calf. Her squeal could have shattered glass. Nice.

"Ms. Westwood? What is it?" Sean's deep voice was hushed and worried. "You see her?"

"No! There's something, oh, oh, crawling on me!"

I scampered up until I was in ick territory, way too close to a pair of sheer black panties, then made a circuit of her thigh, doing a little impromptu break dance that made her squeak and screech. Plenty of room for dancing since she hadn't favored tight jeans. She hopped around, doing a pretty good high kick until she jarred me loose. I slipped down to the top of one boot and almost fell inside, hanging on to the rim with both claws or whatever the hell cockroaches call those things they grab with.

"Hush, now. Someone could hear you. I reckon if there's something illegal goin' on in that shop, your girl could have muscle helping her. You want them to come check this alley?" Sean's voice was soothing, and Viv froze, proving she wasn't as dumb as she looked. "Where is it? Point and I'll kill the sucker."

Uh-oh. I clung tightly to my perch. I really didn't want to end up inside, next to Viv's bare foot. These were obviously last year's favorites, if you get my drift. What had seemed like fun now wasn't.

"Don't hit me." Viv shook her leg. "This is stupid. I don't feel anything now. Must have been my imagination."

Easy for her to say. At least I was slipping down the outside of her boot now and ready to run for freedom.

"There goes your imagination, lady." Sean sounded gleeful. Viv shrieked.

Guess she'd seen me. I put on vamp speed at the sound of Sean's shoes behind me. Could I be one of those flying roaches? I was all set to take wing when I was hit from behind and slammed into the brick wall at the back of the shop. I fell to the pavement and lay dazed and still. I knew better than to struggle to my feet. It was dark and from the sweet smell I figured I'd landed in, oh, great, a puddle of molasses from Mugs and Muffins next door. I'd be invisible to a mortal.

"Got him, Ms. Westwood. Ready to call it a night?"

"Yes. I need to talk to my brother. This vampire thing is nuts. Daddy was, sorry to say it, a little nuts too. That will makes no sense, and I'm not doing this. We need to lawyer up and see what we can do to get the estate settled." Viv sounded determined. "But we need to find Daddy or his, um, body. This Glory St. Clair may have killed him. She looked like the kind of woman who would go after a rich man and take advantage." Viv sniffled. "Poor Daddy. Bet he tried to break up with her and she wouldn't accept it."

How did *I* get to be the bad guy? I wanted to shift and tear out her throat. I even tried to move my foot, but the sticky mess held me prisoner.

"Is some money missing? Maybe you need to check your daddy's accounts."

"Good idea, Sean. I find checks made out to this St. Clair woman, I'll make sure you get a bonus. A very generous bonus." Viv's voice faded as they headed out.

I lay there, utterly miserable, and decided to console myself with a taste of my bed of pain. Because that kick hadn't exactly been a love bump. Molasses. No, maple syrup. Mmm. Too bad I couldn't do more than lick my wing. Mortals would have enjoyed a stack of pancakes with this stuff. I'd heard the coffee shop made killer muffins with maple syrup and brown sugar. I wallowed in self-pity, dreaming of a muffin and wondering if I should try to shift back to my vampire self. I dreaded it. I'd ruin my outfit if I went to Glory form while lying here.

"Glory, what were you thinking?" Rafe stared down at me.

I figured that didn't deserve an answer so I closed my eyes and stayed put, silent and mortified. A cockroach covered in maple syrup. Could I be more wretched? Sure. I could lie here and be reamed out by Rafe. And I had it coming. I'd pulled a stupid, impulsive stunt and had no defense.

"Is she all right?" Nadia.

Well, if that didn't put the icing on my shit cake. I opened my eyes and saw Rafe reaching for me.

"Don't move, Glory, I'm going to be very careful. You don't want to lose a foot or, uh, wing." Damn it, he was trying not to laugh.

"Not funny, Rafe." If my thoughts seemed a little defensive, blame it on the fact that my mouth was sealed closed except where I darted out my tongue for a last lick of that delicious syrup. Rafe didn't say another word, just eased me out of my sticky prison.

Between Rafe's gentle handling and Nadia's excellent self-control—not a smile on her gorgeous face—I would have cried if I thought roaches had tear ducts.

"That woman was the enemy after you?" Nadia glanced down the alley. "We should have left Glory here a little longer and taken care of her when we had the chance, Rafael."

"No, Glory asked us to wait and try to solve the problem

another way, so that's what we'll do." Rafe had me out of the mess. Now he nodded toward Nadia. "I've got shop keys in my left front pocket. Would you pull them out? We need the red one."

"Of course." Nadia grinned and took her time probing Rafe's pocket. At one point he grunted and gave her a look that should have warned her off, but she just laughed and finally held up the set of keys. "Got them."

In moments, we were inside. Rafe stuck his head inside the shop and let the clerk on duty know that we were in the back and not to be disturbed.

"You ready to try shifting back, Glory?"

"I'm covered with syrup. I'm afraid I'll end up with that gunk all over the clothes I'm wearing." I saw Nadia nod.

"She's right. Give her to me. I'll take her in the bathroom I see here and carefully clean off the mess. She may end up a little damp, but better than sticky, eh, Glory?" Nadia smiled and held out her hand.

"Yes, thanks."

"Hey, woman to woman, I understand." Nadia carried me into the bathroom and was meticulous, using paper towels and even cotton swabs to get the sticky mess off me. Finally, she sighed. "That's the best I can do. Shift and let's see what we've got."

I concentrated and ended up hobbling into the back room. Sean's kick had done a number on my backside. I had a feeling I had a boot print on my butt. My own boots stuck a little when I walked across the floor and I needed to wash my hands, but other than that, my clothes and everything else were in great shape. I impulsively hugged Nadia, careful not to touch her with my hands.

"Thanks so much. I know you guys have an appointment and I'm making you late. You went above and beyond here." I smiled, then rushed over to rinse the sticky off my hands.

"No worries." Nadia shook her head at Rafe. "This man wasn't leaving your side until he was sure you were okay."

"And still won't until I've ripped you a new one. Are you

friggin' nuts?" Rafe put his hands on my shoulders. "Sean could have stomped you, and no amount of vamp healing could have brought you back. I was seconds away from shifting and ripping his damned head off."

"But you let me do it my way. Thanks for that. And I get it. I'm an idiot." I put my hands over his. "Sorry I freaked you out. Temporary insanity. Won't happen again." I smiled at him. "Thanks. For sticking around. I do appreciate it. Now go take care of your business. I'm fine. I'll be surrounded by people here, and it's not your job to keep me safe anymore."

"I know. But I can't seem to break the damned habit." He stepped back. "Try not to do anything stupid while I'm gone."

"I've reached my quota for tonight." I rubbed my sore butt. "I'm taking it easy for now. Sean must have been a kicker on his high school football team. He sure drop kicked me."

"Don't remind me." Rafe grabbed the back doorknob. "Let's go, Nadia. I'm done here."

"So I see. Glad you're all right, Glory." Nadia followed Rafe. "Lock the door behind us. I don't like these people stalking you. Anyone who wants to kill one vampire is an enemy to all of us." She shut the door.

Well. I stared at the closed door, trying to work up warm fuzzies for Nadia, who had been pretty cool about this, and Rafe, who'd actually respected my wishes. But my butt was killing me. Bottom line? My playtime *had* been a dumb stunt. Hindsight. Oh, I could do jokes like that all night long. Instead, since I was safe inside, I would do a little work for the shop. Too bad Flo and Aggie arrived just then. They were chattering about the latest Victoria's Secret catalog. Shower research. Fine. Concentrate on the wedding. So I'd make some calls to show Aggie that my party was on track too.

"Simon Destiny, please. Tell him it's Glory St. Clair."

Flo gasped when she heard me. "Glory, hang up. You know he's dangerous."

She was right. The leader of the Energy Vampires could

arrange to have the stuffing sucked right out of you, and had tried to get to me, Rafe, and even my buddy Flo more than once. But recently we'd called a truce, and now he had something I wanted. This bachelorette party had to rock. And the EVs made stuff you couldn't get anywhere else.

"Gloriana. How did you know I was just talking about you?" Simon's snake-oil-salesman voice came on the line. And the idea that he'd been discussing me? Well, it was enough to make the room spin and my stomach camp out in the back of my throat. I'd have sat down, but it wasn't worth the pain.

"Must be boring out there in EV land. What on earth would you have to discuss about me?" I held off Flo and shook my head when she tried to snatch my phone.

"Don't try to deflect, dear. Why did you call? What can I do for you? Is your friend Israel Caine in town again? I read in the paper that he's performing here. Also that you two broke up. So sorry to hear that." Simon oozed fake sympathy. Well, maybe not so fake. He knew Ray could afford his services, including a daylight room and chocolate that vamps could actually eat.

"Don't believe everything you read, Simon. Ray and I are still tight, just not engaged. But I'm not calling for Ray. I'm throwing a little party and want to buy some of your special treats." I smiled when Flo backed off and settled down to listen.

"Now, Glory, I know you like my chocolate truffles, but those are only available here at headquarters." Simon chuckled. "Bring Israel out here again, and you can have my treats. We'll arrange a romantic weekend that should have him yours again in no time."

"Thanks, Simon. When I want relationship advice, I know where to come. But don't you have a menu of things I can do for takeout? Like you do with the Vamp Viagra. Come on, Simon. Flo's getting married. I'm throwing her a bachelorette party. This is a once-in-a-lifetime deal. We hope." I gasped when I got a stiletto in the instep. "We *know*. Anyway, I'm sure Energy Vampires have some great products that a group of ladies could enjoy. Anything margarita flavored?"

Aggie gave me a narrow-eyed look, clearly seeing me trying to steal her thunder. Oops, bad choice of words. She had the thunder all tied up. Rain and lightning too. Anyway, I heard Simon talking to someone in the background.

"Well?"

"Of course. I'll send Greg Kaplan to you with samples. Unless you'd like to suck it up and come out here." Simon chuckled, like he didn't believe I'd have the nerve.

"Yeah, I know what gets sucked up out there. Hate to disappoint, but I've been shifting lately. A lot. My energy level's at an all-time low."

"Sorry to hear that, Gloriana. Your value to me just took a nosedive. But I'd still like to see you. I'll play nice."

"Really? Nice? Somehow that's one four-letter word I doubt you know." I patted Flo's hand when she put her arm around me. She knew how much I hated dealing with Simon. And that I was doing this for her.

"Is that any way to talk to a man who can give you what you want?" Simon's voice cooled, and I figured I'd pushed too hard.

"You're right. I'm sorry. But we're talking business, and I've got Flo's platinum card ready to close a deal. You really don't want me anywhere near your place anyway, Simon. The last time I was out there, my new boyfriend and old boyfriend almost tore the place apart and got you some bad publicity. Besides, that energy-sucking goddess of yours creeps me out. No offense."

"None taken. You're wise to be cautious around our supreme being. Many foolish vampires have ignored her power to their regret. But you'd be perfectly safe *this* time. There's someone I want you to meet."

"No, thanks. I'd rather suck blood from a rabid hyena." I smiled at Flo. "I'm surprised Greg hasn't been sucked dry by now. Seems like he's always on your to-do list."

"True enough. But then he comes up with something

valuable, and I spare him one more time. What can I say? I guess I'm a soft touch." Simon said something to whoever was with him, and I'd heard enough. It wasn't just his goddess who creeped me out. I was going to hang up or hurl right into the phone if I had to put up this brave front one more minute.

"Send him out, then. When can I expect him?"

"Later tonight. No reason to delay. I've heard the wedding is in a few weeks." Simon tossed this off casually while I felt my heart freeze. How did he know that?

"What do you know about Flo's wedding? You're not on the guest list." I glanced at Flo, and she shook her head.

"I know everything that happens in the vampire world in Austin, well, even in Texas, Gloriana. Why, I know a lot about your recent trip to California."

"Oh, yeah? Stay out of my business, Simon. Just sell me some of your goods. That's all." I ended the call.

"Greg Kaplan's coming over with some samples. We can pick out what we want. Aggie, maybe you'll find something you want for the shower too. That's why I asked about the margarita stuff." Guess near death by tennis shoe had rattled my brain tissue. I was actually being nice to Aggie.

"Who's Greg Kaplan?" Aggie smiled, folded down a page in the catalog and tossed it on the table.

"An old flame of Glory's. Ended badly, right, Glory?" Flo picked up the catalog. "No more black, Aggie. I want some color in my underwear drawer. Red, violet, tiger print. *Molto* sexy."

"Let's hear the story." Aggie smiled at me. "He dump you?"

Of course she would assume that. "I don't have a clue. The loser is a vampire who wiped out my memory so I wouldn't remember dating him. Can you believe it? Like he's such a catch I would have stalked him to try to get him back." I grabbed a pink silk bustier from a shelf, ready for a subject change. "Flo, this is vintage, but you'd look hot in it. Try it on."

"I want to hear more about this vamp who made a fool out of you." Aggie snagged the bustier out of my hand.

"This is great, though. Maybe I'll try it on and buy it for myself."

"Leave her alone, Aggie. And she showed it to me first. I try." Flo took the bustier and stalked over to the bathroom. "Greg is a toad, but he has good connections, so we'll be nice to him. Simon Destiny is worse than a toad. He is *il diavolo*. I would kill him with my bare hands if I wasn't afraid of him and his goddess." Flo shuddered and slammed the bathroom door.

"Wow. Is she kidding? I didn't think Flo was afraid of anything or anyone." Aggie was wide-eyed.

"Smart people, vamps, Sirens, whatever, are afraid of Simon Destiny. He's got power on top of power. I've come up against it and almost didn't live to tell about it." I leaned against the table. "It's kind of like that freeze thing you do. I bet your boss can do that to you. Am I right?" Aggie could freeze you in place, and you couldn't even *blink*. It's a skill I'd like to have, I tell you that.

"Yeah, and I hate it. You feel freakin' helpless." Aggie shuddered.

"Well, Simon can do it too. And he can read your mind past any block. Totally blows your defenses." For once, Aggie and I were in sync.

"Bet he couldn't read *my* mind." Aggie's chin went up.

"Not a bet I'd take." I sighed, tentatively tried to sit on the stool and hopped up again. It was better, but it would take a day of vamp sleep before my bum would be 100 percent. I wished for my computer mirror upstairs. I just knew there was a boot print on one or both of my cheeks.

"I'm sure a throw-down between the Storm God and Simon would be quite a sight, but I wouldn't want to be close by. Simon's got a goddess backing him that's from some part of the Underworld. So we tread carefully around the EVs. Unless we have no choice." I grinned. "I almost skewered Simon once. To save Rafe. Simon's never forgiven me. So I don't trust him. I don't doubt he'll try to get even with me someday."

"But you called him and sounded calm as can be." Aggie actually sounded admiring. "Didn't think you had it in you."

"Don't underestimate my BFF. Eh, Glory?" Flo stepped out of the bathroom, a vision in pale pink and lace. When Richard saw her in that, he'd swallow his tongue. "How I look?"

"Gorgeous. That's your shower gift from me. Take it off and I'll wrap it. Save it for your honeymoon." I grinned and got up when I heard a knock at the back door. I knew who it was, could smell him through the door, but asked anyway. "Who is it?"

"Your long lost love, Glory. Who else?" Greg said cheerfully. "Why are there mortals with crossbows and your picture lurking in your alley, lady? Want me to take them out?"

Six

"Get in here." I grabbed Greg's arm and dragged him inside, then slammed the door. "Are you crazy? How many are there?"

"Four. A leader and three bodyguards. That's my take." Greg grinned at Aggie. "Introduce me to this beautiful lady."

"I won't be doing her any favors, but, Aggie, this is Greg Kaplan, the creep I told you about who does grunt work for the EVs. Greg, Aglaophonos, a Siren who can freeze you in your tracks if you do her wrong, so behave yourself." I don't know why I bothered warning him; it would have served him right if he'd ended up a statue in the park across the street.

"Now, Glory, I've risen in the ranks at EV headquarters lately. And I'm not so bad once you get to know me." He ignored Flo, who, muttering Italian curses obviously intended for him, had emerged from the bathroom dressed in her own clothes again. He smiled at Aggie. "Aggie, I'm sure you can make up your own mind about the men you meet." Greg gave her his "I'll seduce the panties off you, but I hope you're not wearing any" look.

"I certainly can." Aggie looked from me to Flo and back to Greg. "That freeze thing is no joke. I can turn you to what amounts to stone with a look, buddy boy." She ran a red-painted fingernail down the front of his blue button-down shirt. "But that's only in an emergency. Seems a shame to turn a hot guy into a cold statue."

"Much as I enjoy watching the mating dance here, we've got a war party in the alley, and I've got an idea." I tapped Greg on the shoulder. "Give me your cell phone."

"Why?" He reached into his jeans pocket anyway, then sniffed. "Glory, anyone tell you your new perfume smells like maple syrup? When I was mortal, I loved the stuff."

"Thanks. If I can't eat, at least I can smell yummy. Now I assume your number is untraceable. Right?"

"Of course. Can't have just anyone calling EV headquarters." Greg grinned at Aggie. "You should come out there. It's an amazing place. I'm sure you like water. We've got a creek and private pool where you can swim as nature intended."

"Glory, I'm either going to throw up or toss Gregory out the door into the alley again. What are you going to do?" Flo shoved him out of the way and stepped to my side.

"Listen." I hit 911 and pressed speaker phone.

"Nine-one-one, what is your emergency?"

"Oh, my gawd. Oh, my gawd. They're going to kill us!"

"Slow down, miss. Where are you?"

"Sixth Street. Near the alley behind where I got my new tat and that coffee shop, Mugs and somethin'. Oh, yeah, Muffins! My boyfriend parked his bike there, and when we went to get it, this gang of guys were like hiding between the cars."

"Did they threaten you?"

"Yeah, yeah! They had, oh, my gawd, spear guns. And Ronnie, he's sayin' what're they doin' next to my bike? And wantin' to take 'em on." I sobbed noisily.

"Is anyone hurt?"

"Not yet 'cause I'm not lettin' him get killed even though he's got shit for brains. Oh, my gawd, oh, my gawd! They're comin' this way! They've got real guns too, not just those spear things." I screamed Ronnie's name.

"Miss, please stay on the line. Help is on the way."

I yelled "No!" then slammed the phone shut.

"Bravo! I forgot you were an actress, Glory." Greg clapped.

"I want to see what happens when the *polizia* come." Flo laughed, and even Aggie grinned.

"Let's go out through the front and hit the roof. We should have a great view of the action from there." I opened the door into the shop and told the clerk I was taking off for a while. There were a couple customers in the store, and we got a few curious looks as we hurried through, my boots squeaking when they stuck to the floor. A quick glance assured me that there wasn't anyone suspicious out front, so David Westwood must have concentrated on the alley this go-round.

I punched in the security code, then we ran up the stairs just as we heard sirens coming down Sixth Street. It wasn't an uncommon sound in this area, and I'm sure David ignored it, figuring there was trouble farther down the street.

We'd just settled on the roof when police cars screeched to a halt at both ends of the alley. Uniformed officers wearing bulletproof vests hopped out and crouched behind vehicles, shouting for the men hunkered down near the Dumpster and my car to lay down their weapons and come out with their hands up.

David cursed and threw down his crossbow. His men tossed guns and rifles into a pile, and I shivered. All this to take me out? Flo put her arm around me.

"You outsmarted them, *mia amica*."

"This time." I leaned against her.

Flo sniffed. "You do smell funny. And walked funny out of the shop, like you're hurting. You want to explain?"

"Maybe later. Look!" I pointed to a man behind the police cars and the officers assigned to keep the interested crowd back while Westwood's gang was being handcuffed.

"I'm worried about you, Glory." Flo wasn't giving up.

"But it's Jerry!" I concentrated and sent him a mental message. We were pretty far up, but he should be able to hear me.

"He sees us!" Flo hugged me. "Now I feel better. He'll come, and you can tell him what's wrong." She glanced at Aggie and Greg, who were whispering. "Those two chummy? I don't like it."

"Aggie's a big girl, and she can be mean as a snake. Remember? She can handle Greg." I had my own worries. Aggie wasn't even in the top ten. Flo was right. Jerry had glanced up and nodded. Message received. Now he was talking to a policeman and giving the silent prisoners who'd asked for a lawyer a narrow-eyed look. Reading minds.

The men still weren't wearing the vamp-detecting glasses. Why not? Had Brent kept those a secret? All *his* guards had worn them. If the innovation had died with Brent, it was an unexpected advantage to us. If these guys had worn the glasses and noticed Jerry was a vampire . . . Well, what would they have done? Yelled "Fangs!"? In front of the police, who were already interested in why they were hanging out in the alley with my picture and weapons?

Oops. My picture. I bet the cops would come calling to ask me about that. I'd have to make up a story. And what would David's story be? Spurned lover? That would make him a stalker. Of course he could afford the sharpest lawyers and would probably get off with a plea bargain and community service. His best bet would be temporary insanity. He could point to his daddy's vampire-hunting Web site. Claim the crazy ran in the family. I heard the door to the roof open. Jerry was here.

Greg's body language changed from seducer to warrior in an instant. Obviously he remembered that Blade wasn't a fan of the EVs or their representatives.

"Aggie and I are going down to my car to try some samples. What she doesn't want for her shower, she'll leave for you at the shop." Greg finally acknowledged Flo with a tight smile. "Florence, guess you should come with us. These are for your parties after all."

Flo glanced from me to Jerry's grim face. "Glory, that okay with you?"

"Sure. Make a list of what you like." I smiled at her. "Jerry and I need to talk. I'll be fine, right, Jer?"

"Of course." Jerry nodded. "Florence, Aggie." He didn't acknowledge Greg. "Be careful, ladies. If you need me, give me a mental shout. I'd be more than happy to eliminate any problems." He gave Greg a warning stare.

"Relax, Blade. I come in peace. Simon sends his regards. No hard feelings on our side." Greg pulled a packet out of his pocket and tossed it at Jerry. It fell at his feet. "Free Vamp Viagra. Don't be such a hard-ass. Glory will thank you for trying it." He yelped when Blade suddenly had him up by his shirt front and dangling over the edge of the roof.

"Why don't I drop you into the alley? The ladies will meet you downstairs." Blade shook Greg, who'd grabbed his wrists.

"Ease up. Can't you take a joke?" Greg cut his eyes toward me. "Glory? The cops are still down there. We don't need this."

"Jerry, he's right. He wouldn't even get a broken bone, and we'd get unwanted attention." I put my arms around his waist and pulled him back. Not that he'd have moved if he hadn't realized what I said was true. "And the Vamp Viagra might be fun. Why not take a free ride?" I stood on my toes and ran my fangs along his neck. "I'm having a stressful night. Might help me relax."

"There you go." Greg landed on the roof and smoothed out his shirt. "Ladies, shall we take off? Seems Glory's got an agenda, and we're in the way." He steered Aggie and Flo toward the door.

"Glory, I only go if you say it's okay. Jeremiah is not in such a good mood." Flo moved away from Greg. "Jeremiah, be kind to her. Glory handled this very well. But she is shook up. *Sì?*"

"Yes, I am. Look at all those weapons." I clung to Jerry. Why was he so angry? Not at me, of course. I threw up a block. As long as no one told him I'd gone crawling into Viv's jeans, I should be golden. Totally the victim.

"Gloriana knows I'm just worried about her. It's those bastards downstairs I'd like to rip apart. You can leave us, Florence." Jerry said this quietly. "I'd never hurt Gloriana."

"Right. Go, Flo. We're fine." I finally let go of him. "See you tomorrow night. Oh, and I forgot to tell you. Nadia Komisky is Rafe's partner. She says she knows you and that we can have the bachelorette party at their new nightclub."

"Nadia! Yes. She gave Damian a run for his life. Hah!" Flo was now all smiles. "And this bachelorette party will be some fun. I'll invite her. You and I will talk tomorrow." She turned on her heel and shoved Aggie and Greg out ahead of her.

"Another Westwood attack." Jerry looked over the wall as the police cars finally left the alley and all was quiet again.

"Yes. But Greg saw them, and I called nine-one-one. The police handled it. I was never in danger at all." I tried to relax.

"Then maybe you can explain why you smell like a cheap pancake house." Jerry didn't look at me. Just kept staring down at the dark alley.

"What do you know about places like that?" I moved closer.

"I know a lot of things that seem trivial at the moment. And don't know what I need to." He finally looked at me. "When I heard there were men in the alley with crossbows and your picture . . ." He slapped the wall, and a piece of concrete crumbled. "Damn it, Gloriana, what the hell is going on here?"

"Seems that arrow attack was more than the revenge thing I took it for. Brent Westwood left a will. He's got two kids. The first one to pop his killer inherits his estate, the whole enchilada. It's over a billion dollars, and that's a powerful motivator." I picked up the baggie of Vampire Viagra. If I could persuade Jerry to use this, I could definitely get his mind off life or death. Does that make me a live-for-the-moment kind of woman? Well, might as well. When you're being stalked . . .

Suddenly I was grabbed by both arms and shaken until my hair flew around my head like I'd been struck by lightning again.

"What the hell is the matter with you? You could have been killed tonight. Did you see the weapons that mob carried?"

"How could I miss them?" I jerked out of his grasp, the rooftop spinning. "Was that necessary? I think you bruised my arms. And after you told Flo you'd never hurt me." And what was with my men tonight? Seems I'd pushed Jerry and Rafe too far for once. And how rude of Jerry to poke into my mind without an invitation. It was something we simply didn't do.

"You'll heal. It's a miracle I haven't knocked you on your arse before now. I swear you are the most damnably provoking woman I've ever known." Jerry ran his hand through his hair.

"Thanks a lot. And, trust me, my arse has suffered enough abuse tonight." I brushed my hair out of my eyes, then pulled up my sleeves as if to check for those bruises. Laying on some guilt. In case Jerry decided I still had a knock on my arse coming. He was seriously steamed. And I understood. If he'd been in this kind of danger and kept it from me . . .

"I'm afraid to ask what the hell that means. God, Gloriana, you could have stepped out of your back door and been shot through the heart." He reached for me again, gently this time, and pulled me to his chest. "I remember what those crossbows can do. Saw my best friend taken down with one right in front of me. Remember?" He said this with his face in my hair, arms wrapping me tight as if he could keep me safe single-handedly.

I swallowed. He was right. Of course this had brought back horrific memories for him. But I wasn't a complete idiot. Hadn't planned to unwittingly step out there without someone checking the alley first. Though if the men *had* been wearing vamp-detection glasses . . .

I cleared my throat and looked up. "They hauled David off to jail. I'm safe for tonight anyway."

Jerry released me and stepped back, under control again. "You said there were two Westwood brats. Where's the other one now?"

"I ran her off earlier tonight. Stepped in maple syrup doing it. That's where the pancake smell is coming from." I glanced down at my shoes. "Anyway, Rafe saw me do it." Oops. Jerry looked like a thundercloud.

"Great. Valdez knows about this, but he didn't tell me."

"He's not your employee anymore. He doesn't owe you—"

"I let him out of his contract, but he does still owe me." Jerry pulled the Vampire Viagra from my hand. "You want to play? Forget the future and live for the night? Why not? Come home with me. I don't have roommates to hear you scream with pleasure. If your life is going to be cut short, I guess we should make the most of the time we have left."

"Jerry, I—" Tears clogged my throat, and I followed him dumbly to the door. Did I want to make love with him? Of course I did. Maybe I didn't like what he said, but he was way better at facing reality than I was. A warrior. And I had a history of running away when things got hot instead of standing and fighting. I hated to do it, but maybe leaving was still my best move. So a night of his lovemaking? Bring it on.

He silently held the door open, and I walked ahead of him down the stairs. My damned sticky boots squeaked with every step. I'd worn tight jeans and a red sweater. I wished I could stop in my apartment to at least change shoes. Or it might help my cause to switch out my bra. What I had on could have carried rocks for David to use against Goliath. The image made my mouth quirk in a smile.

"What's funny?" He slipped his arm around me at the bottom of the stairs.

"Me, us. Always ending up in bed together. It beats talking

when we'll only fight anyway." I reached up and brought his head down to kiss his lips. "I know you're worried about me. I love you for it. Be patient. Give me a night to remember. Tomorrow night, I promise we can take this threat seriously."

He pulled me tight against him and kissed me deeply until I felt that centuries-old connection I needed so badly. "I love you, Gloriana. I don't want to live forever if it's in a world without you."

Tears filled my eyes. "Jerry. That's the most romantic thing you've ever said to me."

"It's the God's truth, but if you tell Valdez I spouted such drivel, I'll call you a liar." He kissed my nose, then hit the code to open the security door. "Stay here and let me check to make sure the coast is clear. Just because you ran a Westwood off once doesn't mean she's stayed away."

"Thanks." I smiled, totally pleased with him, while I waited for him to come back for me. For once I'd relax and let him take charge without a lot of objections. Vampire Viagra. I'd taken it accidentally once with the wrong man. It had made me wild, but I'd been left unsatisfied. It enhanced a vampire's sexual pleasure and prolonged it. Since we already have amazing libidos and the males can last pretty much all night long, this was going to be quite a night. I remembered that it took a few minutes to get going so we'd swallow our pills in the car on the way to Jerry's house. Then once in his bedroom . . .

We never made it to the bedroom. Jerry opened the back door and dragged me into the kitchen. The granite countertop was cold but solid, and I landed on my back, ready to take him on top of me. Thank God, my bum seemed to have healed and it didn't hurt, or at least not enough to slow me down.

My skin was tingling, on fire. I couldn't bear the touch of even a stitch of clothing on my body. Jerry had ripped off my sweater in the car. I'd shucked off my boots there too. My jeans and thong were near the door. Jerry ripped my unsexy bra apart down the front, and it was destined for the garbage. Jerry's shirt hung from the doorknob, and his shoes and pants lay tangled in a heap near the dishwasher.

"Jerry!" I tried to drag him down on top of me.

"Gloriana!" He slapped my hands away, then grinned and leaped on top of the counter to stand behind me. He was being playful. I loved it. He lifted me until I faced him. Good thing he had twelve-foot ceilings in this house.

"You realize mortals would think it's nasty to make love on kitchen countertops." I pressed myself against him, rubbing my breasts against his chest and lower.

"We've never cooked anything here. If Damian ends up selling to mortals, he'll have it cleaned." He teased my nipples, then gently gathered me in his arms and lowered me to the cold granite again. "This is a proper use for a kitchen. Perhaps I can have a meal while I'm here." His grin was full of fang.

"Perhaps. But seems like you want more than a drink from me." I reached between us to grasp him. "You're as hard as this stone beneath my bum. Are you feeling as wild as I am?"

"Like if I don't have you in the next moment, I'll disgrace myself?" He leaned down to take my nipple into his mouth, suddenly rough and hungry. When he raked his fangs across it, he drew blood and I moaned.

"Don't wait." I guided him into me and lifted my hips. At the same time I arched my back and dragged my own fangs along his shoulder. We were bleeding and moving and grinding into each other, as we became more frantic. We'd never abused each other, and yet this was more thrilling than I could remember. Jerry savaged my other nipple, and I gouged his biceps with my fingernails before I sank my fangs into his jugular.

"God, yes!" He cried as he plunged into me again and again. He grabbed my legs and flipped us over until I was on top, still connected to him. I rode him hard, releasing his neck so I could sit up and take him deeper inside me. He'd licked the wounds on my breasts clean, and I felt them healing already.

I looked down and saw his eyes closed as he strained to give me all of him. He pulsed inside me, and I reached down to squeeze his sacs, then raked them with my nails.

"Gloriana. Love!" He came with a warmth deep inside me. Answering spasms shook me from my toes to my heart. I collapsed on top of him and lay there, listening to his answering beat. Faster than usual. The Viagra, or what we'd just done?

Usually we'd lie together and bask in the afterglow for a few minutes. But not this night. The VV made Jerry pull me up the stairs at a dead run. His bed was a king with a comforter that he tossed aside before he flung me down.

"Madness, but I've got to have you again. Right. Now."

I stared up at him. Oh, yes, he was good to go again, and so was I. I held out my arms, and with a Scottish battle cry that made me laugh, he fell on top of me. He sheathed his sword inside me and grinned.

"I haven't been this randy since I was a lad chasing milkmaids into Da's barn." He stroked me, making me gasp at the pressure and the pleasure.

"Catch many?" I shoved him until we sat facing each other.

"A few. God, Gloriana, tell me if I hurt you." He held my hips as he pumped into me.

"Tell me if I hurt *you*." I growled and bit his ear, then licked it clean, savoring the salty sweetness of his blood as release shuddered through me again. I tightened my legs around him and held his shoulders as I screamed and fell back on the bed. He came with me, still moving, still hard inside me while I saw stars and moons and a crazy Scot looming over me as intent as if he were drilling a well.

"I . . . I can't stop." Not my normal in-control Jerry, he was panting and flushed.

I pulled his face down to mine, mouth to mouth, tongue to tongue. I let him know I could go as long as he could, longer. I grabbed his ass, pressing him deeper, and held on until he finally, finally surged one last time. He collapsed next to me, his body slick with sweat and streaks of blood where I'd scored him with my nails when I'd come yet again.

"Dear God in Heaven. That drug." He turned his head to stare at me, then touched my nipple with his fingertip. "You're bleeding again. Sorry. I don't remember doing that."

I leaned over to lick away the blood smeared along his hip. "I don't remember you doing it. I was too crazed." I sighed and laid my head on his chest. "Still feel, I don't know, like I've got an itch inside me that can't be soothed."

"Not sure I like this Vampire Viagra." Jerry ran his hand down my bare back. "Where's the finesse, the foreplay?"

I grinned. "You been reading sex manuals, Jer?"

"Give over, Gloriana. I watch cable. I try to do what pleases a woman. Even a milkmaid liked a bit of sport before she'd lift her skirts in the hayloft."

"I'm getting jealous." I eased my knee over his rising erection. Again. So soon. And I felt that rising urge myself. Crazy. "You've always known how to please me." I nudged him with my knee. "And when there's time, your fore-play is—"

I squealed when he abruptly rolled me off of him, then grabbed me and carried me toward the bathroom.

"If we're to have another go, then we'll shower first." He kicked open the bathroom door. "God help me, if the drug allows it, I'll show you finesse that'll have you screaming my name."

"God, yes." I landed on my feet and pulled him into the huge double shower. We discovered that the VV still rode us hard. Jerry took me standing against the tile wall, the soap giving us something new to play with and Jerry a chance to show that finesse he was so proud of. Scream his name? Oh, yeah.

I took him on the bench seat with the warm water pound-ing against the middle of my back. This time he shouted *my* name and almost knocked a hole in the tile wall when I used some of my own finesse. By the time we'd towel dried and collapsed back on the bed, dawn was near and we could hardly move.

"Guess that stuff's not too bad as long as you don't care about the niceties," I said as Jerry gathered me into his arms.

"Niceties? You mean like making love instead of sex? Guess it would be okay for an occasional hookup." Jerry yawned and watched for my reaction.

"Yeah, I'll keep that in mind." I laughed at his expression. "Okay, fine. I'll admit I'd tear out the throat of any bimbo you hooked up with, so don't go there." I snuggled against his hard body, then trailed a fingertip down his stomach. "And don't get me started on what I'd do to you."

"I stand warned." Jerry kissed the top of my hair, which I'd blown dry in his bathroom while he'd played with my breasts and kissed erotic paths all over my body, front to back, exclaiming over my various healing bruises and bites. I'd put off explanations of those he knew *he* hadn't given me, and he'd let me.

"This VV is dangerous. Do it too often, and you'd never get any work done. I've been neglecting my business lately, and that's got to stop." I had trouble getting too worked up over it though. Eight orgasms—or was it ten?—will do that to you.

"Your business won't matter if the Westwoods get their way. We need to talk about that, Gloriana." Jerry propped himself on one elbow and stared down at me.

"I know. I'm taking this very seriously, Jerry. I am. But can we put this discussion off until we wake up in the evening? Right now I'm limp from being well served, and I don't have it in me to get into this life-or-death stuff." I smiled up at him and put my hand on his jaw, rough with the start of his daily beard.

"I won't argue with you. But heed me, my girl. You'll not keep things like this from me again. I *am* going to keep you safe. Sappy sentiment or not, I love you. I will kill the man or woman who hurts you. But I'd rather keep them from trying."

"I know. I've always known it. I love you for it. Thank you, Jeremiah. Now lie back. The sun's coming up, and I'm out." I fell back, the darkness claiming me. I prayed Jerry didn't live to regret his vows. I sank with a shiver of foreboding.

Seven

Jerry's housekeeper, a shifter who worked during the day, had left my clothes, cleaned and folded, just outside the bedroom door. My cell phone, keys and credit card were piled on top. My boots, no longer sticky, sat neatly next to them. I guess she'd gone out to the garage and found them and my sweater in Jerry's car. Jerry obviously paid her really well. I checked my phone. Six missed calls and three messages. One from the shop, the rest from the Austin police department. Gulp.

I didn't bother to listen, just called the shop.

"Vintage Vamp's Emporium, Lacy speaking."

"It's Glory. What's up?"

"What isn't up, you mean. The police have been here. Seems they arrested a gang of guys behind the shop last night who were holding your picture and carrying enough weapons to start a revolution. They have questions." Lacy sighed. "All those cops in here haven't helped business."

"I'll bet. I have a bunch of messages I want to ignore."

"What are you going to say?" Lacy spoke to someone next to her. "I'm taking this to the back room. Erin's handling the front." I heard a thud. "Door's closed. Rafe came down and gave me the four-one-one. Westwood. He's haunting you from the grave!"

"Yeah, it's the pits." I sat on Jerry's bed. He was downstairs, returning some business calls in his home office. We hadn't had our confrontation yet. Lucky for me, unlucky for Jerry, there was some kind of crisis in a company he owned in Florida. I wished I could sneak out of here before he could grill me. I hated to ruin the afterglow of a hot night.

"What do you want me to say if the police come back?"

"That I'm coming in." I glanced at my watch. I needed to go home and change. Clean or not, I wanted clothes that hadn't touched Vivien Westwood's thigh. "I'll be there in an hour. I'll make up a story that should satisfy them. For now, we don't know who David Westwood is or why he's carrying around my picture."

"That's exactly what I said. That the guy must be psycho. Running around with a crossbow. I mean, how weird is that?" Lacy paused. "Glory, this is serious. You want me to get my family on it? We can handle a mortal, no problem."

Lacy's a were-cat from a large and powerful family. "Thanks, Lacy, but I don't want to answer to your mom if anything should happen to you or one of her other kittens."

"You've been good to me, Glory. Mom knows that. Say the word, and we'll have every cat in Travis County out at the Westwood ranch ready to do a little scratch and sniff." Lacy snarled. "We'll show that dipstick what happens when he messes with a friend of ours."

"Appreciate it, but I don't want to drag anyone else into this. Blade and I are on it. Let me see what we can figure out." I heard the bedroom door open. "Got to go. Thanks for handling things." I ended the call, then met Jerry's gaze. Time to face the music. I just hoped it wasn't a funeral dirge.

I laid it all out for him, all the little details I'd left out before. Richard's help to get David out of my shop and how I'd gotten the police involved on his second try. Then my little adventure with Viv as a cockroach.

"You make this sound like a game." Jerry had practically

walked a trench into the hardwood floor, and he looked like he wanted to shake me again.

"I know it's not. The stakes are too high. A billion has more zeros than I can wrap my brain around." No kidding. I celebrated when my bank balance hit three digits after all my bills were paid.

"Everything you've done so far has just postponed the inevitable. Convince the Westwoods to give up this hunt, or kill them both." Jerry sat on the bed beside me. "I think you know the only viable option."

Sometimes I forgot just how ruthless Jerry the warrior had been back in the day. I guess he saw my lack of self-preservation at all costs as a character flaw.

"Sorry, Jer, but I just can't kill two mortals. Besides, where would their bodyguards be while we're ripping out West-wood throats? Twiddling their thumbs?" I grabbed his hands. "You see how this could turn into a nightmare?"

"It already has, Gloriana. Wake up and deal with it." Jerry was itching to do just that. The old-fashioned way. And vampires didn't take prisoners. The bodyguards would be collateral damage.

"Quit looking like you want to rip out someone's throat, damn it." I started my own stomping circuit of the room. "There's got to be another way. But reasoning with them won't work. They both want the money and surely deserve to inherit their father's estate."

"Maybe, maybe not. We have no idea what their relationship with their father was like." Jerry stopped me in my tracks. "Let's go. You have to talk to the police. Look how these people have already complicated your life. Now you're involved in an investigation."

"I know. I hate it. I remember when the media thought Vintage Vamp's stood for vampires. It got worse when Flo painted that mural on the shop wall that looked like a vampire biting a woman's neck. I had a heck of a time convincing the public that a vamp was nothing but a roaring-twenties hottie."

"Your Goth customers are still hoping for a fang sighting." Jerry pulled me down the stairs. "Forget all that. Tell the police that Westwood's crazy and you're an innocent victim."

"That's true! This vamp hunt is totally unfair. The police should be on my side. I pay taxes. Though pitifully little compared to a billionaire. Damn, Jerry. If it comes to a power play, I'm shit out of luck."

Jerry frowned and jerked open the kitchen door. "Wait and see what the Westwood boy told them to explain his presence in the alley with an army at his back. That'll help us."

The detective who interviewed me was happy to share David Westwood's story. Seems David had my name as a person of interest, someone who'd been around when his father had disappeared. He'd been watching my shop trying to find his missing dad. Cue the violins. Witnesses claimed Daddy had died in the woods near Lake Travis and I'd been seen there that night. Blood had been found in a clearing that private DNA tests had confirmed belonged to Brent Westwood. No one had reported it to the police because his body hadn't been found. No body, no proof of a crime.

The detective shook his head. "Beats me why they didn't even file a missing person's report. If I disappeared like that, my kids would be all over it."

"That is strange. Not sure I'd believe a word this guy has to say." I wondered why David hadn't mentioned that video I'd heard about, but I sure didn't bring it up.

Anyway, according to the detective, David had admitted that his father had been hung up on vampires. The whole scenario had freaked out his kids, and maybe David had over-reacted to Dad's notes that claimed I was one of them. So he'd come to my alley fully armed to try to talk to me. The one time he'd come to my shop, I'd refused to meet with him. And my friends had been big dudes who seemed to run with a rough crowd. So Dave had brought his own reinforcements.

"What a fairy tale. First, this guy showed up in my shop

with bodyguards built like fire plugs and the IQs to match and asked my clerk some questions about me, made my customers uncomfortable. My friend who asked him to leave was an ex-priest. Sound like a rough type to you?" I waited until the detective wrote that down.

"Second, yes, I met his father once. He was creepy, talking about vampires. Who believes in that stuff? I threw him out of my shop. I mean, do I look like a vampire to you?" I tossed my hair, batted my eyelashes and gave the detective my "Glory is an innocent victim" look.

"Nutcase, pure and simple. The whole family obviously has a screw loose. Had him pegged as soon as I saw that crossbow. Sorry to bother you, Ms. St. Clair, just had to follow up." The detective shut his notebook and stuck it in his pocket. "The firepower those guys were carrying was way out of line, permits or not. Looked like an ambush, not a guy wanting to talk."

"Exactly! You see why I'm so freaked out? One of my employees had a car parked back there and saw the whole thing. She said they had my picture, like I was a target or something." Jerry, who'd stayed silent and watchful, was right beside me. "I'm afraid to go out my own back door now. Surely Westwood will face some kind of charges."

"That's up to the DA. I'll turn over my notes, suggest they step up patrols in this area." The detective laid a business card on the counter. "Call me if Westwood bothers you again. Ask for Danny Oleto."

"Why, thank you, Detective. I feel safer already." I walked him toward the door. "If Westwood gets released, will you let me know? I want to be aware . . ." I pulled a face. "In case he's stupid enough to come around again. And he's got a sister. Do you think she might bother me too?"

"I'll talk to her. Warn her off. But it was obvious to me that Westwood realized he'd made a mistake when he got to the station. His lawyer sure reamed him out." Danny smiled. "I think you're okay for now."

"Thank you so much." I smiled and held out my hand.

"No problem, I'll stay in touch." Danny shook my hand, then headed out. Once outside, he walked over to a patrol car parked at the curb. He leaned in and spoke to the officer inside as I shut the shop door.

"Interesting." Jerry spoke from behind me.

I looked around and saw that we had no customers. The patrol car pulled away, and the detective got into an un-marked car. That should help.

A lot of my regular customers were leery of law enforce-ment. Paranormals enjoyed my shop because they liked helping out a fellow freak. Other customers sometimes had an illegal substance stashed in their pockets while they enjoyed my rea-sonable prices on vintage clothes. Then there were some who avoided establishment types on general principle. Sure enough, the door jangled as a couple dressed in black with multiple piercings came in from the coffee shop next door.

Erin waved me off and went to help them, steering them to the cape section. Lacy's shift had ended, and she'd taken off.

"Let's go to the back room." I led the way, Jerry silent behind me.

I turned to Jerry once the door was closed. "If the West-woods aren't believing in vampires now, I wonder what they think happened to their dad? That video, and the two body-guards, made it look like I killed him. Which I did, of course."

"You'll certainly never admit to that. Unless you can convince them that it was self-defense."

"It was! The video is bound to prove that. And every-one knows he was treating me like an animal, hunting me down." I paced the small room. "I bet that estate can't be settled until they declare Westwood legally dead. Both kids are dependent on old Brent's money. I'm sure they'd do any-thing to get it settled quickly."

Jerry watched me pace. "So what do you have in mind?"

"We need to find Westwood's body for them. They'll be so grateful, they'll be more than willing to forget I ever ex-isted. Even better, they might even spring for a reward." I stopped in front of him. "Of course I know exactly where he died. Then you asked your daughter and her friends to clean up the site. Drac should know where they dumped the body." Lily's boyfriend had renamed himself Dracula this century.

"You're right. Let's see what they know." Jerry pulled out his phone and hit speed dial. "Lily, where are you? Is Dracula with you?"

I could see Jerry getting frustrated but didn't use my vamp hearing to eavesdrop. I knew he'd give me the highlights.

"We'll meet you there in ten minutes. Don't move." Jerry ended the call. "Those half-wits are at Damian's trying out a new synthetic blood that's supposed to give you a buzz. We'll be lucky if they're coherent by the time we get there."

"Let's go now, then." I stuck my head out to tell Erin we were leaving and came face-to-face with Vivien Westwood and her bodyguard. She gasped and grabbed Sean's arm.

"Ms. St. Clair? C-can we talk?" Viv didn't look as confident as usual. Maybe because Jerry was glaring at her like he was about to rip out her throat. Oh, yeah.

"Love to. Come into my back room." I threw open the door.

Sean balked. "Out here. Witnesses." He couldn't take his eyes off Jerry. I figured he was getting all kinds of mental messages because sweat was popping out on his broad forehead. I had a few for him too. This was the guy who'd booted my backside.

Jerry was suddenly right in front of Viv. "Say what you've got to say and get out of here. But know this. You ever attack Ms. St. Clair again and—" Jerry leaned forward and whispered in her ear. Vivien paled. He stopped Sean with a hand on his chest, and the big guy froze before he could pull the gun he obviously carried in the shoulder holster under his jacket.

"Listen, Ms. Westwood. I know you've seen some kind of video that involved your father and a crossbow." I waited until she nodded, her eyes wide.

"How did you—"

"People talk. Which you'd do well to remember. Forget this vampire stuff. Totally bogus. Your father obviously had a screw loose. I think he may have had an accident in the woods near one of the lakes around here. He was out there vampire hunting and ran into some totally innocent people camping and partying."

"Oh, my God." Viv gripped Sean's arm.

"Exactly. You can imagine what might have gone down if someone came at you with a crossbow in the middle of the night and you'd been enjoying a substance or two. Know what I mean?"

Viv nodded vigorously this time.

"So it's possible your dad had an accident. I'm going to ask around. See what I can find out. Would you like me to do that?"

Viv was speechless and just nodded her head again.

"Fine. Your brother spent the night in jail. I'd suggest you both lay off the harassment before you end up serving time for stalking. I *will* press charges." I glanced at Jerry. "Or, even worse, let my boyfriend here do what he wants to with you."

"No!" Viv looked like she was going to fall to the floor, but Sean held her up. She took a breath and rallied. "No, that won't be necessary. We're going to have this will my dad wrote about vampires thrown out. It was obviously nonsense."

"Sounds like a plan." I smiled.

"But that means until we find Dad's, uh, remains we can't settle the estate. So while you're, uh, asking around?" Viv wobbled on her high-heeled boots. "Would you see if you can find his, um, body?" Her eyes actually filled with tears.

"It would be my pleasure." I realized that sounded a little strange, but I certainly meant it. I'd hated Westwood with a passion usually reserved for the Devil incarnate.

"Now that we've settled that. I'm sure you won't find it necessary to come into this shop again without an invitation." Jerry's voice was quiet. *I* shivered and knew he was on my side. "You want me to spell out what will happen if you do?"

"N-no." Vivien was shaking now and leaning on Sean, who looked none too steady himself.

"Ms. St. Clair is under my protection. There will be no more attempts on her life in the alley or anywhere by you or one of your hired guns. Is that clear?" Jerry met her gaze, then Sean's. Both of them nodded and backed toward the door.

"Vivien, you and your brother will forget this vampire stuff. No such thing. The invention of a sick mind. Got it?" I moved in on her.

"Sick mind. Daddy was sick." Viv hit the door.

"Exactly." Jerry threw it open. Viv and Sean scurried out.

"Whew. Guess it's safe to head out now." I grinned at Erin. "I swear Jerry had me shaking in my boots."

"You both were awesome, Glory. Don't want you mad at me, Mr. Blade." Erin didn't look scared, she looked more than a little excited. Werewolf. And not long till the full moon. I'd have to be sure her shift was covered then.

"We're out of here." I grabbed Jerry's arm. "Call if you need me, Erin."

"Sure thing. And we've got your number here too, Mr. Blade. For emergencies." Erin looked like she really wanted to use it.

Obviously pumped after the confrontation, Jerry hustled me out to his car and drove at top speed to Damian's castle on top of the hill near Sixth Street. When we got close, we could hear laughter and shouts of partying. Obviously the new synthetic had created more than just a little buzz. The vamps who'd tried it sounded like they were flying high and not as birds or bats.

"This is probably a waste of time, but let's see if they can show us where they dumped Westwood's body," Jerry grumbled as we climbed out of his Mercedes.

"Hey, thanks for what you did back there. Warning off

Vivien." I kissed him as he helped me out of the car. "Totally hot too."

"I thought you didn't want me to protect you." He pulled me close, his hand sliding down to hold me against him.

"Doesn't mean I don't like to see your warrior side occasionally." I grinned when I heard him grumble about never understanding women as we walked up to Damian's front door. It opened before we could ring the bell.

Damian was flushed and had obviously been celebrating along with his company. "Come in, friends. We're just getting to the best part of the evening. Glory, it's strip poker. As I remember, you're a lousy gambler, so I'd love to have you join the game." He waggled his eyebrows.

"Lousy and reformed. I don't play at all anymore." Long story. I'm so bad I had to join Gamblers Anonymous and pay on credit cards for years as part of my recovery. I still can't be around a game without feeling dangerous urges.

We walked into Damian's spacious living room with its breathtaking view of the Austin skyline. But it wasn't the city that made me gasp, it was the sight of Jerry's daughter, her boyfriend Dracula and his two best buddies, Benjamin and Luke, all in various stages of undress. They were surrounded by empty bottles and crystal goblets. Their cheeks were flushed too.

"Don't look, Dad. I'm not very decent." Lily giggled and covered her bare breasts with a throw pillow. She'd obviously been losing because she was down to a thong and two high heels. Leave it to Lily to keep on her shoes while discarding her top.

"You're more than decent, my love." Drac made a grab for the pillow but toppled over. He wore stretchy black briefs that left nothing to the imagination and a knit cap. Benny and Luke had fared better, both of them still in pants and socks, but shirtless. Somehow Damian was the only one fully clothed, unless you counted a missing belt. Cards were scattered across the glass tabletop.

"Ante up, you two. One article of clothing to start." Luke gave me a wicked smile. "Do us all a favor, Glory. Take off that sweater."

"In your dreams, sweetheart." I grinned back, not above noticing that all three male vampires were beautiful men. "Are you sober enough to remember the night I killed Brent Westwood? The night Israel Caine's house burned down?"

"How could we forget?" Benny jumped up, swaying before striding over to sling his arm around my shoulders. "You took down the baddest man in the whole damn town." He grinned at his mates. "Hey, that's a song lyric. 'Leroy Brown,' eh?" He started to sing, Drac and Luke joining him for the chorus. Their group had been a singing sensation in the seventies. I waited until they'd run out of words, stopping Jerry with a look when it was obvious he wanted to shout at them to shut the hell up or knock their heads together. The guys were that good.

"Brilliant. Now we need to know where you stashed Westwood's body." I turned to Lily, who'd put her head on Drac's shoulder, her pillow slipping to show most of her left breast. "Lily, cover up, girl. You were in charge of getting these guys to clean up the mess when I took out Westwood. Remember?"

Damian came in with a tray of full bottles. I read the labels. B-sotted. Blott-O. Oh, and my favorite, Undead Drunk.

"Here we go. Refills. Glory, Blade, try one. You look like you need a pick-me-up." Our perfect host picked up one for himself.

"Maybe later." I had to admit I was tempted. After the night with the Vamp Viagra, I wouldn't mind a little experimentation. But business first.

"Don't give them any more until we get some answers." Jerry put his hand on Damian's arm.

"Wait a damned minute. Who put you in charge?" Benny turned to face Jerry. Or tried to. He lost his balance and landed in the middle of the card table. Glass broke, cards went everywhere, and everyone except Jerry and me thought this was hilarious. When Benny got a cut on his foot trying to pull himself up, a growl went around the room that made Jerry try to put me behind him.

"Stop it! Calm down and answer me." I pushed Jerry out of the way, grabbed another throw pillow and jammed it against the cut on Benny's foot. My own fangs were down, but I ignored them. He did have a delicious blood type. I grabbed one of Damian's bottles and took a swig. Self-preservation. It wouldn't have been cool to lick Benny's big toe.

"Gee, Glory. Watch how you chug that. It's got a powerful kick." Lily grinned at me. "Dad, you may want to take her home after this. It also makes you, um, horny as hell."

"That's enough. Now answer Gloriana. Where did you dump Westwood's body that night?" Jerry picked up a bottle and took a sip. Clearly I wasn't the only one thirsty.

"Nowhere. The guys were messing around. Wanting to cut off his head, take a trophy, which I knew you wouldn't like, Dad. See how loyal I am?" Lily rubbed Drac's knee, and I looked away from his obvious response.

"Where'd you take the body, Lily? And don't say nowhere." I wanted to slap some sense into her. Especially when she let Drac grope her in front of all of us.

She at least had the good sense to shove him away and stand. "I'm telling you. I don't know where in the hell the body ended up. Another vamp came along. He offered me big bucks if we'd let him have Westwood. Said he'd do the cleanup." Lily shrugged and took a bottle Drac snagged for her. "Hey, I could use the money. The guys here are loaded, but I'm not. It was expensive moving here from Transylvania." She wrapped a rich black velvet throw around her, toga-style, and dropped her pillow.

"Sorry, Dad. Since I got here, you've been nice, but even though I'm your one and only child, you haven't offered me an allowance or a place of my own. I had to look out for myself. So I decided we should take the cash and split. What did we care what happened to that body anyway?"

"Yeah, I remember now." Drac took a long draw from

his bottle of B-sotted. "Man, that's fine. Oooh, baby." He grabbed Lily's hands and pulled her close. "We're gonna have to find Damian's love shack soon. I'm hard and hurtin'." He laid a kiss on her that was triple X-rated, his hand moving up her thigh.

Damian rolled his eyes at me. "Young vampires. No manners. Blade, your daughter is lovely, but the company she keeps . . ."

"I couldn't agree more." Jerry took another hit from his bottle and put his hand on my hip as if to show he wasn't just Lily's old man, but in need of a love shack too. "But I can't believe you couldn't handle this one simple task, Lily. Why the hell did you palm it off on a stranger? You had to know this was important to me."

"To me too." I swatted Jerry's hand away. "Who was this man? You don't know where he took Westwood's body? Of all the irresponsible, stupid . . ." My great plan was slipping away just like Lily and Drac were toward the French doors that led outside. "Where are you going?" My voice was nearing screech level.

"Let them go, sweet thing. They are lucky enough to have each other. We didn't know the guy or care. Like Lily said, the girl needed cash. The price was right. You took off in a tearing hurry, now didn't you? If it was so important, why didn't you stay around and see to it yourself? Eh?" Luke looked me over.

"I should have. Valdez and Ray made me leave, and I was shook up. In shock, really. I don't go around plugging men with crossbows every day." I took another gulp of the synthetic and appreciated the heat of it going down. "We should have stayed and handled it ourselves. Jerry, you weren't even there. You met us at the car."

"I didn't want to leave you either. That's why I delegated. Obviously to the wrong people." He glared at his daughter and Drac, making out by the glass doors.

Luke smiled at me. "That's old news. Glory, don't suppose I could interest you in a little two on one with Benny and me."

Blade had Luke up and off the couch in a heartbeat, glass crunching under his leather boots. "The lady is spoken for. You and Benny satisfy each other. I'm sure that's your usual way."

"Hey, man, chill." Luke blew him a kiss from his landing spot on the floor next to the wall. "Benny and me swing either way. No problem. And if you want to join in, I'll take on a hairy Scot, though Glory'd be my first choice."

Lily giggled and stopped at the glass doors. "You're propositioning my dad? I'd pay money to see that video."

"Is there even one of you that has something useful to say?" I wanted to scream with frustration. Just when I thought we'd found a solution to our problem, we'd entered the twilight zone and I was surrounded by pod people.

"Maybe this'll help. The guy with the cash was a dealer. Gave us some of that cool drug. Vampire Viagra." Luke grinned at me. "Oh, look at you, Gloriana. I can see it in your eyes. You've tried it. So you know what I'm talkin' about, sweet thing. Good stuff, isn't it?"

"No comment." I flinched when I felt a hand on my shoulder, relaxing when I realized it was Damian beside me.

"It must have been an Energy Vampire, then, who took Westwood's body. Don't know why you want a pile of bones, but you'll have to deal with the EVs to get the information you need. Maybe Lily will give Blade a description of this dealer." Damian nodded toward where Jerry was talking to his daughter.

Vamp hearing let me know it wasn't that night he was asking about. No, the allowance comment had struck a nerve, and he was offering to support her if she'd find a better set of friends. That was met with a string of profanities, and Lily jerked Drac outside to Damian's gazebo a.k.a. love shack.

I turned to Damian. "Well, no help from those two."

"Why do you want Westwood's body?" Damian took a swallow of his drink and looked around the room. "Never mind. Tell me later. Right now I need to call my own woman. These thugs are right. The drinks are an aphrodisiac. And I figure Blade would cut out my heart if I made a move on you, Glory."

"Damned right." Jerry slung his arm around me. He finished his bottle of Blott-O and slammed the empty down on a table. "One lead. I guess that's more than we might have gotten from this bunch."

"Yes." I walked up to Luke, who was arguing with Benny about whether to leave or call some women they knew to come over.

"Luke, Benny. Focus a minute."

They stared at me, their smiles making it clear they'd taken my command as an invitation. Benny held out his arms.

"Knew you couldn't resist the two of us. Come closer, darling. We've got some Vamp Viagra if that works for you." Benny blinked, like focusing was beyond him. I could relate. I'd drained my bottle of hooch, and though it had been delicious, I was a little woozy myself.

I stayed out of reach. "What did this drug dealer look like? The guy who took Westwood's body?"

"That was months ago." Benny leaned against Luke. "Tall? Kind of hot, I guess. Give us a kiss, Glory, and I might remember more."

"Not a chance. Luke? You remember anything else?"

"Benny's right. He *was* hot. I wouldn't kick him out of bed." Luke's grin was sexy and knowing.

"You wouldn't kick a were-hyena out of bed, you horn-dog." Benny collapsed against the sofa cushions, laughing so hard he choked.

"Stupid sod." Luke pounded him on the back. "Glory needs our help." He looked at me, suddenly almost sober. "He was blond, blue-eyed and, oh, yeah, had a sweet ass." He grinned and opened his phone. "Here, call him. I've got him on speed dial."

I realized my mouth had dropped open. "Are you kidding me?" I grabbed the phone and heard ringing then the voice mail for Greg Kaplan. Well, well. I left a message for him to call me, then handed Luke his phone.

He grinned and slipped it into his pocket. "Now you owe me."

Jerry stepped between us. "We'll keep that in mind. Come on, Gloriana. Let's get the hell out of here."

"Yes. Thanks, Luke. I do owe you." I didn't wait around to play any more verbal games, just followed Jerry to the door. "Much as I hate the thought, looks like we'll have to meet with Greg Kaplan. I'm doing business with him anyway. Maybe Greg will tell me where he dumped Westwood's body."

"I hate for you to deal with one of those devils too. But Kaplan will tell you what you need to know if I have to beat it out of him." Jerry ran his hand through his hair. "Damned drink. Right now all I can think about is getting you naked."

"Naked sounds good. Race you to the car." I slipped out of his grasp and hit the door. We were in the car in seconds and speeding toward Jerry's house again. I felt guilty for abandoning the shop again, but not much. And I hadn't checked in with Rafe. He deserved to know what was going on after worrying about me. First thing tomorrow. Flo too. Then Jerry had his hand inside my pants, and I felt obliged to do the same for him. One thing led to another, and we were doing the wild thing in his car inside the garage.

Forget the kitchen. This time we made it to the den and the leather sofa in front of the fireplace. Ridiculous to keep using artificial stimulants. We'd gone centuries without them. But I had to say the extra boost added a new level to our lovemaking. It had certainly cut out the need for small talk this go-round.

I climaxed for the fourth time and lay atop Jerry, listening to his heart beat. "You're incredible."

"Back at you."

We both jumped when we heard the back door open. Jerry grabbed a furry brown throw and tossed it over us.

"Lily!" I sat up and covered both of us reasonably decently.

"I took your advice, Dad. I dumped Drac, and I'm moving in." Lily dropped a bulging leather bag on the floor and grinned. "Guess you'll have to move your action to the bedroom from now on unless you like an audience." She yawned. "We can work out those details tomorrow. See you in the evening." She picked up the bag and headed for the stairs. "Usual room? Down the hall from yours?"

"Sure." Jerry shook his head. Poor Jerry. He hadn't even known he had a daughter until a few months ago. Now she'd be living with him. And taking an allowance since that had obviously sealed the deal.

I kissed his cheek. "Buck up, old man. You'll do fine. The girl needs guidance. Obviously she's never seen how a decent man goes on. Look at the company she's been keeping."

"Trash." Jerry's jaw tightened.

"Exactly. So you'll show her how it should be." I stood and held out my hand. "Dawn's coming. Let's to bed."

"Aye. You've fair worn me out." Jerry yawned and lifted me up in his arms. "Well worth the effort, lass."

"I hope I always will be." I leaned against him as he walked up the stairs.

Eight

"I'm fine. Quit worrying, Jerry. Rafe will be here any minute. You take care of your business, and I'll take care of mine." I ended the call and concentrated on writing out payroll checks. My business needed attention, and if I didn't pay my clerks on time, I wouldn't *have* a business. I'd just signed the last one, wincing at how low that left my bank account, when there was a knock on the back door. I knew with a sniff that it was Rafe. I threw the double dead bolts and let him in.

"Blade filled me in on the Westwood situation. I don't like the EV involvement." He didn't waste time with a hello.

"Can't be helped." I locked the door again. "You didn't see either Westwood hanging out in the alley just now, did you?"

Rafe gave me a "Get real" look.

"Okay, fine. So we've declared a temporary cease fire. I'm sure Jerry's warning to Vivien helped too." I glanced at my cell lying next to papers strewn across my work table. "I'm waiting for Greg Kaplan to call me back. He took over the cleanup after I killed Papa Westwood. I wonder why he did it."

"That's what's worrying me. An EV never does anything without an agenda." Rafe shoved the papers aside and sat on the table. He looked good in a black T-shirt with a red N-V slashed across it. His dark wash jeans were snug and well-worn.

"We'll find out when Greg calls back." I stacked my papers. "Nice shirt. That your new logo for the club?"

"Yeah, Nadia's design. What do you think?" Rafe glanced down. "She's very tuned in to the club scene."

"I love it. You going to have live entertainment or a DJ?" I shoved the papers onto a shelf and sat next to Rafe. I still wanted him to dance at Flo's party. Especially now that I had hope I might live long enough to hostess the thing.

"A mix of both. In fact, I told Nadia I'd talk to Nathan about getting Israel Caine to perform as our opening act since he's coming to town anyway." Rafe nudged my knee with his. "You have a problem with that?"

"Why would I? Sounds like an excellent plan to me. Ray isn't exactly your biggest fan though." I smiled, remembering how Rafe had run interference when Ray had made moves on me. I'd always thought it was out of loyalty to Jerry, his employer. Now I wondered how much of it was from Rafe's own jealousy.

"Nathan's a businessman and an excellent manager. Nadia's willing to pay big bucks to get this club off to a good start." Rafe grinned. "But if you want to put in a good word with Ray, I wouldn't stop you."

"Asking a favor?" I smiled at Rafe. For a weak and selfish moment I wished that he was still my bodyguard. Then I could have him by my side when I had my meeting with Greg Kaplan and not seem like I was wimping out. I blocked all these thoughts so Rafe, who could read me better than anyone but Jerry, couldn't get them. He had his own obligations, and I wasn't one of them.

"Hey, if you'd rather not talk to Caine, I understand. It took you a long time to convince him to move on. The guy might think you were trying to start up again." Rafe pulled a piece of paper out of his pocket. It was a clipping from a magazine. A picture of Ray with a tall beautiful brunette I recognized.

"Reading the tabloids now?" I tossed it back in his lap and jumped off the table.

"Nadia does. She thought you'd be interested." Rafe dropped the clipping in my overflowing trash can. "Guess you're not. The woman's vampire, Glory. She came on to me in that club in L.A."

"Yes, I remember. Guess Ray finally got his vampire sex." I managed to say it like I didn't give a damn. And I shouldn't. I could have initiated Ray into the ways of vampire lovemaking myself. But I'd been with Jerry. Had always been with Jerry.

"Hey, what's Jerry got on you, Rafe? He says you still owe him. How can that be? Your contract is up, right?" I watched his face carefully. If I didn't know him so well, I might have missed the slight tightening around one corner of his mouth.

"Don't worry about it." Rafe pushed off the table and headed for the door. "I assume you're here for the night? No EV games planned?"

"I don't play games with EVs." I wasn't about to share my plans with Rafe. He needed to work on his club. But if Greg called, I was meeting him. "I'll put in a personal plea with Ray to sing in your club, but I want a favor in return."

"Let me guess." Rafe threw the dead bolts open and had his hand on the knob. "Dancing for your bachelorette party."

"Right." I grinned and stepped up to him. "You don't have to wear your angel costume, just something sexy. To please the ladies." I put my hand on his chest. "And me."

"I'm hiring extra security and putting it on the tab." He grabbed my hand and tugged me closer. "And quit toying with me. It's becoming clear that I need to move on just like Caine has. You're Blade's woman, always have been."

"You're right." I stepped back. But I was more attracted than "Blade's woman" had a right to be. The animal part of him pulled at me on a deeply primitive level. And then there was that heat again. Vampires had a chill that never quite went away. No matter how many times Jerry and I exchanged blood, we never gave each other warmth like I felt from Rafe's body. His blood would be hot, fire on my tongue. He smiled, his dimples so charming that my heart stumbled. Yes, Rafe could be a warrior, but he understood me on a level that Jerry never had, despite our centuries together.

"Come here, Glory. You've had some damned near misses, haven't you. Still feeling shaky?"

"Yes." I slid my arms around Rafe's lean waist and laid my head on his chest. "I'm not toying with you, Rafe. You're my best friend. Please don't ask me to let you walk out of my life and forget you. I . . . I can't." I couldn't look at him because I knew his dark eyes would be pushing to see into my soul.

"Damn it, Glory. I'm still here for you. You want me to stay?" His strong arms held me close. "You can always count on me. Whatever you need. I hope you know that. But I wanted to be more than a friend. Guess that's *my* problem, not yours." He laid his cheek on my hair for a moment. "Enough of this shit. If I'm staying, I've got to make a call."

I pushed back, relieved yet confused. "No, you need to take care of your club. I'll call Ray. Nate too, if necessary. Give me the date you want him to sing." I ran my fingers through my hair, suddenly nervous. Silly to be uncomfortable around Rafael Valdez. I mean, I'd had him sleeping on the foot of my bed for five freakin' years.

"Here's a list of possible dates." Rafe dug in his pocket, pulled out a piece of paper and practically threw it at me. "Nadia's got a crew working night and day to get the place ready. As soon as we get the headliner nailed down, we'll start publicity for the opening. You'll have to schedule your party a night or two before then." Rafe grinned, obviously bursting to get out of there and tell his partner things were rolling along.

"Fine. Go. I've got work here and a call to make." I picked up my cell. "Thanks, Rafe. Seriously. Flo'll be over the moon."

"I know you can't guarantee anything, but I appreciate

the try. Lock the door behind me." Rafe grabbed me around the waist, landed a kiss on my lips, then was out the door.

I touched my fingers to my mouth. Not much there as far as a kiss, but sweet to see him so excited. I hit speed dial on the phone for Israel Caine. We'd pretended to be engaged long enough to have each other's numbers. He picked up on the third ring.

"Glory, babe. Everything okay?" Ray's voice was deep, with the same sexy vibe as the way he sang.

"I'm fine. I've been reading in the press here that you're coming to Austin for the South by Southwest Music Festival. I hope you're going to say hi when you're in town." Still a fangirl, I just managed to bite back a giggle.

"Of course. You were my first stop." Ray laughed, and I heard noise in the background. "Let me go outside. It's crazy in here." I heard music, then silence. "There, I'm on the balcony. I rented one of Chip's houses in the hills, and it's party central here for the band. The guys won't leave me alone."

"Sounds like business as usual." I laughed and sat on the table. Chip was the vampire who owned his record label and a big chunk of real estate in L.A. "How've you been, Ray?"

"Fine. Promoting the new album. Getting into the vamp scene." He coughed. "Finally got a vamp woman to pop my cherry, Glory girl."

Gee, put it right out there. I wouldn't make love with him, and Ray had been desperate for vampire sex. It *was* different when you added the incredibly erotic mutual blood drinking.

"That's good, I guess." So why did I feel like crying?

"Wish it had been with you. Even though it was incredible with the fang banging and all. I'm even writing a song about it. You know how you feel like you're taking in the life force and connecting *so* deep." He groaned, a noise that made me squirm. "Still, I have a feeling the wild thing with you, babe, would have been the absolute best." Ray's voice was a sensual rumble.

"We'll never know." I sighed. "But, Ray, new subject."

"Good idea. This one's killing me. What now?"

"When you come to town, you're bringing the band, right?" I knew he was, it had already been in the newspapers.

"Yes, Chip and Nathan have worked out something to promote the first single on the new album." Ray coughed again. "Damn it, vampires aren't supposed to get sick, but something here is bothering me. It'll be good to get out of L.A. for a while."

"You're not taking weird drugs out there, are you?" I knew Ray liked to experiment. Of course lately so did I.

"No. Well, not much anyway. Now you were going to ask me something else."

"Yes. Two favors."

"I like the sound of that. Then you'll owe me." Ray laughed, the evil laugh that I loved so much. Yeah, I did love him. Jerry too, and Rafe. I did love my men. But I couldn't like the way everyone I knew was suddenly keeping a tally of the favors I owed. I was in debt up to my eyebrows. Money I could handle, but favors? Those could end up biting me on my chubby butt.

"Well, one's really a favor for Flo. You remember my buddy Florence da Vinci."

"Of course, the woman is unforgettable." Ray laughed. "What does she want?"

"She's getting married to Richard again, a big blowout, and would love for you to sing at their wedding. It's while you'll be here anyway." I heard a knock on the connecting door from the shop. "Hang on. Someone's at the door." I sniffed. Greg Kaplan and Aggie? Hmm. I opened the door anyway. After all, I was safely in the back room of my own shop. I waved at Lacy to let her know that I'd yell if I needed her. I made a sign to Greg and Aggie that I'd be with them once I got off the phone.

"Sure, I'll sing at the wedding. Let me know if there's a particular song she wants." Ray coughed again. "I hope like hell I don't lose my voice."

"Healing sleep should fix you right up." I realized I had Greg listening and was careful with what I said.

"What's the other favor?"

"Rafe's opening a club."

"You talking about that mutt who used to be your over-protective bodyguard?" Ray actually growled. "What's that got to do with me?"

"Now, Ray, you've got to admit he saved my life and yours on more than one occasion." I smiled at Greg and Aggie. "I've got company so I can't go into details, but think about doing me a personal favor and singing at the opening of Rafe's club."

"The guy had the hots for you, Glory. Why would I help him score?" Ray sounded like a spoiled child.

"He's not scoring any more than you are, and you know it. I'm Blade's, uh, woman. Rafe said it just tonight. He knows it. Accepts it. Just like you have. The shifter stayed in dog body for five long years just to protect me. I think it would be cool of you to help get his club off the ground. I'd be grateful."

"How grateful?" Ray sounded like the Devil himself angling for a soul.

"Just think about it, Ray. I'll call you tomorrow. Got to go now." I ended the call and looked up to see Greg grinning like he'd learned something useful. Oh, boy, did I hate that.

"I swear, Glory, I don't know how you get all these men dancing to your tune." Aggie tugged down her turquoise knit top in case Greg and I missed seeing the swells of her breasts. "I mean, you are absolutely nothing special, and those hips . . ."

"Thanks for the reality check, Aggie." I stuffed my cell phone in my pocket. "Guess some men have no taste." I looked pointedly at Greg. "Or maybe you two didn't come in together."

"No, we did." Greg grinned. "I've found that Sirens have many talents, some of them extremely useful."

"Yes, Greg appreciates me." Aggie clung to his arm.

"You left a message for me last night. What's the deal? The samples for your party are already here." Greg walked over to the shelf, pulled out a gold bag and looked inside. "Doesn't look like you tried them yet. Go nuts. Then you can order from the list. I've included bottles of three kinds of exotic brews as well as samples of vamp edibles you're gonna go crazy for." Greg grinned like he knew things about me I'd rather he didn't.

Forget him. I glanced inside the bag, my mouth watering at the sight of what looked like real chips and salsa. And a cupcake! It wasn't chocolate—I guess mean Simon Destiny saved that for EV headquarters—but I'd take white with strawberry icing any day. I dipped my finger into the icing and licked it.

"Heaven. But this isn't why I called last night. I have a question. About the night that I killed Brent Westwood."

"Oh? Simon and I call that 'the night Glory finally got her guts.' Brilliant of you." Greg smiled at Aggie. "She turned his own crossbow on the hunter and plugged him."

"Then left Jerry's daughter Lily and her pals to clean up the mess. Now Lily tells me that you came by and paid to take over the job." I couldn't resist. I dug a chip out of the bag and bit into it. Salty and crunchy. My moan of ecstasy was downright embarrassing.

"Yes, it was my own brilliant move of the night. Simon is calling that 'the night Gregory became an invaluable asset.'" Greg laughed, pulled the jar of salsa out of the bag and twisted off the cap. "Dip a chip in this, Glory. It's spicy hot, delicious."

What can I say? I'm easy. I dragged a chip through the bright red salsa and stuffed it in my mouth. Oh, yeah, on fire. I grabbed a bottle of something called Moch-A and took a swig. Coffee flavored. I had tears in my eyes and not from the hot sauce. I was in food lover's Heaven. I hoped this stuff didn't have consequences. I'd suffered after an encounter with Cheetos.

"Wait a minute. Why did taking Brent Westwood's body make you an invaluable asset?" Call me a pig, but I said this around a mouthful of cupcake.

"That, dear Glory, is what you're about to find out." Greg nodded to Aggie. "Do your thing, love bunny."

"Swallow that bite, Glory, and wipe the frosting off your nose. What a pig." Aggie put her hands on her hips.

Mortified, I swiped at my nose, then washed down the cupcake with another thirsty gulp of Moch-A. Man, those EVs knew their stuff. I glanced at the price list in the bag. Good thing Flo was paying because I sure couldn't afford it. But Jerry could. Maybe I should break down and marry him. Was that a terrible reason to say vows? Aggie and Greg just watched me.

"What?"

"This." Aggie smiled and turned me to stone.

Aggie and Greg carried me out between them like a five-foot-five-inch log. When my head whacked the edge of the back door, Aggie thought it was hilarious.

"Quiet. She has a lot of nosy friends around here. We don't need one of them riding to her rescue." Greg hit a remote, and the lights flashed on a black SUV with dark tinted windows.

"Big deal. Then we'd have more statues for the alley." Aggie chuckled and let my hair brush the dirty concrete.

"I don't feel like dealing with the complications." Greg shoved my feet into the back of the vehicle.

And what could I do about it? Zip. Not a damned thing. Couldn't even blink. It had only been a few minutes, and my eyeballs already felt like sandpaper. I strained with every fiber of my being to move *something*. I shouted frantic mental messages in every direction. Apparently no one heard.

"Poor Glory. You want to know where you're going?" Greg patted me on the rump just before he crammed me the rest of the way in. "Not telling. Not until we're well away from this shop of yours. I know you're trying to call for help."

I saw him take Aggie's arm before he slammed the back door, leaving me in darkness. I could hear them arguing. Aggie wanted to come along, but Greg had strict orders to come alone.

"What good is it going to do to have her out there like that? Nobody can take the freeze off her but me." Aggie sounded seriously pissed.

"Trust me, Simon will thaw her out with a glance. Sorry, sweet thing, but we'll go another time. We'll have one of the luxury suites and a romantic weekend. This is business."

Aggie changed tactics. "Combine business with pleasure, baby." I heard some sounds I didn't want to analyze.

"Sorry, but not tonight. Soon. Now I've got to go." Greg was out of breath but determined. Which just proved how scared of Simon he was. Because offer Greg sex and he was usually putty in your hands. Or at least I'd heard rumors to that effect. The overhead light blinked on then off when Greg got into the car and started the engine.

"Guess you heard. So now you know where we're headed. Not to worry, Glory. Simon won't hurt you. Not if you co-operate."

I lay there in the dark, rolling and bumping helplessly with every turn the SUV made, and figured this was it for me. Because I couldn't imagine cooperating with Simon Destiny.

What the hell did he want with me? To meet the mystery man the EV king had mentioned? Oh, yeah. Simon called himself king of the EVs. Didn't wear a crown, or at least I hadn't seen one, but that didn't mean the jerk didn't keep one on his nightstand to impress the ladies insane enough to sleep with him. Another turn and I rolled until I lay face-down on the carpet, the rough nylon smashed against my nose.

Would Simon give me to the energy-sucking goddess the EVs worshipped and feared? They'd built a gold-domed temple to her. The car swerved, and I slid to my back again, staring at a black ceiling and wondering if I could find a way to hurt Aggie before I died. I really, really wanted to take the Siren down.

"Calm down, Glory. You're broadcasting your thoughts pretty clearly, and you can forget hurting Aggie. Maybe this will help you chill. I bought this CD just for you." Ray's voice suddenly filled the car. His new album. Of course I had it at home and in my car. Cut number three was a song Ray had written for me. When it came on, I wanted to cry bitter tears. Damn. Couldn't squeeze out a single drop. I wanted Ray badly. He'd rip out Greg's throat and sing while doing it.

The music changed, faster, rocking hard. I lay there in the dark, awash first with hopelessness, then with a homicidal anger that had no place to go until the last song faded into silence.

"Great. We're here. Good thing. I know he's a big deal, but I couldn't take another second of your rock star's wailing. 'The Glory Years'? Gag me." Greg stopped the car, and the overhead light came on. His door slammed, then the back door opened. "Hey, could use some help here. Got a heavy package to unload."

Greg grabbed my shoulders and pulled me out, then another man took my legs and they carried me across a parking lot to a large brick building. Once inside, they set me on my feet, Greg leaning me against a wall.

"Get Simon, will you?" Greg ordered the other man.

"No need. I'm here." Simon walked into the room, his weasel face all smiles. "Well done, Gregory. I see you used your Siren's skills to subdue Gloriana." He walked close and brushed my cheek with a cold fingertip before he sniffed. "Strawberry?" He laughed. "She really went for that cupcake, didn't she?"

"Oh, yeah. You sure you can undo this freeze thing?" Greg patted my cheek, hard enough to make me rock against the wall. "Aggie really wanted to come out here and do it herself."

"I can take care of it. Leave us." Simon smiled into my eyes. It was like staring into a cobra's gaze, waiting for the fatal strike. I prayed he'd thaw me out, so I could run like hell or shift and fly away.

Greg left and closed the door.

"Gloriana, you know I can read your thoughts. Since you're so hell-bent on leaving, it suits me to leave you in this help-less state awhile longer." Simon backed up a step. "You're not going anywhere until you meet my special guest. That's why I had Gregory bring you out here, since you refused my invi-tation to come on your own." Simon walked over to his desk and picked up a phone. "Send him in, Loretta."

I didn't know who to expect and sure didn't like Simon's secret smile when the door opened and a man walked in. When I saw who it was, I really wished I could blink, rub my eyes, something. No way. Couldn't be. That bump on my head had given me hallucinations.

"Glory St. Clair. I've been wanting to thank you for what you did." The man strode over to stand right in front of me.

Gag reflex. No, not working. Hyperventilate. Breathing didn't function either.

"What's the matter with her?" He put his hand on my shoulder, and I began to slide.

"Frozen. It's a trick some of us higher-level entities can use as a defense. She doesn't like to visit here."

I landed on my back and lay staring at the ceiling. Neither man so much as lifted a finger to help me. Real gentlemen.

"I'd like to do that. Freeze someone. Is she stuck like this permanently? That would be bad. I need her, you know. Able to move." The man squatted beside me and peered into my eyes, so close I could feel his breath on my face.

He'd been drinking from a type-B mortal, and I could see his fangs. Vampire. Hysterical laughter knocked around in my brain, sending my thoughts scattering. One landed front and center. I hated him. Oh, yeah. First chance I got, he was going to hell and staying there. His eyes raked my body, and he squeezed my breast through my sweater. His smile begged to be ripped off his face.

"I can release her at any time. But I'd suggest you be on

the other side of the room when I do it." Simon stood beside his guest and clapped him on the shoulder. "Read her thoughts. I think you'll find them enlightening."

"Oh yeah. I keep forgetting I can do that." He stood, then stared into my eyes. I sent him a very specific message.

"Wow. She's got a mouth on her." He glanced at Simon, then back at me, his smile full of fang. "Sorry, Glory, but Brent Westwood's back, and thanks to you and Greg Kaplan, I'm going to live forever."

Nine

"**Glory,** I'm going to release you now." Simon had taken Westwood's place by my side. "I'd advise you to behave if you want to stay free."

Behave? Instead of fight or try to escape? Why not? I wanted to know what Brent Westwood could possibly need from me. Gross touches or not, it wasn't sex. I'd read his mind too, enough to know he'd just been trying to intimidate me. God, I hated him.

"All right. I can see you've decided to be reasonable." Simon touched my shoulder. I could *move*.

Good intentions or not, I leaped and went straight for Westwood. I threw him up against the wall, my hands on his shoulders.

"Listen to me, you asshole. You ever touch me like that again, and I'll kill you and make sure it's permanent this time. You hear me?" I slammed his head against the wall. Simon just watched, apparently amused. "I'm not ripping out your throat because you probably taste like dirty gym socks. But, remember, you're a fledgling, and I'm over four hundred years old. I can take you down and not even break a sweat."

"Simon? You just going to stand there and let her do this?" Westwood's mouth trembled over his new fangs.

"You shouldn't have touched her. Only a man who can't get a woman any other way would take advantage like that." Simon strolled over to his desk and sat in a black leather chair. "Let him explain his needs, Gloriana. I think you'll see an advantage in cooperating."

I smacked Brent's head against the wall one more time, then let him slide down into a groaning heap on the floor. "Cooperate with *him*? You're kidding. Damned vampire killer. Why haven't you fed him to your goddess in little chunks already?"

"Normally, I would have. But remember who we're dealing with." Simon gestured at Westwood, who was giving me hate-filled looks. "He's a billionaire. Money talks."

"Not that loud. I can't believe Greg turned him. What the hell was he thinking?" I strode over to an armchair in front of Simon's desk and sat. I didn't doubt Simon would keep Westwood from retaliating against me. Obviously I had a purpose here.

"It was genius. I was amazed Kaplan had the foresight to do it, and I've rewarded him." Simon smiled. "You can imagine how surprised our guest was when he woke up."

I grinned. "Hey, Brent, how's it feel to be one of those evil undead bloodsuckers? Where's your crossbow? Want me to put you out of your misery?" That earned me a one-finger salute, and I laughed so hard I got tears in my eyes. "I love the irony. Tell me, Simon, did he cry and beg you to stake him?"

"Shut up, bitch." Westwood threw himself into a chair. "You don't know anything about it."

"What I know is that you hunted down innocent vampires. I saw that Web site. You put your kills on exhibition." I snarled at him. "You don't deserve immortality."

"Tough shit." He smiled and showed fang. "I got it anyway."

"Cool it, both of you. Westwood, remember you need

Gloriana's cooperation. Living forever is an expensive proposition. You said you wanted access to your funds." Simon was
serious now. "Don't get sidetracked by petty concerns."

"It's not petty when I'm attacked. She nailed me in the
first place with my own weapon." Westwood glared at me.
"The pain! Hell, I prayed for death as I tried to stay absolutely still and listened to that bunch of vampires talk about
chopping off my head."

"Too bad they didn't follow through. It would have made
a sweet bowling ball." I smirked at him. "You can appreciate
the desire to take a trophy, can't you, Brent? Where's your
necklace?"

"Figured one of those damned vamps took it." Westwood
looked down at his fists. "But forget that. I'm looking to the
future now." He glanced at Simon. "I want my old life back,
or at least access to my funds. But I'll need your help."

"When monkeys fly out of your butt." I sat back. "Your
kids are already divvying up your fortune. All they want is
your body. Somehow I think they'll be disappointed if you
show up now." I grinned at him. "Not exactly father of the
year, were you?"

"I made some mistakes. Like anybody could." Westwood
stood, looming over me. I jumped up and faced him.

"Yeah, I made a big one. I should have ripped out your
throat. Made sure you were truly dead that night." I looked
him up and down. "But I couldn't bear to get that close."

"Can we drop the pissing contest and get down to business?" Simon pounded his fist on his desk, making his phone
clatter and Westwood jump a foot. Newbie.

I shrugged and sat down again. "Business. Whatever it is,
I'm not interested. This is a waste of time."

"You're not going to turn us down, Gloriana." Simon
smiled, his fangs gleaming in the light. He was basically
ugly as sin—sharp nose, thinning hair and squinty eyes. But
those eyes could promise you the pains of hellfire with just a
glance. He gave me the creeps and scared me more than I'd
ever admit.

"Watch me." I hid my fear with a yawn.

"I've got to prove that I'm still alive." Westwood fidgeted. "I want my money and to resume my old life as Brent Westwood, billionaire. I can't just show up and claim it."

"Why not?" I was interested in spite of myself.

"Because there were bodyguards who got away that night. They saw you take me out. I've been out to the ranch, in disguise of course. I heard what's going on."

"What did you do, shift into your natural form and slither in?" I saw him struggle to keep from lashing out again. Damn, he really did need me. This could work to my advantage. I peeked at Simon. He nodded, like there you go. Be smart.

"I went out there really late one night. I managed to destroy the vamp-detecting glasses, every pair. No one else knows exactly how they work, so we won't be bothered with them again. That was my survival instinct kicking in, of course." Westwood straightened, looking more like a man who'd made billions with his ideas.

"Of course." I waited to see what was coming. Insane, talking to Brent Westwood without a stake aimed at my heart.

"There are statements from several witnesses who saw me go down under fire that night. You were identified as the shooter. One guard even had the foresight to take a video with his phone. It's poor quality, but you can see enough to figure I was down for good. No one went to the police for a couple of reasons."

"Oh? Like maybe the kids didn't give a damn how you died or who killed you as long as they could get to your money?" I loved seeing Westwood lose his cool.

"Gloriana, quit goading him." Simon's quiet voice rang with authority and the implied threat that I could be a statue again if I didn't shut up and listen.

Westwood, half out of his chair, glanced at Simon, then settled for a look that promised me payback.

"A couple of reasons. First, it was clear I had the drop on

you first. You were acting in self-defense." He frowned. "I'd underestimated you, and you managed to turn my own weapon on me."

I leaned back. "The police are involved now anyway. Because of your stupid will that pitted both kids against each other. Did you tell Simon about that?" I turned to the EV leader. "Father of the year? Get this. First kid to take out Brent's killer gets the whole fortune. How's that for an equitable distribution." I saw that Simon wasn't surprised.

"We know all about that, Gloriana. And it seems Brent is now listed as a missing person." Simon nodded toward Brent. "You're going to help find him."

"Again, when those monkeys . . ." I smiled.

"I wrote that will when I still thought vampires were out to get me. Damn, I hate that David ended up in jail." Westwood sighed.

"Fortunately, your children have seen the light. Lawyers are racking up big fees getting that piece of crap tossed aside." I sighed. "Seems Brent here was showing signs of losing his mind at the end. The will proved it. Along with that horrible Web site." I glared at Westwood. "Simon, have you seen it? The pictures of his kills? Westwood, I don't know why the law hasn't come knocking on your door about those murders."

Westwood flashed his fangs. "Because vamps live off the grid. No one was reported missing, no bodies were found."

"You killed my boyfriend's best friend." I blinked back sudden tears. "I'll never work with you."

"Calm down, Gloriana. I'm sure Westwood has regrets now." Simon toyed with a letter opener, sliced his own finger and licked it clean with his reptilian tongue.

I turned back to Westwood. "Screw your regrets. Those pictures and that Web site have to come down."

"I agree. I'm no longer proud of my role in destroying vampires and sure don't want to encourage hunters. But only I can crash the site. I used special codes and equipment I have at the ranch to build it." Westwood's eyes gleamed with pride. I wanted to snatch Simon's letter opener and stab them out. Too bad he'd heal now.

I took a steadying breath. "Slither out there some night then and take care of it."

"No. I want my life back. The ranch, the jet, all of it. I'm sure the Energy Vampires will enjoy some of my homes in other parts of the world. Right, Simon?" Brent looked at his mentor for approval and got a nod. "Good thing they need proof or my children would have already started dismantling everything I built."

"So why can't you just show up now and say 'Daddy's home'?" I was so ready to get out of here.

"Because we need to do this right. There's a pile of evidence out there I've got to refute. I want to prove that the video was bogus and the witnesses who saw what went down were tricked. Got to show that the whole vampire thing, my kills on the Web site, all of that, was a scam too." He darted a look at Simon.

"Yeah, well, what do *I* have to do with anything?" I got up, drawn by a bowl of Simon's famous chocolate truffles near the door. I loved them, but what I'd just been through had given me trust issues with anything made by an EV.

"I want you to reenact the whole death scene with me. I'll take my own video to them when I show up. There we'll be, you aiming the crossbow, me pretending to go down, then jumping up again like it was a hoax. Claim that I was just trying to make myself look good. It'll explain away the whole night."

"And the disappearing act?" I shook my head. "Your kids think you're dead, Westwood. They have for months."

"We'll work out the details later." Simon sounded very sure of that.

"Yeah, right. An increase in their allowances and they'll be okay." Now Westwood wouldn't look at either one of us. Obviously he didn't like having to act the fool to his children or his adoring public who came to his Web site to feed their hatred of things that go bump in the night.

"What would be in it for me?"

"I'll pay you." Westwood's jaw was tight. Aw, did he hate asking me for a favor? I smiled.

"Hmm. That job should be worth millions. Right, Simon?" No way did I trust either of them to actually pay up.

"Don't be greedy, Gloriana. You'd be paid what amounts to a fortune for a working person such as yourself." Now Simon smiled. "Westwood is becoming an Energy Vampire. In gratitude, he'll donate part of his fortune to the goddess and her causes."

Should I warn Westwood that deals with Simon usually ended up with everyone a loser except the king of the EVs? Naw, let him find that out the hard way. By the time Simon got through with him, Westwood would be begging for his own allowance.

"I'm really busy right now. Got Flo's wedding coming up. Lots to do. Sorry, fellas, but I think I'll pass." I got up and strolled to the door. I glanced down at the chocolate again, my mouth watering. Damn, I hated depriving myself.

"Be reasonable, Glory." Simon followed me. He reached into the bowl and took a chocolate, then popped the truffle into his mouth. "These are delicious. Remember when you were out here before? Take one."

Why not? Had to be okay since Simon had eaten one. I selected the biggest and bit into it, savoring the burst of flavor as my taste buds went wild.

"Come on. I'll pay you big bucks. It won't take long to do the video." Now Westwood was on my other side, his voice a whiny irritation that made me take a second chocolate.

"Forget it. I don't trust you. You'd get the footage you want, and then I'd never get a stinking dime." I smiled at Simon. "I know how Energy Vampires operate." I gasped as a pain hit me. Too much chocolate? I didn't think that was possible. I staggered back to my chair.

"Not this time. You'll get paid. Cooperate for your own good, Glory. My kids are trying to kill you, aren't they?"

Westwood actually looked proud of this. "You want to take a chance that they'll be successful before I can call them off?"

"Your kids took a shot, but their lawyers won't have to break a sweat getting that dumbass will thrown out. I mean, vampires? What judge is going to think a competent man wrote that?" I laughed. "So Daddy's crazy, and the kids will split your dough down the middle. They just don't want to wait seven years to do it. Right now I'm their only hope of recovering your body, so I figure I'm safe from them." I bent over as stomach pains hit me hard. "Simon, what was in that candy?"

"A little something to make you more cooperative, Gloriana. You forced me to use it. If you'd just said yes." I heard this as I fell to the floor. The pain! Everything went dark.

I woke up in a room without windows. I was lying on a double bed, and I wasn't alone. I rolled over and saw Rafe, seriously battered and bloody, unconscious beside me.

"Oh, my God!" I carefully touched his swollen jaw and torn lip. Blood seeped from several wounds on his beautiful face. One thing I knew how to do was heal. I touched the cuts I could see. He'd obviously put up a hell of a fight before he'd been thrown in here. But how did he know where to find me?

His eyes opened, and he stared up at me. I realized I was crying when a tear splashed on his scraped chin.

"Ow! Dry up, will you? That stings like a son of a bitch." Rafe lifted one hand up to his face, his knuckles raw and bloody.

"What were you trying to do, take on the Energy Vampires single-handedly?" I sniffed, relieved when the worst of the cuts started healing under my fingertips.

"I knew you were in here. No way was I letting you face these creeps alone." He sat up carefully. "I did some damage before three of them took me down."

"Those are piss-poor odds, Rafe. You should have called in reinforcements. Or waited for word from me." I looked around at what amounted to a jail cell. The walls were concrete and the door steel. Anything useful as a weapon had been removed. The bed was a mattress on top of a concrete shelf. We didn't even have a sheet we could strangle someone with.

"What would your word have been, Glory? From what Aggie told me, you were a statue. Couldn't move or talk." Rafe lifted his shirt, and I saw a gash in his side seeping more blood. I inhaled and had to force back my fangs.

"Damn it, look at you. It's a miracle they didn't toss you to their goddess." I put my hand over his wound and heard him suck in his breath. "Hold still, I'm healing this."

"Yeah, I figured. Thanks." His smile was lopsided because of a swollen lip.

"How did you know where I was? Did Aggie tell you what she did?" At least the bleeding stopped.

"I thought I heard you calling for help after I left your place. So I went back. Lacy said Aggie and Greg Kaplan had come by just before you took off without a word. She was worried." He winced when I pulled up his sleeve. Another cut.

"You shouldn't have come out here. Look at you. Your shirt is a bloody mess. Take it off and let me see what else is under there. I hate that you did this for me. You're off the payroll, you know." I still felt like crying.

"Glory, look at *me*." Rafe put his hand on mine. "Forget the freakin' payroll. I will always take care of you. End of story." He ripped off his shirt. "Now go ahead. Fix me up so I can get us out of here."

"I'm sorry, Rafe. I didn't mean to sound ungrateful." I put my hand on his chest, which was bruised but not cut anywhere. "It means the world to me that you would put yourself through this for me. But—"

"Forget it." He smiled. "A good fight beats paperwork any day. You want to tell me why Greg dragged you out here? Obviously not to decorate the square in front of the golden dome since you're not a statue anymore."

"You won't believe it. I'm surprised Aggie told you where to come."

"Greg pissed her off because he left her behind." Rafe rolled off the bed and walked slowly around the room, stopping to study the solid door. He tried the knob. Locked, of course. "When I tracked her down, she was happy to spill his secret. Besides, where else is an EV going to go?" He stopped in front of me. "Are you okay? What did they do to you?"

"Drugged me with some of Simon's chocolate truffles." I made a face. "Guess I'm pretty predictable around food. As soon as Simon ate one, I was all over them."

"Hey, I get it. How are you feeling now?" He brushed my hair back behind my ear.

"I'll live. The drug's worn off." I sighed. "But what's next? Water boarding?"

"Why did they bring you out here?" Rafe sat beside me on the bed again. "Why the drug?"

"Seems Brent Westwood's alive and 'Livin' La Vida Loca' out here as a new vampire." I still couldn't believe it.

"You're shittin' me. I saw you take him down."

"Yeah, well, he didn't stay down. Wild, isn't it? He's now the one thing he hated most." I studied Rafe's pale face. He'd lost a lot of blood, and I wondered if I could get him to drink some of mine.

"Damn it, we were sloppy that night. I should have confirmed that he was dead." Rafe swayed.

"Yeah, well. You had your hands full, taking care of me. You know, you don't look so good. Lay back, and I'll tell you the rest." He didn't argue, which meant he really was weak. He even closed his eyes while I laid out the facts. Rafe's bare chest rose and fell, and I wondered if he was asleep. I snagged his discarded shirt and draped it over him. He grabbed my hand.

"I'm awake. Barely. Must have a concussion. Talk to me.

Shouldn't sleep." He opened his dark eyes. "You going along with Westwood's plan?"

"No way. I'd like to see him staked out in the sun to fry."

"Yeah, that would be cool." Rafe's eyes drifted shut again.

"Wake up, Rafe. Listen. I'm going to pretend to cooperate, or Simon will never let us go." I jiggled his shoulder. Was he out again? Damn it. I bit open my wrist and pressed it to his mouth. "Drink. Pretend this is from a juicy rare steak."

He groaned and reached for me, his hand on the back of my head. "Glory." At least that got some of my healing blood into his mouth. I saw him swallow, then grimace.

"Don't stop, keep drinking. Damn it, Rafe, I need you healthy. Do it for me." I pressed my wrist harder against his mouth and laid my head on his chest. His heartbeat was strong and reassuring. I felt him swallow and smiled. "That's right, buddy. Drink Glory's magic juice. Then you'll be all better."

He shuddered, then his arm tightened around me. With his other hand he shoved my wrist away and rolled me under him. His mouth came down on mine, and he kissed me like he was about to take his last breath. I went with it, savoring his taste, the heat of his mouth and the feel of his hard body. Rafe. I couldn't bear it if I lost him. The kiss seemed endless and stirred all sorts of feelings deep inside me. Then I heard the scrape of a key in the door lock.

I shoved him off and jumped to my feet. I'd rip out the throat of whoever thought they were going to beat on Rafe again. Then he was by my side, standing close and in the same defensive posture I'd taken. Fine, we'd kick butt together.

"Children, please relax." Simon and two of his EV muscle-men stood just inside the door. "While I admit the preceding scene was quite illuminating, I want to talk now. Unless you make these guards take a rough road instead of an easy one."

"You saw . . . ?" I glanced at Rafe.

"Of course, my dear. Have you forgotten that I have every nook and cranny of this compound wired for sound and picture? I wonder what your lover Jeremy Blade would think if I sent him a short clip of you two rolling around on the bed?"

"If Jerry knew I was out here, he'd be at the head of the army ready to take you down." I wasn't about to lower my guard. "Once a voyeur, always a voyeur. How pathetic is that?"

"Not pathetic, Gloriana. Useful." Simon smiled and gestured to his men. "Jerry, as you call him, will not be in such a hurry to rescue you if he thinks you've been out here with your new lover." He laughed. "And he'll wonder what's been going on all those years he had you on his payroll, Valdez."

"Why you—" Rafe lunged for Simon, but the two guards stepped between them. One of them aimed a weapon and there was a sizzle, then Rafe staggered and went down.

"What did you do to him?" I ran to where he lay flat on his back, scowling and twitching one foot.

"Taser." Rafe growled at the two men. "Assholes, I'd like to see you try to hold me back without that."

"Why should they, Mr. Valdez? It's such a handy tool. Lucky for you I told them to keep it dialed back. Otherwise you wouldn't be able to speak; you'd be in a drooling coma." Simon chuckled. "Your big tough bodyguard came running to your rescue, Gloriana, but obviously he's gotten careless since he's fallen for your voluptuous charms. We caught him before he'd gone a foot inside the compound." Simon flicked me with a look that made me want to check to see if my breasts were covered.

"Don't listen to him, Rafe. He's playing mind games." I helped Rafe up. "What do you want, Simon?"

"To finish our earlier conversation. About Westwood. I'll hold your 'friend' here as a guarantee that you cooperate." He nodded, and one of the men aimed the Taser at Rafe again.

"No! Leave Rafe out of this. I'll do what you want, just let him go." I jumped in front of Rafe when he tried to get at Simon.

"Don't listen to him, Glory. You know you can't trust him." Rafe looked battered, pale and determined.

"It's okay, Rafe. Simon and Westwood need me. And Simon knows he has to hold up his end if he wants me to hold up mine." I sent Rafe a mental message to trust me. He wasn't happy, and I could tell he wanted to take another shot at those guards.

"Come along, Gloriana. If you've truly come to your senses, Mr. Valdez will be waiting for you when we're done, no worse for wear." Simon gave Rafe a warning look. "Be aware, Valdez, that your actions can endanger Gloriana. She's right, we need her. So relax and heel like a good dog." Simon laughed when Rafe lunged and got a jolt from the Taser that sent him to the floor again.

"Stop it! Let's go." I didn't look back at Rafe, just followed Simon out the door. God, I hated this. But with Rafe as a hostage, what choice did I have? We were both going to be out of this evil place before dawn no matter what I had to do.

Ten

Another face-to-face with Westwood, who was waiting in Simon's office. I turned to the EV leader.

"Simon, I'm never helping this murdering rat bastard."

"Gloriana, pay attention." Simon pointed to the chair where I'd sat before my chocolate swan dive.

"I don't trust either of you." I dropped into the chair. "You're wasting your breath."

"Listen up, lady. Simon and I can make your life a living hell. You believe that?" Westwood was obviously in a better mood now, which worried me.

"Sure, Simon's powerful and has lots of evil tricks up his sleeve." I smiled at the thought of Westwood getting his energy sucked out while Simon spent his billions. "Slither out from under Simon's skirts, and I'll show you how vampires deal with each other. It'll be fun for you, fledgling."

Westwood's snarl needed work, but he was definitely furious. "I fight with my brain, not my new fangs. I'm a computer genius, and that's not bragging. It's how I made my fortune. So I can hack into your records, empty your bank accounts, give you a criminal history, even issue warrants for your arrest in foreign countries. That could be fun for *you*."

His superior smirk begged to be slapped off of his very forgettable face. Westwood was average in every way—height,
build and bland features under close-cropped mouse brown
hair. It had made him a dangerous hunter who could blend
in with a crowd.

Simon must have read my mind. "Gloriana, focus. I know
Westwood's not your type. You go for big men with short
tempers."

I smiled. "You're right. I like tough guys, real men who
aren't afraid to stand and fight instead of hiding behind a
piece of technology."

"Listen to me, Gloriana." Simon gripped that letter opener
like he wanted to use it on me. "Westwood has his tricks, and
you're right, I have mine. We *can* make your life a living hell.
And then there are your friends. Like Mr. Valdez."

I flashed to Rafe's bloody body. And with Westwood's
hacking skills, even Jerry could become a pauper. So not fair.

"Blackmail? Getting desperate, aren't you?" I managed a
superior look.

"Your friend Florence is having a wedding soon. It would
be a shame to have the festivities ruined by an unfortunate
event." Simon dropped the letter opener, obviously assured
he had my full attention now. He steepled his long fingers
and tapped them together. "And you've been so looking forward to it. Florence too, of course. Even your friend Israel
Caine will be here. How would things play out if you had
some uninvited guests?"

Westwood laughed. "Got you on the ropes now, don't we?"

He was right. I couldn't risk my friends or their happiness
because I hated this creep. Make a video. Okay, not a big
deal. And if I could squeeze some money out of this, so much
the better.

"Ah, I think you're finally getting it, Gloriana." Simon
stood and walked around the desk. "We have some details
to work out. It will be up to you to keep people like your
Valdez from interfering as we take care of this. Can you do
that?"

"If I have to." I hated being backed into a corner. No way was I telling Jerry any of this. He'd want to charge right out here and make sure we had a Westwood body with us when we left. But Simon had an army of EVs and those damned tricks. Jerry wouldn't stand a chance.

"Here's the plan. You go back to your little life. Communicate to my children that you have a line on proving whether I'm alive or dead. That should keep them off your case while I get things set up." Westwood leaned back.

"No problem. I already told your daughter I might be able to find your remains. Know what? She didn't even shed a tear. Did a happy dance around my shop 'cause that meant she'd get to your cash sooner rather than later." I smiled when Westwood looked sick. Aw, did I break the big bad man's heart?

"Don't be a bitch, Gloriana. Chocolate?" Simon strolled over and dropped one into his mouth. "The others were just to make sure you stayed around long enough to see reason. And you have, haven't you?"

"What I see is that I have no choice. Unlike you two social rejects, I *do* have friends. And I won't have them bothered on my account. Don't interfere in Flo's wedding or hurt any of them, financially or otherwise." I was over chocolate. Just the smell had my stomach doing jumping jacks into my windpipe.

"Cooperate and everyone near and dear to you will be fine." Simon smiled and went for another candy. Sadist. "Sure you won't have one? These are excellent. I may let you have some for your little bachelorette party."

Bachelorette party. Like I could think about that now. It seemed so normal and impossible.

"Let's get this over with. Bring out the camera." I looked from Simon to Westwood. "Let Rafe go as a sign of good faith."

"Not so fast, Gloriana. As I said, we have things to arrange first. But you and your"—Simon winked—"*friend* may leave. You understand the consequences if you try to back out of this deal now, don't you?"

"Yes, yes. Just tell me when and where, and I'll do it." I grabbed the doorknob. To my surprise, it turned beneath my hand. "Release Rafe and we're out of here."

"Why not? I'll have Gregory give you a ride." Simon walked toward his desk and picked up the phone.

"Forget it. We'll shift and get back on our own. Call and tell them to release Rafe." I glanced out into a hallway but had no idea exactly where they were keeping him. Simon had led me through two buildings before we'd arrived at his office. "Have him meet me outside." I could see the glass door to the grounds at the end of the hall. "Now."

"So demanding." Simon picked up the phone. "Send the shifter to the front of the temple. Tell him you're taking him to his girlfriend, but put an extra guard on him, he'll probably give you trouble. Release him when she gets there." He hung up and looked at me. "Satisfied?"

I didn't bother to respond. I hurried to the door and pushed it open. I was in the area in front of the gold-domed temple where the goddess resided. I heard an ominous groan coming from there, and my nerves shredded. When I saw Rafe being half dragged from the opposite side of the clearing, I ran to him. The guards just dropped him at my feet and stepped back.

"Was this necessary?" I snarled at the guards. They didn't bother to answer. "Bastards!"

"Rafe, what the hell happened?" I knelt beside him and touched his forehead. He was bleeding from a new gash.

"Taser again. I wanted to know if you were okay and where they were taking me. They didn't like questions." Rafe held on to my arm. "What now?"

"We're free to go. Can you shift? I can get us a ride, but I thought we could just fly the hell out of here." I glanced at the stony-faced guards. One of them had a bruised chin and the other the beginning of a black eye. All right, Rafe.

"I can manage." He looked at the guards. "Let's jet." He visibly pulled himself together. With a groan, he changed into a bird in a blur of motion.

I did the same and we headed out. Not that I had a clue which way to go, but I figured Rafe had found me out here, he could lead us home.

I was right. We landed less than a block from the shop and apartment. The flight had been a long one, much longer than I was used to, but Rafe had been watching out for me to make sure I didn't stray too far from him. We shifted back, and both collapsed on the grass under a tree.

"I want to hear what you had to do to get us out of there, but home first. It's late." Rafe slung his arm around me.

I leaned against him. "You've been Tasered and kicked around. Can you stand up?"

"Think so." He pushed himself up, using the tree for leverage, then put his arm around me again. "You did great, Glory. Shifting like that."

"Thanks. And I'll tell you everything when I wake up. It *is* late, and you need to lie down before you fall down." We walked toward the alley, Rafe limping but surprisingly strong. He was still the bodyguard, scouting out the area first before we got close to the back door of the shop. Luckily Rafe still had his keys. Mine were inside where I'd left them.

In the back room, I grabbed my purse, then remembered that my cell phone was in my pocket. Three missed calls and a voice mail from Jerry. Later.

We checked in with Erin, who promised to phone Lacy and let her know I was all right, then headed for the apartment. I opened the door and almost walked into Nadia, who'd just come out of the kitchen with a glass of her favorite synthetic.

"Rafael, where the hell have you been? I needed you there tonight." She came closer. "What happened? You look like you were in a fight and lost."

"Thanks a lot, Nadia. I got my licks in." Rafe headed into the kitchen. "Here, Glory, drink one of Nadia's power drinks. I figure you need it."

"I do." I smiled at a frowning Nadia. "Sorry we disappeared on you. It was an emergency. Let Rafe heal, and he'll be all yours again."

"Are you sure about that?" Nadia sat on the couch and crossed her long legs. "He seems to be very . . . attached to you. I bet he got hurt riding to your rescue."

"I can rescue myself, thanks. And—"

"I can talk for myself." Rafe sat beside Nadia on the couch, an opened package of Twinkies in his hand. He crammed one into his mouth and chewed, closing his eyes for a moment.

"So talk. What are you eating?" Nadia hadn't quit frowning.

"It's comfort food. Look at me. I was stomped, Tasered and generally beaten like a junkyard dog." He winked at me. "And I don't do dog duty anymore."

"Not funny, Rafael. We had papers that needed signing. Work you should have supervised. And you disappeared for most of the night. What am I to think? Are you serious about this club, or do you want to go back to guarding your lady friend here?" Nadia took a deep drink of her synthetic, and we could see her fangs.

I twisted the top off a bottle and chugged some myself. God, but I needed that. The drug Simon had given me had worn off, but I was exhausted from all that flying. And the stress!

"I'm into the club thing. This was a loose end. Something I should have handled while I still worked here. I owed it to Glory to follow up." Rafe bit into another Twinkie, then got up. "I need a beer. Glory, if you're going for a shower, you'd better hurry. It's too close to dawn."

"Yes, right." I walked over to the hall and stopped at the bathroom door. "I'm really sorry, Nadia. Rafe's all yours. I promise I won't distract him again."

"That's not your call." Rafe stood in the kitchen doorway and took a pull on his beer. "Nadia, I have some loyalty here. Deal with it. If that ruins our arrangement, I'll let you buy me out, or we can just cancel the whole thing."

"No, I understand loyalty. I prize it." Nadia drained her glass and set it on the coffee table. "And I have good news. Israel Caine's manager called me. We're coming to terms." She smiled. "Thanks to Glory. So I forgive you both this time."

"Ray's going to do it?" I couldn't believe it.

"For a very steep price. His manager said he was doing it as a favor to you, Glory. I owe you." She got up and stretched, a tall and elegant woman all in red this night. Her dark hair gleamed, and her lipstick matched her two-piece outfit perfectly. She was beautiful, and I knew she was on her way to Rafe's bedroom. They were just friends, and once dawn hit, there'd be no "hokeypokey," but until then . . . ? I couldn't blame Rafe if he decided to let her ease some of his pain.

"I'm going to fry up a steak, rare." Rafe grinned. "For some reason I've got a craving. I'll see you ladies when you wake up tonight. And, Nadia?" He put his hand on her shoulder. "I *am* sorry. I never should have flaked out on you like that without some kind of explanation. Won't happen again."

I left them talking and heard Rafe promise to spend some daylight hours at the club. I grabbed my robe, then shut the bathroom door. I stood under the hot water and scrubbed every inch of my body. If only I could wash away the memory of what had happened at the EV compound. Westwood alive. Ridiculous. And then Rafe's kiss. Oh, wow. Even wounded, he knew how to make me feel things and forget for a few moments where we'd been. Trapped by Simon. Damn the EV king and his plotting. I'd get him for that if it was the last thing I did.

When I woke up that evening, I realized I'd never listened to Jerry's voice mail.

"Gloriana, I've called you three times. I know you have caller ID, so why aren't you picking up? We need to talk. I have some ideas about how to handle this jam you're in. I even came to your shop, but you apparently took off without informing your staff. I thought you were serious about your business, so perhaps you're merely avoiding *me*. You must know I intend to help you. Call me. Immediately."

Had to love the logic there. Sure, Jerry, it's all about you.

But I wasn't going to tell him about Westwood. Best case, Jerry would try to take over, and we'd have a vampire war with my friends as casualties. I told myself that he meant well with this protective thing, but the way he issued orders . . . I put that problem on the back burner. Obviously I needed to come up with a story that would satisfy my bossy lover.

First, I had to make sure the Westwood children had declared a cease fire. I found a phone book, but the Westwoods weren't listed. A few minutes on the Internet got me what I needed.

"Westwood."

"David Westwood?" I really hated that last name.

"Yes, who's this?"

"Glory St. Clair. I want to talk to you about your father."

"Yeah, well, my lawyers have advised me not to contact you." He sounded sullen and not a bit happy.

"*I* contacted *you*. To try to clear up this crazy misunderstanding." I gathered my thoughts. "Have you talked to your sister since she visited my shop yesterday?"

"Yes. Hate to say it, but my dad was obviously nuts toward the end. Have you seen that Web site he put up? Must be early Alzheimer's."

"So the will that demanded you stalk a supposed vampire?"

"My lawyers are all over it. Dad was even leaving money to this stupid vampire-hunting organization he started. Ridiculous. Vivi and I agree on this."

"Good." I had to like the idea of Westwood arriving home and his kids throwing him straight into an asylum.

"Yeah, well, you can relax. Vivi and I aren't going vamp hunting again. Guess we went a little nuts ourselves. Should have checked with the lawyers sooner. Sorry if we scared you."

An apology. Did I smell a potential lawsuit? Oh, if only I were a simple mortal with a grudge. Sigh.

"Your sister traumatized me with that crossbow, you know. And then you showed up with an army at my back door. Scared away my customers." I sniffled. "I should probably get my own lawyer, press some charges." More sniffs. This was fun.

"Now, Ms. St. Clair. Feel our pain. We've just lost our father. And to make matters worse, we don't have a body to bury." David sighed. "It'll take years to settle this thing and have Dad declared legally dead. Even if you won a lawsuit, you wouldn't be able to collect anything."

"Tied up? That's tough. I'm sure you and your sister don't deserve to wait for your rightful inheritance." I oozed concern.

"Exactly! I'm glad you understand. You see, one of Dad's bodyguards swears you were with my father that last night. I even saw a video, though it was pretty poor quality. It looked like you and Dad facing off."

"I was in the woods that night, near the lake and with some friends. We were camping out, partying if you know what I mean. Is that where he was?"

"My buds and I used to do that when I was in college." David chuckled. "Smoked some weed. Whatever. And Dad? The bodyguards said he was chasing some vampire. Claimed it was you. Not sure of the exact location."

"Well, now you're really convincing me he was crazy. I mean, you've seen me. I run a business. I don't have fangs. Come on, David, do you really think I'm a vampire?" I laughed.

"I'm sorry. It sounds really insane, doesn't it? But that video . . ."

"I can't imagine what you've got, but you said it was at night, right?"

"Sure. And on a cell phone. Quality was the pits. Can't see much. But it sure looks like Dad and a woman and his stupid crossbow. The guards swear it was."

"Well, maybe you should do a background check on those dudes. See what they might have been smoking, you know?" I sighed. "All I know is I did meet him once. He came into my shop and claimed I was one of those demon vampires. 'Cause of the name of the place, I guess. Scared me to death waving around a stake of all things. You need someone to testify he was nuts, I'm there."

"Good to know." David sighed again. "But where the hell are his remains?"

Gee, get all choked up about your dead father, why don't you?

"Like I told your sister, I'll try to help you with that. Maybe he followed me out there that night. I told you he thought I was a vampire. Maybe some of my friends who were with me saw something. If you offered a reward . . ." Did David know Austin had had one of the worst storms in its history that night? Perfect for a camping trip. But then his dear old dad had been hunting in that torrential rain too.

"Yeah, sure. Pass the word. Big bucks for absolute proof Dad's gone."

"I'm on it." I heard a knock on my door. Nadia was in the bathroom, and Rafe had been gone when I got up. "I'll do my best to help you. For the reward, of course."

"Listen, I do apologize. For before. Vivi and I both went a little nuts at first." David actually laughed. "Billions will do that to ya. But we're on the same page now. Fifty-fifty split. All we need is a body, and we're good to go."

I felt a chill. Papa Westwood was a first-class creep, but his children were colder than . . . Not my problem. "Okay, then. If I find out anything, I'll give you a call."

"Great. If we don't come up with a body though, enough reliable witnesses who can testify they saw him die might do the trick. Would you be willing to say you saw Dad take his last breath?"

Another, stronger knock, a sniff, and I knew it was Jerry outside.

"Sorry, but that wouldn't be true, David. Please accept my sympathy for your loss." I couldn't resist that parting shot as I slammed the phone shut and ran to the door.

"Gloriana, I could hear you on the phone. Were you talking to young Westwood?" Jerry dropped a kiss on my mouth,

then strode inside, full of purpose and obviously ready to
take charge.

"Yes, I told him we were working on finding his father's
body. He's through vampire hunting."

"That's good." Jerry smiled and pulled me into his arms.
"I was worried about you. Where the hell were you last
night?"

"Um, Rafe and I went out to the woods where I shot
Westwood and tried to find the body. No luck and no signal
on my cell phone." I kept my mind blocked from Jerry's
probing.

"You should have called me to go with you. The shifter
has his own life now, as you've reminded me. I guess he was
good protection, though. At least you didn't go out there
alone." Jerry looked down and saw the bottle of Nadia's good
stuff I'd started on. "What's this?"

"New brew. Rafe's new business partner Nadia Komisky
is staying here. She bought it." I decided to let Jerry's attitude go. Protect me? Hell, who'd arranged for Rafe and me
to leave the EV compound? I was practically Superwoman. I
picked up the bottle and offered it to him. "Try it."

"No, thanks. I fed on the way here." Jerry still drank from
mortals and knew I disapproved. No doubt he'd whammied
some poor sap who'd gone too close to an alley, taken just
enough to quench his thirst, then wiped the donor's memory
and sent him on his way.

"You can search those woods if you want to. I promised
Nadia I'd leave Rafe out of this from now on. He's got enough
to do with their new club."

"Yes, he does." Nadia walked into the room, this night
elegant in a long silver top and black leggings. Her hair was
pulled back from her face, highlighting her cheekbones. I'd
seen my cheekbones once, for about five minutes. I loved that
top but figured it wouldn't look half as cute in extra large.

"Nadia, Jeremy Blade. Jerry, this is Nadia, Rafe's partner." I finished introductions, then watched Jerry's reaction.

His smile was genuine as he took her hand and bowed over it like he was meeting the queen. Damn.

"It's a pleasure. We've met before. In Kiev. It's been a century or more, and the country was in turmoil so you may not remember. I was Jeremiah Campbell then."

"Yes, it's coming back to me now. I rarely forget a handsome man. What a small world this is." Nadia clasped his hands and kissed both his cheeks. Didn't mean a thing; it was a European greeting. I swallowed a jealous growl and stepped between them to break up the action.

"Ray's going to sing at their club opening." I figured mentioning a man Jerry had been insanely jealous of would get his attention back on me.

"No kidding. Israel Caine agreed to do Valdez a favor?" Jerry raised an eyebrow. "Or was it a personal favor for you?"

"A little of both." I smiled at Nadia. "He's charging them a paw and a tail for the performance."

"It'll be worth it. With a headliner like that opening our club, it'll be an instant success." Nadia slinked toward the door, slipped her long, narrow feet into silver ballet flats, then picked up a black leather handbag large enough to hold a laptop. "I've got to go. So much to do before then. Nice to see you again, Jeremiah. You must come to our opening." She nodded to me. "Both of you. I'll save you a special table. Glory has been kind enough to let me stay here."

"Yes, well, I think Rafe's lined up a house for you. Maybe tonight. You'll be so much more comfortable there than bunking with Rafe." I said this with a smile. Jerry tried to be discreet, but I saw the way he studied her body. We'd been monogamous for a while now. Maybe that was hard for him. I had my own problems with monogamy. Why hadn't it occurred to me that Jerry did too?

"Yes, I've been imposing." Nadia opened the hall door.

"I didn't mean . . . You're welcome to stay as long as you want. Really."

"I appreciate that, Glory, but you're right." She gave my

tiny living room a quick glance that said it all. "I need more space. I'll let you know what my plans are. Good night."

"Imagine meeting her again after all these years." Jerry sat on the couch. "She's Rafe's partner? And sleeping with him. Bet that's an interesting story."

"She uses his bed during the day. They're just friends." I needed to shut up on that subject before Jerry thought I was a little too concerned about Rafe's love life. "Don't know how they met. But Rafe used to work for her." I didn't share the dance thing. Jerry would deride that. Let him assume Rafe had done the bodyguard gig for her too.

"She's wealthy and smart. She owned several really nice vampire clubs in Kiev." Jerry pulled me down beside him. "You going to tell me what you have going on tonight, or are you going to disappear again?"

"I need to see Flo, work on wedding plans. I am her maid of honor, you know." I smiled. "And you're Richard's best man."

"Yes." He pulled me into his lap. "You want to make it a double ceremony? Finally tie the knot?" He slid his hand up to cup my breast while he breathed against my throat with just a hint of fang.

"First, Flo would die if anyone tried to horn in on her big night. And, second, Jerry . . ." His mouth settled over mine. His kiss was familiar, comfortable and still exciting. Sort of. I was in big trouble. I grabbed his hair and leaned in, rubbing my hand over his hard thigh. Of course I loved kissing him. We had this thing. I reared back, breathing hard. What the hell was the matter with me? I couldn't stop thinking, analyzing . . .

"Glory? You okay?" Jerry slid me down to lie on top of me on the couch. "What freaked you out just now?"

"I, I have a lot to do, Jerry. A lot on my mind." I gently shoved him off of me. Oh, my God. Had Jerry picked up on my thoughts? I smiled at him, reassured by his concern. He wasn't blocking *his* thoughts, and they were all about a manager robbing him blind. "Rain check?"

"Sure. I have work too. That mess in Florida is getting worse. If I thought you were really all right, I'd fly out there." Jerry sat up and pulled down my sweater.

"You should go. I'm fine. The Westwoods and I have called a truce. They're having the crazy will thrown out and agree their dad was a few bottles short of a six-pack with the whole vampire-hunting thing."

"Glad to hear it." Jerry stood and pulled me to my feet. "Good. I'll head out for a few days. Back in plenty of time for the wedding preparations. I've got a company out there . . ."

Jerry went on about his labor problems, but I wasn't really listening. He was here now. I should be crawling all over him to send him off with hot memories. Instead, I couldn't walk him to the door fast enough. The giant secret I was keeping from him—that was my problem. This guilt was all about the Westwood video deal, nothing more. Right?

Eleven

"I can see why you sent Blade off on a business trip. He'd never allow you to deal with Westwood like this." Rafe had come in a few minutes after Jerry left and made me tell all. To say he thought the whole thing was nuts was an understatement.

"Jerry doesn't get to allow or not allow me to do anything, thank you very much. Neither do you. I hate dealing with both Simon and Westwood, but what choice do I have? You'd still be locked in a cell being Tasered every time the guards wanted their jollies if I hadn't agreed."

Rafe paced the perimeter of the living room, not a bit happy with me. "I can take care of myself, was already working on an escape plan." He finally sat across from me and zeroed in with dark eyes that saw way too much. "I'm free now so you can forget it. Or can you? Why are you going along with this?"

"I'm stuck. Westwood can give us hell with a computer—clean out bank accounts, you name it. And then there's Simon. You know how he is." I didn't back down, matching him stare for stare.

"Yeah, what's Simon got up his sleeve this time?" Rafe

stalked into the kitchen. He came out with a bag of Cheetos and ripped it open. Let the torture begin.

"Do you have to eat those in front of me?" I sniffed and got a jolt of salt and deep-fried cheese that made my eyes water. God, I loved stuff like that. Damned liquid diet.

"I'm hungry. And I'm waiting for some answers. Spill. What's Simon threatening you with now? His energy-sucking goddess again? Don't listen to him. You've been shape-shifting your ass off lately, so you're not nearly the energy fat cat you used to be." Rafe examined an extra-large cheese puff, then popped it into his mouth.

"Don't use the 'f' word when you refer to me or my ass, damn it." I stomped into the kitchen. "You keep crunching in front of me, and I'm going to rip out your throat." I grabbed a bottle of Nadia's premium synthetic. It wasn't close to the same, but at least I wouldn't hear my stomach growl again.

"Oh, yeah?" He blocked me when I turned to go back, and pointed to his neck with a grin. "Help yourself, Blondie. Just be gentle. And I expect a nice thank-you kiss afterward."

I shoved him out of my way. "Get serious, Rafe."

"Okay, then. Quit evading and tell me why you're doing Simon's bidding." No smile now. Too bad.

"Okay, here it is. He'll ruin Flo's wedding if I don't go along with this. He's got his eyes on Westwood's fortune. With billions on the line, he'll do whatever he has to, and he doesn't care how many local vampires he alienates."

"Bastard. He'd be happy to disrupt a big shindig like that to make a point." Rafe finally closed the bag and set it on the floor.

"You see why I have to cooperate?" I swallowed some synthetic.

"When's this video going down?"

"I don't know. I'm going on business as usual and getting this bachelorette party organized. Acting like there's nothing in the wind." This wasn't going to be easy. Flo knew me too well.

"So he's going to let you know when the video is happening, and you're to drop everything and show up for it." Rafe stopped next to me. "It won't end there, Glory. You'll probably have to back up Westwood's story, verify everything. He's got a lot to explain away—like his lifestyle before he 'died.' Fake video, phony vamp hunting."

"At least they promised to pay me for my part in this. Westwood's son is offering a reward too, in case I come up with a body." I frowned. "If Simon wasn't involved, I'd be happy to take another shot at that bastard and deliver his body personally."

Rafe put his hand on my shoulder. "You're dreaming if you think you won't get screwed over in this deal. No good ever came from working with an EV."

"You think I don't know that? That's why I'm so freaked out." I put my hand over his and squeezed, comforted instantly.

We both froze when we heard a knock on the door. Bad news that neither of us had sensed someone coming up the stairs.

"Glory, I hear you in there. Open up." Flo was here. Let the acting begin. I got up and unlocked the door.

"Is the bachelorette party all set?" Flo had Richard with her, and he was weighted down with packages. "Put them on the kitchen table, *amante*. I want to show Glory what I bought."

"Just ironing out the details now." I pasted on a smile. "Have you tried Damian's synthetics with a buzz?"

"*Perfetto.*" Flo was all smiles. "I'll make sure he donates several cases of his very best for the party."

"Rafe, Glory, hope you're not sick of this wedding already." Richard dropped the bulging sacks on the table. "It can't get here soon enough for me. You'd think we were planning a coronation instead of simply renewing our vows."

"Excuse me? Is that the love of my life talking? The man who finally captured my heart?" Flo put her hands on her hips. "We can call it off. Just because there are dozens of our friends flying in from all over the world—"

"Relax, darling." Richard put his arms around her. "It's all good. I just like to see you fired up. You're so sexy when you're mad." Richard grinned at Rafe. "You ever tie the knot, run off somewhere with strangers as witnesses. No muss, no fuss. Which is what I thought I'd managed when we eloped. But no, my dearest has to do it again in high style."

"Flo does everything with style." Rafe was smiling, but there was something wrong, and it wasn't just the secret we were keeping. I actually didn't know a thing about his background. Whether he'd ever "tied the knot" or even his age. He had awesome powers too. More than you'd expect from a shape-shifter.

"It'll be wonderful, you'll see." Flo turned to me. "Is Israel Caine going to sing for us?"

"Absolutely. Ray said he'd be happy to do it for you, Flo. A personal favor." I peeked into the sacks. I couldn't solve the riddle of Rafe's background now, and I had to keep Flo out of my thoughts. "What's this? A new nightgown? Flo, you should have waited to see what gifts you get at Aggie's shower."

"I couldn't stand it. A sale, Glory. I bought one for you too. As a little thank-you for all you're doing for me." She hugged me, then pulled a sheer piece of silk and lace from the bag. "Look, it's your color and your size." She didn't have to say that it was twice as big as the one she'd gotten for herself.

"It's beautiful." I held the turquoise silk up to my chin. "My color?"

"Who's going to notice the color when you've got something like that on?" Rafe grinned and grabbed the edge of it. "I can almost see straight through it."

"Exactly." Flo looked from Rafe to me. "Glory will look very sexy, *sì*? And it does bring out the blue in your eyes, my friend. I know what I'm talking about."

"Always, darling. You got Israel Caine to sing at the wedding?" Richard grinned. "How'd you manage that, Glory?"

"No problem. He loves Flo and—"

"Will do anything Glory asks. He's even singing at my club for the opening." Rafe dropped the gown and put his arm around me. "Thanks to our girl here, the place'll be a guaranteed hit."

"I don't know if he'll do *anything* I ask. He was going to be in town anyway." I glanced at my watch and eased away from Rafe. Flo was pro-Jerry, and she looked like she was ready to step between us if she had to break Rafe's arm to do it. "I hate to interrupt this, but I've got to get down to the shop. None of my clerks could work the late shift tonight so it's on me."

"You should hire more staff." Flo pulled out a skirt and a sweater. "Look at what else I got. For the honeymoon. Richard won't tell me where we are going this time."

"It's only our sixth—or is it tenth?—one." The usually reserved Richard couldn't stop grinning. "I'm not counting, just happy to belong to this woman." He shoved Flo's finds into the bag and picked up everything. "Come on, darling."

"Flo, you can always come help out again." I hid a grin. Flo had subbed for me right before I got back from L.A. The store would never be the same. She wouldn't wait on "frumps" and had declared some of my vintage finds "tacky" and "too old" to sell. She'd rearranged shelves, stuffing rejects in the back room. I still couldn't find all my merchandise, and was afraid some of it had ended up in the Dumpster in the alley.

"No, thanks. So many people have no taste, and would they listen to my advice? No." She laid my new nightgown on the table. "Here is your gown, Glory. Enjoy."

"I will." I touched the fine lace and imagined how it would look against bare skin. I glanced up to see Rafe staring at me. Hmm. I had a feeling he was picturing the same thing. I smiled. "Thanks, Flo. It's gorgeous."

"Put it to good use." She sniffed at Rafe. "With Jeremiah. Where is he?"

"Off to Florida. A business crisis. But he'll be back in time for the wedding." I walked Flo and Richard to the door.

"He'd better. I figure he owes me a bachelor party, since Florence is getting hers." Richard opened the door. "I imagine a naked mortal woman in my favorite blood type served to me on a platter would be about right. Or at the very least a poker night and some of Damian's potent brews."

"Poker, definitely. No naked women for you, *amante*. And you come home sloppy drunk, and it's the couch for you, I tell you." Flo scolded him all the way down the stairs and out of sight.

"You did great. She has no idea her dream wedding depends on you dancing to Simon's tune." Rafe picked up the nightgown. "You sure you have to hurry down to the shop? Maybe you should try this on, see if it fits."

I snatched it out of his hand. "It'll fit, and you'll never see me in it, bud."

"Wouldn't count on that." Rafe grinned and followed me to my bedroom where I carefully put the gown away. "I think I'm making headway in taking our relationship to the next level. You were really upset when those guys Tasered me."

"If you'd seen yourself when they did it, you'd have been freaked out too. You looked like you were break dancing without music." I sighed and shut the drawer. "You're my friend, I care about you. But nightgowns like this one . . ."

"Are meant for only one thing." Rafe moved closer until I was against the dresser. "You kissed me back out there, Glory. I didn't imagine that."

"Any response on my part was involuntary. I was an emotional wreck, and you had a concussion. I felt sorry for you."

"Just a bump on the head. And you're never an emotional wreck." He leaned in, his body hard and hot against mine.

"Hah! I should record you saying that. And Simon's chocolates were drugged. I was under the influence."

"The more excuses you trot out, I figure the more I got to you." He pushed his hand into my hair and massaged the tight muscles at the back of my neck. It felt so good I wanted to moan and weep with relief. It had been a hellish rollercoaster ride of a twenty-four hours. But encouraging Rafe wasn't fair to him or to me. Though I was having trouble pulling together the exact reason why with his hands working their magic.

"Don't, uh, don't make too much out of it, Rafe," I said to the N-V on his chest. Another logo T-shirt, this one red with black letters. Envy. Maybe I did envy Flo her excitement and her big wedding. Not to mention all those honeymoons. To be so crazy in love . . . How long had it been since I'd felt so completely lost in a man's arms, wild for his touch. Oh, wait a minute, that happened every time I was with Blade. Right? Or did it? The Vampire Viagra had helped. But without it?

"It was just one kiss." I stiffened when Rafe pulled me closer.

"Then maybe you need another, for comparison. To see if the response is still there. What if it wasn't just the circumstances? What if there's more to this? Is that such a bad thing? I've made no secret of the fact that I want you." He rubbed my back in a slow circular motion that was erotic and yet comforting at the same time.

Yeah, he wanted me. I could feel how much below his belt buckle pressed hard against me. I laid my hands on his chest.

"I can't do this now, Rafe. I've got to go. Seriously. And what you're suggesting could take a while."

"Now you're talking." Rafe grinned, his dimples punctuating his relief as he released me and stepped back. "Go. But we're definitely getting back to this later."

I didn't bother responding to that. I'd left the door open, which was wrong, wrong, wrong. I should just shut Rafe down. Instead I grabbed my purse and left without another word. Down in the shop, I took over from Erin and settled in for the night. We weren't very busy, and I had way too much time to think. I'd just about talked myself down from my EV freak-out and fantasies about Rafe when Aggie walked in. Did she think I'd be glad to see her? I met her near the door, ready to go to war.

"What the hell are you doing here?" How's that for customer service?

"I thought we should discuss Flo's shower since you're the expert on all things bridal." She eased around me and began to flip through my cocktail-dress rack.

"Last time I saw you, you were happy to turn me into a freakin' statue. I won't forget that any time soon." I wanted to snatch the sea green dress she was holding out of her hand. Damn it, she acted like nothing had happened.

"I was wrong. I admit it. Greg had convinced me I'd be doing him a favor, and he'd, well"—she smiled and winked—"he'd do some favors for me."

"Then he left you here. Why didn't you just thaw me out then and leave him in the lurch? Make *him* a statue?" I glanced at the price tag on the dress she was holding. Good profit potential. I'd like to toss her butt out of here, except if she was going to buy something . . . Damn, I hated that my finances didn't allow me the luxury of alienating a paying customer. Westwood's cash payoff couldn't come fast enough.

"I sent your buddy Rafe out there to save you, didn't I?" She held up the dress and looked at herself in the full-length mirror next to the dressing rooms. Yeah, she has a reflection. Me, not a glimmer. It's a vampire thing.

"You sent him out to be beaten and tortured." I itched to claw the smile off her face. "You buying that dress or not?"

"Sorry if Rafe's visit didn't go well, but that's not my fault." She swept her eyes, the same color as the dress, over me. "You look like you survived okay. Greg said they just wanted to talk to you, so why shouldn't I help him?"

"I'm fine, no thanks to you or Greg. But believing anything Greg says isn't smart. Haven't you figured that out yet?" Had to stay on track here. As far as Aggie knew, I *had* just gone out there to talk. Greg wouldn't have told her any EV plans. She'd blab to Flo if she thought she had a juicy tidbit.

"Sure. Now I have. But, unless your shifter suffered permanent damage, I'd say you need to relax and cooperate with me. We're both supposed to help Flo have the wedding of her dreams. Am I right?" Aggie didn't wait for an answer, just stepped into the dressing room. "I'm trying this on. Tell me what I need to do at a shower besides invite people and feed them."

"You think I've been to a wedding shower?" I heard the rustle of her clothes behind the curtain. "All I know is what I've seen on TV and in movies. I think they play games. Oh, and wrap the bride in toilet paper. I have no idea why."

"Making Flo into a Charmin mummy sounds like fun but I doubt she'd stand for it. Might not be a good look for her." Aggie threw back the curtain. "Fits perfectly. What do you think?"

I thought that I'd kill to have her kind of figure. The vintage sixties shift could have been made for her. It was a size five, six max. The color did amazing things for her skin and eyes, and the hem hit her mid thigh. She had great legs that seemed to go on forever. Panting men would follow her anywhere in that dress. The short length would even allow for her fish tail if the Storm God got mad at her again. That thought made me smile. I'd like to see Aggie stuck on a rock singing for her supper again like a Siren should.

"Perfect. Where are you going to wear it?" I swallowed my snark for the sake of a sale.

"The bachelorette party. We should dress up, right?" Aggie bit her lip. "You said it's at Rafe's nightclub."

"Sure, sure, dress up." I couldn't believe I was having a civil conversation with her. But she was more powerful than I could ever hope to be. I didn't want to end up a statue again.

"What kind of games should I get for this shower? I'm not usually into them myself. Though I played strip Scrabble once." She stepped back into the dressing room and shut the curtain. "I'm really good with words, but I lost on purpose. The guy I played with was unbelievably hot, but he didn't like to lose."

"No word games. Flo's English isn't so great. Do some research. Search the Web for bridal-shower games. See what comes up. You do have a computer, don't you?" I took the dress she handed out to me. I realized I had no idea where Aggie lived or *how* she lived. As far as I knew, she still called a cave in the middle of Lake Travis home. But she dressed well and seemed to have plenty of money. Siren magic. I really didn't care as long as she didn't give me a rubber check for this dress.

"I'll figure it out. Maybe I'll see Greg again. He has a computer." She stuck her head out. "I told you he has his uses."

"Whatever. Just don't plan to bring him to the wedding as your date. Flo won't want any EVs there. Now I'll write up this sale. Come out when you're dressed." I headed to the cash register. In a few moments, Aggie came out and stopped in front of the mirror again. She fluffed her hair and pulled a lipstick out of her purse, retracing her pink lips. Finally, she walked over to watch me fill out the sales slip.

"You know you could tell me what they wanted out at the EV headquarters." She leaned on the counter. "I can keep a secret."

"Yeah, right. Forget it. It was my personal business, none of yours." I clipped the tag off the dress.

"Be that way." She made a face. "At least tell me what the place looks like. Greg raved about it. That's why I was so mad when he didn't take me along." Aggie handed me a credit card. The name on it was A. Sirena. Hmm. It went through without a hitch, so I was happy to answer her.

"It's beautiful and scary as hell. Imagine a gilded mosque with an energy-hungry goddess inside, in the middle of a pine forest. If you were with Greg, you'd be safe, but the king out there, Simon Destiny, and I don't exactly love each other. I've tried to kill him; he's tried to kill various friends of mine. His goddess acts like a giant Shop-Vac, sucking energy out of paranormals. I used to be loaded with energy, so I had a near miss out there. I avoid it like plastic flowers on flip-flops."

"Obviously. That's why the statue thing was necessary. And the EV leader did snap you out of my freeze. Impressive." Aggie signed the credit slip without even checking the total.

"Sure, if you like weasels. Be careful around EVs, Aggie. Ask your boss about them. He'd probably tell you to steer clear." I figured I'd done my good deed for the night. Now I was ready for her to leave. I stuck the dress on a hanger and slipped a plastic bag over it.

"I don't tell the Storm God squat about my love life. He'd try to interfere, and I've definitely decided to give Greg another go. He *is* amazing in bed."

"TMI, Aggie." I held up a hand. "I really don't want details of your love life either."

She grinned and took her purchase. "It's too bad you don't remember your time with Greg. He said he wiped your memory because you were too clingy. He didn't want to be bothered by your whining when he broke up with you."

"If you choose to believe that liar, go ahead. I'm glad I can't remember being with him, obviously a low point in my life. But when a guy and I decide to part ways, I don't cling or whine." Apparently Greg and I had been together in New York City. I'd had other vampire friends there too. I'd tried my luck on Broadway but soon realized matinees ruined my chances of actually being in a show, and I'd ended up working as a waitress. I could remember all of that, but not a speck of my time as a couple with Greg Kaplan. The blank spot made me insane.

"Well, he's the best I've got right now. Maybe at the wedding I'll have better luck. I always wanted to hook up with Israel Caine. You know how I love his music." Aggie stuffed her charge card and receipt into her purse.

"You tried to kill him, Aggie. I doubt he'll be happy to see you again." When would she leave? A new customer

entered the shop, so I figured that was her cue to take a hike.
I was right.

"You never know, Glory. You and I seem to have patched
things up." With that, she sashayed to the door like she
owned the place. I just stared at her, my mouth open. Patched
things up? Not even close. She stopped next to the new customer, looked her up and down, then glanced back at me.
She mouthed a word, then hit the door and was gone.

I reached for the stake I kept behind the counter. A vamp
can't be too careful when she's alone at night. And Aggie had
said a word I didn't hear too often. "Demon."

"May I help you?" I kept the stake out of sight, not sure
it would do much good anyway. Some demons were suscep-
tible to them, just like vampires; others laughed when
plugged. I wished I had something else, like holy water or a
Bible. But then they didn't always work either. Instead, I
threw out a mind probe. Nada. Not surprising. Demons
aren't into sharing their thoughts.

"I'm looking for Glory St. Clair, and obviously I've found
her." The woman smiled and showed off a pair of fangs. She
was posing as vampire. Didn't fool me. I knew a demon
when I smelled one. The evil has a sweet odor like baking
donuts. It would make you hungry if you didn't know it
came straight from hell.

Of course she was beautiful; demons usually are when
they're in public. This one had long dark hair and amethyst
eyes with long lashes against pale perfect skin. She was about
Flo's size, short with the same tiny waist and size-six figure.
She wore an expensive designer outfit in a deep purple silk
that set off those exotic eyes.

"Yes, I'm Glory. How can I help you?" I kept the counter
between us. I'm a churchgoing Christian and try not to con-
sort with demons as a matter of principle. Not to say that I
haven't hit a few low spots in my long, long life and been
tempted to make deals with the Devil. A girl's got to do what
a girl's got to do to survive. Am I right? But I'd squeaked by

without resorting to that. So I was fairly calm. Unless someone had put a contract out on me . . .

"Relax. I'm not here to take you out. I'm here to find someone." She smiled, and the fangs were gone. "Obviously you've figured out what I am, so I won't try to play games here."

"Yeah, I get that you're from the dark side. So what's your business, and who are you looking for?" Now I was worried. Someone close to me. Who could she possibly want and why?

"I'm looking for Rafael. I believe he's using the name Valdez this century." She'd quit smiling and was suddenly on my side of the counter. "I know he's been near you. I can smell him." She sniffed my blouse. "He's been touching you."

I almost jumped over the counter to get away from her. Almost, because she'd hooked me with a silver-painted fingernail, and I wasn't going anywhere. It wasn't brute force; it was more like an electrical current that jammed my feet to the floor. Similar to Aggie's statue trick except I could talk and blink and move my arms. She looked up, her eyes gleaming.

"Why's he been touching you?"

"He's my bodyguard. Sometimes he has to get close. What's it to you?" I tried to shove her away. Nope. I didn't like where this was going. Powerful entity and demon. I knew nothing about Rafe's history. Maybe he'd made a pact with the Devil, and this thing had come to collect a debt. I tried to wrench free and couldn't make headway. Rafe was strong and clever, but against this? I was afraid he wouldn't stand a chance. Could I get a message to him to run like hell?

"Bodyguard. That's okay, then." She removed her claw and gave me an inch of space. "So you have a business relationship."

I didn't bother to correct her. I mean, it was true. Somehow I didn't think she needed to know that Rafe was also my best friend. I sent out a mental message to him to meet me upstairs if he could hear me, then realized this creature had been reading my every thought since she'd stepped through the door.

"What do you want with Rafael?"

The demon smiled and her eyes glowed red. "I'm his wife."

Twelve

"You and Rafael are married?" I jumped over the counter then. I needed some air not tainted with a sugar rush.

"Yep. And this is our anniversary. Bet that bad boy forgot again. I try to check in every decade or so." She sighed and made a move that put her in front of the same mirror Aggie had preened at moments before. "I don't know why he's so difficult to pin down. It's not like it wasn't a love match." She smiled, then pulled a brush from a leather shoulder bag and proceeded to fuss with her hair.

Rafe and a demon, even a beautiful one. I didn't get it. I mean, Rafe is good. Honest. I knew him. Had spent five years close to him, as close as two creatures could get, and had never seen a hint of a dark side. Well, unless he was in fighting mode. All warriors dredged up a little hell then, even Jerry. That didn't make either of them evil, just tough. For the guy to have hooked up with this, this thing . . . Well, it just didn't compute.

"Compute this, Glory." She'd stowed her brush, too close to me again. "We have an open arrangement. If you and Rafael are doing the dirty, it's not going to get you staked.

But I'm not a 'thing.' I'm a third-level demon, one of Luci-fer's favorites." Her eyes were back to that incredible violet.

"Sorry. Rafe and I are just friends." I backed toward the door and flipped the sign to Closed. I didn't want a customer walking in on this. Should I run? I didn't think it would do me much good. And right now she honestly seemed to mean me no harm.

Get a clue, Glory. Demons don't honestly do anything.

"Just friends? Too bad." She grinned wickedly. "You gay or something? The man can bring it, girlfriend. But then if you don't roll that way . . ." She was suddenly mere inches from me and touched my shoulder. "I can bring it too."

"Uh, no. I mean, you're beautiful, but I've got a guy. I'm in a committed relationship. Rafe was just my bodyguard. That's all." I was pressed against the shop door and felt it hit me hard between my shoulder blades when someone shoved at it.

"Let me in, Glory." Rafe was here.

I moved away, relieved and yet worried sick about what would happen next. Demons lied all the time. Maybe this creature wasn't his wife but a hired gun here to take him out. Stuff like that happened. I spied a nineteenth-century prayer book and a rosary on a shelf of collectibles and used a vamp move to snatch them. Maybe they'd work in a show-down.

The look on Rafe's face assured me this wasn't some demon for hire but someone he knew well and wasn't happy to see. I stayed out of their way and waited with my weapons. I wanted to bawl. What else hadn't Rafe told me? Of course I had plenty of secrets myself. Enough already. *Concentrate.*

"Alesa. What the hell are you doing here?" Rafe's greet-ing didn't exactly say loving husband. He radiated fury from his tight jaw to his fists hitting his thighs.

"It's our anniversary, Rafael. How could I ignore it?" She smiled, her eyes red again. Really creepy. Rafe stepped closer.

"Easy. You go back where you came from and do your thing. I do mine. That was the agreement." Rafe glanced at

me and shook his head. Shorthand for "I'm sorry"? Not
nearly good enough.

"The agreement sucks. I want a child, and you're going to
give me one. You owe me that after what you put me
through. Your rejection made me a laughingstock where I
come from. I need to gain back my pride. I'm not leaving
until you give me what I want." Her eyes were really heating
up the place, and I looked away before my eyeballs got singed.

"No way. I don't owe you a damned thing." Rafe stepped
to within inches of her. God, but the man had stones. I
wanted to escape out the back door and leave them to hammer out their own domestic details. But what if Rafe needed
me? I shivered but gripped the soft leather prayer book in
one hand and the cross dangling from the rosary in the other.

"Please, darling." She dragged a silver nail down his
cheek, drawing blood. He never moved. "I'm getting older,
and my fertile time is almost over. You've got to—"

"Bullshit!" He grabbed her shoulders and shook her, his
fingers digging into her skin and ripping the fine silk of her
blouse. "I've heard this all before, Lesa. I'm not tying my
family to yours or damning a child of mine. I promised my
grandfather, and that promise I'll keep. The marriage was
annulled in the Mayori court. I'm sorry if you don't want to
accept that, but it's done. Over. Go back to hell and take a
lover there. Or creep into a mortal bed and get a spawn that
way. But you'll never have a child of my blood. Ever." Rafe's
eyes suddenly glowed red too.

I gasped and clutched the book and rosary to my breast,
so shocked I felt my knees buckle. Rafe's eyes red? That
could only mean one thing. The room darkened right before
I hit the floor.

When I woke up, I was in my own bed and I was alone.
What the hell had happened?

*Not much, Glory. Just everything you know about Rafael Val-
dez is suddenly wrong, wrong, wrong.*

I glanced at the clock and realized I'd been out for about an hour. The shop! I sat up, but when the room spun, I fell back again.

"You're awake. Sorry about that scene earlier and then the blackout. Alesa is hell on wheels when she's pissed." Rafe stood in the doorway, a bottle of Nadia's synthetic in his hand. "Here, drink. Maybe it'll help get you on your feet again."

"Are you telling me that demon knocked me out?" I took the cold bottle and held it against my forehead, not ready to drink yet. I felt shaky inside and out. "She didn't touch me."

"She didn't have to. It's one of her tricks. She gave you a psychic right hook. Sent you straight to the floor. She didn't like having an audience, since I was rejecting her." Rafe looked like he wanted to hit the wall next to the bed. "She's gone for now, but I'm afraid she'll be back. The woman's on a mission." He slammed his fist into his palm. "Damn it, Glory. I'm sorry she dragged you into this."

"She said she was your wife." I struggled to sit up again. Rafe was there instantly, arranging a pillow behind me. When I waved him off, he frowned but stepped back. "I can handle this." I leaned against the headboard and sipped from the bottle. "Is she? Your wife?"

"No." Rafe pulled his phone out of his jeans pocket and answered it. Guess he'd had it on vibrate. "Yes, sir?" There was a long silence while he listened to whoever was on the other end.

I could hear enough to know the guy wasn't happy. Neither was Rafe. He burst into a different language, one I'd never heard before, and began pacing around the bedroom. Another long silence. Judging by Rafe's body language, this was serious. You know the phrase "blind with rage"? Well, that was Rafe. I lay very still, not sure I wanted to draw attention to myself.

"No!" That outburst was followed by another long silence, Rafe listening, then suddenly ending the call.

"You okay?" I still didn't move but decided it was safe to ask the question.

"No. Damn it!" He turned off the phone, shoved it into his pocket and faced me again. "I owe you an explanation."

"Only if you want to, Rafe." I held out my hand. "Come, sit and cool down first." I hated to see him so upset. He was my calm-in-a-crisis buddy. Now I wanted to wrap my arms around him and hold him till he collected himself.

"You sure you trust me that close to you? I know you saw my eyes earlier. My demon eyes." He came close to the bed now but still hadn't taken my hand.

I swallowed. Yes, there was that. But right now I saw the same soft brown eyes of the guy who'd risked his life for me countless times. They weren't teasing me, and I sure wasn't seeing the dimples that came out when he grinned. But I loved everything about Rafael Valdez, and I wasn't going to throw away our friendship without giving him a chance to explain.

How can he explain demon eyes, Glory?

"Come here, Rafe." I grabbed his hand, pulling him down to sit on the bed. The movement made me a little woozy, and I sank back against the pillow. "Your ex really did a number on me. I still feel like I've been shaken, not stirred."

"She's a vindictive bitch. She was the biggest mistake of my life." Rafe smoothed back my hair. "Thanks for hanging in with me, Glory. I hope you won't be sorry."

"Never. How on earth did you ever fall for such a creature? And who was that on the phone?" I held on to his hand. "Never mind explaining about her. I can't say much. I apparently once carried on with Greg Kaplan. Brain farts. Hormones override common sense. It happens to the best of us. Alesa is beautiful when she's looking like a human."

"Yes, she is. And I was young and rebellious. My grandfather, the guy on the phone, had warned me to stay away from demons. So naturally I was hell-bent, pardon the pun, on trying one." Rafe laughed, but it wasn't a merry sound. "Kids can be stupid pricks. I sure was. Alesa and I had a hot time and even made it legal during a wild weekend."

"You did marry her." I wanted to jerk my hand away but

decided that would be childish and stupid. I was jealous. I had no right. I'd been married before. Of course my husband had been dead for more than four hundred years. Then there was my relationship with Jerry. *He* figured we were as good as married.

"Yes. Big mistake. Once she thought she had me tied to her, she let the worst parts of her evil side hang out. Man, was I stupid." Rafe took my now empty bottle of synthetic and set it on the nightstand. "So I went crawling home to my grandfather, and he helped me get the marriage annulled."

"From what Alesa said, she's never accepted that." I gripped Rafe's hand, imagining a young, impressionable shifter in the hands of a demon bitch. "I'll bet those creatures are never naïve and always know exactly what they're doing."

"That's the argument we used in court. The Mayori court is the governing body of the shape-shifters. Demons don't obey their edicts. So it suits Alesa to pretend we're still married. I know we're not." He smiled at me. "Vampires don't acknowledge our court either."

"I know that. We're free spirits. But I've heard of the Mayori." Blade and Damian actually admired the shape-shifter power structure. It kept them off the human radar. You didn't read a lot of scary shifter stories like you did the Dracula thing, now did you? I was finally feeling better and sat up straight. "So what's your grandfather got to do with them, and how did you end up with demon eyes?"

"Please. Only part of me is demon. The rest is pure shifter. Grandfather is head of the Mayori court now." Rafe stood and pulled me to my feet. "He'd like to pretend it never happened, but my mother, his only daughter, was the result of his own romp with a demon bitch."

"Oh, the sins of the fathers . . . or in this case, the grandfathers." When my knees started to cave, I slipped my arms around him, absorbing his warmth and strength. "No wonder he was giving you hell on the phone. He wanted this all to go away permanently, didn't he?"

"Oh, yeah. And he'd flip if Alesa had a child of our blood."

Rafe held on to me. "Of course I won't let that happen. Being part demon has made me something of an outcast among my kind." He breathed against my hair.

"Poor Rafe." I ran my hands up and down his back.

"I handled it. Grandfather would have bought me acceptance, but I've always made my own way." He put his hand under my chin. "But if sympathy gets me something here, I'll take it."

"What does he think about you consorting with vampires?" I looked up and caught a glimpse of white teeth and dimples.

"Hates it." Rafe slipped his hands down to my waist and pulled me closer. "Which makes you even more desirable."

"Still the rebellious youth, I see." I didn't resist, and his eyes darkened. "How old are you anyway?"

"Eight hundred and seventy-two." He lowered his head and took my lower lip between his teeth, then gently sucked it into the heat of his mouth.

Hmm. No youthful fumbling here but rather a world of experience. He kissed me as if he could dive into my soul and pull me into his. I shoved my hands into his hair and lost myself in the moment, reveling in the taste of him, the heat of his mouth and the magic of his hands moving down to grab my butt.

He lifted his head. "You sure you're okay?"

"Getting there." I really was feeling stronger. I ran my hands over his back, his muscles bunching under my fingertips.

"Maybe you'd better lie down again." He eased me back to the bed until I was sitting on the edge, then knelt in front of me. He kissed me again, his mouth hot on mine as he slid his hands under the back of my sweater. One went up to the clasp of my bra, and one went down to slide into the back of my jeans.

"Mmmm." I fell back on the pillows, dragging him with me, our mouths still connected. This was feeling very right, very—

"Rafe, Glory?" Nadia slammed the hall door, and I could hear her heels tapping as she headed across the living room.

We sprang apart like guilty children, then grinned at each other. Rafe ended up next to the dresser, a book in front of his bulging zipper. Like he'd been reading me a bedtime story. I finger combed my hair.

"In here, Nadia." I sat up and grabbed one of my shoes lying on the rug next to the bed and slipped it on. "I had an accident, and Rafe was taking care of me."

"Accident? What happened?" Nadia looked concerned, but I could tell it barely covered a combo platter of curiosity and aggravation.

"A blast from my past came by. In the form of a demon bitch. She knocked Glory around a little." Rafe gave up on the book, took Nadia's arm and steered her back to the living room. "I need to warn you in case she comes back. And I'm pretty sure she will. She lives to cause trouble."

"Who is she? What does she look like?" Nadia was now all business. "I need you on track here, Rafe. This is the second night in a row you've disappeared on me, damn it. This club isn't going to open on time if this keeps happening."

"I'll tell you all about her on the way to the club." Rafe turned to me. "Glory, about your shop . . ."

"Rafe, did you just lock up?" I stuck my foot in the other shoe and followed them to the living room. Nadia's attitude had snapped me back to reality in a hurry.

"I had no choice, Glory." Rafe acted like abandoning my shop hadn't been a big deal. Aggravating.

"Sure, fine. But now that I'm recovered, I need to get back down there. I'm missing sales and ruining the track record we had for being open twenty-four hours."

"Can't you let it go for one night? Alesa might come back." Rafe was in my space, staring worriedly at me while Nadia tapped her foot and looked like she wanted to say something. It didn't take mind reading to know she was over the whole Rafe-and-Glory connection and ready to pull the plug on their partnership. I couldn't let him ruin this club thing over me.

"I can't afford to do that, Rafe. I'll call Richard. He's an ex-priest. He'll know what to do about a demon. If nothing else, he'll stay with me until the next shift comes in. You and I can talk later. How's that?" His eyebrow went up. Okay, so we hadn't exactly been talking when Nadia had come in. I saw my purse and dug in it for my phone. Silence. I looked up and saw Rafe staring at me. Mr. Inscrutable.

"I'll be careful." I pulled out my phone. "Calling Richard now." I patted Rafe's chest, then pushed him toward Nadia. "Go. This is important to you. I want the club to be your number-one priority until it's opened successfully. I'm a businesswoman too, Nadia. I totally get where you're coming from."

"Listen to her, Rafael. Now let's go. There are a million details, and I can't handle them all by myself. I called your cell, and it went straight to voice mail. This is no way to run a business." She opened the hall door and gestured for Rafe to precede her. "Are we going?"

"Yes, I guess we are. Don't go down without Richard, Glory. I'll be back before sunrise." He gave me a look that was a promise of something interesting later, then walked out. Nadia's glance actually said thanks, then she slammed the door.

"All right, then." I picked up my phone and called Richard. Voice mail. Knowing Flo, that probably meant they were practicing for the honeymoon and she'd made him turn off his phone. I left him a message that this was urgent and involved a demon in my shop. More than a little shaky about my decision, I grabbed some supplies, stuffed them into my purse, then headed out.

The first hour was uneventful. I had a few customers, including two who had tried to come earlier and were disappointed that we'd been closed. The sales I made convinced me that I'd done the right thing reopening. When the bell rang over the door and Aggie came in, I was relieved. Reinforcements. I hoped she'd fight on my side if a demon showed up.

"I had Greg look up shower games, Glory. Tell me what you think." Aggie plopped papers on the counter and sat on the stool in front of me. "Some of these are pretty funny."

"Funny's good." I picked up a paper. "Unless you're making me look ridiculous. 'Stack cotton balls on your head. The person who can balance the most wins a prize.'" I crumpled the paper and dropped it in the can behind the counter. "I think not."

Aggie grinned. "Aw, come on. Where's your sense of humor? I can see you now, a stack of those fluffy things on your head, Miss Cottontop, while we all laugh and cheer."

"Next." I picked up another paper. "What's this? 'Kiss Flo's ass.' Are you nuts?"

Aggie snatched it. "You didn't read it all. You blow up a picture of her head and draw a body. Then we each put on a ton of lipstick and a blindfold. The person whose lips end up closest to Flo's cute little ass wins a prize. Isn't that fun?"

"In Siren land maybe." I grabbed the paper and tore it in quarters, dropping it in the can. Okay, maybe I wasn't in a game-playing mood. Getting drop-kicked by a demon will do that to you.

"Fine. Be that way. I'll pick my own games, and you'll just have to go with the flow." Aggie laughed. "Get it? Flo, flow?" She stared at me. "Never mind. What's got you so bummed? You're usually a little more upbeat than this. Is it something to do with that demon I saw come in here earlier?"

"You could say that. What do you know about demons?" I sat on the stool I kept behind the counter. Aggie was right. I was down and sinking fast. I'd even lost a sale earlier because I hadn't smiled and faked interest in a customer's dress choice. Now Aggie and I were alone so I could vent.

"I know they're trouble." She pulled another sheaf of papers out of her Louis Vuitton tote. "Games for the bachelorette party. X-rated. That should cheer you up."

"Damn it, Aggie, I can't think about games right now. The demon may come back anytime, and she's hurt me once." I pulled a vial of holy water out from under the counter, then draped the rosary around my neck. "Think this stuff will help?"

"Couldn't hurt." Aggie picked up the holy water. "Well,

I take that back. Fake. Whoever sold it to you ripped you off. I can tell the real deal from a mile away. Gives me the heebie-jeebies. Not that I'm evil or anything, but I've got enough of the bad stuff in me to have a sense of things like that."

"Well, shoot. Got it off the Internet. I had high hopes for it." I dropped the vial in the trash can. "What about the rosary? I had it in front of me, along with a prayer book, when she was here earlier and she didn't approach me, but she did treat me to a kind of psychic knockout punch."

"Yeah, they don't like touching stuff like that. But it depends on what kind of demon you're dealing with. There're good demons and bad. I assume you're going at it with a bad one." Aggie was checking her manicure like this was no big deal. I wanted to cram her stack of papers down her throat.

"Yes, definitely bad. She's really after Rafe. Wants to have his baby, of all things." I propped my chin on my fist. Visions of that coupling made my skin crawl.

"Ooo. Now you've got me interested. Sex with a demon. Tell me more." Aggie leaned in.

"She's Rafe's ex. Now she claims her biological clock's ticking, and she wants her little hellbaby to be his. Rafe's not interested. She hit me, so maybe she's thinking it's because I'm in the picture. Of course that's not it. He wouldn't do her if she were the last female in Heaven, hell or any part in between." I glanced at the bachelorette games. Ring toss with an inflatable penis? Oh, joy.

"He'd better be careful. She could sneak up on him. Knock him out like she did you, and then take him while he's unconscious." Aggie started to stuff her papers back into her tote. "Don't ask me how, but demons can get men up when they don't want to be there. It's happened before. The Storm God has told us some really cool stories about it."

"Not sure with Rafe. He's part demon himself."

"No frickin' way." Aggie stopped in mid stuff.

"I was as shocked as you are." What was I doing spilling Rafe's secrets to Aggie like she and I were girlfriends? "Don't you tell anyone I told you that. Swear it, or I'll tell the Storm God you love your shoes more than you love him."

Aggie blinked. "Gee, Glory. Play hard ball why don't you? Fine. I won't tell a soul." She crossed her heart.

I looked up when the bell over the shop door rang. Customer? No. I nudged Aggie. She turned around. We knew immediately that we had a problem on our hands.

"Well, well, well. A vampire and a Siren. I just love a twofer." The demon glanced back, and my sign flipped on its own from Open to Closed. The dead bolt clicked shut, and we were trapped with her.

"Love this." Aggie threw up her hands like she did when she was about to turn someone to stone.

The demon just laughed and threw up her own hands. Aggie was frozen in place. Yep, stuck on her stool like a permanent fixture. I gaped at Alesa.

"Alesa, wait a minute. Why start something when we really don't have a problem here?" I picked up the Bible I'd brought from my apartment and rounded the counter. I didn't have a clue what to try, but hoped my religious objects would at least keep me mobile. I glanced at Aggie. Still frozen.

"No problem? Honey, you think I can't read your every thought? You're into Rafe, and I bet you a thousand dollars that he's into you. You're just his type, so sweet, so freakin' good." She gagged. "I don't know how in the hell he stands the stench of all that decency. You reek of it."

"Forgive me, but that's not a problem I care to fix." And who was she to talk? The woman was giving off so many sugar fumes a human would gain five pounds just breathing in the air around her.

"You're a vampire. You're supposed to kill, drain people dry. Come over to the dark side with us and use your powers to do our master's work." Alesa had been roaming the shop, ripping a piece of silk here, smashing a fine porcelain there. I wanted to screech at her and toss my Bible at her head. She needed to see my dark side? Let her ruin one more piece of merchandise.

"Rafe and I aren't together. I told you that. But it wouldn't matter if we were. Rafe doesn't want you. Why do you demean yourself by going after a man who has rejected you?" I couldn't stand it. She was aiming for a designer dress that would bring me several hundred dollars. "Get away from there!"

"Why, Glory, am I bothering you?" Alesa plucked the dress from the rack and held it up to her. It was much too big. Would have fit me if I hadn't decided I couldn't afford to keep it.

"Put the dress back, Alesa."

"Of course." She gave it a look that stained the red wool with a smear of black oil, then slid it back onto the rack, careful to smudge it against two other expensive dresses on either side. "How's that?"

"You bitch!" I flung myself at her, fangs down, claws out. I landed on the floor because she used a lightning-fast move to get out of the way.

She laughed and stepped on my back. "Missed me." She dug her high heel into my spine until I heard a bone crack. "Vampires have such lame skill sets."

I bucked and rolled away, diving under another dress rack before I sprang to my feet.

"I'm going to rip out your throat, take you down and drain every toxic ounce from your evil body." My taunt just earned a cackle that made me back up until I hit another rack behind me.

She'd dropped the mask of beauty, and I cringed away from her hideous hawkish face. Nut brown skin stretched over her beaklike nose, with deep grooves on either side. I heard her breathing as she circled around the rack, and I leaped to the other side of the shop. Her eyes glowed bright red, and her lips peeled back in a grin that exposed rows of sharp teeth that would rip me to shreds if I let them get close.

I was definitely having second thoughts about that. Forget an attack. I saw my Bible where I'd dropped it on the floor. Would that keep her away? My rosary sure hadn't. My back ached where she'd dug her heel into me, and I could smell my own blood and the stench of hellfire coming from her flaming eyes.

The shop door banged open, and there was a definite change in the atmosphere. Alesa's face changed too. Her mask of beauty slipped back into place, and she smiled.

"What have we here? More help from a vampire? Another Goody Two-Shoes at that." She flew over the dress rack and landed behind me, her hand clamping around my throat, her nails digging into my jugular. I knew then that she'd been playing with me. I'd never been any real match for her.

My vision darkened. I grabbed her arm, tearing desperately at her skin to try to relieve the pressure. Black liquid oozed from her wounds, but she didn't give an inch.

"Let her go, demon." Richard's voice came from far away.

"Make me." She ripped her nails down my throat, and my own blood poured down my chest. I had to do something, or I was going to die right here in my own shop. Through a haze of pain and terror, I lifted my feet and slammed them down onto hers, grinding my high heels into her insteps just like she'd done to my back. Her bones shattered, and she finally released my throat with a screech. Free, I lunged away from her, falling to the floor and rolling under another dress rack.

Cool water splashed my jeans as I fell. Alesa's screams bounced off the walls as I crawled through skirts until I collapsed against the cool metal legs supporting the rack.

I reached up to my wet, torn throat. There was a terrible hole where my jugular belonged. The demon had known exactly how to kill me. I fought away the darkness and held my flesh together, praying healing thoughts. I couldn't let evil win. Church. This Sunday. Night service.

"Glory, can you roll this way a little?" Richard calmly tried to coax me from my hiding place. Or was it a trick?

I cautiously cracked open my eyes, afraid to wiggle even

a finger or she'd know I still lived. Masculine brown leather boots and dark jeans. Richard. Or was it? Demons could be so cruelly clever.

He murmured a prayer in Latin. I didn't know Latin, but I knew Jesus and God when I heard them called on, something a demon would never dare. All right, then. I reached out my trembling hand.

Oh, Glory, when did you get so weak? I eased toward him until he pulled me into his arms.

"Richard? Where's the demon?" I leaned against him, not caring that I was getting his blue shirt bloody. I'd buy him a new one. Two new ones. He was my hero.

"Gone. Holy water got her."

"Shit, that was close." Aggie peered over his shoulder. "You look like crap on a cracker, Glory."

"Thanks. How did you get out of that freeze?" I whispered. Whatever the demon had done to my throat hadn't healed yet.

"Guess when Richard watered her down, it broke her spell. Never saw anything like it. Well, except in that movie *The Wizard of Oz*, when they threw the water on the bad witch. Anyway, he tossed the holy water, his was the real deal, and there she went, dissolved like Kool-Aid powder. Amazing stuff that holy water." Aggie was clearly buzzed. She patted Richard on the back, following him as he carried me to the door.

"You did a great job, preacher man. Flo's a lucky gal. Glory, don't worry about your little shop here. I'll stay till your helper arrives. Should be soon. Dawn's only an hour away." Aggie grabbed the shop door and pulled it open so Richard could carry me out. "Wait!"

"What is it, Aggie? I need to get Glory upstairs. She's in pretty bad shape." Richard was obviously losing patience. He looked tired. I guess facing a demon, especially after a night of pleasing a bride in the bedroom, took a lot out of you.

"Glory, I'm sorry if I've been a bitch to you. You were awesome tonight. Really went after that demon." Aggie put her hand on my arm. "I'd like to be your friend."

"Thanks, Aggie." I blinked back tears. God, but I hurt and I was weak. Now I was supposed to have some kind of sweet make-up scene with Aggie? Not sure I could handle it. "Talk to you tomorrow." I'd disappointed her, but that was all I had in me.

"Sure. Tomorrow." She thrust something into my lap. "Here's your purse. I wrapped it in a plastic bag so you wouldn't get blood on it."

I sighed. Okay, so she was acting like a friend. "Thanks, pal." That got her to smile. Good thing because she could be a really bad enemy. *Hold that thought, Glory.*

Richard carried me up the stairs while I dug for my keys. I was desperate for healing sleep. But when I saw who was waiting for me in the apartment, I knew I wasn't going to get it yet.

Thirteen

"Look at you." Flo hovered over me after Richard deposited me on the bed. She shooed him from the room, then cleaned me up herself and put me into my new nightgown. I protested weakly, thinking this was a real waste, but she ignored me. "You are so terribly hurt. Wearing pretty things will make you feel better."

"Yeah. I'm weak too." I blinked and wondered why she didn't turn on the lights.

"You lost too much blood. Here, *mia amica*."

Before I could stop her, Flo had ripped open the vein in her wrist and pressed it to my lips. What can I say? I'm a vampire and needed the nourishment. I drank and realized the lights were on. I'd been closer to death than I'd been in a long, long time. Finally, I sighed and pulled away. Flo wiped my lips with a cool washcloth and settled me back against the pillows.

"It's almost dawn. I want to hear the whole story about this demon, but I don't think you're up to telling me. Aggie can tell me some of it. Your day help arrived, so she came up. She's in your living room talking to Richard. You can tell me the rest tomorrow. Will you be all right if I leave you now?" Flo still sat on the edge of the bed, her hand next to my head.

"Sure. Thanks, dear friend." I reached for my throat, relieved it was almost healed. A good feeding will do that for you. After I slept, I'd be 100 percent again. "I need to thank Richard. What he did was dangerous. And awesome."

"Ah, he was in his element. When he got the call to come fight a demon? You should have seen him when he pulled out his holy water—blessed by the Holy Father himself, he said—and stuff he has in a special trunk. He even prayed over it." Flo smiled and stood, then leaned over to kiss my cheek. "I am very proud of him. He is a good man, no?"

"Yes, the best. He saved my life." I sighed, really exhausted. "So did you. I love you, Flo."

"Me too, Glory. Rest now. Rafael is arriving. He will guard you through the day, but the demon is no more. Ricardo did the trick." Flo stopped at the door. "Should I call Jeremiah?"

"No!" I tried to sit up but couldn't manage it. "No need to worry him. It's over. I'll be fine when I wake up. I'll tell him about it when he gets back." Maybe. But probably not. If I could persuade Richard and Flo that Jerry didn't ever have to know about it. Did Jerry know he'd hired a bodyguard who was part demon? I'd like to know the answer to that. I heard doors close, then saw Rafe in the doorway. His eyes were dark, hot and—

"Rafe."

"You almost died because of me." Right beside me in an instant, he gazed down like he wanted to take me in his arms but was afraid he'd hurt me.

"No, I almost died because of *me*."

"How can you say that? I brought Alesa here."

"I'm the one who *had* to open the shop." I held out my arms. "Would you hold me? Please?"

He sat on the edge of the bed and gently gathered me close. He smoothed my hair like I'd once run my hands over him when he'd been in dog body. The thought made me smile.

"Well, she's gone now. For good. That ought to make you and your grandfather happy." I leaned back and looked at him. "You're petting me. You realize that?"

"What?" He looked puzzled.

"I used to do this to you when I was hurt or upset. You'd lie next to me on the couch, and I'd run my hands over your furry coat. It made me feel calm and protected, you know."

"And I had to lie there and take it. Because I was a friggin' dog." He grinned and studied that sinfully beautiful nightgown I wore. "Of course you never pranced around in stuff like this. You favored granny gowns and robes you found in thrift stores."

"Vintage chenille. Valuable stuff and comfortable." I was very aware that I hid nothing under the gown.

"Is this comfortable?" He ran his finger under the tiny satin strap.

"Almost like being naked." I smiled and fell back on the pillow. "Is Nadia here?"

"Nope. She got a house and decided to spend the night there. She took a change of clothes in her tote when she left earlier." Rafe was looking his fill, but he frowned when he got to what was surely an ugly red scar on my neck.

"Richard, Flo and Aggie?" I adjusted the sheet, which reached my waist. At least he couldn't see what was probably a nasty looking heel mark on my back. It still ached.

"Gone. The vamps had to beat the sun home, and Aggie wanted to get back to her watery digs." Rafe yawned. "Guess I'll hit the hay. Been a long day."

"Would you mind lying here next to me and just holding me?" I knew nothing could happen. In about a minute I'd be dead. Then he could go to his own bed.

"Sure. Squeeze over." He stepped out of his jeans, surprising me with a pair of white jockeys, then pulled off his black

T-shirt. He eased into bed, treating me as carefully as a piece of the finest porcelain. "I'm sorry you went through that. A brush with hell isn't something you soon forget." He gently touched his lips to the scar on my neck. "When I think of what she did to you . . ."

"It's over, Rafe. I survived, thanks to Richard. I don't know why she didn't just knock me out again, but she didn't." I snuggled into him. "This feels good. Safe."

"You *are* safe. I swear it. And I'm sure she didn't knock you out because she was toying with you. Figuring she'd have fun tearing you apart before she finally took the kill. She didn't count on a former priest showing up to do his thing."

"The real holy water do it?" I could barely speak. The combination of blood loss and shock were getting to me along with the coming dawn.

"It helped. Richard's had dealings with demons before. He had some special prayers too, I guess. Anyway, he managed it in fine form, and I'm telling Grandfather about him. The Mayori needs to know there's someone they can call on for situations like this." Rafe kept talking, his hand warm on my back. But my lights winked out, and I didn't hear any more.

I woke up with my nightgown twisted around my legs, and Rafe hard against me. I did a quick inventory and realized I'd healed, all aches and pains gone. He stirred next to me, as usual hyperaware of me and my movements.

"How you feelin'?" He stretched, his arms hitting the headboard, his feet a good six inches beyond the end of the mattress.

"Perfect except for a desperate need to brush my teeth. Be right back." I bolted for the bathroom and took care of business, even washing my face and brushing my hair. What was I up to? A major right turn in my life. I knew in my heart that Rafe was there with me. I posed in the bedroom doorway.

"Flo was right about that nightgown." Rafe brushed by me, his hand grazing my breast. "It does bring out the color of your eyes." He stepped into the bathroom and shut the door.

My eyes? What the hell was he doing looking at my eyes? I stomped over to the bed and sat. Then jumped up again. Took a trip to the kitchen and grabbed a bottle of synthetic. Chugged it. Marched back to the bedroom and slammed into Rafe, who stood just inside the doorway.

"Something bothering you, sweetheart?" He grinned, his dimples deep and sexy as hell.

I looked him up and down. Hmm. Guess maybe he *had* noticed something besides my eyes if that bulge stretching his shorts was anything to go by.

"No. Something bothering *you*?" I ran a finger down the center of his chest, then popped the elastic on his briefs.

"Oh, yeah." He jerked me to him and covered my mouth with his. The kiss was wet heat and a slow melting of my senses. I knew this taste. Knew this firm body. Could find this scent in the dark. I had his hair in one hand and his taut ass in the other. God, how I wanted him. What had taken me so long to do something about it?

I jumped, wrapping my legs around his waist and felt his hands on my butt, holding me hard against him. My aching breasts jammed against his chest, and I couldn't get enough of his mouth, his tongue, the edge of his teeth. I scraped a fang over his lip and sipped at his blood, moaning with pleasure at the salty tang.

He walked us over to the bed and eased me back on it, dragging one of my legs off so he could stroke his hand up my thigh. I clenched around his roving fingers, so on fire I wanted to scream at him to hurry and take me then and there. He broke the kiss and leaned back, his face flushed, his hair wild.

"God, Glory, what's come over you, girl?" He smiled and eased my straps down. "Slow this down. A lot. I've waited five long years to see you go wild for me. I'm taking my time."

I helped him get the gown down to my waist, unable to speak. Not that we needed words. We were experts at mind reading. I sent Rafe a graphic message that made his eyebrows go up. But he had his own ideas about where to go as he stroked his tongue around one nipple, then sucked it into the heat of his mouth.

I held on to his shoulders, desperately trying to slow down too. But my bloodlust was on fire, urging me to scratch him and make him bleed, needing that scent to bind us. No, he wouldn't like it, wouldn't want to feed me. Before we were done, I was so going there. I writhed beneath him as he moved to the other breast, his mouth clever while his hand dove between us to search out that aching place between my thighs that wept for him.

I opened my legs and stroked his chest, exploring his nipples, while I traced his contours with my tongue and teeth. Control. I couldn't lose it. Didn't want to scare him off. Oh, who was I kidding? It would take hell's legions to scare away this bad boy. He traveled down my body with his hot mouth. I gasped and lost it, clawing at him. Rafe just growled and used his own teeth until I bowed off the bed.

His eyes gleamed as he rose above me and carefully stripped away my gown—he knew how much I prized such beautiful things—and tossed it toward the dresser before he pounced, saying my name in a way that made me hot and cold and hungrier than ever. He murmured words in that language I didn't understand, kissing and licking his way up my body again. I still couldn't speak more than his name. But every time I said it, his eyes darkened.

Finally he took my mouth again in a deep, ravenous kiss that left me breathless. We were coming to the point of no return, and we both knew it. A point that would change things between us forever. He pulled back and stared down at me. I met his gaze, so hot, so hungry, yet still so very kind.

Forget kindness. I wanted passion, to be taken completely. And I knew we'd already crossed that line a dozen kisses ago. Rafe, Valdez, my bodyguard, a man Jerry had trusted . . . No, wouldn't think about *him* now. Only Rafe. He wanted me. I wanted him and was way beyond pulling together a single reason why I couldn't have what I wanted. I shook with pleasure when he moved over me, his hand caressing my breast, his mouth gently touching mine before he asked a question I wished he hadn't.

"Are you sure?"

I dragged his mouth down to mine, then pulled him to me, crying out at the exquisite rightness as he pressed hard and deep inside me. Sure? Was I ever certain of anything? But I couldn't keep wondering if I'd been wasting time waiting for another man to change. This man was here now, and he knew me, *really* knew me, and accepted me, Glory St. Clair, as I was. He wasn't taking *me*. I was taking *him*.

I rose to meet him and felt something else shift besides my body. What was I doing? Oh, yeah. Setting myself free. And it felt damned good. As Rafe moved, I opened my eyes and looked directly into his. I smiled and felt the pure pleasure of moving with him. He grinned and put his hand behind my neck to pull my mouth toward the vein I wanted like a wanderer lost in the desert. Every heartbeat, every pulse that throbbed through him, called to me in the most primitive way.

"Drink, Glory. I know you want it. Take it, baby." He drove into me, his eyes on my face.

I couldn't say a word, but of course he'd seen and felt my fangs down since the first kiss. My body already trembling on the edge of satisfaction, I sank into his vein, the shifter's blood hot and sweet like I knew it would be. I shuddered with the exquisite pleasure, then let go for a kiss long and deep. I felt Rafe's release inside me before he stilled and sighed my name. His head landed next to mine on the pillow.

We lay there for a few moments, just breathing, until I reached over and touched the fang marks I could see on his neck. I propped myself up so I could lick them closed.

"Thanks, Rafe. Maybe I shouldn't have—"

"No, I told you to. And I kind of got off to it." Rafe

grinned at me, then pulled me on top of him. His shorts had long ago disappeared, and he was so beautiful naked. "I've always known you were a vampire, Glory. And you're not my first. I know feeding ramps up a vamp's pleasure." He drew a circle on my hip that made me shiver. "And I'm all about pleasure."

"Mmm. I can see that." I wiggled against his stirring erection. "But now I'm disillusioned." I dropped a kiss on his lips, obscenely happy. "I wanted to be your first."

"Remember how old I am. Bound to have had a little experience. The demon chapter was a onetime deal. I learned from that mistake. I'm really sorry you had to pay for it." He ran his hand up my back. "Sure you're all healed?"

"I think I just proved that. But why don't we jump in the shower, and you can examine me for yourself? Front and back." I sat up and pulled him with me.

"Sounds like a plan." He laughed and gathered me in his arms for a long, lusty kiss. "You know I'm going to have to meet Nadia at the club in a little while."

"Then we'd better hurry." I glanced at the clock. I was late getting down to the shop, and I was pretty sure Blade had called at least once in the last two days. I hadn't even glanced at my cell phone. I ran into the bathroom and pulled a shower cap over my hair. No guilt. Just fun. I was sick of being Glory the good, the decent, the boring.

I watched Rafe adjust the water temperature, admiring his taut butt. Maybe I'd regret this later, but I laughed when Rafe jerked me under the warm water. There, I did a few things that actually surprised him. And he did a few things to me . . . definitely no regrets.

"I forgot to tell you. Looks like opening night is Thursday. Ray will be here before then so we can set up for him. You'll have to have your bachelorette party on Wednesday night. It'll give us a chance to make sure the sound and lighting systems all check out. If you still want me to dance . . ." Rafe ran a comb through his wet hair in front of the bathroom mirror.

"I don't know. Show me your moves again, Angel Man." I licked my lips, then realized what he'd said. "Wait a minute. Wednesday? This is Saturday. Not much notice, Rafe." I stuffed my feet into red heels and stomped into the bathroom. Rafe hadn't put on a shirt yet, and the sight of his bare chest stopped me. I was turning into a fool over a hot body.

"Can't help it. Nadia's already pissed at me. She set the schedule. I've got to go along. If you want the party at our club, that's the date." He turned and grinned at me. "What are you looking at? Waiting for a demo?" He did a bump and grind that sent every bit of blood straight to my, well, you know.

"Forget it." I turned and flounced out of the room. Or tried to. Rafe caught me around the waist and pulled me to him.

"Liar. You were lusting after my body."

"Yeah, well. And thinking what a shame you had to play dog all those years and sleep at the foot of my bed"—I ran a fingertip around one of his dark brown nipples—"when you could have been in a much choicer position."

"You know why that couldn't happen." Rafe slipped open a button on my silk blouse and slid his hand inside my white demicup bra.

"Yes, I know. Not going there. So I'd better get down to the shop. Saturday night is busy. And now I've got to call the list of people Flo wants at this bachelorette party and invite them for Wednesday night." I sighed when he found my nipple and squeezed it between two fingers. "I'm already late."

"Me too." Rafe groaned because I'd eased my hand down the front of his jeans. No underwear tonight. Which was fine by me.

"We're torturing each other." I pulled his head down and kissed him, amazed that I was so comfortable doing this. Rafe as my lover. I still hadn't checked my cell but figured there would be missed calls and voice mails from you know who. I couldn't seem to give a damn.

"A quickie?" He licked my ear and pulled me toward the bedroom.

"A very quickie." I drop kicked my thong across the room. "Leave my clothes on. Jeans down to your knees, mister." I lifted my skirt. He was ready, I was ready. I pushed him back to the dresser so he could lean against it, and he helped me climb on board, wrapping my legs around his waist.

"Oh, wow!" I felt him sink home, the pleasure so intense my toes tingled. My head fell back, and Rafe kissed my neck, then the vee exposed by my open blouse.

"Glory!" He held on to me and worked my hips against his, the motions fast and hard until we both gasped and bumped heads, laughing at our own crazy passion. A book I'd been reading about relationships, *Should You Be Committed?*, had hit the floor along with a box of necklaces and earrings, jewelry flying everywhere.

I glanced at my watch. "Six minutes. Not bad, big boy."

"I don't exactly pride myself on my speed, sweetheart." He eased me onto my feet. "I'll get you a washcloth." Rafe grinned and pulled up his jeans. Then he headed into the bathroom while I found my thong and ran a brush through my hair.

Once we were cleaned up, we kissed and made a promise to meet back at the apartment two hours before dawn for a more lengthy session. I was grinning like an idiot when I walked into the shop. Flo and Richard were waiting for me.

They exchanged looks that warned me I was in for some explaining. I pulled them into the back room, then held up a hand.

"Stop. Don't say it. I'm a big girl. I can do what I want on my own time."

"Glory." Flo's eyes filled with tears. "I'm worried about you. You had a near miss with a demon, and now you are falling into bed with Rafael." This time *she* held up a hand. "Don't bother to deny it, girlfriend. Ricardo and I can both smell sex and him on you. And Jeremiah is still out of town, isn't he?"

"So what?" I couldn't look at her. Nice play of the guilt card. "I had a good time. Flo, you of all people understand that sometimes you just want to have fun. Jerry and I aren't married. I can take a lover if I want one. Rafe and I have known each other for five years. I love him. He's a dear friend."

"Ricardo and I are your dear friends too. We should have stayed with you." Flo bit her lip.

"No, you were wonderful. Both of you." I sighed. "Come on, Flo. I had a near-death experience. It reminded me that life can be shorter than we think. So Rafe and I took our friendship to the next level. I'm allowed. Right?" I pulled my cell phone out of my purse. Good diversion. I glanced back at my friends.

Flo pursed her lips but didn't say anything else. Richard frowned but obviously had nothing to add either.

"Rafe's club is opening this weekend, so we have to have the bachelorette party on Wednesday night. Will that work for you?" I added a smile, trying to get this back on a friendly basis.

"Sure, why not?" Flo glanced at Richard. "You have the list I gave you of people to invite? I have a few to add." Flo pulled a paper out of her purse. "Here, there are names and numbers. It should end up thirty-five, maybe forty women in all. Is that too many?"

"No, the more the better. We'll have the whole club to ourselves." I kept smiling. "I wish I could pay for this myself, but with my budget I'd have to have this in my apartment with a movie rental." I looped my arm through hers. "But I'd be sure to get one with naked hot guys."

"Tempting." Flo laughed when Richard grumbled. "But let's do it in the club. Like I told you, it's on me." Flo had definitely thawed out. Richard just looked ready to escape. I grabbed his arm.

"Richard, would you please not tell Jerry about Rafe and

me? I know Jer's your friend, but why get him all stirred up if this is just an experiment? Post-traumatic stress or something?" I stepped back at the look on Richard's face.

"You want me to lie to him?"

"Ricardo! Glory didn't say that." Flo stepped between us. "You want to be the one to break up her relationship with Jeremiah permanently?" Flo glanced at me. "Spare your friend the pain of jealousy. You know how bad that feels, am I right?"

"*I* wouldn't be the one breaking them up." Richard didn't say it, but his stare clearly proclaimed me an unfaithful slut. "And I won't lie to him."

"Of course not, *amante*." Flo walked him to the back door and turned the dead bolt to unlock it. "You just won't volunteer information. If Jeremiah asks the question, you will tell him what you know. Glory won't expect anything more."

"Right, Richard." I relaxed. Jerry and Richard never discussed their love lives. The most personal info I'd ever heard them exchange had been the name of the shifter who handled a stock transaction for Jerry. "I haven't thanked you properly. You saved my life last night. I'd be dead or in hell if it wasn't for you."

"Not sure you should thank me yet, Gloriana. Fights with a demon can have lasting effects." Richard still wasn't smiling as he kissed Flo's cheek and stepped into the alley. "Be careful with Rafe. It isn't like you to have what Florence is calling a fling. Think about that."

Flo closed the door and grinned at me. "I love him, but he is a bit old-fashioned, eh? You and Rafael? Tell me everything, girlfriend."

After Flo left I headed into the shop and assisted customers. I may have lost a few sales, but suddenly I was talking first, thinking later.

"Honey, big ass flowers on a big ass? Never in four hundred years will that look good. Trust me, I know." I pushed the woman over to a nice pair of pin-striped gabardine pants that would make her look taller. "Of course you could always lay off those strawberry Pop-Tarts for breakfast if you really want to squeeze into a twelve." I ignored her gasp. "Here, try these on and don't torture yourself. Fourteen."

The woman's face was red, and she was wondering how I knew about the Pop-Tarts, but she ended up buying those pants and two blouses in an extra large, not the large she'd tried to cram her boobs into.

"Glory, what's gotten into you?" Erin watched the woman leave before she turned to me. "You were pretty, uh, blunt."

"I just told the truth. Come on, Erin, you know that sideways stripe made her look fat. I sure don't wear them."

Erin gasped. "We don't use the 'f' word in here."

"Get over it." I frowned and picked up my cell phone. Ten more calls to make and I'd have the bachelorette party locked down. I'd thought of a theme, and every woman I'd called had gotten excited about it. Still had to arrange the munchies, but Greg Kaplan would come through on those. The EVs wanted my cooperation, so I was sure there'd be no problem there. Damian was going to provide some of his buzz-producing synthetics, so I'd have to go on the Internet for some drinking games. Did I still want Rafe to dance for the crowd of women? Now that he was my guy . . .

I flinched when the phone in my hand vibrated, then rang.

"Hello."

"Glory, it's Westwood. I want to meet tonight to work out the details on that video."

"No can do." I glanced around the shop. We had a lull going. I signaled to Erin and headed for the back room. I'd had a brainstorm about this video, and I was going through with my plan.

"I don't think you have that option. Remember your pal's wedding?"

"Sure I do. But I want a little down payment before I start any preproduction work on this video." I shut the door and picked up the newspaper I'd looked at earlier.

"I don't have any money yet, vampire."

"I'm sure Simon will spot you some. Here are my terms." I smiled and focused on the ad that had caught my eye. "I want a brand-new red convertible." I rattled off the make and model. "Must have the extended warranty, and the title will be in my name, free and clear. It should be delivered to the alley behind my shop and my old Suburban towed away. Once that is done, I'll be ready to play your video game. Got all that?"

"You're out of your friggin' mind." Westwood actually growled.

"No, I'm being smart. Bet you didn't give me credit for that, did you?" I slapped the phone shut and sat staring at the picture of my new car. Boy, did I look forward to this. Paid for by the EVs. How sweet. Much better than cash that could be stolen away with the click of Westwood's computer mouse. For once, I actually think I had outsmarted the bad guys.

My phone rang. Westwood calling back? I glanced at the caller ID, my stomach twisting. Earth to Glory. Jerry. Time to decide just what kind of future I wanted.

"Not now, Jer." I shut off the phone without answering.

"Was that Mr. Blade?" Emmie Lou Nutt shimmered in front of me.

"Yes. I didn't feel like talking to him." I sat on the stool and saw that Erin or someone had piled the three dresses Alesa had ruined on the table. Infuriating. So much lost revenue.

"You okay now? Never saw such a horrible fight. The way you and that demon were goin' at it." Harvey Nutt stood next to Emmie Lou. "I figured you were a goner fer sure."

"Me too. I'm fine now." I sighed. "Richard saved the day."

"The preacher was awesome, but we helped." Emmie smiled at Harvey.

"Sure did. When we seen your friend was fixin' to throw that holy water, we shoved your shirt rack outta the way." Harvey had his thumbs stuck in the straps of his overalls.

"Honey, not a speck of water got on your fine silk blouses. And that demon got enough holiness in her face to send her straight back to hell where she belonged." Emmie grinned at Harvey. "It was flat amazin'."

"I had no idea you helped." I would have hugged them both, but I knew they were nothing but cool air and a vision. "Thanks so much."

"Proved somethin' to us, I tell ya." Harvey put his arm around Emmie's waist.

"What's that?" I glanced down at the dresses and wondered if a good dry cleaner could salvage any of them.

"Look at us, Glory." Emmie's voice was suddenly quieter. I looked. "You're fading out. What's up?"

"We finally got the message." Harvey pulled Emmie tighter against him. "When I first laid eyes on this little gal all those years ago, right in this here building, I knew she was the one for me."

"Oh, Harvey. I knew it too. I was just stubborn enough to make you court me proper for two years before I'd say yes." Emmie's eyes sparkled, and she sniffed. She wasn't wearing the cowgirl costume she'd been wearing when Harvey had accidentally run over her in his pickup truck. Now she had on a beautiful wedding gown, a fifties-style satin that must have been what she'd worn on their wedding day. She looked about twenty, and her gray hair was a soft brown.

"And we were happy for many a year." Harvey kissed her cheek. His overalls were gone and so were about thirty pounds. He had on a black suit and a white shirt with a black western tie. Wedding suit. "If I just coulda given you children . . ."

"Hush now. I was happy. Didn't need no kids. You were a handful, and that's a fact." Tears ran down her face. "I've always loved you, Harvey Nutt. Always will."

Now I was crying. Because the more they talked, the more they faded out.

"We're leavin' ya, Glory. Finally goin' upstairs now that we've figured things out." Emmie took a blue bandanna from Harvey and dabbed at her wet cheeks. "Be happy, girl. I hope ya find a good man ya want to keep by yer side forever. But iffen ya don't, well, be safe and take care of yourself."

"And stay away from them demons!" Harvey shouted. But it was hard to hear him. Because he and Emmie Lou were winking out.

I blinked and rubbed my eyes, then realized I was truly alone in the back room. I looked down and saw a blue and white bandanna on the floor. When I picked it up, it was still damp from Emmie Lou's tears.

That did it. I lay my head on the table and sobbed like my heart was breaking. And maybe it was. To have a love like that . . .

"Babe? Glory? What the hell is wrong?"

I looked up. One of the men in my life. A good one? Maybe. *The* good one? Probably not.

Fourteen

"Ray?" I mopped at my eyes with that bandanna.

"Tell me, what's wrong?" He pulled me up to face him.

"The Nutts are gone." I sniffed and tried to make myself presentable. I hadn't seen Israel Caine in ages, and now I had to face him with a red nose and swollen eyes.

"You can't eat nuts anyway. Why're you crying about that?" He smiled and pushed my hair back from my face. "Get a grip."

"No, I mean Harvey and Emmie Lou Nutt, my resident ghosts. They made up after fighting for decades, and now they're finally on their way to Heaven. They'll never haunt my shop again." I choked back a sob, still sad but realizing that was pretty selfish of me.

"That's a good thing. Can't have creepy stuff like that scaring the customers." Ray looked down at the ruined dresses on the table. "Whoa, what happened here? Looks like motor oil."

"Long story." I wasn't about to share my run-in with a demon. He and Rafe already had issues. If he knew Rafe had brought a demon into my life . . . "My ghosts left my customers alone as long as they were good people. The Nutts hated vamp hunters and were a big help when Westwood was after me." Now maybe this was something Ray would like to hear about.

"Okay, fine. Good ghosts." He looked around the back room. "So where's your knight in shining armor?"

"Which one?" I smiled, wondering if Ray was jealous. I have and always will be a fangirl for this hot rock star.

"I was thinking Blade, but maybe you have the dog panting after you now too." Ray tried to put his arm around me, but I slipped out of reach.

"Rafe's a shape-shifter, not a dog. I love dogs, by the way, but now he's staying in human form and he's my roommate. When you sing at his club, you'll have to treat him with respect, Ray." I kept some distance between us. "Where's your new girlfriend, the vampire who, as you so delicately put it, popped your cherry?"

"That was a temporary thing. We've moved on. Sienna came with me to check out the music festival."

"Oh? You and Sienna—" Sienna Star was another singer, and they'd had a hit together but nothing more as far as I knew.

"Not together, though the tabloids think so, especially since our duet went platinum." Ray came close and ran a finger down the vee of my blouse. "I'm still available if that's what you're asking."

"No, I'm not asking. Guess who's still alive and kicking. No. Guess who's undead and annoying as hell." I moved out of reach again.

"I'll bite." Ray grinned and showed fang. "Who?"

"Brent Westwood." This time *I* grinned as I waited to see his reaction.

"No way. I saw you take him out with his own crossbow." Ray sat on the stool.

"The ever-helpful Greg Kaplan, drug pusher and EV, turned him, and he's now one of those evil vampires he hated so much. Don't you love it?" I sat in the chair on the other side of the room. I really didn't want Ray too close to me, if he picked up on smells like Richard and Flo had . . .

"I say let's get a stake and put that creep out of his misery." Ray was right in front of me and pulling me into his arms before I could stop him. "He almost killed you, Glory."

"He's over that urge. Now he just wants me to help him get his billions back. Trust me, I'm going to make him pay through the nose before I think about taking the bastard out again." I watched Ray's face and knew the moment he figured out my scent.

"Son of a bitch!" He shoved me back and put a good five feet between us. "You're having sex with that damned shifter."

"Now, Ray." I could see he was furious. With me, with Rafe, even with himself.

"All those weeks I played the fool, begging you to sleep with me. 'Oh, no, Ray, I can't. I'm saving myself for Jerry.' Damn it to everlasting hell." He picked up the wooden stool and threw it at the steel back door where it shattered with a crash.

"Ray, I didn't plan it. It just happened. I've known Rafe for five years. We've lived together. He's saved my life." I shut up when I saw this was futile and sounding desperate. I held out my hand. "Ray."

"Don't touch me. Not unless you plan to strip off and fuck me right here and now." Ray's face was hard, and I'd never seen him look so cold or sound so bitter and heartless.

Something sick and twisted inside me reared its head and shouted, *"Wow!"*

"You want me, Rock Star?" I slid my panties down my legs and kicked them across the room, then cleared the table and jumped on it. "Come and get me." I grinned and spread my legs. "What are you waiting for?" I hiked my skirt in case he wasn't clear on the "get me" part.

"Glory, what the hell is this?" Ray stared at me like I was a stranger.

That look brought me down to earth. What the hell *was* I doing? I sat up and swiped at stupid tears.

"Missed your chance." I pulled down my skirt and hopped down. "Besides, that would only prove that I care about your feelings enough to help you get even with Rafe. If you're keeping score." I dropped back into my chair. Dear God, but I'd almost made a huge mistake. What was the matter with me? Ray still looked at me like I'd lost my mind. He wouldn't be wrong. "You want me to do it out of pity, Ray?"

"What the hell? If I didn't think you'd hate me later, I'd be inside you right now." Ray picked up the pieces of the stool and slammed them on the table. "How could you sleep with that shifter, Glory? I thought you were in love with Blade, so I could kind of respect that. Where is the Scot, by the way?"

"Out of town." I probably shouldn't have said it. It only gave Ray ammunition.

"Excellent. So how long has this affair been going on? Were you two going at it the whole time Valdez was playing bodyguard?" Ray shook his head. "Never thought I'd feel sorry for Blade, but this may do it. Dumb bastard was paying the shifter's salary, big bucks from what I understand, and the V-man was getting a little somethin' somethin' from you on the side as well. Pretty good job, I'd say."

"It wasn't like that, Ray. When you and I were together, Rafe and I had never . . ." I sighed. "Hell, why am I explaining myself to you? You think I'm a slut? Fine. I guess that's all I am to you. I'm sorry I've hurt your feelings, but who I sleep with is really none of your concern."

"Right. I'm just the fool who came here because you asked me to." Ray picked up the broken stool leg, which looked very much like a stake, and I shuddered. "The idiot who agreed to sing in your lover's club. As a favor to you."

"They're paying you. And wait till you meet his partner, Nadia. She's just your type. Beautiful with a world of experience." I stalked over and jerked the piece of wood out of his hand. "You're making me nervous."

"What? Afraid I'll stake you in a fit of jealousy?" Ray shook his head. "The hell of it, Glory girl, is that I *am* jealous. And as much as I'm hurting, I'd never hurt *you*." His expression promised pain of another kind.

"Ray, you're scaring me." He was. Not for myself. I knew he wouldn't lay a hand on a woman. Had always known it. But there was a violence simmering inside him now that I'd never seen before. It made his bright blue eyes into laser beams that were almost painful to stare into, but I couldn't look away.

He wasn't the fledgling vampire, who'd needed me to guide him, anymore. This man had come into his power and knew it. He could be dangerous but leashed it now. Barely. Insanely, part of me was turned on by it and still wanted to jump his bones. I backed up, to give myself space.

"Jump his bones." I swear I heard a voice in my head saying it.

"The person I'd like to ram that piece of wood through isn't you, sweet thing. It's that damned shifter. That dog who's tasted you"—Ray jerked me into his arms—"seen you naked and made you scream his name when you came." He nuzzled my neck, his fangs scratching across my jugular. "He did make you come, didn't he, babe? Because if he didn't—"

"Stop it, Ray." I shoved him away, my heart pounding, the makeshift stake shaking in my hand. "I can't do this, play this twisted game."

"Oh, yes, you can." I told my inner bad girl to shut the hell up.

"It's not a game to me." Ray's eyes dimmed. "I was never playing with you. That's the hell of it."

My heart stalled at the pure misery in that confession, and for a moment I wanted to soothe him and kiss away his pain. Couldn't do it because something in me wasn't sure I'd be able to stop at just a kiss. I bit my trembling lip.

"I'm sorry, Ray. All I can tell you is to remember you're a professional. Sing in Rafe's club. Sing for Flo's wedding. Do whatever you need to at the music festival, but forget about anything we once had going."

"We never had anything going, Glory." Ray jerked the stake from my fingers as easily as if I hadn't gripped it tightly. "That's the problem. I played things too safe with you. Like I would with a human female. Obviously I didn't have a clue how to deal with an ancient vampire." He smiled and walked to the back door, turning the dead bolt. "But I'm going to find out. Maybe this Nadia will give me some pointers. Then I'll be back. Because for some reason, maybe because you aren't easy to get, you fascinate me. And now that I know you can be unfaithful to Blade? All bets are off." He tossed the stake onto the table. "See you around." He stepped outside and closed the door.

"Go after him."

I shivered, tempted. Wrong. I rubbed my forehead. Concussion. Hearing voices now. Could things get any worse? The phone rang again. Guess so. Blade. I had to answer it this time. At least he couldn't smell me from Florida. My cheeks went hot with guilt as I punched the button to answer the call.

"Hey, Jerry."

"Gloriana! Why the hell haven't you been answering your phone? Are you all right?" Jerry sounded truly worried. Which just made me feel even worse.

"I'm fine. Lost my phone. Finally found it tonight. Sorry if you were concerned." How easily I lied. Had I always been this glib? This manipulative?

"Everything all right there?" His voice was quiet, as if there might be someone else in the room with him.

"Sure. How's your business coming?" I picked the stake up off the table. I was saving it. You never knew when one could come in handy. I might use it on my own forehead if this voice didn't shut up.

"Don't even try it."

"It's a mess here. I'm interviewing new managers right now. Then Richard called me."

"Oh?" I dropped the wood with a thud.

"He wants a bachelor party. It'll have to be pretty close to the wedding. I'll be here for a while yet."

"Do you need my help? With the party?" I collapsed in the chair with relief.

"No, I'll handle it from here. Thank God all he wants is poker and cigars. I'll get Damian to bring some of that potent brew we had at his house. We'll get the man roaring drunk and have a fine time."

I heard a knock on my back door. "Sounds great, Jerry. I've got to go, someone's here. See you when you get back."

"Right. Take care." He hung up without another word.

Hmm. Pretty abrupt, but we didn't gush at each other, usually exchanging love words only in bed. I couldn't stress about it. I walked to the door.

"Who is it?"

"Greg Kaplan. Let me in. We need to talk about your party."

"Just a minute." I hurried to shove the broken pieces of stool into the bathroom, leaving the one leg that would work as a stake under a soiled dress, then opened the door.

"What about the party? I thought you had my order all figured out. But the event's now this Wednesday night."

"Yeah, well, if you want good eats, you never should have played hardball with Westwood on the phone. Simon's furious." Greg strolled in, a shit-eating grin on his face. "What the hell were you thinking?"

I slammed the door. "I was thinking that Simon and Westwood would try to screw me out of my payoff for helping them. So I needed some of my reward up front." I put my hands on my hips. "I'd think you'd get that, Greg. You've been around Simon long enough to know how he does business."

"Yeah, he always comes out on top." Greg frowned down at the stained dress. "That one's ruined."

"Yes, an accident. So what are you here for? To spank me?" I got between him and the table.

"You go, girl."

"Glory, Glory, that sounded like an invitation." His eyes lit up, and he had a look on his face that seemed vaguely familiar. "If you'd been that much fun in New York, I might not have wiped your memory clean."

"Get over yourself, Greg. Am I getting my car or not? I won't do the video without one, and I want it up front." I poked his chest.

"Oh, I brought you a car all right. A loaner." He tossed a set of keys on the table. "The tow truck will be here later to haul away that piece of crap you used to drive." He chuckled and sat in the only chair. "How long you had that?"

"Doesn't matter. It will cost more to get it fixed than it's worth, so it's salvage now. I don't need a loaner; I need a car that I can own, free and clear. I told Westwood that."

"Westwood's broke. He can't buy you a pair of roller skates, Glo. And it's Saturday night. Even Simon can't get you a clear title on a new car until Monday." Greg opened a bag he'd brought with him and pulled out a tortilla chip. He shoved it into his mouth and crunched. "Mmm. Don't know how Simon makes these, but they taste like the real deal. Want one?" He held out the bag.

"No. Last time I ate some of Simon's food I ended up unconscious." I inhaled corn and listened to more crunching. Could I trust the food at Flo's party? "It had better be okay at the party. No funny business."

"With all those area vampires there? Simon's a businessman. He's counting on using this party to get his catering gig up and running. We'll make big bucks on these snacks." Greg ate another chip. "Don't be paranoid, Glory. You want your party to be a success, you'll get this stuff and serve it. Wednesday?"

"Yes, well, it's when I could get the club." I knew the ladies would flip if I brought out chips and salsa for vampires. Combined with a hot male dancer, it would be a party Aggie sure couldn't top.

Greg smiled. "Get with the program, Glory. If Westwood calls for you to come do the video, you'd better show up, new car or not. If I can't take back a guarantee from you on that, I'm afraid bad things will start to happen to those you love." Greg crammed another chip into his mouth. "And we'll blow off the p.r. opportunity. No snacks at your ladies' night."

"I don't like threats, Greg. This is *my* deal. Leave my friends out of it."

"Even Israel Caine? That fledgling vampire just left here. He'd be Simon's guest at the energy vacuum pump right now if I'd had orders to take him out." Greg laughed. "Caine never even saw me in that alley. You'd think he'd remember all the trouble you've had back there."

"Damn it. Leave Ray alone." I would call Ray the minute this creep left and warn him to keep his bodyguard with him. I assumed he still had Brittany, his shape-shifter, on the payroll.

"Go ahead and warn him. Warn the bride too. She was shoe shopping at the mall earlier. Two of our men tailed Florence into Nordstrom and would have had no problem getting her and her three pairs of shoes back to the compound." Greg finished the last chip and crumpled the bag into a ball. "Seems she favors black patent for spring. Couldn't decide on the pumps or the sandals so she bought both."

A chill shuddered through me. "Richard will turn that compound into a wasteland if you harm one hair on Flo's head."

Greg smiled. "He could try. Note to Glory: Holy water doesn't work on Simon or our goddess." He aimed his bag at a trash can in the corner of the room and hit the shot. "Score!"

"The only scoring around here is the zip your team gets when it tries to harm my friends." I slammed my fist into his nose and blood spurted. "Westwood and the EVs can kiss his billions bye-bye if any of my friends are dragged off to EV central."

"Damn it, Glory. You broke my nose." Greg glared at me, his hands trying to stem the blood flow.

"I'm making a point, Gregory. I want my new car, and I'll

come when Westwood calls. No car, no video. I'm essential to Westwood's plans, and he'd better not forget it." I grabbed Greg's shirt and dragged him to the door.

"What the—" Greg gasped but kept his hands over his bloody nose. I think he was in shock at my sudden attack, because he didn't fight me.

"And if one vampire gets so much as a twinge from any of the EV goodies, there will be hell to pay." I opened the back door and used my foot on his backside to shove Greg out into the alley. "Ask your girlfriend, Aggie, about this. I've got a demon connection now, and I'm not afraid to use it." I slammed the door and locked it.

"Demon connection is right, girlfriend. You have no idea how close a connection it is." The voice in my head laughed until I wanted to tear my hair out.

"Would that demon connection be me?" Rafe grinned at me from across the room where he'd obviously come in from the shop side.

"You'd better believe it." I ran to him and wrapped my arms around his waist. "You have any idea how glad I am to see you?"

"No, why don't you show me?" He leaned down to kiss me, his mouth hot and dangerously knowing.

I indulged myself for a long and satisfying moment until Rafe pulled back.

"Now tell me what that was all about. Kaplan threaten you?"

I slid out of his arms. "Worse. He threatened Ray and Flo." I rummaged among the dresses on the table for my cell phone. "I've got to warn them."

"Do that." Rafe frowned down at the broken stool leg on the table. "What happened here?"

"Ray found out about you and me. Didn't take it well." I hit speed dial for the rock star and got voice mail. I left a message for him to call me back. "He might not return my call. I wonder if he brought Brittany with him. We should call her."

"I'll do it. Come here first." Rafe pulled me into his arms

again. "How badly did he take it?" He glanced at the stool leg. "He didn't hurt you, did he?"

"No, but I wouldn't recommend you get alone with him in the alley anytime soon." I leaned my head against his chest and listened to his strong heartbeat. "It was horrible, Rafe. He was hurt, furious. You remember how he was with me."

Rafe's arms tightened around me. "Hell, yes. He ran around naked in front of you every chance he got. Tried everything to get into your pants. Never did, though, did he?" There was a world of satisfaction in those words.

I leaned back. "As far as you know." I shoved and put my hands on my hips, then remembered that my panties were still on the floor in the corner of the room where I'd tossed them. Wouldn't that be fun to explain. "Let me make things clear. I am my own woman. I can sleep with whomever I please." I still held the cell phone, too aware of the man I'd talked to earlier.

"So Caine got to you." Rafe wasn't smiling as he dug out his own phone from his pocket. His jeans were snug enough to make me lick my lips. Ridiculous to notice that right now.

"I felt sorry for Ray."

"Now that's okay." Rafe's grin was back. "Poor pitiful rock star. I can work with that."

"Call Brittany."

"Got her on speed dial." Rafe pulled out his phone.

Rafe and Brit had been an item once but had parted in L.A. and not on such good terms. Both shape-shifters, Brittany thought I took advantage of Rafe's loyalty and worked him way too many hours. The fact that she'd been right had ramped up my guilt and left us on not great terms either.

"Isn't that convenient." Oops, my jealousy was showing. Better deflect. "Anyway, remember, Ray's supposed to sing at your club Thursday. If he doesn't because you two get into it over me, Nadia will be pissed."

Rafe pushed me against the back door. "Might be worth

it. Caine's arrogant, called me a dog. Always wanted me in my place, which in his world was at his feet or on the floor. It wasn't easy doing my gig knowing you were sharing his bed." He pressed his body against mine, his breath hot against my cheek. "I wanted to be the one holding you through the day."

"Rafe." I slid my arms up around his neck. "Nothing happened between Ray and me. You know that, don't you?"

"Things happened, all right. Just not what Caine wanted." Rafe lowered his head and kissed me tenderly. "So I'll steer clear of the bastard. Cause *I* got what *I* wanted. Plan on getting it again too. Real soon." He kissed me again, this time with a hunger that could have headed toward something more if there hadn't been a knock on the door from the shop.

I tugged on his hair, the soft curls much finer than the Labradoodle fur he'd worn. "Got to get that."

"Yeah. And we need to warn your friends. We'll continue this later." Rafe eased back.

I took a breath, then walked to the door and opened it.

"Glory, I'm swamped out here. Can you give me a hand?" Erin was flushed, and I could see she had a good half dozen customers roaming the shop with items in their hands. Good business.

"Give me two minutes to make a phone call." I smiled and slammed the door, then hit the speed dial for Flo. Voice mail. Left a message for her to call me. Same for Richard. I just hoped they were together and practicing for the honeymoon again. I heard Rafe on the phone with Brittany. He was telling her about the EV threat, so she was here and on Ray guard duty. Okay, then. I opened the door again and stepped into the shop.

"Hold up, Goth Girl. Step away from the black. Try on this silk blouse. It's definitely your color, and think how shocked your parents will be when you wear it at home on spring break. Daddy tight with the purse strings since you pierced everything? Play it smart. Go home and pretend you've seen the light. Take out the safety pins, put on colors and watch Daddy melt. After he raises your allowance, come back and buy this!" I took her arm and steered her to the Goth girl's dream, a black satin cape and thigh-high black leather boots studded with silver.

"Blue?" She looked uncertainly at her friend, who was even more pierced than she was.

"I'm gagging." The friend was no help.

"If you hate it, after the break, have it dry-cleaned, and I'll buy it back from you."

That got her attention, and she decided to try it on, and two other colorful blouses. I could hear her muttering about her dad stroking out when he saw her, obviously an added incentive.

Two hours later, I had rung up six sales and convinced three students that I was psychic. Okay, so I used my mind reading to help things along.

I moved in on another student who was fumbling through the blouse rack. "You're student teaching kindergarten this semester, am I right?"

The girl gasped and looked at her boyfriend. "How did you know?"

"Guess I overheard something. Anyway, you look fine if you were planning to teach Serial Killing 101. But you're scaring the little kiddies." I dragged her to the skirts. "Try one of these print skirts. And ballet flats instead of combat boots."

"I like her in black." The boyfriend was obviously not on board. But then he probably had trouble seeing her through his guy-liner and mascara. I could have told him a fresh tube would take care of his clumping problem.

"I bet you'll also like her when she's hired next year and earning a paycheck. Am I right?" I smiled and assessed him. Slacker. The girl could do better. I handed her three skirts to try on and herded her toward the dressing room. "He's not going to class, Stacy. Check him out. This guy will never graduate or work, as long as you will."

"How did you know my name?" Stacy was wide-eyed and

glanced back at eyelash boy, who was deep into the vintage comic books.

"You've been in here before. It's on your credit card."

"Oh. How do you know so much about Rod?" She held up the print skirt, then grabbed a red blouse to go with it. Definitely getting with the program.

"Gut feeling. He's reading comics. When's the last time you saw him reading a textbook?" I had her attention now. "Check things out. Ask someone who's in those classes he's supposed to be taking. You've got a lot on the ball, don't sell yourself short." I smiled and saw Erin wave at me. "Good luck."

"Thanks." Stacy stared at the blouse rack, a thoughtful look on her face.

Erin grabbed me. "I almost forgot to tell you. Rafe left a message before he took off. He's picking you up at three o'clock to take you to see his new club."

I glanced at my watch. "It's a quarter till now. How's my hair?"

"You could use a quick brush and some lipstick." Erin headed back to the register, and I followed her.

"Okay, then. Can you handle things alone now?"

"Sure. It's slowing down. Go. Have fun." Erin began taking tags off of Stacy's new skirts. "When's Mr. Blade coming back?"

I stopped in my tracks. "Uh, not sure. This week sometime. The wedding's on Sunday. He has to be back before then."

Erin started punching numbers into the register but paused to glance at me. "You two over now? Since you and Rafe . . ."

"I have no idea how things are going to shake out. But keep my love life to yourself. Okay?" I grabbed Erin's arm. I figure I must have squeezed pretty hard because she suddenly looked alarmed. "Hey, I'm not going to fire you or anything, but just don't mention Rafe to Jerry if he drops by and I'm not here. I've got a delicate situation going."

Stacy was all ears. "Boyfriend trouble?" She glanced back

at Rod who'd dropped a stack of comics on the counter, obviously expecting her to add them to her credit card bill. "I get it."

"I'll figure things out." *If the guys don't kill each other.*

"Don't worry, Glory. I'm not saying a word to anybody." Erin looked a question at Stacy, and the girl sighed and nodded. "Can't we give this girl a discount on these comics?"

"Sure. Ten percent." I smiled at Stacy and headed for the back room. Oh, boy, but I didn't want to think about Jerry and Rafe meeting face-to-face. Truth though was that I missed Jerry. Just talking to him on the phone had reminded me how I loved his voice, loved the way he could take charge of a situation and you knew, just knew, that everything would be all right.

Yeah, but what if you didn't like the way he wanted things to go? Oh, hell. I was so mixed up, I didn't have a clue *how* I wanted things to go.

I grabbed my purse, quickly fixing my makeup and hair by feel. I spotted those keys on the table. A loaner car. What could it be? A Mercedes like Jerry had tried to give me once? Or maybe a nice Cadillac. Not sporty but reliable. I'd take it.

I unlocked the back door and cautiously stepped outside, looking both ways to make sure there was no danger before I checked the parking lot. My old Suburban was still there. The workers from Mugs and Muffins parked out back, a couple of beat-up economy cars. Diana, the owner, had a sleek Jaguar, and it was in its usual spot. Next to it was a beige—or maybe it was a dirty white—four-door station wagon. It had to be at least fifteen years old, and the back door was scraped and dented. I looked down at the keys in my hand. No way. I hit the remote and sure enough, the lights flashed. Damn Simon Destiny. He'd sent me an ancient beater. Oh, but he was going to pay for this.

My phone rang, and I dug it out of my purse. Maybe Flo had finally gotten my message.

"Hello."

"Gloriana, I see you've found your car."

"Screw you, Simon. This is—" I stopped in mid harangue. "How do you know where I am?"

"You forget, my dear, that Westwood is a genius where surveillance is concerned. It took a matter of moments for Gregory to plant bugs that give me sight and sound in your alley, your shop and your back room, of course." Simon laughed as the implications of that sank in.

"You slimy worm!"

"Ah, I see you're getting it now. I have you exactly where I want you. Unless, of course, you don't care if I send a certain rather interesting video to Jeremy Blade's cell phone. I have several to choose from." Simon waited a beat. "There's the one where your friend Florence says she can smell sex on you and you admit you're sleeping with your shifter."

I closed my eyes, imagining Jerry's fury and pain.

"Or there's the more graphic image of you and Rafael kissing against the door. Then you tell him the rocker never had you, but of course *he*, Rafael, could have you anytime, anywhere." Simon hummed. "Or perhaps that's just implied in the body language. I'm sure Blade can figure it out."

"Shut up, Simon."

"Now, Gloriana, be nice. I know you want me to cooperate. Unless you no longer care what Blade thinks of you? But surely you care if he comes gunning for your new lover." Simon tsked. "Ancient vampires like Blade are so predictable. Always wanting to tear out someone's throat. But how would that work against a man with demon blood?"

Of course Jerry would rip first and ask questions later. Because Rafe had betrayed his trust. And what about me? How would Jerry feel about what I'd done? I had a sick feeling that I was going to find out before this was all over.

"What do you want, Simon?"

"It's really very simple, Gloriana. Stop making demands. Do exactly what I say, when I say it. I'll be in touch." The line went dead.

I stared down at the phone, knowing Simon could probably see my reaction. I looked around, but the cameras were well hidden. Back inside, I tore the back room apart until I finally found a minicam and microphone on top of a dusty shelf. I smashed them to bits with the seat of that broken stool. But there could be more. Didn't matter. Simon already had what he needed. I sank down on the chair and waited for Rafe. I'd been outmaneuvered. I had no choice now. I was Simon's bitch.

"My bitch too, Glory. Wondering about that voice in your head? Guess who? It's Alesa. Alive and well and inside your chubby self. Get ready for some fun 'cause you're a hell girl now."

Fifteen

I had a demon inside me. Talking to me. No. Had to be some kind of hallucination. Weird meltdown from all the stress I'd been under. Should I tell Rafe about it? I started to, but he was so excited to show me the club that I didn't have the heart.

"It's beautiful, Rafe." I couldn't believe the dark, cavelike place he'd shown me before had been transformed into this trendy club. It was still dark, but now it had a sexy vibe. Deep purple walls glowed under special lighting, and those red N-V logos were slashed behind a sleek chrome and black bar and in neon on a black leather-wrapped stage. One end had been cleared of the comfy clutter of tables and chairs and now would be a mosh pit in front of the stage when it wasn't a dance floor. Cushioned booths lined the walls, and there were even private balconies hugging the edge of a vaulted ceiling.

"It wouldn't have come together without Nadia." Rafe grinned, his arm around my shoulders. "When she takes on a project, she brings in her own crew and there's no stopping her."

"What happened to the ceiling?" I looked up, impressed by the wooden beams and vintage chandeliers.

"She had them blow it out. There used to be storage up there, but a weak floor. Now we've got great acoustics and those balconies. Wait till you hear the sound system." Rafe nodded toward where technicians were rolling in massive speakers. "Ray's crew just arrived. They're already setting up. He's wasting no time."

"Obviously. Has he seen you yet?" I doubted it. Rafe wasn't bruised or bleeding, but then I hadn't seen Ray either. Was his body out back in the Dumpster? I didn't want to think about how the two would deal with each other. And what about Simon's latest threat? I sure hadn't shared that with Rafe. He'd probably be all for sending Jerry that video. No, I'd just do Simon's bidding and deal with this hatred that burned like acid in my gut all by myself.

"Not yet. But he's been here. One of the crew said he left with Nadia." Rafe shouted to a man who came in carrying a load of glasses. "Hang here for a minute. I've got to handle this."

"Sure." I just stood there. Ray and Nadia already. No one could accuse Ray of dragging his feet.

"Your fault, clueless. You shoulda had him on that table in the back room when you had the chance. Now the rocker's moved on. Listen to me next time."

So I hadn't imagined this. But did she really think I'd take advice from a demon who'd managed to get stuck inside me? From her attitude, I'd guess if she could move on, she would have. Just my luck. But how could this happen? Richard had doused her with holy water. Prayed. What next? Would she make me do demonic stuff like bite the heads off of chickens or have wild monkey sex with one of the good-looking shifters working on the lighting? Believe me, the urge was there. For sex anyway.

Forget her. Bachelorette party coming up. Such a big space. How would we fill it? And did I give a rat's ass? I had to, for Flo's sake. She'd called me back while I'd been waiting for Rafe, and I'd told her about Simon's threat. So she and Richard were alerted. But I figured they could paint targets

on their backs now and Simon wouldn't aim, not with the
ammunition he'd loaded in the gun he held against *my* heart.

"Isn't this a great venue?"

I jumped a foot. Fantastic. Now my vamp skills totally
blew. "Nate!" I hugged him and smiled. "Sorry. Daydream-
ing. Flo's bachelorette party is coming up. I'm looking for a
male dancer. You want to throw on a G-string? Strut your
stuff?" I winked at him. I'd seen his "stuff," and he was hot
chocolate on a cold night. "You could earn big tips."

"There you go. Get him to strip off now and audition."

"Tempting. But Ray's got rhythm. Me? Not so much."
Nate grinned.

"You have other talents. Ray's lucky you've put up with
him and his new lifestyle." I'd already checked out the crew
here. Except for an occasional delivery guy, everyone was either a shifter or a vampire. Nathan Burke, Ray's manager and
still a mortal, was in danger of being on someone's menu.

"I've known since grade school that Ray was special, but
a vampire? Hell, we both thought they were comic book fiction till he woke up as one." Nate looked over his shoulder.
"Speaking of . . . I'm not making this up. That guy by the
amp is giving me thirsty looks. I'm beginning to recognize
the signs, not to mention his fangs are showing. See what I
mean?"

"Hard to miss." I sent the guy a serious mental threat to
his future sex life, and he turned away. "That AB negative
running through your veins is like fine champagne to us
fanged ones." I linked my arm through his. "The guy's going
to leave you alone for now, but just to be safe, don't come
here again unless Ray's with you. Most of this crew is on a
liquid diet." I fought my own fangs. AB negative was my
personal favorite.

"So who are you with these days, Glory? The way you left
Hollywood after the Grammys, I figured you were finally on
your own." Nate pulled me close. "You want to sip some of
my wine? Come back to my hotel room. We can get comfortable, then you can have all you want."

"Why not?" I grabbed his hand and tugged him toward the door. From the look on his face, I'd shocked him.

"There you go. Now you're acting like one of us." Alesa was proud.

"Where are you going?" Rafe was suddenly right in front of us and looking dangerous, even with a smile on his face.

"Nate invited me back to his hotel for a late night snack." I smiled and leaned against him. "You know what I am, Rafe."

"Yes, I do." He touched his throat, and there were snickers from a few of the vamps working. He turned to glare at them, and laughter was quickly drowned out by the buzz of power tools.

"You trying to stop her?" Nate didn't let me go, which made me respect him and pity him. He didn't have a clue how far in over his head he was.

"Ooo. Are they going to fight over you? Bloodshed. I love it."

"No need." What had I been thinking? I didn't drink from mortals. I had to get a grip on this demon inside me. I shoved my fangs and my urges back where they belonged and kissed Nate's cheek. "Thanks for the offer, Nathan, but better not. Now head out and be careful."

"You sure, Glory?" Nate glared at Rafe. "This guy's not forcing you—"

"I'm my own woman, Nate." I said this to Rafe too. I shoved Nate toward the door. "Good night."

Nathan grabbed a suit jacket and briefcase, and practically sprinted for the door. I'd like nothing better than to take a hike myself. I actually took a step toward freedom.

"Oh, no, you don't." Rafe grabbed my arm. "So you're your own woman. Not mine, obviously. Does that mean you're going back to Blade when he hits town?"

I looked down to where he gripped my arm. He was strong, and his fingers would leave a mark. He let me go with a curse.

"Give me a break." A wave of heat hit me. What was that about? "We hooked up. Does that mean I'm yours now? I don't think so. And if I don't want to hurt Jerry any more than necessary, that's my choice." I glared at him.

"You tell him, girlfriend." Alesa approved.

"Yeah, well, it drives me crazy when other men come on to you." Rafe glared back. "What am I supposed to do? Act like it means nothing to me? You know—" He put his hand on my shoulder. "Damn it, Glory. You know it meant everything to me."

I couldn't stay mad. I slid my arms around Rafe's waist. "I get that, Rafe. But I saw what our news did to Ray, and he and I were just friends. Jerry and I . . ."

"Yeah, I get it. He made you. You two have been off and on for centuries. Blah, blah, blah. I've heard all this before." Rafe stayed rigid, not even relaxing when I ran my hands up and down his back. "You forget that when I was at your feet, wearing a fur overcoat, I heard all your excuses, all your reasons why you couldn't give up on old Jer." He backed away, throwing my hands off of him. "Guess nothing's changed. Except that I got to enjoy your bed *and* your body for a change." He looked me up and down, like he was wondering if it had been worth the wait.

I smacked him right across his handsome face, then stared at my hand like it was an alien being. Inside, Alesa laughed like a wild thing. Damn her.

"You really shouldn't have done that." Rafe grabbed my hand and pulled me to him, the look in his eyes warning me that I had started something dangerous.

"Rafe." I slipped a button free on my blouse. "I'm sorry. I don't know what got into me. Things *have* changed. I swear it. I'm confused, that's all. I can't just throw away those centuries with Jerry if this isn't . . ."

"What? The real deal?" Rafe shook his head. "What's real and what's not? I sure as hell don't know. I've heard you lie to people and never blink. I can do the same. It's how we survive. Damn it, every time you block your thoughts"—he gave me a hard look—"like you're doing now, I figure you're lying about something, and it's killing me."

"Back at you, Rafael." I understood. I eased closer. I sent

him a mental message about what I wasn't wearing under my skirt. That hard look heated up. Progress.

"Quit trying to play me, Glory. I thought I meant more to you than that." He pulled me closer. "I won't sneak around with you and then watch you go hit it with Blade when he gets back. I did that for too damn long, and it hurt too damn bad."

"Rafe, I'm not going to treat you like that. You do mean more to me . . ." But I didn't want to hurt Jerry either. I looked around and realized this was a hell of a place for this kind of conversation "Can you leave? Can we go back to our place?"

"Not till Nadia gets back. There's too much to do before the opening." Rafe dropped my hand and whistled to a man behind the bar. "Jimmy, take Ms. St. Clair home. Make sure she's inside her apartment with the door locked before you leave."

"Got it, boss." Jimmy nodded. He was a shifter I'd met in here once before, when Rafe had first rented the place.

"I don't want—"

"Just go, Glory. I'll see you tomorrow." Rafe waved me away, then strode over to talk to the men with the sound equipment.

I watched him, so strong and confident and so damned right. I guess I was a coward, afraid to make a choice. Afraid to come clean with Jerry. Modern women managed more than one man well enough, or seemed to on the TV shows I'd seen. Problem was, I couldn't seem to get the hang of modern ways. I dressed modern, talked modern, but I was obviously still stuck back in the 1600s in some ways. Stupid. Because that was the very thing that bugged me about Jerry. He always treated me like that ancient female he'd met back in the day, helpless and in need of a keeper. Damn, I'd hate to think he'd been right about me all along.

No. Ancient males were possessive and wouldn't change. Unfortunate it was the ancient ones that attracted me—Jerry and Rafe. Ray wasn't ancient, but I'd like to have a go at him too. Why couldn't I have them all?

"You can, you should. The more men, the merrier." Alesa was all for it. But I knew better than to think that would work. Who did I want? Rafe or Blade? Both of them meant so much to me. And I didn't have to choose yet. Rafe was here. Blade wasn't.

I locked the apartment door and waited until Jimmy clomped down the stairs. Did Rafe really think he could just send me to my room? No freakin' way. Sure he had work to do, but I was going back to that night club and talking to him. I had a point to make and knew just how I'd do it. I changed clothes, then unlocked the door, stuffing my cell phone in one pocket of my jeans and my keys in the other.

I was going to try a different approach, a surprise attack that would catch Rafe off guard and hopefully make him listen to reason. I slipped down the stairs and out the front door. I looked both ways, hugging the shadows next to the building. I didn't want anyone to see what I did next.

It was really late, almost four in the morning now, and the street was deserted. Fine. I shifted and headed toward Rafe's club. It wasn't far, just a few blocks. Even if Simon had surveillance on the front of my apartment building, I doubt he'd have noticed my change. I picked up the pace. Rafe was going to be so amazed, he was bound to soften toward me. I was counting on it.

The back door of the club was locked of course, but I waited until a delivery truck pulled up at the loading dock and the driver got out. I hid in the shadows as he rang a bell. Nadia must have paid a premium to get tables delivered this late.

The steel door swung open and there was conversation, then the huge garage door came up with a groan and a crash. I darted inside while three men stepped into the truck. I kept to the shadows, slipping into the main room and looking for Rafe. He was behind the bar, and he'd pulled out a bottle of Jack Daniel's and a glass. Great. I'd driven him to drink.

"What the hell?"

Oops. I'd been spotted by the human truck driver. I ran across the empty dance floor to the bar.

"Ignore her." The shifter carrying two tables laughed. "One of the owner's pets if I'm not mistaken."

Rafe's head came up, and he stared at me. He shook his head and drained his glass. I just sat down in front of the bar.

"What do you think you're doing?" Rafe poured another drink and knocked it back.

Several of the men had stopped working to watch. A few of them laughed.

"Hey, boss," one of them called. "Who's the bitch?"

Rafe leaped over the bar and was on him in a heartbeat. "You want to ask me that again?" He had a fistful of the man's shirt. "Maybe you don't need this work."

"No, man. Sorry." The man glanced at me, then at the rest of the gang who all got really quiet, then busy with hammers and electric drills and saws.

"That's it for tonight. Clear out." Rafe grabbed the clipboard the delivery man thrust at him and signed. "All the tables inside?"

"Yes, sir." The delivery man was confused as the work crew packed up their tools with quiet efficiency and exited the building in record time.

"Out." Rafe followed him to the door, and I heard the garage door come down with a noisy clang.

I just sat there, not so sure this had been a good idea. If he'd just smiled . . .

"So what's this about?"

I didn't say anything, just laid down and looked at him with big eyes. What had he done to show he was sorry in the past? Oh, yeah. I rolled over and showed him my tummy.

Finally, he smiled with just a hint of dimple. "A golden retriever?"

"It matched my hair." I wiggled and thumped my tail against the floor. Mental messaging seemed to be the way to talk to him.

"So I see." Rafe knelt down and rubbed the fur under my chin. "Soft. How does it feel? To be a dog when I'm human."

I didn't like it one damned bit to tell the truth. I rolled over again. The tummy up position had been way more vulnerable than I could deal with for more than a minute at a time.

"It's not great. How did you stand it all those years?"

"I'm a shifter, not a vampire, for one thing. We look at these things differently. And I was getting a big paycheck for the inconvenience." Rafe sat on the floor beside me. He put his hand on my head. "Seriously. I want you to remember this feeling. I had to live with it a long damn time. Watch you go about your business, and see you as a desirable woman while I knew you never saw me as a man."

"I'm sorry, Rafe."

"It's okay. It's over. I'm not doing that again." He looked around the club. "But this has to be a success. I'm through with the bodyguard thing. When I cut myself off from my family's wealth, I had to take some jobs that weren't so great. Like dancing in Nadia's clubs. And doing dog duty for Blade. And those were the best of the lot." He turned to stare into my eyes. "Never again."

"Why'd you cut yourself off?" I wondered if I should change back but felt maybe Rafe would share more about himself if I stayed in this dog persona. I wasn't physically uncomfortable. I didn't have fleas or anything. And the concrete floor wasn't cold. But I was definitely in a subservient position, and I didn't like that at all. Alesa hated it, and I was hot again. Guess that was my punishment when she was displeased. I mentally shot her the finger, then sucked it up and stayed put.

"Granddad is head of the family. Because my branch has the demon taint, we have to be model citizens to be accepted in the shifter community. We're supposed to marry the right women, have the perfect children, always be above reproach. My brother pretends to go along with it, but I wanted to do things my way. So I took off." Rafe stroked my head like I used to do when I was upset.

"What do you mean, your brother 'pretends' to go along?" I sighed. His hand felt good on me. Warm, soothing.

"We do have demon blood. It makes us enjoy being a little, okay, a lot wild at times." Rafe's eyes gleamed. "Ethan keeps his stunts on the down low. I never bothered. It caused my family some grief. I haven't shown you that side of me yet, Glory. Because it would probably be too much for you. Like now."

I stiffened, reading his mind. *"No, I won't do that. You just veered into ick territory."*

He grinned. "Thought so. Brittany was up for it, but then she's a shifter. Like I said. Different point of view."

"Changing the subject now. I saw your eyes go red at the shop. That's part of the demon thing, right?"

"Yeah. I've got a few dark powers. Trust me, you don't want to see me go there. But if I need them, I can call on the forces of evil." Rafe lifted his hand from my head. "Payback's a bitch, though." He frowned. "Do you hear that?"

"Rafe, your dog is ringing." Nadia walked into the room, her high heels tapping on the concrete floor. "And why the hell is the crew gone early?"

"They got enough done. The sound system and lighting are installed. The tables arrived. I let them go. The vamps needed to feed before dawn and the shifters . . ." Rafe shrugged, then jumped up and faced her. "They'd earned a break. The second crew will be here in a few hours. I'll come back and supervise." He frowned down at me. "Glory, shift and answer your damned phone."

I hated to. Blade? Simon? And shifting in front of the sophisticated Nadia made me feel awkward and vulnerable.

Rafe grinned. "What? You naked inside that dog body?" He'd done his guard duty clothing optional.

Damn, I should have thought of that. But Nadia being here would have ruined that scenario anyway. I gave up and stood. The phone had stopped ringing, but I heard the sound that meant I had a voice mail. I trotted behind the bar, then shifted.

"I'm not naked, just felt a little weird about shifting again." I straightened, then walked around to face both of them. "Not my usual thing."

Nadia shook her head. "I don't care what games you two play on your own time as long as the club gets ready." She glanced over her shoulder. "I see Ray's men were here and set up his special sound equipment. Now we've got to rent a grand piano."

"That's a little much, don't you think?" Rafe walked with her toward the stage while I dug my cell out of my pocket.

Uh-oh. Missed call from an unknown caller. I had a feeling that meant Greg, Simon or Westwood. I pressed a button and listened to the voice mail while at the other end of the room Rafe and Nadia argued over Ray's performance and the expense.

"Gloriana, we think we've got the right location for the video shoot. Meet Kaplan behind your shop in ten minutes, and he'll lead you there. We want your input." Simon's voice. A command, not a request. I glanced at Rafe. He wasn't going to like this, but I had to go. I owed it to Rafe to tell him about it. No secrets. Our relationship was hanging by a thread already.

"Rafe?" I eased up behind him.

"One minute." Rafe put his hand on Nadia's arm. "Go ahead with the piano. It'll be like his Grammy performance. Right, Glory?"

"Sure. It was sensational. Ray really gets the crowd going when he sits at a keyboard." I forced a smile.

"Exactly." Nadia laughed, clearly pleased to have won the round with Rafe. "Run along and enjoy the rest of the evening. I'll tell Ray. He's staying at my house." She gave me an inquiring look. "I know you two used to be together, Glory. I hope that doesn't cause a problem."

"No, have fun." I even managed a smile.

"Oh, I'm sure we will." Nadia laughed. "As I told you, there are no safe hotels for a vampire here in Austin. It will be so much better for Ray at my house than having his

shifter keep housekeeping out of the room during the day."
She nodded at me. "You understand."

"Perfectly." I understood that Ray was putting his plan
into motion at warp speed. Nadia would give him an up
close and personal lesson in how ancient vampires played.

"Sounds like a winner." Rafe didn't bother to hide his
satisfaction at the news. He picked up a paper. "Here's the
invoice for the tables. I'll lock up. Ray's already moved in?"

"He was getting his luggage." Nadia frowned. "Glory, he
said you'd left him a message. For some reason he didn't
seem inclined to call you back. Was it important?"

I gritted my teeth at the slam. "Ray and I had a misunderstanding earlier, but I still care about him. There's been a
threat against some of my friends. Rafe talked to Brittany,
Ray's bodyguard, so she knows all about it." I smiled. "I think
I've got it handled now, but Ray should still be careful. I assume you have excellent security."

"Of course. No vampire can sleep during the day without
it." Nadia picked up the purse she'd dropped on a table and
slung the strap over her shoulder. "Don't you worry, I'll keep
an eye on Ray." She winked. "Sorry about the fight, but
seems you and Ray have both moved on. Rafe, I'll talk to
you tomorrow night. Have fun, you two." She left without a
backward glance.

"Now are you going to tell me who called? Was it Blade?"
Rafe kept a table between us, not exactly taking Nadia's
"have fun" to heart.

"No. Simon. He wants me to check out the site for the
video. I've got to meet Greg in the alley behind the shop
in"—I glanced at my watch—"about five minutes."

"I don't think so." Rafe moved in front of me and laid his
hands on my shoulders. "I don't trust those assholes."

"It's okay, Rafe. I'm going to do it. It's the only way to
keep my friends safe. But come along, keep an eye on everyone if it makes you feel better." I put my hands over his. "It
would make *me* feel better."

"I don't get it. Why so cooperative with Simon all of a

sudden?" Rafe didn't release me, just gave me one of his probing and very intense looks.

"I had time to think about it. Seriously, what choice do I have? And maybe I'll get a paycheck at the end of this." I stepped back, and he released me. "I can't live in fear, worried that he'll hurt someone I love to try to coerce me."

"Okay, I guess I see your point. But I sure as hell don't have to like it." Rafe followed me to the back door. He pulled a key ring out of his pocket. "We'll both keep our eyes wide open. Any sign of a double cross, that this is a trap to bring you down, and we're out of there."

"Seriously, Rafe, if Simon or Westwood wanted me dead, I'd be gone already. Out at the EV compound I was unconscious. The goddess there could have sucked me dry, and I couldn't have done a damned thing about it."

"You're right. My fault. I never should have gone out there without backup." Rafe locked the door, set an alarm, then walked beside me around the building until we were on the sidewalk. It was really late now. This would have to be a quick trip.

"Nothing is your fault. Simon and Westwood are the bad guys here." I stopped Rafe and gave him a quick kiss. "Please be careful. I can't bear to see you hurt. Just watch and listen. Maybe we can learn something that can help us later."

"I'm a man of action, Glory." Rafe put his hand behind my head and kissed *me* this time, his mouth hot, a claiming kiss.

"Mmmm. A man of action. I can feel that." I held on to him.

"Yeah, action. I told you he could bring it." Alesa sighed. *"Takes me back. We once spent a solid week in bed."*

I shuddered. How creepy to think about Rafe and the slime sister inside me together. No, had to forget that. My plate was full enough with this video.

"Let's go." I grabbed his hand and dashed down the street. When we got to the shop, I could see my clerk inside reading a paperback book. No customers. Couldn't worry about that now. Rafe and I ran to the alley and found Greg sitting on the hood of that ancient white car.

"About time. What's he doing here?" Greg jumped off the car.

"I'm coming with her. You got a problem with that?" Rafe shoved Greg until he hit the bumper.

"Naw. Knock yourself out." Greg smiled. "Glory, we're shifting out of here. Keep up. Simon's waiting." He whirled and, always a cliché, did the bat thing.

Rafe and I were right behind him. We flew out and over rooftops until we left the city lights behind. We were headed toward a part of Lake Travis I recognized, so Simon and Westwood had figured out the approximate location. When we came to the edge of the lake behind some houses, we landed and shifted back into our human forms. Simon and several other men walked out of the woods nearby. Westwood carried a crossbow. I wanted to hurl.

"What the hell?" Rafe jumped in front of me.

"It's a necessary prop. We also have wardrobe." Simon gestured, and a man brought out a video camera and tripod. Another carried a large suitcase. "We're doing this right."

"Then change locations. We're too close to those houses. This is all wrong." I looked around. "We climbed out of the water on a strip of rocks and sand. No houses in sight."

Simon frowned. "Kaplan, you and Bevis go up and look around. See if you can find a spot like that."

"Right." Greg the bat and the suitcase guy took off.

I turned to Westwood. "You pick this place?"

"I didn't remember a damned thing because I was shot, remember?" He looked defensive.

"You're supposed to be this great hunter." Rafe stayed close to me. "I'd think you'd have scouted out the area pretty well in advance."

"No kidding. And how'd you even find me in the first place? You weren't shot then." I was stalling. I really didn't

want any part of a play where I had to stand in front of a
crossbow. To my relief Westwood laid it on the grass and
looked around.

"It was all spur of the moment. We missed the shot at
Caine's house but finally got word from my men on the water
that you'd escaped that way. So we parked and walked in. We
tracked you for miles." He looked up when Greg landed.
"Find anything?"

"Yeah. This way, just a hundred yards or so. Perfect spot.
You can walk it." Greg led the way through the trees.

When we came out into a clearing, I shuddered. If this
wasn't the same spot, it was damned close. I remembered that
night too well. We'd had to swim for our lives, leaving Ray's
house burning to the ground after Westwood and his men
had shot flaming arrows into it. Ray, Valdez and I had
climbed out of the freezing lake thinking we were finally
safe, only to face Westwood's hellacious crossbow.

"This is perfect." Westwood looked at me. "Check out
Glory's face. I'm right, aren't I? This is like the place where
you plugged me."

"Lay off, Westwood." Rafe shoved Westwood back when
he got too close to me. "Can't you see this is upsetting her?"

"Aw, poor little vampire. Having a flashback?" He smiled
and aimed the crossbow right at my heart.

That did it. Something snapped, and I pushed Rafe aside.
Before Westwood had time to react, I'd snatched that crossbow
and flung it into the lake where it landed with a splash.

"You son of a bitch! You aim that thing at me again, and
I'll stuff it down your throat." I was shaking, but I wasn't
backing down. I swallowed, the urges to throw up or scream
both fighting for first place.

"Damn it! We need that weapon for the video. Simon?"
Westwood didn't even have sense enough to know I was on
the edge of doing something I really wasn't going to regret.

"Kaplan, jump into the lake and retrieve the bow." Simon
actually looked amused. "Gloriana, calm down. We're just
acting here. Westwood isn't going to hurt you."

"Damn right he's not." Rafe tried to put his arm around me, but I wasn't having it. I brushed him off, my focus on Westwood and his smirk. It was the damned superior look of a man who still thought he was the great hunter. No fang necklace, but I remembered it. Could imagine it hanging around his neck. Trophies from vampires he'd killed like they were animals and not people who had friends and lovers who would grieve for them forever. A tear slid down my cheek, and I angrily knocked it away with my fist.

"Westwood, we need her cooperation. Try to get along with Gloriana." Simon obviously issued an order this time.

"Don't be ridiculous." Westwood glared at me. "I'm not making nice with this bitch. She's done nothing but insult me. And now she's acting like she's got all these tender feelings." He curled his lip. "I'm not buying it. Come on, Glory, you tellin' me I was the first guy you killed?"

I heard Rafe growl but ignored him as I leaped for Westwood's throat. Fangs down, hands wrapped around his scrawny neck, I heard him squeak as I lifted him off the ground. Rafe was at my back, holding off Simon's men, but he didn't interfere.

"Hell no, Brent. I've killed men. So many I've lost count. You're just the first one who didn't stay dead." I tightened my grip and heard him wheeze. One more minute and I was going to finish him, twist off his head and toss it into the lake like I'd done his crossbow. Damned if I wasn't.

"Simon, help me. She's going to kill me. Look at her eyes. They, they're glowing." Westwood gasped again. "Red!"

Sixteen

"You really want to do this, Glory? Simon can be a bad enemy. I'm with you no matter what. You need my demonic powers, you've got 'em." Rafe's voice was inside my head as I squeezed Westwood's neck, watched his face go dark and his eyes pop.

"No! The price is too high, you said." God, but I wanted this worm dead and lying at my feet.

"Listen to him, Glory. Even if you get out of here alive, you'll regret it. If I lose this man's fortune, I'll make sure everyone you love or ever have loved will die." Simon's voice was in my head now too, cold and determined.

"He can't get away with what he's done." I couldn't let go, but I didn't squeeze harder either. If Rafe asked for hell's aid, what would it cost him? Red eyes. Oh, God. What would it cost *us*?

"He won't. As soon as his money is mine, he'll pay in other ways." Simon gave an unearthly chuckle. *"He'll wish he'd died tonight before my goddess gets through with him."*

"You swear? On your goddess?"

"Yes. I swear on her soul. I'll make sure Westwood regrets taking a fang from a single vampire." Simon sounded convincing, and

I believed him. I also believed Westwood hadn't heard any of this.

I let go and stepped back. Westwood collapsed on the grass, grabbing his crushed windpipe. I was sure he'd curse me but not without some serious healing first.

"Take off. We'll start filming here tomorrow night, midnight," Simon said, as a soaked Greg, moss dangling from his shoulder, emerged from the lake with the crossbow. Aggie would have loved the look and been all over him.

"Damned thing sank to the bottom. Next time you want to make a point, Glory, throw it into the woods." He sloshed over and dropped it on the ground. "I hate water."

"Yeah? Join the club." I turned to Rafe. "Let's go."

"You need me to guide you?" Greg pulled off his shirt, wringing it out, then did a double take when he saw Westwood struggling to his feet. "What the hell happened to him?"

"Gloriana." Simon smiled at me. "You'd make an excellent Energy Vampire now, my dear. Think about it."

I shuddered, pretty sure I'd just been insulted.

"We can find our own way back. Come on, Glory." Rafe shifted into a bird, and I was right beside him. We flew as fast as we could back to our building.

By the time we hit the door to the apartment it was close to sunrise. I collapsed on the couch, exhausted and yet jazzed. I'd kicked some butt out there. No, I didn't want to become an EV, but for Simon to say I was worthy was actually pretty awesome.

I jumped up, stalked into the kitchen and grabbed a bottle of synthetic, chugging half of it before I hit the couch again. What the hell was the matter with me? Awesome? Clearly I was on a slippery slope sliding straight down to hell. Rafe grabbed a beer and opened it.

"Are you going to ask?" Rafe took a drink. "About your eyes?"

"Guess I wasn't surprised by the red thing. Alesa's been talking to me, in here." I set my bottle on the table and tapped my forehead. "Still not sure how she got inside, but I'm desperate to get her out. Am I a damned demon now too?"

"You're kidding me. Alesa's in you?" Rafe tugged me up and looked me over. "That has to be a pisser."

I laughed. "Understatement of the year. She's irritating, prone to giving me heat attacks and even tries to order me around."

"A typical demon." Rafe pulled me close. "Damn, I'm sorry. No, you're not a demon, just her vessel. How to get her out? Well, we'll have to work on that. As to how she got in, that's easy." Rafe settled us both on the couch face-to-face, lots of eye contact. "You were both wounded in that battle in the shop. Right?"

"Yes, bleeding heavily. Her blood was an icky black. Gross. Smelled like raw sewage." I put my hand on his knee. "Am I infected? What's next? Horns and a tail?"

"Do I look like a cartoon devil?" Rafe grabbed my hand. "Her blood must have entered your open wound. I should have realized . . ." He leaned in and sniffed, then smiled with a sad twist of his lips. "Ridiculous that something so nasty can smell so sweet. It's faint. Your vamp friends probably aren't even picking up on it, but of course you have the taint. Takes one to know one, as they say."

"Oh, God, Rafe." Tears filled my eyes. "No matter what I told Westwood, I'm not a stone-cold killer. Only if it was them or me." I shook my head. I wasn't dredging up things from hundreds of years ago. Life then had been different for vampires. No synthetics, no security systems.

"I know that, Glory." Rafe wiped a tear from my cheek. "I'm sorry I drew her here. If it's any consolation, I'm sure Alesa hates being inside you. You've got the kind of good and decent soul she despises. That's why she wanted to kill you in the first place."

I shuddered and leaned on him. "You're giving me too much credit. Tonight I could've killed Westwood without a speck of remorse. Hell, I *wanted* to rip his head off." I sat back. "I've changed since that fight with Alesa. Said things without thinking, acted out in crazy ways. Even used the 'f' word."

"Whoa. Blade would be shocked. You know he's rabid about treating you like a lady." Rafe leaned back and smiled.

I laughed and hit him. "Not *that* 'f' word. Fat. I called a customer fat. Was mean to a couple more. I keep on like this, I won't *have* customers."

"Like I said, totally a pisser."

I lost my smile. "I don't want to be like that, Rafe. Without a conscience." I sure wasn't telling him how I'd offered to do the wild thing with Ray. I put that totally on the demon.

"That's not going to happen. And don't worry about what you did to Westwood. His death would be a public service." He kissed my forehead. "You look exhausted. Being a badass is hard work. I should know."

I surprised myself by giggling and felt him smile against my skin. "I *am* tired. Thanks for being there for me."

"We'll talk about this again when you wake up. Work on finding a way to cast out that demon."

"Now you're talking. If it wouldn't turn me to dust, I'd bathe in holy water." I stood and pulled him up with me.

"Talk to Richard about it." Rafe looked down at me. "We'll figure something out. Don't worry."

"Yeah, well. Hope it's soon. Alesa doesn't worry about anything. She just urges me to act out. Then I have to deal with the fallout. Fun for all." I felt the dawn and the bone-deep exhaustion that came with it. "There's no time for more than a cuddle tonight, and I know we still have issues, but will you just hold me and let me conk out in your arms?"

Rafe suddenly looked fierce. "Issues be damned. Simon could have ended you tonight. No way am I wasting a second worrying about tomorrow. Forget Blade. I'll take what I can get now."

"Oh, Rafe. I hope this doesn't end up hurting you." I saw what I wanted to see. A man who cared about me. Add that sensual vibe that pulled at me until I wanted to crawl all over him, and there was no way I was denying myself his comfort. Both of us demons. Bizarre and maybe a twist of fate, a sign. I pulled his head down and kissed him with everything I had.

One thing I knew. When I got up in the evening, I was going to church. If a demon could still pray, I was giving it a shot. Alesa kept her mouth shut. I figured that meant I was on the right track.

"I think it's lucky for a bride to go to church before her wedding," Flo announced as she waited for me to buckle my seat belt.

Rafe had been gone when I'd gotten up at sunset. His note had promised we'd see each other later, after he'd taken care of some club business. So I'd crammed myself into Flo's car with Richard and his mother. Mother Mainwaring wasn't Flo's biggest fan, and she stayed silent beside me in the backseat.

"Love the new car." I didn't love the fact that I'd had to climb into the tiny backseat in a pencil skirt. At least Flo had picked me up behind the shop, so only one homeless man and a stray cat had been witness to my cursing, inelegant effort to get aboard. "I thought Richard gave you an SUV though."

"Oh, he did. I exchanged it for this." Flo blew him a kiss. "He meant well, but I must have a sexy car. *Sì?*"

"The SUV was a much safer choice and better for carrying passengers." Richard adjusted the seat and closed the passenger door before buckling himself in. "The way my dearest drives, I'd have bought her a tank if it were permitted on these roadways."

"Pah! A tank is not sexy, Ricardo." Flo pulled away from the curb without looking, and there was a screech of brakes and a frantic horn honk.

"Florence! The rearview mirror is for more than checking your lipstick." Sarah Mainwaring squirmed, but she and I were jammed hip to hip in the backseat.

"Quite a wedding present." I smiled at Richard's mother. Rumor had it she was the source of Richard's money.

"I simply manage Richard's money, Gloriana, because I'm so good at it. He's quite wealthy in his own right." Sarah smiled, then gasped. "Florence, you just forced a car to the shoulder of the road. Do you even look when you change lanes?" She grabbed the back of his seat. "Richard, why aren't you driving?"

"Florence won't let me drive her new car, Mother." Richard had closed his eyes and gripped the door handle.

"No, I won't. This is my pretty little car." Flo swerved to pass a tractor trailer truck, and we all braced ourselves. Except for Richard, who kept his eyes closed but murmured Hail Marys.

I breathed a sigh of relief when we made it around the truck before the oncoming traffic hit us head on. Which was a miracle. I leaned forward to pat Richard on the shoulder.

"Thanks for the prayers. Keep it up."

"I dare not stop." He never even peeked. "Just tell me when we get there. But remember, darling, we have plenty of time. Church doesn't start for another half hour."

"I know. But some people don't seem to know the speed limit, *amante*. It's not a suggestion. You must go that fast or get off the freeway!" She yelled this and added a hand gesture at the car in front of her. "Am I right?" Flo turned to look at me.

"Uh, whatever. Just watch the road!" I grabbed Sarah's hand as Flo swerved to pass the car she'd decided was moving too slowly. My friend always drove fast. And tailgated. Now that she had a new convertible, she was even more reckless, convinced she had to "blow out the carburetor," whatever that meant. Apparently it included gunning the engine at every light, so she could race the car beside her to the next corner. The new car was turbocharged, a fact Flo kept throwing into the conversation.

Tonight the top was up as a concession to Richard's mother, who always wore a hat and gloves to church. Flo had complained, always happy to stick a pin in stuffy Sarah Mainwaring, but I'd jumped in and asked to keep the top up too, claiming I didn't want my hair blown because of a late date. I actually liked Richard's mom and took pity on her. Flo would be a tough daughter-in-law, a tough friend too. She almost put the top down anyway once she heard Jerry was still out of town.

"Flo, I never told you how to run your love life, so I know you won't tell me how to run mine." I leaned forward since the traffic had cleared and we weren't in imminent danger. "Thanks for coming tonight, Richard. You always make me feel safe."

"Yes, Glory, tell us why we are supposed to watch our backs. Are you and Simon Destiny feuding again?" Flo poked Richard. "Look at Glory. See what is happening with her."

"No, your backs are okay now. Keep praying, Richard." Sarah's nails dug into my palm. "Flo, you just ran a stop sign. Uh, that truck almost hit us. Guess his engine isn't turbocharged, or he'd have clipped Sarah's door back here."

"Pah, missed us by a mile." She poked Richard again. "Praying? I've never had a single wreck, Ricardo, not in all the years I've been driving."

"Probably made a deal with the Devil," Sarah muttered.

My own Devil's disciple muttered a profanity so vile I shuddered. I eased my hand from Sarah's. She had some serious mind-reading skills, and I didn't want her deep diving into my brain right now.

"Seriously, Flo? Even I've had a few fender benders."

"That's because you go too slow, Glory." Flo swerved around another car, barely missing it, and we heard a crunch as it scraped a guard rail behind us. "See? She is too slow and can't keep up with traffic. So she bends her fender. *Idiota.*"

I looked back, sorry for the driver who'd gotten in Flo's way. Time for another change of subject. "Flo, I've called everyone on the list for the bachelorette party. Looks like we'll have a great crowd."

"Can't wait. What are we going to do? Please, no silly

games." Flo glanced at Richard. "Open your eyes, *amante*. I'm pulling into the parking lot. See? You made it here alive."

"And in record time." Richard crossed himself, and his mother murmured a "Thank you, God."

"The entertainment is a surprise, but I have a theme. Come dressed as your favorite seductress. How does that sound?" I sat back and unbuckled my seat belt as we came to a rocking stop.

Flo laughed and put the car in park. "I love it. Decisions, decisions. Wait a minute. Of course I'm my own favorite seductress." She gave Richard a secret smile. "What do you think, *marito*? Who is your favorite seductress?"

"You, darling. Who else?" Richard glanced back at his mother, straightening her hat. "Mother, are you all right?"

"Richard, don't be hen-pecked. You've had some very accomplished seductresses make runs at you through the years. My son is so handsome, you know, Florence. You're very lucky to have snared him *this* century." Sarah smiled when Flo's eyes narrowed. "And of course I'm all right. I've survived much worse than Florence's driving. Though I believe I'll shift for myself in order to get home." His mother put her hand on my arm. "Gloriana, dear, surely you're going to invite me to this party. When and where?"

I finally found my voice. "Wednesday night, ten o'clock at Rafe's new club, N-V, on Sixth Street."

"Wouldn't miss it. I always fancied myself as Mata Hari, the World War I spy. She wore the most adorable jeweled bras." Sarah reached out her hand and let a startled Richard help her out of the backseat. Flo and I forced our mouths closed.

"Well, then, see you there. I haven't decided on my own costume yet." I pulled myself out of the other side, trying not to flash thigh at the rest of the parking lot. The massive building that housed the Moonlight Church of Eternal Life and Joy loomed in front of us. I'd always liked coming here for the positive message by Pastor John and the great music.

As I followed Flo and Sarah and a crowd of other worshippers from the parking lot toward the sanctuary, I began to hum to the soaring organ music coming from the speakers mounted on the outside of the building. Surely everything would be all right. I had good friends, had always tried to lead a fairly decent life, even after getting my fangs, and Richard, alert to any danger, was a comforting presence close by. But when we reached the arched doorway, flanked by two large gold crosses, I stumbled.

"Glory? Is there a problem?" Richard took my elbow, looking down in case I'd broken a heel.

I'd worn some great vintage pumps, four inches and crocodile, I'd found in a thrift shop. They were holding up just fine. The brown went perfectly with my beige pencil skirt and red twinset. I carried a designer knockoff purse that you'd need a magnifying glass to tell from the real deal. I looked pretty good if I do say so myself. But I suddenly didn't feel so great, and I really couldn't blame it on the skirt's tight waistband. I studied the church doorway and knew what my problem was. Hell's handhold twisted my tummy, and I swallowed.

"You really don't want to go in there," Alesa growled.

Like I'd let her stop me. Now I was determined. "Give me a minute." I sank down on a stone bench a few feet from the door. I opened my purse like I was searching for something. Maybe a tissue or Rolaids. Yeah, like a vampire ever carried *those*.

"Ladies, go on inside. Give us a minute. Save us seats." Richard smiled and waved Flo and Sarah away. "Sit near the back, right side on the aisle." Both his mother and Flo looked ready to argue, but after they glanced at me, they must have seen something that changed their minds.

"Please." I was shaky, like maybe I was going to throw up. The crosses . . . Guess Hell Girl didn't go for those. The closer I'd gotten to them the queasier I'd felt.

"Gloriana, talk." Richard sat beside me. "What's wrong?"

I had a vintage hanky in my hand, one from the shop I'd tucked into my bag. Good thing, because I'd teared up.

"I'm infected, Richard. By that demon." I dabbed at my eyes. "Now those crosses are making me sick." I gasped as Alesa hit me with heat. "I don't think I can go inside the church."

"What makes you think that?" Richard put his hand on my shoulder, then jerked it back. "You're hot. Is that . . . ? I can't believe it. I usually have a sense of these things."

"I hear her, Richard. She speaks to me. Sends me these heat waves." I knew I owed it to Rafe not to share his demon secret. "Rafe says because I had an open wound and Alesa, the demon, was bleeding from her own injuries, I got infected by her blood when you, uh, put her down. I'm tainted." I swallowed again, afraid I was going to be sick all over my pretty brown shoes.

"Yes, I've heard that can happen. Sending a demon back to hell is a tricky business. What I did was drastic, call it overkill. That demon isn't in hell. I thought I had annihilated her." Richard frowned, obviously thinking things over. "I was careful to hit her head-on. Of course she'd have tried to find a host, but I didn't think she had time. Surely whatever little bit you absorbed from her blood wouldn't be enough to make you a full-fledged demon. Remember, you were wearing a rosary that night with a cross. So you had some protection." Richard smiled encouragingly.

I looked at those enormous crosses. "Full-fledged or not, I'd hoped coming to church would help get rid of her. But now, feeling like this . . ." I pressed a hand to my heart. "I can't get past those giant crosses."

"I don't believe that, and neither should you. You're good. That evil can surely be driven out if we work at it." Richard's voice was so kind I wanted to cry all over his expensive gray suit, handpicked by Flo, of course. His wife would be looking for him, might even come out here, and I'd have to explain . . .

"I'm afraid I'm going to hell, Richard." I blotted at my tears. "And now I can't go inside my own church." I heard new music starting, one of my favorite songs. Was I doomed?

"Nonsense. I refuse to believe that a basically decent person can be corrupted by a simple accident. Come on." Richard put his hand under my elbow and hoisted me up. He'd probably made a good priest back in the Dark Ages. Too bad he couldn't handle celibacy. "Let's try this again, slowly."

"I don't think—" I didn't want to fight with him, but the closer we got to those crosses, the worse I felt.

"Yes, we're going inside. Careful now. Don't look at the crosses. Look past them at the sanctuary. Focus on all the happy people singing. There's Pastor John, smiling and welcoming the congregation. His arms are open wide, and he wants you to join him." Richard eased me down the sidewalk. When I got next to those crosses, I fought a sudden horrifying urge to spit on them and jerked against his strong grip on my arm.

"Stop! This is wrong!" Alesa gave one last jab at my forehead, and I went blind. I held on to Richard and kept going.

"Steady. Straight ahead. Feel all that positive energy." Richard pulled me past the crosses and down the aisle.

Gradually the warm atmosphere of the place worked its magic. Alesa finally whimpered, and I felt her give up. Hallelujah! My vision cleared, the sickness eased, and I concentrated on the music, the joyful sound lifting the rock lodged against my heart. I found my place between Flo and Sarah, and a hymnal was thrust into my hands. When I'd come to church before, I'd enjoyed the music so much that I'd sing along. I'm not a great singer, and my habit of levitating with certain songs was pretty embarrassing. As the evening progressed, I hoped I'd rise again. Sarah watched me, expecting it to happen. But my feet stayed planted firmly on the carpet. No heavenly pull for me.

By the time we piled back into Flo's car for the ride home, I was completely depressed. I did manage to get Richard aside when he helped me out of the car in front of the shop and ask him to keep the demon thing our secret. He glanced at Flo, who sat at the wheel with the motor running. He obviously hated to keep anything from his bride, but finally agreed.

"We've got to find a way to get rid of this bitch." I held on to Richard's arm, feeling desperate.

"Watch your mouth, you pious pinhead." Alesa was back.

Richard patted my hand. "I'll do research. Relax, Glory. You're not alone. You have lots of friends you can count on."

"Yeah, right." I realized that sounded ungrateful. "I mean, thanks, Richard." I saw that Flo had gotten out of the car after all and hummed "Here Comes the Bride."

Flo grabbed Richard's arm. "Come, *amante*, I want to hear about all these seductresses your mother said you've known. Every detail." She smiled at me. "Thank you for the bachelorette party, Glory. It will be great fun. Can't wait."

I waved them off, laughing when Richard looked like he was being dragged off to the guillotine. I knew the feeling as I trudged upstairs to change for my video shoot.

"Glory, if you don't want to do this video, say so. We'll ditch it and figure out a way to get Simon off our backs." Rafe came out of his room, and I nearly jumped out of my skin.

"Jeez, Rafe. I don't know why I didn't sense you were here." I kicked off my heels. "What's wrong with me?"

"Stress." He walked up and turned me around, gently massaging my knotted neck muscles. "How was church?"

"A disaster. Alesa freaked." I told him about my reaction. "Didn't I take you to church with me before?"

"Sure. But I was a dog. I stayed outside. Remember?" Rafe turned me around. "Good thing because, since I've got demon blood, crosses give me a bad case of 'No way.'"

"Seriously? I got inside, but it took some help from Richard. Alesa's making me pay for it." I winced when she stabbed me between the eyes for the fourth time in five minutes.

"I'll bet." Rafe pulled me down to the couch. "If she makes you do things you don't like, fight her."

"I'm trying." I sighed. "I never suspected you had any demon in you. How do you control that side of yourself?"

"You forget that I've had a lifetime to learn to cope." Rafe slid his hand under my hair to trace my ear with a fingertip, his thumb on my jugular.

"I'd think a demon bodyguard might be cool in some cases." I eased away from the distracting fingertip. "Did Blade know about your demon part when he hired you?"

"Yes." Rafe put his feet on the coffee table. He wore leather boots with his jeans and a vintage Harley T-shirt that molded to his chest.

"You're kidding." I sat up straight. "That didn't bother him?"

"He saw it as an asset. Which it can be." Rafe stared at his boots. "We met during a dustup with some rough characters in Europe. Blade and I ended up on the same side. He saw me take out the bad guys with my dark powers and was impressed. He wanted that kind of thing on his own payroll."

"You're being very vague." I needed to know more.

"That's all you get, Glory." Rafe looked at me. "Blade and I agree. I won't tell his secrets, he won't tell mine."

"I know almost everything about Jerry." I crossed my arms under my breasts.

Rafe smiled, a knowing smile that made me instantly uneasy. "You want to bet?"

I jumped up and glared at him. "What are you hinting at? Trying to drive a wedge between Jerry and me? You think I don't know he's had other women besides me? We take breaks, you know. When we're on a break, we can do who or what we please. Big freakin' deal. So I wouldn't suggest you go there."

That wiped the smile off his face. Too bad. I loved that smile and those dimples.

"It was worth a shot. All's fair . . ." He was up now too. "You have Blade on a pedestal, Glory. He's just a man. A warrior. Like I am. We do what we've got to do. And blow off steam any way we can." Rafe watched my face.

I sat again. "I can relate. Right now I'm so stressed, I could use a way to release it." I sighed. "But Blade and I didn't exactly take a break when he left. Sure I've had other lovers too when Blade and I have been apart. But this time . . ." I shook my head. "There's no way I can rationalize what we've done, Rafe. It's cheating, and I feel—"

Rafe put his fingers over my lips. "Stop with the guilt trip. You didn't plan this. It just happened." He sank down next to me. "You wouldn't be the woman I care about if this didn't bother you. But, Glory, what we did wasn't some casual lay and you know it." He pulled me close. "You ask me, this thing between us was long overdue."

I should get out of here. Stop things before they got even more complicated. But this was Rafe, and I knew he was right about one thing: What had happened had been building for a long time. I threaded my fingers through Rafe's silky hair and looked into his gleaming eyes. Desire. Is there anything sexier?

"Finally. Forget that religious kick. This is what I'm talkin' about." Alesa slithered around in my midsection. It was almost enough to make me back off.

"What do I have to do to convince you that you've wasted a lot of time on the wrong man?" Rafe didn't rush me, just waited for me to make up my mind.

I couldn't ignore that look in Rafe's eyes. If Jerry was the wrong man, could Rafe be the right one?

"Convince me, Rafe." I brushed my lips across his, just a tease, but that's all it took. He crushed me to him. I fell back on the sofa with him on top. That damned tight pencil skirt ripped when he pushed it up to slip his hand along my thigh.

I ran my hands under his T-shirt to touch his hot skin. He stopped kissing me long enough to pull off my sweaters, then helped me tug his cotton shirt up and off. His bare chest was beautiful, well muscled from a long lifetime of work.

"Sorry about the skirt," he murmured as he opened my bra and tossed it aside.

"It's okay. I hated it." I moaned when he took my nipple into his mouth and gently bit it. "Rafe."

"Mmm." He finished the job on that poor skirt and threw the pieces of fabric on the floor, then drove one hand inside

my bikini panties. I was damp for him and arched against his
fingers as they slid inside me. I moved in time to his stroking
and cried out as a quick orgasm shuddered through me.

"You're so good." I pulled his hair, then kissed him again.

"Just wait." He grinned and picked me up, carrying me
to the bed. He laid me down gently on top of the chenille
bedspread and looked me over, his dark eyes gleaming. Overhead light on. Too bad. But he had the same excellent night
vision I had so it didn't matter. I wished I had something
pretty and filmy to wear. My pink bikini panties did me no
favors. Wide hips and thighs. They haven't been popular
since way, way back in the day. I pulled at the spread, desperate to hide.

"Quit looking like that. I told you once I love a woman
with curves. You're just what I want, Glory. Don't cover a
thing." He stripped off his boots and jeans, then stood in
front of me, beautiful in a totally masculine way. "I've got
scars. War wounds. Hell, look at my back."

He turned, I guess to show me some old injury, but all I
saw was a perfect ass that begged to be touched. I sat up
and gave it an open-mouthed kiss, making him sigh with
pleasure.

"Damn, woman. If you tell me to take a hike when Blade
gets back, I may just have to kill both of you."

Seventeen

I froze, my lips just inches from his warm skin. I did not just hear him threaten me. He'd been kidding of course. A bad joke. I eased back onto the bed and glanced at the clock. We had an hour before we needed to head to the lake and the video shoot.

Rafe crawled onto the bed to lie beside me. He tugged on my hair, using a curl to tease one of my nipples, and I stared into his dark eyes, relieved that there was no trace of that evil red.

"Tell me what you want, Glory." His voice was low, his smile offering me everything.

I shivered and stretched out my arms, my inhibitions floating away on a rising tide of lust. Had any man asked me that question and truly meant it? I swear if Alesa said one word now, I was going to drink holy water until she drowned. She got the message and stayed blessedly silent.

Rafe waited, clearly ready to satisfy my every desire even if he never got his. I savored the power, the absolutely delicious possibilities holding me still for a breathless moment.

"Read my mind, Rafael, and I'll give you a play-by-play."

I licked my lips. "Kiss me first. One of your 'I'm your man and don't you forget it' kisses."

He grinned. "News flash. Now that you're on demon turf, no one can read your mind except another demon. A nice perk. Me? No problem. Send me that playbook." He leaned in, his mouth easing over my mouth while he threaded his fingers through mine. Our arms were wide, our bare chests just brushing each other, the slight friction an erotic tease lifting me off the bed to seek more. That kiss did claim me and left no doubt that Rafe meant business.

I sent my first mental message, and he pushed one knee between my legs, starting a rhythm that he'd match with his tongue and his cock before we were done. But not yet. First he'd do clever things to every other part of my body, front to back and then front again. And let me drink from him. Then more of those soul kisses that made my body weep for him. Finally, I'd let him come inside and take me hard and fast.

Of course I should have known Glory as tough bitch in charge wasn't going to fly for long. Because Rafe was too good. Before I got through half my erotic wish list, I fell apart.

"Now, Rafe. I need you inside me now." I straddled him, sighing as he filled me. "That is *so* good." I closed my eyes and just enjoyed the moment. "Now move."

"I thought you wanted this to last." Rafe smiled up at me.

"It's lasted. Now get on with it." I sat up and felt the hard heat of him inside me. Mmm.

"You sure? I've got more pleasure in store for you, Glory. Much more." He lifted me off of him. "Lie back. Close your eyes. I think you'll like this."

"Rafe, please." More pleasure? I couldn't imagine it. Of course my brain had left the building somewhere between orgasms number two and five. I'd been kissed, nibbled and licked in spots that even Jerry hadn't discovered. But I wasn't about to wimp out now. I closed my eyes.

"I'll be right back." The bed dipped. What was he doing? Getting a toy? I wouldn't mind that, though I wasn't into pain. Or at least the old Glory hadn't been. Alesa whispered that whips and chains and all sorts of erotic tortures were worth trying. I ignored her. The bed sagged again.

"Keep your eyes closed. Now open your legs. No matter what you feel, don't look."

"You trying to scare me? Not easy anymore, my friend." I smiled and opened my legs, excited and, okay, scared. I gasped when something cold slid inside me, followed immediately by the warmth of his flicking tongue. The thrill startled a shriek out of me, and I jerked against Rafe's steadying hands on my hips.

"Hands. Whew. For a minute there I thought you'd shifted into a snake or something." I shut up when I felt another jolt of cold. Ice? Soft, not hard. Whatever, it was crazy exciting. I quivered, and his clever tongue went to work again. Oh. My. God. So incredibly, um, good. Tremors shook my hips. One of Rafe's warm hands pressed on my tummy to keep me from bucking like a bronco. His mouth, so insanely talented. Chill, heat and I lost it, tossing my head and keening as I came.

"Keep your eyes closed and open your mouth," Rafe ordered, sliding up my body and wrapping my legs around his waist so that his hard cock teased my unbelievably sensitive cleft.

Since I'd forgotten how to form words, I did what he said. Cold again but against my tongue. I tasted . . . My eyes popped open.

"Strawberry!"

"Strawberry ice cream. Figured you'd be off chocolate after what Simon pulled." He slid a spoonful into my mouth, grinned, then drove into me.

I swallowed, grabbing his hair to give him a kiss that would have devoured him if he hadn't been giving as good as he got. He tasted delicious, of sin and danger and everything a woman bound for hell could ever want. He rammed into me, the headboard banging against the wall. I wanted him, needed him, needed . . .

I inhaled. Oh, yes. My hands still in his hair, I jerked his head aside and struck like a cobra at that vein pulsing in his neck. I tore into it, not caring if I hurt him, and sucked at his life force. The hot jolt of energy pushed me over the edge again, and I released his hair to dig furrows into his back with my nails as I came, screaming his name in my head.

The heat and force of his release inside me finally brought me down to earth. I gasped and let go, dropping back to the bed to stare at his ruined throat in horror. Dear God, I think I would have killed him if I hadn't stopped just then.

"Rafe, I, I'm sorry." I waited to see how he'd react, what he would do.

His hair was damp, his face pale as he opened his eyes and gazed down at me. Blood dripped from his wounded neck, and it was smeared across his shoulders. Then he grinned, those dimples deep and begging to be kissed.

"Damnation, Glory. I believe that was the best sex I've ever had in my life."

"You can't mean it." I reached up with a shaking hand. "I don't know what came over me."

"Hell, yes, I mean it." He kissed my fingertips. "I told you I like it wild. A little of your healing touch, a rare burger and I'll be good to go."

I pressed my fingers to his wound, sealing the edges and thinking healing thoughts. He needed blood—and not decorating his body. The rare burger and a shower were definitely in order.

He glanced at the clock. "Hop in the shower. We'll have to hurry if we want to get out to the lake by midnight." He stood and held out his hand. "Or maybe we should make Destiny wait."

I enjoyed the view. Totally sexed out, aching in spots, sticky where I shouldn't be and still I wanted to smear the ice cream I could see melting in a bowl on the night stand all over his perfect body and lick it off. Mmmm.

"Tempting." I pulled him down to give him a deep and thorough kiss. "That was incredible for me too."

He grinned and nuzzled my breast. "So we ditch Simon?"

"No, better get this over with. Lots of wedding stuff coming up. Aggie's lingerie shower for Flo is tomorrow night. Got to keep Simon happy, so he'll leave things alone. With luck we can knock out this charade tonight, and that'll be that."

"Quit giving me hot looks, then, lady." Rafe grinned. "Clean up. I'm eating first, showering next. For some reason I'm feeling a little weak." He pulled me out of bed, slid his hand down to my bottom and squeezed, then aimed me at the bathroom.

I watched him strut toward the kitchen. Oh, yeah, he was feeling pretty proud of himself. Can't say I blamed him. I stuffed my hair into a shower cap and stepped under the warm spray. Best sex he'd ever had.

I sagged against the tile wall. Oh, God. Jerry. Jeremiah. Couldn't blame steam from the ancient water heater for the room blurring before I pressed my face into a washcloth to muffle my sobs. How many times had Jerry and I made love? A thousand? Two? Ten thousand times? On furs in front of a fire in a cave in the Highlands. In a luxury suite in Paris on silk sheets. The place never mattered. To Jerry I was always a goddess, his beloved.

No beloved here. Not a single word of love had been spoken on that bed where we'd gone at it like animals. I scrubbed my aching thighs and heaved the washcloth across the bathroom where it landed in the sink. Luck was with me, and it didn't break anything, or Rafe would have come running. What had I done? Sure I loved Rafe. He was a friend who'd always been there for me.

Get a clue, Glory. There was a paycheck involved, and he wanted what Jerry was getting.

I turned the water to cold and punished myself, holding my face under the spray to reduce the swelling on my eyes. Makeup would have to do the rest. I was going to have to untangle myself from this mess I'd made of my life. Nice if I could blame the impulse that had made me invite Rafe into my bed on "The Devil made me do it." Would Jerry buy it?

Not in a million years. To be honest, I'd been attracted to Rafe and sending "Come and get me" signals long before Alesa jumped on board.

And what about Rafe? Would he be willing to go back to friendship now? Pretend this "fling" as I'd called it to Flo had never happened? He was more likely to take the murder route.

I was so screwed. And not in the super-cool multiorgasmic way either.

"I should have known you'd figure out a way to spoil the afterglow. Toss the halo, numbnut, and join the dark side. You just had a sample of the fun here." Alesa gave a throaty chuckle. So she'd gotten her rocks off too. I grabbed my toothbrush and attacked my teeth, wondering if I'd ever feel clean again.

Eighteen

We were about to head out to the lake when my cell phone rang.

"Rehearsal is canceled. It's raining at the lake, and I don't want my camera equipment to get wet. I'm sending you a copy of the script. Look it over and get back to me." Simon didn't wait for my response, just hung up.

"Well, that's a relief. No rehearsal." I smiled at Rafe.

"You want to come with me to the club? I've got plenty to do there." Rafe leaned against my dresser while I brushed my hair.

I glanced at the clock. Still hours till dawn. Why not? I had an idea for the bachelorette party and wanted to talk to some of his hired help. It would also do me no good to avoid Rafe. I had to figure a way to wiggle out of this friends-with-benefits deal while keeping the friendship. I slapped on a smile along with some "Kiss and Tell" lipstick.

"Okay. I'm almost ready. Would you grab a bottle of synthetic for me out of the fridge while I do something with this makeup?" I reached for my eye shadow.

"Got to warn you. Ray will probably be there, rehearsing and getting a feel for the stage." Rafe watched me for a reaction.

"Have to face him again sometime. Better in a private set-ting and not at the wedding, don't you think?" I never missed a beat and moved on to eyeliner. I was a star-quality actress. Inside, my gut knotted. Showing up on Rafe's arm was bound to trigger a scene. Rafe just nodded and headed for the kitchen. Maybe I was giving myself too much credit. Ray was probably all into Nadia now.

I finished my makeup, downed the blood substitute while trying not to cast longing glances at Rafe's neck, then left for the club. The rain had stopped here, and Austin's Sixth Street had been washed clean. I glanced in the shop window. Every-thing was locked up tight like it should be on a Sunday night.

We walked around to the back of N-V and heard the deep bass of one of Ray's rock hits. So he was here practicing. Rafe unlocked the back door, and we eased inside, keeping to the edge of the dance floor and enjoying the music as Ray and the band tore into it. Colored lights pulsed with the beat. Nice effect. The song ended with a final crash of drums, and the small work crew clapped and whistled.

"Thanks!" Ray waved, then turned to confer with the band members before they began packing up their gear. "Roll out the piano before you leave, Steve. Then take off too. It's late."

"No problem." Steve, with the help of another of Ray's road crew, pushed out a baby grand piano then walked off the stage.

Ray sat on the bench and played a few chords before he turned and pinned Rafe and me with a sober stare.

"Knew you were there from the moment you hit the door. Didn't think my guys needed to hear this." He slammed down the lid on the piano.

"My guys don't either. Come into my office." Rafe ges-tured to a room next to the stage.

"Why not?" Ray stood and walked in that direction.

"Listen, you both need to cool off." Understatement. I could feel the heat of Ray's anger from the twenty feet sepa-rating us. Rafe's was starting to catch up.

Ray stopped and turned to smile at me. That turned the thermostat down, way down to glacier level. "We're cool, Glory. Just need to clear the air. You want to wait out here?"

"No way in hell." I stalked up to him. "Don't you try to start something with Rafe, Israel Caine. Who I do or don't do is nobody's business but mine."

"Yeah, I get that." Ray looked me over. "I so get that."

"Let's take this out of the public eye." Rafe grabbed my elbow. "My crew is loyal, but big bucks from a tabloid would be a temptation I wouldn't expect anyone here to resist."

My stomach twitched. "I've had enough tabloid headlines to last me a century."

"Comes with the territory. You don't want to go public with the V-man, Glo? Can't say I blame ya." Ray gave Rafe a sneering inspection. "What do they say? Lie down with dogs, get up with fleas?"

"You son of a—" Rafe pushed Ray toward the office door, which I managed to open just in time for them to stumble through.

"That's enough." I shoved between them after I got the door closed. "I know you're not fighting about *me*, because you've decided I'm not worth it. Right, Ray?" I had my back against Rafe and could feel his tension.

"I'd never say that, babe. But I took your advice, got with someone willing to show me the vampire ropes." Ray grinned and winked. "*All* the ropes. And chains and even a few gadgets I'd never heard of before."

"Ooo. I really like this guy. Come on, Glo. Can't we do him too?" Alesa urged me toward Ray. I told her to stuff it. That earned me a stab to the eye and a hot flash.

"Nadia. Yeah, she's been around and won't get hurt when you take your show on the road." Rafe backed up. "Which you always do. Am I right?"

"You in a hurry to see me leave, shifter?" Ray kept smiling. "Feeling threatened, are you?"

"Not in the least." Rafe slipped his arm around my waist. "I've seen you in action, remember? Seen Nadia's action too.

You're a matched set. A lot of fun and games, and then 'See you around, sucker.'" Rafe tightened his hold on me.

"Nadia said you'd been there, done that." Ray sat on the edge of a crowded desk. "We'll see who gets bored first, won't we?" He smiled with a hint of fang. "Hope that doesn't tie your tail in a knot, Valdez."

"Nadia and I are just business partners. Go for it." Rafe released me and walked over to open a laptop. "Sounds like you're off the hook, Glory. Nadia can mentor your fledgling now."

"Ray, I'm glad you're having fun." Yeah, right. My hellbound side wanted every hot guy I knew to stay mine all mine, but I stuffed her back down again. "But I'll always be here for you, if you need me." I ignored Rafe's grumble. "For mentoring." Oh, I was so good. Alesa gagged.

"Offer a trade. You give him vamp tips, and he can show us those ropes and chains." Alesa *really* liked Ray.

"Sure. I get it." Ray looked from me to Rafe. "Can't wait till Blade gets back in town. I want a front-row seat."

Rafe was by my side again, his frown ferocious. "Glory, didn't you say you wanted to talk to some of the guys out there about working for you Wednesday night?"

"Yes, I do." I fake smiled at Ray, who was way too easy to read. If it wasn't for Nadia, he'd have already told Rafe to forget the club opening. Distraction time. "I'm throwing Flo's bachelorette party here."

"Nate said you propositioned him. You hiring male dancers?" Ray began unbuttoning his shirt. "How about me? I can bump and grind. I'll even audition."

"You wouldn't—" I laughed, couldn't help it. A famous rock star strutting his stuff would make my party impossible for Aggie to top.

Alesa was all over it. *"He can bump and grind me anytime."*

"Glory's got the entertainment covered. She's looking for waiters and bar help." Rafe really wanted to toss Ray through a wall. Didn't take mind reading to see that.

"Then maybe I can stop by and sing a song." Ray hadn't rebuttoned a single button. Such a yummy chest.

"Flo would love that, if she's sober enough to remember it." I grinned just thinking about it.

"Oh? How're you getting a vampire drunk?" Ray was suddenly really interested.

Uh-oh. Ray had been a week away from rehab for alcoholism when he'd been turned vampire. Besides sunlight, the thing he'd missed most since his vamp initiation had been booze.

"I really hate to tell you this, as your mentor and all, but there's a synthetic blood, several actually, with an alcoholic kick. Blott-O, Undead Drunk, to name a couple. You can get a pretty decent high." I glanced at Rafe. "Like the Vampire Viagra, they also make you horny. We're going to have plenty of it at the party, courtesy of Damian, Flo's brother. He's a local supplier. I didn't realize it before, because it's not in my budget, but apparently he'll sell to anybody who's got the cash to order an exotic brand. I'm surprised you didn't discover it in L.A."

"Chip probably made sure I didn't. I have way too many people in my life who try to run it. You know what I mean?" Ray moved close despite Rafe's growl.

"You bet I do." I smiled because Ray and I were friends in that moment. "But we just want you to take care of yourself, Ray." I put my hand on his arm.

"I get that." He ignored Rafe, who was looking dangerous and ready to pounce. "I appreciate it, sometimes. Right now I'm going to practice my acoustic number on the piano, then I'm heading out. I'll let you know if I decide to drop by Wednesday. But anytime you need me, Glory, you have my number. That hasn't changed." He slid his thumb down my cheek, then opened the door and walked out.

"Always makes a move, doesn't he?" Rafe glared after him.

"Was that a move? Didn't notice." I shrugged. "But I hated turning him on to the blood with alcohol. He's going to run straight to Damian, I know it."

"He's a big boy, Glory. If he gets addicted, tough shit." Rafe settled at his desk again. "Let me know which guys agree to work Wednesday night. I'll send the bills directly to Flo. You did say she's paying, didn't you?"

I sighed and sat on the edge of the desk. "Yes. I hate that I can't afford to do this for her on my own."

"Well, that's the way it is. Not many working stiffs could. She wants everything first-class, and that's what she's getting. It's making her happy so just relax and enjoy. You're arranging some neat things. If getting asshole Ray to dance in the buff would make the party better, hell, call him and say come on." Rafe grinned. "I'll take pictures and sell them to the tabloids. Make us both some serious coin."

"I'm sure Alesa would say go for it, but don't you dare." I heard the piano and Ray's sexy voice start in the other room. "Great acoustics, Rafe. Just listen to that sound. Ray'll make this club opening a tremendous success. I doubt it's in your best interests to throw him to those tabloid wolves."

"Damn, I hate when you make sense." Rafe stood and kissed me. "Go on out there. You know you're dying to listen. I've got paperwork. Just keep your distance. Now that you're mine, I'm not sharing."

I eased out of his arms when he tried to make the kiss into foreplay. So possessive. Man, was I in deep. I should call him on it, but then I'd miss hearing Ray. So I just smiled and walked out to sit and listen while Ray did a complete set, much more than he'd do for the opening. He'd always been able to seduce me with his music. It was all a fantasy, of course. He'd pulled his shirt out of his pants, and it was open over a chest still and forever bronzed from when he'd been a sun-worshipping human, prefangs. He sang of love found and love lost and lovers who needed each other.

I sighed and just drank him in, lost in the whole Israel Caine mystique. I could have had him once. *Yeah, right, Glory. And he would probably already be tired of you by now. Rafe was right about that. Ray has a pattern. You made a study of the rock star. Remember?* That was my own common sense talking. Alesa was silent, just soaking up Ray's sexy singing.

When he'd sung the last note, Ray just got up, nodded in my direction without even a smile and walked away. I heard the back door click shut behind him. Israel Caine. If I'd had this bit of demon in me back then, there was no way I would have put him off and not sampled every bit of what he had to offer. A little heartburn later would have been so worth it.

Rafe came out of his office, took one look at my dreamy face and stomped back inside, slamming the door hard enough to make glasses rattle behind the bar. I didn't want to hurt him, but a little space between us right now wasn't a bad thing.

I got up and approached Jimmy, who'd been busy setting up shelves. Flo's party had to be priority one for now, and sighing over lost opportunities got me zilch. Guess that's why I couldn't beat myself up for what had happened with Rafe. I had always wondered. Now I knew. It had been incredible. And if Jerry hadn't already owned my heart, I could probably be perfectly happy with Rafe. I doubted that would be much consolation for my shifter. I just hoped I could find a way to fix things so we could still be friends.

Alesa cackled and heated me to near boiling. *"Good luck with that, sister. My money's on my demon honey. Somehow I doubt this Jerry can beat him in the love department."*

I asked Jimmy for a glass of ice and rubbed it on my face. Alesa was so wrong. But I hoped she was long gone before Jerry got back. Had to be. This torture had to stop.

A lingerie shower. And of course Flo wanted to drive me out there in her new car. How could I say no? I sure didn't want to drive that horrible old car Westwood had given me. It started, but when I'd used the window defroster, there'd been a terrible smell, like maybe a small animal had died inside the dash-board. Eww. Add a weird whistling noise, and you had creepy *and* eww. The driver's seat had a loose spring. Hit a bump and you were spanked. I was not accepting the junker. Either Simon or Westwood were buying me a new car. Alesa cheered me on.

Flo and I zoomed over the hills with the top down toward Aggie's shower at a famous Mexican restaurant with a view of the lake. I was determined to enjoy it since I'd gotten a call from Simon that we'd be taping the video later tonight.

"Love this car," I shouted as we did a curve at eighty miles an hour. What can I say? I'm immortal, and the front view was way better than the one from the backseat.

"Yes, it's *perfetto*. How you like the red?" Flo grinned and slammed on the brakes. "Sorry, but did you see the deer? I cannot bring myself to dent my fender on such a creature."

"Good driving. I love the color. It's you. Matches your lipstick." I sighed as she took off again. Turbocharged. That's what I'm talking about. I added it to my list of features.

"Matches yours too." Flo turned into the parking lot. "I hope Aggie knows what she's doing with this shower. Nice setting." She gestured at the half-empty lot. "But where are the people?"

"First, the restaurant is closed on Mondays. We have the whole place to ourselves. Good call for our Siren." I unbuckled my seat belt and pulled a brush out of my purse. "Hold on a minute. Let me untangle this mess." I went to work on my hair. "And, second, some of your guests obviously will shift to get here. Am I right?"

Flo stopped in the middle of her own hair brushing. "Not with a package for me. But maybe they carpool. For a moment I had a doubt. Am I not popular?" She put her hand on my arm. "I know one thing. Until I came here, I never had a real girlfriend. Men? Pfft. I could always get men. But I didn't get really close to other women until you, Glory."

I reached across and hugged her. "I love you, Flo. You're like the sister I never had, only Italian." I laughed and sat back. "Hey, why so serious?"

"What you're doing for me. With the wedding." Flo's eyes glittered. "It means everything to me, *mia amica*."

I sniffed, all the emotions I'd been stuffing down lately welling up. I'd like to tell her how mixed up I was about Rafe and Jerry, even Ray. I hated hurting any of them but saw no way around it. Ray had been hit first, and it had killed me to see his pain. I knew now that I'd have to let Rafe down too. And he was my best friend. How could I reject him like that? And when Jerry found out what Rafe and I had done . . . I didn't deserve Flo's love. Didn't deserve anyone's. God, but I was tempted to lay my head on Flo's shoulder and sob. But she was the bride, and this was her week to have no worries at all.

"I'm so glad you have Richard, Flo. And that he makes you happy. I just want this wedding to be perfect for you." I hugged her again. "Now we'd better fix our makeup and get inside."

"*Sì*, I want to see who Aggie dragged out here for this." Flo pulled out her makeup bag.

"Everyone loves you, Flo." I grinned at her. "Well, except maybe your mother-in-law. Aggie says even she's coming."

"Great, now I'm dreading this thing." Flo finished powdering her nose, then opened her car door.

"One more thing to dread. We're playing games." I got out of the car and faced her across the open top. "Please be nice and go along with it. Aggie's never done this sort of thing before. You want more gal pals? Pretend to have fun. There will be booze. Drown your dislike of games. Okay?"

"Booze?" Flo's eyes lit up. "You mean blood with a kick?"

"Yep. Let's get hammered." I walked around the car and linked my arm through hers. "And we'll play Aggie's stupid games. This place faces the lake. How about we throw her off the balcony at the end of the party?"

"Girlfriend, I can suffer through anything if I have that to look forward to. I've never forgotten how that Siren turned me into a statue." Flo laughed and pulled me toward the door. "Payback time. And lots of new lingerie. What could be better?"

Aggie greeted us at the door. She looked gorgeous in a

designer dress that I'd never be able to afford. The green print matched her eyes, and her blond hair was pulled back with a silver clip that looked like a piece of sculpture. Wow. My own red pantsuit screamed end-of-year clearance.

"Here's our guest of honor now!" Aggie gushed. She thrust a basket at us. "Pick a number. We're playing a team game or two, so you'll need to see which team you're on."

I grabbed a folded paper. One. Flo showed me she'd drawn a two. Opposite teams. Oh, well.

"Grab a drink. Would you believe I found margarita-flavored blood on the Internet? Try it and tell me what you think." Aggie nodded, and a waiter in a serape came forward with a tray. He was obviously human and terrified, the glasses shaking and rattling. His name tag said Rudolpho. Aggie patted him on the shoulder. "Would you relax? I told you. No worries. These ladies are harmless." Aggie turned to me and winked. "AB negative, Glory."

I snagged a glass and sipped. Okay, I could get used to this. It definitely kicked. Another waiter came by with the EV chips and salsa. I dove in. My kind of party.

"Gloriana, Florence. Darlings, I don't know where you met this Siren, but she throws a great party."

"CiCi!" I grabbed my dear friend and surrogate mother, Countess Cecilia von Repsdorph, and hugged her. Flo claimed her next. CiCi had been in Paris for months but had flown in for the wedding with her son and his partner. I desperately needed her sane advice but couldn't drag her off to burden her with my angst now. Not when there were margaritas on hand.

It seemed like every paranormal female in Austin, and quite a few from Europe, had shown up for this shower. I added a few to my guest list for Wednesday night. Flo was thrilled, especially by the large table full of wrapped packages.

Aggie clapped her hands for attention. "Ladies, please get into your teams now. There are four of them."

I was on margarita number three and eyeing Rudolpho

for a nightcap. Hmmm. Definitely feeling a buzz, and my hellish side was picking up steam.

"Go ahead and snack on the waiter. Hell girls don't hold back." Alesa giggled, obviously feeling the buzz too.

"First game. Check your purses. Here's a list of oddball items. You have ten minutes, and the team that finds the most things on that list in their purses wins."

"Wins what?" I shouted, definitely thinking Rudolpho would make a nice prize. Three other vamps on my team noticed where I was staring and grinned.

"Each team member gets a choice of a case of margarita Blud-Lite or a one-hundred-dollar gift card at the mall."

"Woo-hoo! Game on!" Lacy was on my team, and she grabbed a copy of the list from Aggie.

"Time starts now." Aggie looked at her Rolex.

"What's on the list, Lacy?" I could go for some Blud-Lite to take home.

"We're toast. This is stupid. Who carries a corkscrew?"

"I've got one." This from Erin, one of my night clerks. Hmm. "Is there a flask on there?"

"No, but how about a box of condoms?"

The shifter who cut my and Flo's hair offered up one of those in a jumbo size that raised a few eyebrows.

"Hurry, my dear. Team three has six items already." CiCi snatched the list. "Eloise, get over here."

I'd met Eloise Duval briefly. She was a witch who Flo and CiCi knew from Europe. Apparently she'd come in with the countess and had been happy to jump in on all the wedding festivities. I smiled because I knew we were set to win now. Eloise was the only witch here, and she glanced around the circle at her teammates. We all nodded, not a conscience among us.

"Now you're getting it!" Alesa crowed. And didn't that make me think through my alcoholic haze.

"Oh, look!" Eloise cried, digging into her black patent designer tote. "I have an empty beer can and a jock strap."

That last one cracked me up, and she threw it at me. I caught it and dropped it next to the box of condoms.

"What luck! It's jumbo too." We all laughed.

"Two-minute warning. Team three is ahead with six items. Who knew that Diana carried around a sex manual in her purse?" Aggie danced around with excitement in her Louboutin pumps while team three high-fived each other. Team two, with Flo complaining bitterly that she should have carried her tote instead of the cute little clutch, dug frantically in their purses. Team four had settled into heavy drinking and eating, obviously not competitive.

"Come on, Eloise. What else ya got?" I grabbed another drink from Waiter Boy, setting my empty on his tray and inhaling his blood type. I flashed fang, and he ran as fast as his loaded tray would let him.

"Hey, I have a hotel room key." Lacy pulled it out of her hobo bag. She grinned. "Souvenir of a great weekend."

"And I've got the massage oil." The beautician tossed it on the pile.

"We're tied!" Maybe I'd check my purse. Sure Eloise could conjure up a dead cat if we needed one, but winning by cheating wouldn't be all that satisfying. When Alesa jeered, I realized I still had enough conscience left to want to play fair. There was a squeal as team two reached six items.

"One more minute."

"CD of love songs!" I threw it on the pile. I'd planned to use it in my beater to try to drown out the weird sounds. No luck. The Hell Hauler, as I'd dubbed it, only had a tape player.

"Wow, here's a tube of lube." I flushed as all eyes on me widened. "Not for me, of course. A joke for Flo, at the bachelorette party."

One more grab into my designer knockoff, and I jumped up, the room spinning. "Picture of naked man, full frontal. Another bachelorette thing!" I tossed it on the pile just as Aggie called, "Time!" My team leaped to its feet, and I was rushed and crushed in a group hug.

"We won!" Lacy threw herself at Aggie, waving the list. "Blew them out of the water!"

Flo gave Eloise a narrow-eyed look. Her friend threw up her hands.

"Fair and square, *chéri*. Gloriana's purse is a den of iniquity, *n'est-ce pas*?"

"Whatever." I fell onto a chair, truly blitzed. "I want my stuff back as soon as Aggie's done the official count." I crooked my finger at my favorite waiter, but he rushed off in the opposite direction.

"When do I open my presents?" Flo had clearly had enough of games. She didn't take losing well.

"Everyone out on the patio. Achy wants to do his thing." Aggie grimaced, but her look begged us not to complain.

"Sure, can't wait." I helped her herd the gang outside. "The Storm God's gonna light up the sky. No rain, I hope."

"No, I asked him to hold the waterworks." Aggie smiled.

"Wow!" Flo grabbed my arm. "Look at that." The lightning display was awesome. Thunder shook the building, and the lights flickered but never went out. For about fifteen minutes we saw a truly spectacular and colorful show in the night sky. The capper was the waterspout that narrowly missed the balcony.

"That was great, Aggie. Tell your boss he's incredible."

Aggie made a face. "Oh, I do. Nightly. It's all part of my, um, job." She gestured for us to go inside.

"Gifts now?" Flo started toward the loaded table.

"One more game, Flo." Aggie grabbed Flo's arm but released it when she got a death glare. "Come on, sweetie. That last one was fun, admit it."

Flo picked up the picture I'd printed off the Internet. "Glory, this man looks a lot like my Ricardo. You aren't secretly lusting for my man, are you?"

"No! Hell, no." I stumbled up to her. I'd had two more margaritas during the light show. "It was for a joke at the bachelorette party. Does look sort of like him, doesn't it? Of course Rich is way better looking than this guy."

"Ladies, please. This is unseemly. This man is naked."
Sarah Mainwaring had arrived fashionably late. She practically
tore it out of Flo's hands and returned it to me facedown.

I stuck it in my purse and grabbed another margarita for
each of us. "Flo, I'd sure never go after my best friend's man,
no matter how wonderful he is. You know that, right?"

"Of course." She smiled at her mother-in-law. "No more
games, Aggie. Time to open gifts. I can't wait to see what
you brought me, Mother Mainwaring."

"We'll see, won't we?" Sarah looked ready for the queen's
garden party in a demure cornflower blue shirtwaist dress,
panty hose and pumps, but the look in her eyes promised a
surprise Flo wouldn't like.

"Fine. Whatever the bride wants." Aggie grabbed Flo and
hauled her toward the laden table. "Time to open presents."

Flo tore into her first gift and exclaimed over a black bra
and panty set. Lacy came to stand beside me to watch, then
glanced at the buffet table laden with Mexican food where
the shifters from team four had congregated.

"I'm ready to eat. Great food, too bad you can't enjoy it."

"I'm enjoying the vamp treats. Aggie's done a terrific job.
Didn't think she had it in her." I saw Flo hold up the vintage
bustier I'd promised her, and CiCi exclaimed over it. Trust
my old friend to appreciate a fine piece.

Lacy nodded. "Nice present you gave her. Are we still
closing the store Wednesday?"

"Sure, why not? I can do it once in a while. I want all of
you to come to the bachelorette party. I promise it'll be fun.
Remember, come as your favorite seductress."

"I know, I've been thinking about that. May have to bor-
row something from the shop to wear." Lacy bit her lip.

"Fine. Whatever." Ah, my waiter was back. I snagged another Blud-Lite and winked at him. Off he ran. Then I watched
Flo open more presents. I glanced at my watch. This had to be
my last drink. I hated to think about it, but I was going to have
to head to the video shoot later. Showing up soused wouldn't
help me there.

Flo held up a long white cotton nightgown that would cover every inch of her. One guess who'd given her that. I jumped in front of Sarah before Flo could toss her off the balcony. What a party. I'd have to go some to top it. I hit speed dial.

"Hey, honey, how'd you like to dance naked for a bunch of drunk ladies?"

Nineteen

"Gloriana? What the hell is the matter with you?"

Oops. What had I done? I looked at my phone like it had betrayed me. Nope, it had been my fumbling fingers that had hit Jerry's number instead of Ray's.

"Uh, hi, Jerry." I laughed and walked away from the squeals and laughter as Flo held up a pair of crotchless panties from Lacy.

"Dance naked for drunken ladies?" Jerry's voice dropped into a low and sexy growl. "I'm not much for dancing, but if it's just you and me, I'm more than willing to give it a shot."

My inner thermostat jumped a few hundred degrees. Whoa, but I'd underestimated my guy. I spotted a chair behind a tall plant.

"I admit I've always liked your horizontal moves." I heard my husky laugh like an out-of-body experience. "Your dancing? Strip you down and who'd notice whether you had rhythm. Forget sharing. Blame that suggestion on this stuff I've been drinking." I polished off my last, I swear it, margarita.

"Where are you? And why are you wasting a good buzz when I'm not there for the payoff?"

"I'm at Flo's lingerie shower. Aggie's supplied some blood

with a kick. I'm kicking pretty good. Wish you *were* here." I sighed.

"Let's get back to the naked part." Jerry's chuckle made my thighs clench. "You're there too. Naked, of course, and stretched out on my bed. Touch yourself. Do it now."

"Phone sex? This guy has potential." Alesa giggled. *"What are you waiting for?"*

"Mmm." I sagged onto the chair and looked around. Coast was clear. I slid one hand between my legs. Too much fabric and no Jerry. "Not good enough. When are you coming home?" Refused to think about what would happen then.

"Not sure. When's the bachelorette party with the dancing naked men?" Jerry's voice hardened from sexy to serious. "And who the hell are these men if I'm not one of them? Which you've got to know I'm not."

"You just killed my mood." I sat up straight. "Wednesday night. I've got some shifters lined up who claim they can shake their butts. No big deal. Not really naked. It's standard fare for bachelorette parties, Jer. A bride's last chance to check out other guys. Don't stress over it." The laughter and cheers got louder in the next room. Must have been something really special.

"Won't just be Florence checking out those men. I know you, Gloriana. You've always had an eye for a well-built man."

"Don't you know it, big guy," I purred. "Come on home, and I'll show you how I appreciate a Scottish warrior's, um, build." I slid my hand between my legs again and moaned.

"By God, Gloriana, I'd be in the air right now if I could." Jerry sounded desperate. "Wednesday night. That's as soon as I can manage it. Probably close to dawn. Save me Thursday night."

"Hee, hee, hee. And if he and Rafe meet up then? Bloodbath. My favorite kind." Alesa poked me in the stomach.

"Thursday?" My voice cracked. "That's Rafe's club opening, Jerry. He's counting on our support. Nadia's reserved a special table for us, Flo and Richard. CiCi's in town, with Freddy and Derek. We could make a party out of it." Safety in numbers. Witnesses. Whatever. As an extra added attraction, Ray there singing and dying to let Jerry know what I'd been up to while my Scot had been out of town. "We can have a private party of our own later." If any of us survived. Or were in a partying mood.

"If we must. But it'll be the private part I'll look forward to."

"Me too. See you Thursday, then, Jer. Can't wait. Now I've got to go. Flo's opening her presents."

"Right. Wedding duties. I've arranged for Richard's bachelor party on Friday night. Seems I'll need a naked woman now for that." Jerry laughed when I snorted. "It's only fair. But I'm sure as hell not asking you to stand in for that. I keep my woman all to myself."

I bit my tongue. Another possessive male. I loved and hated that about Jerry. I really shouldn't have had that last margarita. The room was a blur, and I wanted to strip off and do nasty things to Rudolpho while I drained him dry. I was pretty sure it wasn't my demonic urges calling the shots either.

"Glad to hear it. Finally, you admit you've got your own bad girl. So let's par-tay."

I swallowed and gripped the phone. *Focus.* "Stick to poker and cigars. I've heard Flo's lethal when she's jealous. Me too." My fuzzy head flopped back, and I stared at the ceiling.

"No need to be jealous, Gloriana. I am and always will be yours. Thursday, after the opening, I'll show you what a good boy I can be." Jerry hung up.

My mind filled in the blanks. Mmm. Rudolpho made the mistake of coming too close. I squeezed his ass, then snagged another drink. What the hell? I was way past drunk as a skunk and had the damned video to look forward to. I figured I was probably a better actress sloshed anyway. And of course Rafe the great protector would go out there with me.

A damned shame that I was going to break up with him before Jerry got home. I tossed back the drink and wished it would knock me unconscious. This week looked to be the worst in my life. Alesa laughed hysterically, more than high herself and looking forward to every painful moment of it.

I staggered out to the gift area in time to see Flo hold up a pair of tiny panties that wouldn't have fit me after the age of ten. I smiled and propped myself up against a wall. Couldn't hate her. Loved her. She'd tell me to do whatever it took to keep Jerry *and* Rafe happy. Alesa was right there with her and flashed me with hellfire to prove it.

Damn. I ripped off my jacket and grabbed a handful of ice from the bowl of boiled shrimp on the buffet table. I shoved it down my bra until I chilled out. A handful on my cheeks went a long way toward getting me sober again. Or at least less shit-faced. The party was winding down. Flo tore into the last package, a sheer apple green silk teddy and panty set that made my mouth water. Not close to my size, of course.

"Thanks, Aggie, and thanks for a great shower." Flo actually hugged the blushing Siren. "Guess Glory and I won't toss you into the lake after all."

"What? Are you kidding me? That would be the perfect ending to this night." Aggie reached back and unzipped her dress, then stepped out of it and kicked off her shoes. "Anyone else up for a moonlight swim?" She looked trim and perfect in an emerald green bra and matching bikini panties.

To my amazement several shifters shouted "Hell, yeah!" and began stripping off to go with her.

"Great party, Aggie." I got to her as she was climbing up on the stone wall that circled the patio facing the lake. The water was at least a hundred yards below, and there were some pretty treacherous rocks near the shore. One shifter had already made a squealing leap off the cliff, though, and had landed safely beyond the rocks. Now she was egging on the rest to hurry up. Immortals. What did they have to lose?

"Thanks, Glory. The party favors are by the door. Each vampire gets to take home a case of Blud-Lite." She grinned and stood poised to dive.

"Wow! Thanks." Obviously Aggie had spared no expense. "See you Wednesday?"

"Wouldn't miss it." Then she took off, her feet changing into her mermaid's tail in midair.

I heard a crash and turned to see Rudolpho slouched on the floor, hyperventilating with his head between his knees and surrounded by broken glasses. Guess he'd finally seen enough.

"Quite an interesting woman." CiCi stood next to me.

"Someone had better do the whammy on the mortal wait-staff, Glory." Lacy crammed her gift card, a naked-man picture and enough food to feed her entire were-cat family into her tote. She reached forward and plucked something out of my cleavage. "Nice accessory, but that's kitty food." She popped a boiled shrimp into her mouth.

CiCi gave me a funny look. "Are you all right, Glory?"

"No, not really. Tell you later." I pulled out my damp tank top and peered down my bra. "Sorry, Lacy, but that's it." I glanced at the empty buffet. "You're shrimp out of luck."

"Too bad. Aggie put out a generous spread, but you know shifters. Fast metabolisms. Of course you see how we eat, hanging with Rafe now and all." Lacy smiled at CiCi. "Glad you're back, CiCi. Glory needs a friend. Flo's been way too busy with this wedding to help her." She glanced at the door. "Oops. Got to jet." She ran to join two other were-cats with bulging tote bags for a kitty car pool.

"You and Rafe? I can't read your thoughts. Who is this Rafe?" CiCi touched my arm. "Can we sit and talk now, Glory?"

"Sorry but I've got to go. Seriously." I glanced at my watch. "Late date. Rafe is Valdez. You remember my shape-shifter, the dog. He's done with his contract as my bodyguard, and now he's in human form. Hot human form. He and I . . ." I grabbed my purse and my case of Blud-Lite. "Well, we got together." I couldn't look at CiCi. She was solidly in Jerry's camp, like most of the ancient vampires in Austin would be. Seems they thought vamps should stick with vamps. Some people would say that's racist. I wasn't about to start *that* debate.

"You and Jeremiah broke up?" CiCi was on my heels all the way to the door.

"No, not officially. Not at all, actually. But . . ." I sent CiCi what I figured was a desperate look. "Can you come by tomorrow night? Maybe you can help me figure things out. I've got a hell of a mess on my hands."

"I heard that, girlfriend." Flo was suddenly right next to CiCi. "We'll both be there. I don't care what wedding stuff is going down. Your friends are here for you. See you right after sunset in your apartment. Am I right, CiCi?"

"Of course. And don't worry about the waitstaff." CiCi watched a wild-eyed Rudolpho scurry past, his tray full of debris. "I like that one's type. I'll take care of him and the rest. Glory, are you going to help Florence with her gifts?"

"*Grazie.* But that's not necessary. There are too many, and my convertible is too small. I called Ricardo to pick me up in his big car." Flo glanced back at the huge pile of gifts. "A great haul, eh? But now I need a favor, Glory."

"Sure, anything." My buzz really was fading, and I needed to get moving. I wondered if Flo would take my case of drinks since I was going to have to shift to meet Rafe at his club.

"Will you drive my car back to your apartment? You can take your prize and just keep the keys for now. I'll get them tomorrow." Flo dropped them into my hand.

"You want me to drive your car? Your new car?" I stared down at the keys. "I can't believe . . ."

"It's fine. Thanks. Pick up an extra case of the Blud-Lite. Aggie had plenty." Flo licked her lips. "Delicious. I'm ordering some." She picked up a sheer flame red nightgown. "It's made me very amorous too. I told Ricardo to hurry. Tonight we start a new honeymoon." Flo turned to speak to a departing guest.

I sighed, totally jealous. I'd been fighting my own hunger for something more than EV nachos since I'd started knocking back those margaritas. Jerry's phone call had made it worse. But I couldn't just use Rafe to scratch an itch.

"Oh, yeah? Men live to be used like that, honey. Admit it, you want him again. The man knows what he's doing."

No way. I pushed my good versus evil war to the back burner and hugged Flo.

"Thanks, I'll be super careful with the car. I swear."

"I know. Run along. I bet Rafael is waiting for you. Am I right?" Flo glanced at CiCi. "Don't frown at me. Glory can have a little fun with a handsome man. Remember the time you . . ."

I left them arguing about CiCi's affairs in Paris and ran out to the car. I popped the trunk and carefully stowed my two cases in the back, then settled into the driver's seat, adjusting it until my feet touched the pedals just right. The car started with a roar.

"Going somewhere?"

I paused with my hand on the gearshift. "Looks like it." I grinned. "Want to ride with me to Rafe's club?"

"You sure you're okay to drive? Someone told me you've been hitting the joy juice pretty hard. Don't blame ya. It was good stuff." Ray laughed and jumped into the passenger seat. "Sweet ride. Tell me you finally gave up on that junker you were drivin'."

"Yeah. This is Flo's, but I've got one on order for myself." I put the car into reverse and backed out of the parking spot. "Looks like you tried the joy juice yourself."

"Sure. They even have a Scotch-flavored blood. I'm feeling no pain." Ray leaned back and grinned.

"My buzz is fading fast, but if you're scared to ride with me, jump out now."

"No, I've always liked to live on the edge." He did buckle his seat belt.

"Hang on. Let's see what this baby's got." I put it in drive and hit the accelerator. "What are you doing out here?"

"Met with the owner. He's a shifter. My record label is throwing a party here. Part of the music festival." Ray didn't have to shout over the wind noise; our vamp hearing did its job.

"It was a great venue." I was on the open road now and having trouble concentrating on what Ray was saying. The car drove like a dream.

"Looked like you girls were havin' a good time. Felt sorry for the mortal waiters. I saw one of them being taken down a pint out by the Dumpster and two other vamps in line." Ray put his hands in the air to feel the breeze.

"Yeah, one tempted me. AB neg." I was really rolling now, taking curves like I was practicing for the Indy 500. Ray put his hand on the back of my neck.

"Pull over. That stuff I drank made me horny as hell. You still up for a pity play?"

Boy, was my hell side ready to rock and roll. Guess my buzz was still there too because I actually thought about it for a second. But a second was all. My rational side knew better than to start something with Ray now. Not fair to him, definitely not fair to Rafe or Jerry. And even if I could get my conscience to take a hike, showing up to meet Rafe with rocker sex all over me was suicidal.

"Gee, Glory, take the stick out of your ass and say yes. Ever hear of a bath? Air freshener? Perfume? Rafe'll never know. Rocker boy can scratch that itch. Pull over and get with it."

I sighed, not about to let my demon have her day, er, night. I managed to shake my head.

"Sorry, Ray. As flattering as that offer is, I'll have to pass. Obviously that ship has sailed. Right now I've got to go out to the lake. We're remaking *Titanic* only without the ocean liner. Simon's directing." Nice water thing going here. My demon screeched, ready to drown me in the nearest puddle.

"What the hell?" Ray flinched when I almost clipped a guardrail. *Someone* had pulled the car toward a rest stop for that scratching session.

"Sorry." I fought it back to the road.

"Just be careful. Dent her new car, and Flo would—"

"Kill me if she could find me. I'd know better than to make it easy." The car swerved again before I dragged my eyes from Ray's pretty blue eyes and hot body. Tonight he had on a black silk shirt, unbuttoned low, and snug jeans. Horny? I squirmed in my leather bucket seat.

"*Titanic*? Simon?" Ray kept his hand on my neck, one finger sliding up and down my jugular. "What's up?"

"We're"—I had to clear my throat—"uh, we're making a video so it'll seem like we staged Westwood's death. Then the hunter'll hop up at the end and show he never died. Confess he didn't really kill any vampires. That all the stuff on his Web site is bogus. He's going to take the video to his kids and get access to his money again."

"Rise from the dead." Ray let his hand graze my breast. "Why're you helping him? He threatenin' you?"

"Simon." I plucked his hand off of me. Fumes. Ray had really hit the alcoholic blood hard. "Simon's the one with the threats. He's got video of me with Rafe. Says he'll send it to Jerry if I don't cooperate." We were out of the hills and into a populated area now, and I stopped at a red light. "I can't hurt Jerry that way. If I want to tell him about Rafe, I will. But to have it just show up in an e-mail . . ."

"Yeah, that's cold." Ray yawned when the light turned green. "So Simon's got you. Bastard. But then he's always been one. No news there." He dropped his hand on my knee. "Sorry, babe."

"I've got a script in my purse." A messenger had dropped it off right after Simon's call. "Check it out. Simon's got us talking like we're in a bad horror flick."

Ray pulled my purse from the backseat and found a picture first. "Naked man? Obviously these guys you hang with aren't taking care of you right." He slid his hand up my thigh. "Glory, baby, don't you know you can call, anytime, and I'll be glad to give you the real deal?"

I shivered and managed to lift his hand off despite Alesa's screeches in my head calling me all kinds of an idiot.

"That picture's part of a bachelorette game. Not going to use it now. No games at the party. Flo really hates them." I'd printed half a dozen. I was surprised Lacy had left me one.

Ray naked. Oh, boy, did I remember the perfection of his body. "Grab the thick pack of papers, Ray."

He skimmed it, laughing. "No one talks like this. 'You'll rue the day you ever killed a vampire, you evil monster.'" Ray laughed. "Sorry, honey, but seems more likely you'd have called him a sack of shit. Don't remember what the hell you said that night, but Destiny would do better to make it a silent picture than have you spout junk like this."

"You're right. That's a good idea. Westwood can say the audio went out." I turned onto Sixth Street. "Thanks for being a friend, Ray. I mean it. I needed to just talk about this. I haven't been able to with anybody except Rafe."

"Yeah, and Dog Breath is all about being the big protector, am I right?" Ray rubbed my knee. "Let me out here, a few blocks from the club. I'll walk the rest of the way. Need to clear my head before rehearsal. I admit that blood with a kick knocked me for a loop. I sure as hell don't feel like another face-off with your furry friend when I'm not in top form."

"Rafe *is* my protector. Being out there in the middle of a bunch of Energy Vampires isn't easy. Rafe makes me feel safe." I pulled over and stopped.

"But does he make you feel this?" Ray leaned in and kissed me, one of his deep and searching kisses that never failed to heat me from head to toe. Spots in between lit up like he'd put a torch to them. The booze cooperated, and I clutched his silky shirt, then ran one hand inside to stroke his cool skin.

"Woo-hoo! This cowgirl could take this stallion for a ride tonight. What are we waiting for, Glo? Turn the car around and head for the nearest horizontal surface."

I wouldn't listen to Alesa, who, for a change, seemed to make sense.

"Sure you don't feel sorry for me tonight, Glory girl?" Ray whispered as he palmed my breast and licked my jugular. "You don't owe that dog your loyalty, now do you?"

"A woman would have to be a fool to feel sorry for you, Israel Caine." I eased back and took a breath I didn't need. Alesa shrieked so loudly my ears rang. "Not saying you aren't temptation wrapped in a hot body, but my life is way too complicated already." I sighed. Yep, my life was so far off the rails now, I couldn't even imagine fixing things.

Ray stared at me, trying to read my mind. No luck of course. "I thought I had you there for a moment. I swear I did."

"Yeah, you're good. No doubt about it. But this is where you get out." I smiled and ran my hand over his cheek, rough with an early-morning beard.

The look on Ray's face made me yank my hand away. I closed my eyes against the dare in his. Suddenly I felt his fangs drift across my jugular, and my eyes popped open.

"Relax, babe. I'll make it great for you. Turn off the engine, and we'll ditch the car. Go somewhere private. No one will ever have to know." He stared down at me, willing me to forget everything and go for it.

Go for it. Alesa urged me to go for it too, and it took everything in me to ignore her screams to take Ray up on his offer.

"Sorry, but *I'd* know. I'm not doing this, Ray, and when you sober up, you'll realize you didn't want it this way either." I shoved at him gently. Damned demon. Damned alcohol. I never should have kissed him back, but something in me couldn't seem to resist him. The world swam as tears filled my eyes. Ray didn't deserve my "now she wants me, now she doesn't" act. He proved it when he didn't force the issue but leaped out of the car.

"Guess I did drink too much 'cause I'd told myself I'd never beg you for it again. Do me a favor and forget this happened. I just made a damn fool of myself." He shrugged, his smile crooked. "Good luck with your men, Glory girl. Count me out of the panting pack. Israel Caine is finally movin' on."

He whirled and became a hawk, silently flying out over

the rooftops, away from Rafe's club. Hopefully the flight would sober him up. I sighed, pulled my clothes together and pressed my head against the steering wheel. No way could I drive yet. Not with tears blurring the street in front of me and my hands shaking. I had the sick feeling that I'd lost Ray forever this time.

I should have known Alesa would feel the need to comment.

"You are the dumbest dipshit I've ever had the misfortune to inhabit. Now don't screw up things with this next guy, or I'll really make your life a living hell." One final jab with what felt like a stiletto heel right between the eyes made the street go out of focus for a moment. Then she settled back for the ride.

I tried to think about what had just happened. Ray had always just been a fantasy man, the rock star I'd been lucky enough to attract by accident. Dumb me didn't know what to do with a man who treated me as an equal from the get-go. A twentieth-century male.

Ancient males. Yep, that was my type. Always had been. Then I bitched and moaned about the reality of their bossiness and possessive attitudes. Jerry and Rafe were just the current members of the club. I banged my head on the steering wheel until I realized I might damage it and couldn't afford the repairs. Time to make a move.

I pulled up in front of the club minutes later. Rafe stood out front. His eyes widened when he saw what I was driving.

"Flo's car?" He leaned in and looked it over. I saw him sniffing the air but ignored it. He didn't ask about Ray so maybe he assumed Flo had taken him for a ride recently.

"I have to put it in back of the shop. Are we shifting out to the lake?" I dreaded it. The weather was cool and clear, a perfect Austin spring night. But shifting was one more stress I didn't need.

"No, I'll drive. I'm parked behind your shop. Meet you there."

"Fine." I gunned the motor, almost hitting a car traveling down the street. Great. I had to get a grip and *pay attention*.

By the time I'd settled into the passenger seat in Rafe's SUV, I was calm enough and had a story ready if he asked about Ray. He didn't. Which worried me.

"How was the shower?"

"Super. Flo got lots of presents, and Aggie was a good hostess. She and some shifters jumped in the lake when it was all over." I opened the window and let the night air hit me, desperate to get rid of Ray's scent. Rafe's nose twitched from time to time, but he hadn't called me on it.

"Because he's already planning how he'll rip Ray's head off and use it for batting practice right after his club opening. That's how a demon takes care of a rival."

Thanks for the info, Alesa. I swallowed, all those margaritas and chips I'd devoured suddenly fighting with each other for a chance to see moonlight.

"Sounds good. Did you get a chance to work on that script?" Rafe never took his eyes off the road. We were on a twisty route that did require some concentration but not that much. Was he mad? I eased closer and put my hand on his thigh. To my relief, he smiled.

"Not really. It's hopeless. Simon should shoot the video without sound. Think about it. That night the camera would have had to have been far away. What do you think?"

"Yeah, that's better." Rafe put his hand over mine and rubbed his leg with it, easing it toward his zipper. Uh-oh. "This whole thing is stupid and dangerous. No way am I letting Westwood point a loaded crossbow at you." Rafe's hand tightened on mine.

"I'm not crazy about the idea either. But how are we going to make it look realistic?" I glanced out the window. It took a lot longer to get to the site when we had to drive. We were late. But Simon hadn't called. Or had he? I dug in my purse, which was a good excuse to get my hand back. I'd turned off my phone after talking to Jerry because my battery was almost dead. I turned it on. Yep, missed call from the great unknown. Simon, of course. I didn't bother to listen. I was on my way. What more could I do?

"Screw realistic. All Westwood's kids have to see is that their dad is alive, this video with a supposed vampire and a crossbow was a setup. That's it. This elaborate film is just pandering to Simon's ego. I say whatever gets taped tonight is it. End of story." Rafe's jaw was set. I sure wouldn't want to argue with him. Of course what did *he* have on the line?

"Let's see what happens when we get there." Finally I saw the road where we turned off into the woods. I did want to wrap this up tonight. After that, I hoped I never saw Brent Westwood again.

Simon was all business as he directed his cameraman and blocked out the shot next to the lake. The wind had picked up, and the water was rough.

"Valdez, since you insisted on tagging along, you may as well do your dog thing. I'll play the part of Israel Caine, since I can make myself look just like him." Simon smiled and ran his fingers through his thin hair.

That boast would have made me gag except it was the truth. What I couldn't figure out was why Simon didn't put on a better looking façade all the time. Right now he was in his regular weasel face. Oops, a face Rafe had pushed too close to.

"Hey. I'm not here to play dog. I'm here to keep Glory safe." Rafe frowned down at my hand on his arm. "Relax, sweetheart, this fanged Spielberg wannabe and I will get this straight. I'm sure he's got other shifters or vamps who can do the dog thing."

"Gloriana is perfectly safe as long as she plays her part. As to the dog . . . ? Fine. Kaplan can do it." Simon snapped his fingers twice, and Greg strolled out from the trees.

"You need me, boss?" Greg smiled at me. "Ready to get started, Glory?"

"Can't wait." Now *I* smiled because I knew what was coming.

"You'll play the dog, Kaplan." Simon pointed at the lake.

"The three of us will crawl out of the water and confront Westwood."

I laughed as Greg's face fell. "But we need Ray's body-guard, Brittany, a shape-shifter. She flew overhead, shifted, then walked up with us."

"That's right. Guess Greg can be Brittany, who's tall, stacked and blond, or the dog. Take your pick, bud." Rafe looked Greg over.

"Another character. Did she have lines, Gloriana?" Simon made a note on his clipboard. "What about wardrobe?"

"Didn't say a thing. She was just ready to rip apart any-one who got near Ray." I glanced at Greg. "Wore jeans and a T-shirt. What's it going to be, Greg?"

"I'll take the damned dog. I don't do women." He winked at me. "Except when I *do* women."

"Bevis, get out here." Simon paced until the man walked up. "You'll shift into a tall blond female. Caine's bodyguard. What you're wearing should do for the role."

"This'll be choice. Two women with hot bodies in wet T-shirts. This goes on my Facebook page." Greg gasped when I grabbed his ear.

"Post one second of anything with me in it, and I'll make sure you never 'do' a woman again. Understand?"

Simon clapped. "Well said, Gloriana. Listen to her, Gregory. Our work here is for my private use and Westwood's." Simon turned to glare at a whining Bevis. "You have your orders. Get with it or have a private meeting with the goddess."

"How's this?" Suddenly Bevis was Brittany. Only not so much.

"My eyes!" Rafe pulled out sunglasses. Of course none of the vampires even owned a pair, but we wished we did.

"Sorry, Beev. Could you go for a little less bride of Fran-kenstein and a little more Britney Spears?" I didn't bother to hide my smile. We all watched Bevis tweak his look.

"Oh, give it up. No one is going to ask you to the prom, fella. You'd better stay behind Simon a.k.a. Ray when we shoot." Greg shook his head. "But, for the record, nice chimichangas."

"Kaplan, show Valdez and Gloriana your dog. See if they approve." Simon sat in a director's chair with his name stenciled on the back. Definitely channeling Spielberg.

"I'm trying to remember how you looked, Valdez. Shift and show me the real deal." Greg smirked at Rafe.

"Not interested. Let's see what you've got." Rafe crossed his arms over his chest.

"Asshole." Greg huffed, then changed. His dog was a black Labrador retriever. All wrong.

"I was a Labradoodle. Curl the hair." Rafe glanced at me. "What else, Glory?"

"You were much cuter, of course." I tugged at Greg's ears. "Hairier and rounder ears."

"Brown eyes. Roll over and let me see your package. Or have you been fixed?" Rafe's dimples were showing.

"That does it." Greg was back to his human form again. "I figure I was close enough to pass. And I'm not showing you my package, asshole. Ask Glory. I have definitely not been fixed."

"Me? I don't remember a thing. Which means what you have must be highly forgettable." I put my arm around Rafe's waist. "Don't worry, Greg. It was dark during the face-off. You and Brittany Ugly will be in the background."

"Let's get serious here." Simon was back with his clipboard. "Gloriana, are you satisfied that Gregory can do the job?"

"As a dog? Oh, yes, he has a natural talent for it." I smiled at Greg.

"Your costume is in the tent. I bought several sizes." Simon looked me over in a creepy way that made Alesa giggle and me want to hurl. "I think I'm a pretty good judge of what you might wear. Go change."

"Fine." I followed a man to a large tent, Rafe right behind me. "Can you believe Alesa has the hots for Simon?" I said as soon as we were inside.

"Figures. Destiny's probably got a straight line to Lucifer. Alesa knows and loves evil. You saw her real face, didn't you? Looks attract her but aren't everything. It's what's inside that counts. The nastier, the better for her." Rafe pulled my sweater off over my head.

"My honey gets me. Isn't he sweet? I think you two have time for a quickie, Glo. Get with it." Alesa shoved me toward him.

I staggered and stepped back. "That doesn't make me feel good about having her in me, you know." I sifted through my costume choices. Simon had my sizes all right. I ignored his creepy underwear choices, sticking with my own.

"Glory, you don't have to do this. We can shift out of here. Think of something . . ." Rafe put his hands on my shoulders.

"Thanks, Rafe. But let's just get this done." I sighed. He had no idea how Simon was forcing me to play this game. If Jerry got a steamy video of Rafe and me together while he was in Florida . . . Well, I was not going to let that happen. End of story.

We came out to find Simon dabbing fake soot on his face. I refused to do it.

"I know we had just escaped from a burning building, but I'm going to be wet. It'll probably wash off anyway."

"You may be right. We'll see. This will just be a dress rehearsal." He signaled the cameraman. "Now let's swim out a few yards, then come in parallel to the beach. We'll crawl out, exhausted." Simon panted like he'd struggled ashore. "Gloriana, you were an actress once. Can you do this realistically?"

"Sure. I lived it, remember?" I shivered as the wind gusted. Honestly, Simon's Ray looked right, but he had the acting skills of a jack-o'-lantern.

"Westwood will be waiting for us onshore with the crossbow. But we won't worry about that right now."

"Film this for real, Simon. I'm not jumping in that water twice." I saw that Rafe was standing next to a glowering Westwood and had taken charge of the crossbow. Good.

"All right. I'm not crazy about swimming in that lake

either. Kaplan, are you ready?" Simon looked around, and Greg as Valdez trotted out and jumped in when we did.

The cold water was a shock, and it was rough enough to be tough going. I hated the creepy, crawly things that brushed my bare feet and legs as I swam the yards I needed before we started back. I remembered then that Ray had held me because I'm such a poor swimmer, but I didn't mention it. No way was I letting Simon touch me. I managed to keep from drowning long enough to get to where my feet touched bottom again. I wasn't acting as I staggered and fell to my knees, crawling out to the strip of rocky shore.

"Cut!" Simon shouted as we stood next to each other out of the water. At least he had liked the "no audio" idea, so we were saved from having to learn lines. A subdued Westwood approached us carrying his crossbow. Now Rafe had the arrow.

"How the hell is this going to work? The shifter won't give me back my arrow," Westwood whined.

"The camera is far enough away that it won't matter." Simon was losing patience. "Just stand there and pretend to yell at Gloriana like I'm sure you did that night."

"I'll jump over to you, grab the crossbow and aim it at your heart." I leaped until I was in front of Westwood.

"Right." Simon nodded to the cameraman. "We'll stop shooting, Valdez can hand you the arrow, and you'll fall down with it stuck between your body and your arm."

"That won't work. Vampires aren't real in this film, remember?" Greg pressed against my leg, and I had a feeling he was trying to see up my skirt. I kicked him away. "Ouch. Anyway, you'll have to run up like a mortal girl."

"Great, now I'm going to come across like I'm an ass, bested by a woman." Westwood threw down his crossbow. "This isn't going to fool anyone."

"Earth to Westwood. You *are* an ass." Rafe strolled up, kicked the crossbow out of reach and handed him the arrow. "Now fall down and show us death throes. We're all anxious to see you dead." Every vampire there smiled.

"I'm sick of this. Where's the respect? I could buy and sell the lot of you." Westwood cut his eyes toward Simon, who was conferring with the cameraman. "Except for Simon of course."

"Of course." Rafe smiled. "We *have* no respect for you, Westwood. You killed friends. Terrorized innocent people. You're surrounded by people who want you dead. Feel lucky you haven't had your head handed to you on a plate yet."

I admired the way Rafe intimidated the billionaire who'd backed up a few steps.

"And the way Rafe looks in those jeans? He deserves a reward, don't ya think? No way are you breaking up with him yet. The hell-raiser deserves a little more hell fun."

"God, but I'm sick of this."

"Me too, Glory. That wind's damn cold." Greg stood too close again. "Simon, can't we finish this?"

"All right. I've figured this out." Simon, still looking like Ray, strode to my side again. "Places, everyone. We'll use a wide angle to get the group of us here on the beach and Westwood. Then follow Glory as she attacks. Valdez, move and take that arrow with you."

Rafe snatched the arrow and got behind the cameraman.

"Gloriana, shout at Westwood, I don't care what. Without audio we'll just be seeing that you're steamed and reaming him out. Then charge and snatch the crossbow. We won't show his face until after the arrow's in, then zoom in for the kill."

"If only." I waited until the cameraman gave me the go ahead. "You murdering slimeball! I hate you. You killed Jerry's best friend, and he never did a damned thing to you. I'm going to tear out your throat." I ran up to him in what felt like slow motion but was probably normal human speed and ripped the crossbow out of his hands. My own hands shook as I aimed it at his heart.

"Cut!" Simon clapped his hands. "Perfect. Real emotion. You're a fine actress, Gloriana."

"Who was acting?" I jabbed Westwood with the crossbow

until he doubled over. "I hate this son of a bitch. Give me the arrow, and I'll finish him for real this time." I heard Alesa cheering and saying something about murder being terrific foreplay.

"No, you won't." Simon stalked over to Rafe and took the arrow. "Man up, Westwood, and take this." Westwood had been swearing and threatening to get even with me. "Now fall on the ground and play dead. We'll edit the film to make it work."

"I don't think it *will* work. Load the crossbow and let's start over." Westwood had a gleam in his eyes and forgot to block his thoughts. He wanted to kill me. Now that he was vampire, he thought he could do it right this time.

"No way in hell." Rafe was right there, standing between Westwood and the crossbow, the arrow in his hand. There was a crack and the arrow broke into two pieces.

"Damn it. That was my last arrow. I had those custom made, you know." Westwood stomped his foot.

"Save your tantrum. We're not impressed." Simon nodded at Rafe. "Good idea. Use the feathered end. Gloriana, pick up the crossbow and stand over him. Here's your motivation. You probably felt glad Westwood was dead but horrified too. Because you're not usually a killer."

"Simon, I was there, remember? And this is a home movie, not in the running for an Oscar." But I did think about that night and how I'd felt. Sick, relieved to have rid the world of a sadistic vampire hunter but in shock too.

"I don't want to make a shoddy product, Gloriana. Work with me here." Simon stood stiffly beside the cameraman.

"Fine. I didn't laugh and dance on his body, but I wasn't sorry either." I picked up the weapon. "Let's finish this so I can go home. Dawn is too damned close, and I'm feeling it." I was also coming way down from whatever high I'd enjoyed from all those margaritas. I was wet and cold and sick of everyone around me except for Rafe, who looked ready to body-slam anyone who touched me. I smiled at him gratefully.

"We're all feeling the dawn, but we have more than an hour left, plenty of time to get this right." Simon shouted out directions and everyone stepped out of the scene except for Westwood and me. "Action!"

I held the crossbow against Westwood's body and looked him in the eye. "I hate you. That fang necklace you wore taunted every vampire who saw it. I hope you die at the hands of a hunter someday and that the last face you see is someone who treats you like an animal instead of a human. Now die, you son of a bitch!" I shoved the crossbow into his stomach.

He overacted, of course, falling back with the piece of arrow clutched to his chest and making squawking sounds. I smiled and looked down at his twitching body, kicked him for good measure, then tossed the crossbow at his head. I turned and walked away, not sparing him another glance.

The other vampires in the crew clapped. Greg, who'd gone back to human form and was wrapped in a towel, even whistled.

Rafe tried to pull me into his arms, but I was too fired up.

"Let's get out of here. We're done, right?" I saw Westwood stand and brush off his clothes, the piece of arrow in his hand.

"With your part of the filming? Yes. Take off. You did well. I won't forget it." Simon looked at me with the promise that Westwood would pay for everything he'd done as soon as his money was safely in EV hands.

"Red convertible. Add turbocharged to my list of options." I smiled and headed for the tent. I'd had enough. Whatever Westwood did with his stupid video, I wanted no part of it. Just my reward. I wasn't being greedy.

Alesa called me stupid and started listing all the things I *should* have asked for. I let her yammer on. At least she wasn't tap dancing on my brain for a change. Noise, I could tune out.

Rafe was quiet as we walked to his car. I knew some kind

of showdown was coming. My stomach lurched as I climbed into his SUV. For once I wished the dawn would come quickly. If I fell into my death sleep, Rafe couldn't expect me to talk about what he was waiting to get into. I'd changed back into clothes that reeked of Ray. Oh, man.

Twenty

Rafe pulled into a deserted scenic overlook and parked. He turned off the engine, then looked at me.

"You have something you want to tell me?"

"Uh, what makes you think that?" We were in the middle of nowhere. Well, not exactly. From this hilltop, I could see the lights of downtown Austin in the distance. Things got dicey, I could shift out of here and fly home.

"Wuss. Things get dicey, you get naked and show the man what you've got. He'll forget his mad, and we'll have some fun." Sex. Alesa's solution for everything.

Rafe opened his car door and got out. He strode over to stare at the city. Keys in the ignition. I was so tempted to just hop into the driver's seat and put the pedal to the metal. Nope, I owed him this. I resigned myself to a confrontation and followed him.

"You stink of Israel Caine. You going to deny being with him tonight?" Rafe didn't look at me, just stayed focused on the incredible view. A romantic setting. What a waste.

"I gave him a ride from the party. He was checking out the place for his record label. They're having a thing out there." I put my hand on Rafe's back. "He was drunk on high-octane blood. It stirs you up, so he made a move. I just happened to be handy. Any woman would have gotten the same treatment. I said no."

Rafe finally turned to study me. "Why?"

"Because he wasn't the right man." Honesty. I couldn't fake a smile because I knew what came next was bound to hurt him. God, I hated that.

Rafe's mouth firmed. "I guess I don't have to ask who you think *is* right. You've been uncomfortable around me ever since our last time together." He picked up a rock and threw it into the darkness below, then turned to give me a crooked smile. "Guess I wasn't convincing enough."

"I'm sorry, Rafe. You know me better than I know myself sometimes." I sat on a large boulder a few feet away from the edge of the cliff. I didn't want to be the next thing he threw. "You were great. Wonderful. Most of this is *my* problem. But you've changed since we became lovers." I sighed. "Really since you dropped the guard-dog act. You never call me Blondie. Never tease me like you used to." I saw his fists clench. Obviously I was hitting one of his hot buttons. "What's the deal, Rafe? I hardly know you now."

"Miss your guard dog? Shit, Glory. You never did know the real me." He moved closer. "Yeah, I called you Blondie and used a voice I heard in a movie once. It was a persona I put on with the dog body."

I stood and reached out to take his hand. "Damn it, Rafe. You know I never looked down on you. Certainly never treated you like a dog. We were best friends. I was comfortable with you. Always."

Rafe sat on the boulder and pulled me down beside him. "No, you treated me with respect. One of the many reasons I fell for you, I guess. You have any idea how much I hated staying a freakin' dog around you? You did it for five minutes. Try five years. The wisecracks helped keep me sane." He laughed. "If I am, after all that time with four legs and fur."

"Why'd you sign up for the gig if you hated it so much?" I leaned against him, comfortable again. *This* Rafe I knew.

"Blade. We had a contract. It's a deal he made with my grandfather, and it became a matter of honor. I couldn't let the old man down by breaking it." Rafe shook his head. "No way was Blade giving me a break and letting me out of it."

"He's a businessman. A contract is a contract to him." What else could I say? "I'm sorry, Rafe. But you're off the hook now."

"Are you kidding? Blade claims I still owe him. Like there's a loophole I didn't jump through. Back to the honor thing. I don't want Blade complaining to Gramps."

"Your family means a lot to you, doesn't it?" I squeezed his hand.

"A shifter's family is a lot like a Highlander's clan. We're tight, loyal." Rafe hit our clasped hands on his hard thigh. "I served my time, Blondie, but your sire made it clear in L.A. that we weren't done. Seems he didn't like the way I helped you keep secrets from him."

"You were being loyal to me!" I bumped against him. "I'll talk to him, Rafe. This isn't fair." Easy to promise, but could I deliver? Especially when he found out . . .

"Save your breath. At least he paid me. When Blade calls in his next favor, I'll handle it and we'll be even." Rafe pulled my hand to his lips. "When's he coming back?"

"Thursday, for your opening." My insides quaked. "God, Rafe, what's he going to do when he finds out we were together?"

"He doesn't own you. But you mean a hell of a lot to him. Let him know that if he kills me, you'll never forgive him. Am I right, Blondie?" Rafe grinned, showing those dimples I loved, and ran his tongue across my knuckles.

"Hell, yes, you're right. But I wonder if he'd care what I thought after such a wound to his pride." I put my free hand on Rafe's chest. "Maybe it would be safer if we took a break."

"Safer for who? I'm not afraid of him." Rafe's eyes narrowed, and his grip tightened. "He's never hurt you, has he?"

"No, of course not. But I won't be responsible for anything happening to you, Rafe. Look at this great opportunity you've got with the club. A new life." I ignored Alesa stabbing me in the forehead. This was the right and kind thing to do.

"Like hell." Stab. Stab.

"This is it? You're done with me?" Rafe jumped to his feet, dragging me with him. "Why am I surprised? Friends. Comfortable friends. Shit." He stared down at me. "And the hot sex? Was that just friends with benefits?"

Tears filled my eyes. "Rafe, I love you, you know that. But I think we do make better friends than lovers." I felt a tear slide down my cheek.

"I really don't think I can go back to just sitting at your feet, Glory. I love you too. But it's way more than as a pal." He looked away for a moment, his chest heaving as he took a breath. When he looked back, his eyes were glowing red. "Damn it, it's always been him. Your Mr. Right. I know where this is going. You're going back to Blade, aren't you?"

"If he'll have me."

Rafe's eyes threw off a heat that made me back up a step. He spun, and a bush across the clearing burst into flames.

"Rafe!" I jumped toward the car. Before I'd gone two feet, he was beside me, holding me, the bush just a charred, smoking stump and pile of cinders.

"I'm sorry, Glory. Say you don't mean it." His eyes were back to brown. "The Scot doesn't deserve you. And what we have . . ."

"Oh, God, I'm sorry." Tears spilled down my cheeks. I hated to hurt him. "We, uh, had a fling. You're a wonderful lover. But Jerry . . ."

"Forget Jerry. He's a bad habit. Give me more time to show you that what we have together can be so much better. You love *me*, Glory, and not just as a friend. Friends don't scorch the sheets like we did." Rafe jerked me closer.

"That was just sex, Rafe. I don't deny you lived up to your reputation. Like Nadia said, you're talented. But you know how I feel about Jerry. Listened to me whine about it often enough." I touched where his dimples would show when he smiled. Please, please, smile again. Not happening. "I'd like to stay friends with you if we can. I miss laughing together, Rafe."

"We can laugh again." He turned his head and captured my thumb with his lips, gently sucking it into his mouth.

Yeah, I let him do it too. What was the matter with me?

"You're getting with the program. Remember how this guy was in the sack, kiddo." Alesa sighed. That was enough to get me to jerk my hand away from Rafe's incredibly sexy mouth.

"Stop this. You're only going to get hurt, Rafe."

"No, I won't. Don't you see? What we have now is so much better than before. We can be friends *and* lovers. I love you, Glory." He tried to kiss me, but I shook my head.

"I know that, Rafe, and it means the world to me. But this won't work. And what was with the red eye?" I pushed him back with my hands on his shoulders. "You scared me just now. You burned a freakin' bush to the ground. What happens if you get mad at me?"

"I'd never hurt you. Surely you know that." Rafe slid his hands around me. "You can trust me, Glory."

"I always have. But then I didn't know you had demonic powers." I shivered. "I know pure hellfire when I see it. I feel heat myself when Alesa wants to jerk my chain." I ripped off my jacket and tossed it to the ground when Alesa blasted me to prove the point.

"I'm sorry, Glory. I won't do that again. I'm usually more in control than that, but you blindsided me." Rafe looked around. "To be honest I'm surprised this whole hilltop didn't go up in flames. The thought of you with Blade again . . ."

"It may not happen. I'm going to have to tell him about us. His pride may not allow him to take me back after that." I could see that thought cheered up Rafe. Me? I felt my heart tear and my gut twist. Not Alesa's doing either. She could care less about Jerry. But then she didn't know him. Didn't have a clue about love and our history. Jerry had said he didn't want to live forever in a world without me. How much worse would it be to live in a world with him in it but know he wanted nothing to do with me? I shuddered and realized Rafe had read my thoughts. He slid his arm around me and gave me a hug I needed badly. Still my friend. Impossible.

"I hate to say it, but from where I sat for five years, seemed to me you could usually bring Blade around." Rafe didn't smile, but he wasn't giving off hell heat now either.

"We'll see how it goes." I dredged up a smile. "Thanks, Rafe. Is it any wonder I love you?" I made myself put some space between us. "Can I do what you just did? Flame something?" Might come in handy. As long as I was stuck with Alesa, I should get something out of her.

"You could. And turn people into crispy critters too." Rafe clearly struggled to stay in friend mode.

"Cool. Wish I'd known that. I'd have loved to set Westwood's hair on fire."

"For God's sake, promise me you won't ever do anything like that." Rafe grabbed me, his hands biting into my arms. "Every time you use one of your powers, you remind Lucifer you're up here. Hate to think he'd send a minion to see what's up." He let me go and looked around, doing a three-sixty of the view. "Damned dumb of me to remind him I'm around. I've had to do a couple of jobs for him. They're a bitch." He shook his head and turned back to me.

"I'm sorry, Rafe." Now I was really freaked out.

"Aw, Glory, this just makes him more interesting. Don't dump the guy. Kiss and make up." Alesa poked me in a few places to make her point.

"Promise me you'll never try to flame anyone or anything. You hear me?" Rafe pulled me into his arms.

"Loud and clear. I've got enough problems with Hell Girl here. I sure don't need a visit from her buddies down below." I leaned against him. My legs felt heavy, and the sky seemed to be lighter in the east.

Rafe noticed. "I'd better get you home. Ray didn't score any points with you tonight?"

"Nope. The pass was more of a kneejerk reaction than a serious effort. Anyway, drunk or sober, he's done." I sighed and slipped away toward the car.

"He's a fool, then. Because I'm not." Rafe beat me to the SUV and opened the passenger door. He pressed me against the steel frame, his arms blocking me in. "We've got lots going for us, Glory. When Blade finds out about us, you'll need a friend. That's me. Here for you, always."

His hard body felt good against me, and I tried not to react to it. Too bad I remembered how we'd been together.

"This guy is a keeper. Don't be stupid, Glory." Alesa pushed me closer, but I wasn't having it.

"You won't tell Jerry about us, will you?" My heart dropped to my toes, then bounced around my body a few times before landing in my throat, a bowling ball in a pinball machine.

"No, that's on you. But too many people have seen us together. If you don't want him to find out the hard way, you'd better get to him quick." Rafe slid his hand down my arm, reminding me that we did have chemistry. My demon girl shouted a *"Hell, yes!"*

I slid into the seat, feeling that tinge of morning in the air weighing me down and dread smothering me. Rafe slammed my door, then got into the driver's seat and started the engine.

"So it's all going to come out. Nice of you to stand by ready to play catch when Jerry kicks me to the curb."

"Yep, I'm your man, Blondie, and don't you forget it."

"Call Westwood's ranch and arrange for the children to meet at your shop tonight at midnight." Simon wasn't asking, as usual.

"Tonight?" I glanced at Flo and CiCi, who'd just arrived at my apartment. They were here for moral support and good gossip. I'd just handed out some Blud-Lite and wasn't in the mood for Simon the dictator.

"The video's ready. I'm sure you'd like to get this done."

"You're right. I'll make the call. Hope they can make it."

"Tell them you have positive proof that'll help them get their father's estate settled by end of business tomorrow. That should light a fire under them." Simon laughed. "I'll meet you in your back room at half past eleven to fill you in on the story we're using. I think you'll enjoy it."

"Oh, I'm sure. Everything to do with this has been a laugh riot. If they can't make it, how do I—" I was talking to dead air. Okay, I guess Simon was counting on them to jump on this and counting on me to do his bidding.

"Sorry, ladies, I've got to make this call." I'd programmed in David Westwood's number and hit speed dial.

"Westwood."

"Hi, this is Gloriana St. Clair. You asked me to call if I had proof your father is dead."

"Yes! Are you telling me you found something?" David sounded excited, not grief stricken. He obviously realized it. "I mean, of course we hoped the old man would be found okay, but either way, we need to know what happened, you know?"

"I get it, David. Can you meet me at my shop tonight at midnight? I have commitments before then." If I'd had a father like Brent Westwood, I'd be shooting off fireworks at his funeral.

"Sure, I'll bring my sister with me." David cleared his throat. "You really have something? The lawyers keep putting us off, and we're stuck here on the ranch with this ridiculously inadequate allowance. You wouldn't believe it."

"Just bring that reward you mentioned because I'm going to have proof that will help you settle the estate by tomorrow." I ignored the questioning looks I was getting from CiCi and Flo.

"You're kidding me! Finally!" David couldn't hide his relief. "We'll be there. Midnight."

I ended the call, then turned to face the music.

"What's this about, Glory?" CiCi put her glass on the

coffee table. "Westwood? And I heard Simon Destiny's voice on that first call. What are you doing consorting with that creep?"

"Seems Brent Westwood's now a vampire. I didn't kill him after all. Simon's got him out at the EV camp. He wants Brent's money. We made a video so it looks like Brent's whole vamp-hunting Web site thing was bogus. He'll reveal himself to his kids tonight so he can gain access to his money. Simon will get it, then Brent is going to pay in more ways than one." Whew. How was that in a nutshell? I collapsed on the couch.

Flo sat next to me and hugged me. "So stressful. How did this video go? Was Rafael with you every minute?"

"Yes, he was." Tears. Of course he had been. Like he always was. Why was I dumping him? Oh, yeah, in a desperate effort to keep Jerry, the love of my life. As if a prideful Scot would want me once he found out I'd cheated.

If only we could have a sizzling reunion first. A night that would convince him Glory was still his girl no matter who else she . . . Oh, hell. I knew better. Jerry would have his broadsword out and up Rafe's butt before I could stop him. Then he'd drop me like a hot rock. My friends were staring.

"What?"

"You made a video. What's in it?" CiCi sat on my other side. Her presence was a great comfort. I wanted to bawl.

"I pretend to kill Westwood again, but he jumps up afterward." I sighed. "Tonight we'll show the kids the video. Westwood will appear and confess to being a lying loser and a nutjob. Not sure how Simon is setting up this scenario." I managed a smile. "Simon's rewarding me, so it's not all bad."

"But you didn't want to do this. Why'd you go through with it?" Flo frowned. "No reward is worth it."

"Blackmail. Simon hid a video camera in the back room. He has tape of me confessing my fling with Rafe. Then another of Rafe and me kissing, making it obvious we were lovers. He threatened to send it to Jerry while he was in Florida. I couldn't hurt Jerry that way."

"That bastard!" CiCi hugged me. "No wonder you were drinking so heavily at the shower. Drowning your sorrows. Did you have to work on that video last night too?"

"Yes! And that's not all." I let some tears fall. "I'm possessed! Richard tried to kill a demon in my shop, but he didn't. It's—it's inside me. It talks to me, urges me to do bad things. I'm pretty sure that's why I slept with Rafe in the first place." I knew as soon as I said it that I was lying. At least about Rafe. I'd had fantasies about him way before Alesa had moved in.

"Exactly. You wanted that hottie first. But giving him up was stupid. No demon would ever do that. You've been one tough nut to crack."

Exhausted by Alesa's nonstop harping on the subject, not to mention my own agonizing over the hurt I'd caused Rafe, I sobbed and fell against CiCi's shoulder. Oh, probably shouldn't have done that. She had on a nice cream Chanel jacket that my mascara was ruining. But when I tried to pull back, she held me firmly against her.

"You're hysterical, Gloriana. Calm down. That's probably just your conscience talking to you. Cheating on Jeremiah with a shifter. That's not like you."

"CiCi, I think she's telling the truth." Flo patted my shoulder. "Ricardo chased a demon in her shop. He said prayers, threw the holy water on it. But I guess it's possible it climbed into our Glory's body. *Aye, Dio!*" Flo crossed herself. "What can we do?"

"Call Richard." CiCi said firmly. "Obviously we need an exorcism or something." She crossed herself too and pushed me back to study me. "Still, we can't rule out guilt. What were you thinking, Gloriana? You had Jeremiah, such a fine man, wrapped around your little finger when I left here."

"Hah! That man can't be wrapped." I sighed. "What I mean is, I love him, but Rafe, well, we got really close. And he's a fine man too." I looked to Flo for confirmation.

"He is. He saved our lives, CiCi. And he's handsome." Flo kissed her fingertips in a classic Italian gesture. "Glory wanted a little something extra. Who can blame her? He lives in this very apartment in my old bedroom. Temptation, eh?"

"A recipe for disaster." CiCi disapproved.

"Or for *amore*, right, Glory?" Flo winked.

I sat up, wiped my eyes and decided to come clean with them and myself. "It's leaning toward disaster. I can't blame the demon for this. Rafe is sexy, made moves, and I let it happen. But now I've decided Jerry's my guy, and I want to be with him. If he'll still have me. As for the demon, I'm dealing with her. She hurts me sometimes, but I've got her under control."

"Control? As if, bitch. Someday I'll show you what I can really do." A megahot flash had me bolting for the kitchen. I opened both refrigerator doors and stuck my head in the freezer until a blast of cold air hit my cheeks.

"What are you doing? What's the matter with you?" CiCi and Flo had run after me.

"The demon—Alesa is her name—punishes me by giving me these heat waves." I grabbed a handful of ice from the icemaker and shoved it down my bra. "I'll be all right in a minute. Sit. Finish your drinks. I've got to go down to the shop in a little while, and we haven't figured a way out of my man trouble yet."

"So when is Jeremiah coming back?" Trust CiCi to get back to the issue at hand.

"Late tomorrow night, but I won't see him until Thursday. We'll all be at the opening of Rafe's club. Rafe and Nadia have arranged a special table for us on one of their balconies." I sighed, hoping that part of the evening went smoothly.

"I saw the ad in the newspaper. Israel Caine is performing." CiCi raised an eyebrow. "The tabloids had you engaged to him. Interesting story there?"

"Not nearly as interesting as it should have been." I polished off my bottle of Blud-Lite, a tingling awareness reminding me of its side effect that would torture me for the rest of the evening. "If Jerry's it for me, I can't go messing around with every guy who makes a pass, now can I?" I turned to Flo. "Flo, you can understand. It's like you are with Richard."

"Monogamy. Yes. I admit I'm surprised I am in it. But a man like Ricardo? He's enough for me." Flo waved her hand with the diamond ring on it. "So *arrivederci*, Israel. What about Rafael?"

"I told him we're done too. He's not happy, but he's accepted that we can only be friends again." I said it but wasn't sure I believed it. "Maybe he's just going along so he can pick up my pieces when Jerry explodes and dumps me."

"You really think when Jeremiah finds out that you and Rafael . . ." Flo stared down at her hands.

I grabbed one of them. "You've got to make Richard keep his mouth shut, Flo! At least until I can tell Jerry myself."

"I'll try to stall him, but, Glory, Ricardo is determined to tell Jeremiah as soon as he sees him. His conscience is bothering him." Flo looked up, her eyes sparkling with unshed tears. "I'm really sorry, *mia amica*, but you'd better hurry up and spill the garbanzos. The *merda* is about to hit the fan."

"Westwood's staying in the back room, and we'll bring his children here for the reunion." Simon rubbed his hands together, clearly in high spirits. "You'll love the story we've cooked up for the time their father's been missing."

"I don't love any part of this." I opened the door and glanced into the shop. I did have a business to run and should get out there and help Erin deal with customers.

Greg grinned. "Brent's been in rehab." He slapped Westwood on the back.

That got my attention. The former hunter had been silent since they'd arrived at my back door promptly at eleven thirty. Guess he was nervous about seeing his kids after months of making them think he was dead. Serve him right if Viv brought her crossbow and plugged him herself for the deception.

"Rehab? Drugs? Alcohol? Oh, wait, sex addiction. That's a trendy one." I looked him up and down. "But a tough sell."

That earned me the first spark of life from old Brent.

"Bitch. I've had many beautiful women. I wouldn't waste my time on a fat ass—" Brent shut up because he had Greg's fist in his mouth. Wow, who knew?

I grinned. "Thanks, Gregory. What brought that on?"

"Hey, you and I hooked up. The man insulted my taste in women. Can't have that." Greg shoved Westwood toward the bathroom. "Stay inside until Simon calls you out. Shut the hell up until you're told to speak. Got it?"

"Another hot guy you did? Wow, Glory. Let's do him again."

I ignored my horny demon and Brent's glare when he wiped his bleeding mouth with his sleeve.

"Gee, Brent, look. You're bleeding, and my fangs can't even work up interest. Bet you had to pay top dollar for those beautiful women." I grinned when he growled but just stomped into the bathroom without another word. "What have you done to him, Simon? Shown him the energy vacuum pump?"

"Among other things. He has to realize he's a fledgling in our world." Simon smiled. "I'm keeping my offer open, Gloriana. Female Energy Vampires are unheard of, but I may make an exception in your case." He put his hand on my shoulder. I blamed my demon for letting it stay there. "I sense an interesting new element in you."

I stared into his eyes and let the red show. How I could do it on demand I didn't know, but the heat shooting up into my eyeballs told me it worked. Simon's hand slid off. Oh, he tried to hide the freak-out, but I wanted to high-five myself for giving him a scare.

"When there's a snowstorm in Hades, I'll be in touch. For now, you know where to shove that offer." I strolled over to the door and opened it. "I'll be in the shop and let you know when the Westwoods get here." I strutted out of the room, shutting the door with an emphatic click.

"That's showing him, girlfriend. You join any club, it'll be the one downstairs with my boss."

Oh, swell. Now I had Alesa's approval. Which convinced me telling Simon off wasn't my smartest move, since I still wanted that car. But it had been so worth it for the look on his loathsome face. Bet he couldn't read my mind now either. Hah.

I'd love a chance to go mano a mano with the EV leader now. Even if I had to try on my new demonic powers, it would be great to grind that SOB into dust, flame him into ashes or—

Oops. The Westwoods were here. Vivien wore a turquoise print wrap dress and heels straight from Paris. Her purse cost more than my entire shop inventory. Guess she'd bought it before the pitiful allowance edict. David didn't hurt my eyes either, getting most of his looks from his mother's side. He wore snug hand-distressed jeans and a vintage T-shirt, obviously not seeing this as the formal occasion Viv did. Or maybe Sis was just desperate for a place to show off and figured a vintage-clothing dealer would give her duds the respect they deserved. I did a quick mind scan. Yep, got it.

"Well, hello, you two. Glad to see you're not swathed in depressing black." I smiled. David's shirt was a faded red.

"What's the point? It won't bring Dad back." Viv brought a lace hanky to her eyes. Oh, how fake was that? "What've you got, Ms. St. Clair? It's late. This better not be a lame attempt to shake us down."

"Viv, ease up. Glory . . . if I may call you that." David smiled at me when I nodded. "Glory is helping us. I told you she thinks this will get things settled quickly." David looked around. There were two customers browsing the dress rack, and Erin, of course, obviously interested in our conversation. "Is there somewhere we can speak privately?"

"My back room. Follow me. I have something to show you there anyway." I led the way. How easy was this? Of course both of them balked when they saw Simon and Greg waiting.

"Who's this?" David put his hand protectively on his sister's arm.

"I'm Dr. Simon, and this is my associate, Mr. Kaplan. We're sorry you've been going through this trying time." Simon was all concern and sympathy. It worked with the kindly face he'd put on. He looked middle-aged and had silver hair. He'd even slipped on a white doctor's coat while I'd been in the shop.

"A doctor? What does this have to do with Dad's disappearance?" Vivien looked at me. "Was Daddy sick?"

"You could say that." Simon nodded to me. "Gloriana, why don't you show the children the video their father made right before he 'died.'" He gestured toward my laptop set up on the table. "It's ready to go."

"We saw a crazy video one of his bodyguards took with Dad being shot by one of those so-called vampires. One that looked a lot like Glory here." David smiled at me. "Nonsense of course."

"I admit now it *was* me. He asked me to play vampire that night to his hunter. I tell you it was just the last straw. Watch this, and you'll see what I mean." I walked over and pushed the button to play the DVD. We all gathered around. I had to admit this was a five-star production. All that was missing was the swelling music and credits. Instead we got a scan of the lake as swimmers came into view.

There we were—me, the Ray look-alike and Valdez the dog. We crawled out onto the beach, and Brittany came into the picture. Westwood stalked up, ranting about something. He was clearly agitated and totally overacting before he aimed that crossbow.

"That's Dad!" Vivien leaned closer. "It looks like he's going to shoot you, Glory. That's insane."

"No kidding. And the lake was freezing. I was shivering."

David leaned in. "It's obvious you were cold." He was trying to hide a grin, and I wanted to smack him. This from a grieving son? Of course I knew how to rock a wet T-shirt.

"Just keep watching your father." I moved back so David

could get a closer look when I ran up to confront Westwood. The camera came in for a tight shot of my face and those boobs. I jammed the crossbow into Brent's stomach. Then he was down, rolling around with the arrow until he gasped and "died."

"Oh, my God!" David paled. "That's the proof we need."

"Shut up, Davy. That's Daddy lying there." Vivien was crying for real now, mopping at her tears with that piece of lace. I grabbed a paper towel and handed it to her. Who knew she had a heart under that sophisticated veneer?

"Keep watching, you two." Simon kept a sympathetic face, but he practically quivered with excitement.

David and Viv leaned closer. We all saw me throw down the crossbow, kick Westwood, then strut away, Valdez and Ray already out of the shot. The camera stayed on Westwood's body. Suddenly Brent sat up, tossed away the arrow and brushed off the dirt and leaves. He looked directly into the camera, gave it a thumb's up and made a cut motion with his hand across his throat. The screen went black.

"What the hell was that?" David looked at Vivien, then at me. "Glory? Did you or did you not kill my father?"

Greg opened the bathroom door, and Westwood stumbled out.

"She did not."

Twenty-one

"**Daddy!**" Vivien rushed into his arms, sobbing. He hugged her, his own face wet.

David didn't join in the family reunion, clearly unsure what he was feeling. I put my hand on his shoulder.

"It was a setup, David. I'm sorry I couldn't tell you sooner, but I was sworn to secrecy. Insane, wasn't it?"

"Why? What's this all about?" Vivien was drying up fast and pushed back, remembering she'd been jerked around by this act.

"Where the hell have you been, Dad?" David stared at his father, still not making a move to get closer.

"Uh, rehab." He looked at Simon. "The doctor here has been helping me figure out some things. I'm sorry you were worried."

"Worried? We thought you were dead!" David looked ready to smash my laptop. I grabbed him before he could start.

"Oh, no, you don't. Hit *him*, hit your dad, but not my hardware." I aimed him at Westwood. "This is his fault. He wouldn't let his own children know he was alive."

"Why? And what's the rehab for? Drugs? Alcohol?" Viv

put a good distance between her and her father, clutching David's arm.

"Sexual dysfunction." I saw Westwood jerk like he'd taken a hit from Simon's Taser. "After Brent made his billions and sold the company, his problem got worse. So he set himself up as a great hunter to feel powerful. Overcompensating, the doctor said." I strolled over to slide a fingernail along Brent's collar. I felt hatred coming off him in waves, but he was struck dumb, courtesy of Simon. I loved it. "The vampire thing? Well, you know what they say about the fine line between genius and insanity." Uh-oh. Brent was close to stroking out.

"Why'd the doctor tell *you* this?" David looked from me to Simon.

"Gloriana was trying to help your father. They were in a relationship that clearly wasn't working. She's the one who got him to seek help after the night of the video." Simon was nothing if not quick. "Your father agreed but hoped for a magic pill." Simon shook his head. "Not everything can be fixed with medication."

"Why vampires? That's so weird." Viv obviously couldn't wrap her head around this. "Really, Daddy, what were you thinking?"

Simon steepled his fingers. "Vampires are a classic phallic symbol. Powerful, eternal. By pretending to kill them, your father acted out a sexual fantasy."

Greg nodded, happy to get in on this. "Even using the crossbow is significant, isn't it, Dr. Simon?"

"Oh, yes." Simon was clearly on a roll. "The penetration—"

"Enough!" David flushed and looked everywhere but at his father. "I wish you'd come to one of us, Dad." He glanced at me. "Glory, I guess we should thank you for sticking with him."

Viv scanned me from head to toe. I had on my usual uniform of slimming black pants and a colorful top, this one purple with a deep V-neck that made the most of my assets. None of it was expensive, but I didn't look like a pauper either.

Easy to read her thoughts. I may be four hundred plus, but I look early twenties. Shopkeeper looking for a sugar daddy hooks up with middle-aged billionaire?

"I never took a dime from Brent, did I, baby?" I dared him to disagree.

"No. Hell, no. Else why would she still be working in this dump?" Brent, allowed to speak, showed some of his old spark.

"It's not a dump, Brent." I turned back to Viv. "Sorry, but this mess has ruined our relationship. That stupid video did it for me. His plan was to kill me acting like a vampire, but I couldn't stand it. So I stuck it to *him*. I'd had enough." I felt Brent tense, but he knew better than to argue with Simon in command.

Simon and Greg nodded solemnly.

"When I confronted Brent later, he broke down and admitted he needed help and let me call the doctor. I'm sorry, but your father decided he'd rather you think him dead than acting so crazy. Especially if he never got better. Isn't that right, sugar lump?" Brent nodded when I jerked his hair.

"Daddy? Are you better now?" Viv eased closer.

"Yeah. Totally over that vampire shit." Brent elbowed me, and I let him go. It had been gross touching him anyway.

"See? All better." I smiled at Viv. "But he and I are history. Brent never respected my devotion to vintage and classic clothes. Love what you're wearing. Paris?"

Viv's face lit up. "Yes! From the cutest little shop—"

"Cut the crap, Vivien. David, did you alert the lawyers that things are going to be settled soon?" Brent shot Simon an anxious look, obviously told to get down to business.

"Yes, sir. We didn't know . . ."

"That's all right, son. Glory's correct. I wasn't in my right mind. But I'm ready to get my life back now."

Westwood glanced at Simon, who gave him a nod of approval. "Yes, you've made remarkable progress." Simon smiled.

Brent turned back to his children, who looked shell-shocked.

"I'll be at the ranch tomorrow night to meet with the lawyers. I'm sorry I put you two through this. Wasn't thinking straight. Obviously." He walked over to Simon. "I'll need more time in Dr. Simon's hospital. It's an excellent facility right outside of Austin, and where I've been staying."

"Nice to know that *now*, Dad." David had moved from shock to bitterness.

"Let's start over, son. I'll see that you both have a generous increase in allowance. David, you can have that yacht you wanted and, Vivi, that Swiss chalet."

"Thanks, Daddy." Viv hugged him and kissed him on the cheek.

David held out his hand. "I'm sorry, Dad. Vivi and I talked about your Web site. It didn't make sense coming from the dad we knew. We should have come to you. Tried to help you ourselves."

Westwood clasped his son's hand. "Well, it's over now. No more vampire talk. You two can go back to your lives, and I'll go back to the hospital till I get my head on completely straight."

"Sexual dysfunction?" Viv glanced at me. "I don't see—"

"Trust me, you really don't want to know." I smiled and opened the door into the shop.

"You're right." Viv looked at David. "Let's go. Dad, we'll see you tomorrow night. You can't come with us now?"

"No. Tomorrow. Have the lawyers there. I want access to my money." Brent smiled at Simon. "So I can make a donation to the hospital. They're miracle workers."

"Sure. Will do." David finally hugged his father. "Glad you're back, Dad." He pulled an envelope out of his pocket. "Since you knew where he was all along, Glory, I don't think you should get this check." He smiled and ripped it in half.

"That was rude." I watched them hurry out of the shop. Bet they couldn't wait to discuss dear old dad and his "condition."

"Glory!"

I turned and shut the door to the shop. Wouldn't want the customers to see the weirdos in the back room.

"Yes, Brent?" I smiled. "Or should I say, sugar lump?"

"Sexual dysfunction? Was that necessary?" Brent's hands were fisted.

"Sorry, guess that was a low blow." I laughed when Brent lunged, but Greg caught him in a headlock. I turned my back on him. "Dr. Simon, I hope you're satisfied and that we're done."

"Oh, yes. Well satisfied. Your reward will be in the alley tomorrow night. Red, you said?" Simon gave me an approving look.

I grinned. "Turbocharged. I'd kiss you, Doctor, but I haven't had a tetanus shot. Please spare my customers and leave by the back door. Good night."

I headed into the shop, so relieved to see the last of that crew I wanted to cry. Just being in the same room with Westwood and pretending to tolerate him had taken all my acting skills. I felt drained and sank down on the stool behind the counter. Alesa whined and complained, clearly hot for Simon. No surprise there. If anyone was marked for hell, it was Simon Destiny.

Flo's bachelorette party. Favorite seductress. Too bad I'd been so busy I hadn't figured out who mine was. Luckily owning a vintage-clothing store gave me a treasure trove of costumes to choose from. After taking care of all the last-minute details for the party and a trip to the alley to sigh over my beautiful new car, I threw together an outfit.

By the time I strolled into Rafe's club, I knew I looked pretty good and felt in full seductress mode. I was early so I could supervise the setup. The music was on and booming through Rafe's awesome sound system. Great choice, the kind of tune that made you want to bump and grind into a hard body. I grinned when a hunk in a loincloth, his perfect body oiled, showed up on cue with a tray of Blott-O.

"Nice job, Trey." I took a glass. "And the costume is perfect. Tarzan?"

"I tried to get Rafe to put up a vine. Don't you think the ladies would go for a jungle yell and me swinging their drinks to them?" The shifter grinned and flexed his pecs.

"They'd have loved it. But this works. Just watch your neck." I sipped my cocktail and checked out the scene. The club looked great, the lights dim with colored spots high-lighting the tables. I'd arranged for centerpieces, and they'd been delivered during the day. I strolled over to inspect the bouquets of Flo's favorite red roses decorated with party fa-vors of lipsticks and nail polishes in all the colors my friend loved.

"Nice arrangements."

"Rafe!" I turned and sighed when I saw him. No loincloth for him. He was elegant in a tux and white satin shirt. Not a button or stud held that shirt closed, exposing his very fine tanned chest down to where the shirt was tucked into slim black tux pants. Yum. I knew it was a bad idea but couldn't resist moving in to kiss his smile.

"Your club looks fantastic."

He hauled me against him. "Thanks. I'm proud of what we've done in such a short time." He slid his hand down to cup my bottom. "Like the costume. Seductress. Who are you, exactly?"

"I'm a woman I knew during my gold rush days in Cali-fornia. She could have any man she wanted. Sang in the sa-loons and couldn't carry a tune." I smiled and ran a finger down that delicious band of bare chest. Not wise. Didn't care. I was into my seductress role, and Alesa egged me on. "No one noticed. She'd flash lots of cleavage and some leg, and guys fell at her feet."

"Sounds like someone I know." He grinned, then backed up. "You dumped me. Quit teasing." He looked me over and frowned. "That dress was any lower, you'd be showing nipple."

"So?" I swished my red silk skirt. "How do you like my garter?" I was playing a dangerous game but couldn't seem to give a damn. Seductress. I'd never been one, but a girl could dream.

"Hey, together we can get any man we want. Go for it, girl-friend." Alesa had a point. I'd noticed she was getting more powerful and harder to resist.

I put my foot on a chair and slid my skirt up to show Rafe the red and black garter high on my thigh. I didn't need it to hold up my black fishnet panty hose. But what made him swallow was the fact that I hadn't worn panties under those hose.

Rafe had his warm hand on my leg before I could have a second thought. "What's gotten into you tonight? You said you're going back to Blade. Tomorrow night. What is this? An invitation for a farewell—"

I put my hand on his mouth. "No. Forget it. I'm obviously out of my mind. But I can't stand the idea of never being with you again either." I sighed when he moved between my legs, shielding me if one of the waiters came by. "I'm going crazy, Rafe. Alesa's gigging me with hard, pointy objects whenever I try to think."

"I'm starting to like her. And I wouldn't mind gigging you with something hard myself right now." Rafe bent his head to tease my lips open, barely tracing them with his tongue. His fingers were doing the same, tracking along an erotic path where the seam of those hose hugged the damp crease between my legs.

I sighed into his mouth. "I . . . can't, Rafe. You know why."

"Sure you can." He pulled me toward his office, making me stumble as my leg fell off the chair. "We've got a few minutes, and we've proved we can have a lot of fun in a few minutes. I'll take a farewell quickie."

I balked at the door. "No. This isn't fair to you."

"Screw fair." Rafe grinned. "No, screw me instead." He coaxed me inside and shut the door. Before I could stop him, he had me against it, kissing me like there was no tomorrow. Wait. There *was* no tomorrow. Not for us. I shoved, and he lifted his head, giving me a look that promised endless pleasure. This whole scene was so on Alesa. I had to figure out how to get rid of her. Fast.

"I'm so sorry, Rafe. This is not happening. Now I've got to go. My guests will be here soon." I jerked open the door and made my escape. I couldn't look back. Didn't want to know what he was thinking. Stupid costume. And damned stupid demon. A wave of heat hit me, and I gasped. "That's a cheap shot, Hell Girl," I muttered and headed to the bar for a glass of ice. "Heat me all you want. Set my hair on fire. I don't give a damn. I'm not playing with any more men. Tonight's about Flo."

"This is the most amazing party ever." Aggie was a Siren, of course. The ultimate seductress. She'd left the fish tail at home, not good on dry land. Her tiny top was made of mother of pearl, and her blond hair flowed to her waist. Her low-riding mini was made of more mother of pearl scales. The tiny starfish nestled in her hair were actually alive. Sort of an ick, but cute too when they waved at you.

"Your party was really the gold standard." I belted back more of the hard stuff, hoping it would lift my mood. My fake smile was wearing thin. At least everyone else seemed to be having a good time. Cleopatras, Marie Antoinettes and several Marilyn Monroes scarfed down drinks, flirted with the waiters and hit the lavish buffet. Diana was Scarlett O'Hara, and CiCi had come as Catherine the Great.

"I love your waiters." Flo was channeling, well, Flo. Only she'd dragged out a vintage Flo. I loved her roaring-twenties flapper dress. The iridescent beads were a brilliant red and gold. She wore the dress with new high heels and had already persuaded a waiter in a tiny toga to dance with her.

"You're not the only one. Did you see Richard's mother?" I grabbed a refill from Jimmy the bartender, who kept jumping over the bar and strolling through the ladies in his Speedo and a gold medal that looked like the real deal. He and the waiters had large bills in their waistbands even though the drinks were on the house. I didn't ask how they earned their tips.

"Are you kidding?" Flo laughed. "Now I've got something on her. Let Mother Mainwaring try calling me out again, I tell you. I'll threaten to tell her son how she acts around hot guys." Flo clinked glasses with me.

"She's been gone a long time. And I'm sure not paying that shiftless shifter for those hours." I'd noticed Mata Hari a.k.a. Sarah Mainwaring in her beaded bra and harem pants slip away to one of the balconies with a waiter in tight bike shorts over an hour ago. I actually thought she was lucky to have someone to take care of the urges this Blott-O stirred in all of us.

"Should have done Rafe." Alesa sounded a little drunk and didn't bother to throw heat at me. I ignored her.

"Are we playing games?" Aggie was getting antsy, and I didn't blame her. Standing around drinking and listening to music wasn't cutting it. Then the lights dimmed.

"Ladies, gather close to the stage. The entertainment is about to begin." The male voice was achingly familiar. Was Rafe going to dance after all? Did I want him to? For this crowd?

"Of course we do. Take it off!" Alesa started a chant that rattled my brain.

"Entertainment?" Flo grabbed my arm. "What is it?"

"Wait and see." I was caught up in the sea of women—there were about fifty of us with all the out of towners—and we surged toward the stage. The lights were down to pitch black when a throbbing beat started. Sex, that's what it sounded like, throbbing, pounding, skin-to-skin, hot and sweaty sex. A spotlight hit the man on center stage, and my heart stalled. He wore a black satin mask, but I knew who filled out that tux.

He moved and the women sighed. Those hips. No surprise that they handled the beat perfectly. All that blood with a kick I'd gulped pooled right where I knew it would. I wanted to jump on that stage and drag him away by his dark hair. Oh, yeah.

Mine. No, he wasn't. I'd rejected him. As a lover anyway.

He danced close to the edge, daring us to touch him and using those hips to toy with us. When a vamp from France tried to grab him, I wanted to rip off her arm and beat her with the bloody end. Rafe just grinned and danced out of reach.

Oh, God, give me strength. The place smelled like lust, every woman there screaming for him to come and get her. My mouth was dry, my fangs down while I gripped the rim of the stage, flanked by Flo and CiCi. They both looked as fired up as I felt. His shoes were shiny black and caught the light as he turned so we could see his super fine butt flex in tight black pants after he tossed away his jacket.

"Ahh." The ladies loved the butt action.

He'd worn a loose bow tie around his neck. Now he jerked it off, twirled it and tossed it to CiCi in the crowd. Another grin and his dimples forced a moan from me. CiCi clutched the tie like she'd won a big prize.

"Take it off. Take it all off," my elegant friend crowed.

I wanted to slap her.

He just winked and toed off his shoes, kicking them aside before he ripped his belt out of his pants and cracked it like a bullwhip. One of the werewolves in the crowd howled and begged him to crack it her way. He flicked it twice more before he threw it behind him and slowly unbuttoned his cuffs.

"Oh, yeah. Keep going, *generoso*." Flo looked like she wanted to crawl onto the stage and bump and grind against him.

"What would Richard say?" I whispered.

"Who?"

He pulled his shirt out of his pants, then turned his back on us again. Oh, yeah, teasing. He shimmied and shook the shirt off until it puddled on the floor. We yelled as his back flexed and he raised his arms to show off his muscles.

"Gawd, I like a man who knows what he's got." Aggie leaned closer and lost a starfish. She didn't even bother to pick it up.

He turned to face us again and unbuttoned his waistband.

Except for the throbbing music you could have heard a pin drop. I swear none of the vampires bothered to breathe. And when the zipper slid down? Every woman there leaned forward, me included. I should have put up a barbed wire barrier. One of Lacy's were-cat friends looked ready to spring.

Black satin briefs. Very skimpy briefs. Oh, my. Yes, I'd seen what stretched that satin, but none of the others here needed to. My guy was turned on doing this. Yes, he was. He stared at me, his eyes dark and intent. Like we were alone in this enormous room surrounded by women who whooped and hollered like they'd managed something wonderful. There were high fives all around. I wanted to clear the room and take Rafe where he stood. I licked my lips and felt Flo and CiCi bump against me, dancing to the music. Reality check.

"Keep goin', big guy." CiCi did not just say that.

Suddenly the lights went dark, total blackout, and the shock kept even the vampires from seeing. When the lights came back up a minute later, we all stared at the stage, empty except for a pair of black satin briefs.

"Oh, *mio Dio*, but I need a drink." Flo leaned against me on one side, CiCi on the other.

"What a floor show." Aggie grinned. "That guy was so totally hot. I'd like to know where he went."

"Yes, well, he's not dessert on the menu." I tried for a smile but failed, finally handing Aggie her starfish and gesturing toward the buffet I'd ordered for the paranormals who could eat. As usual, it was getting heavy play. Lacy and Erin flirted with two of the waiters as they filled plates and fanned their flushed cheeks.

"You know, I think I recognized him." Flo gave me a sidelong glance. "But I won't say anything. Any more surprises, Glory?"

The lights flickered, then dimmed again. "Ladies, here to perform for his special friend and the bride, Ms. Florence da Vinci, N-V presents Israel Caine!"

"Oooo." Loud squeals, and there was a stampede toward the stage again.

Tears pricked my eyelids as I followed a thrilled Flo and CiCi. That Ray would do this for her . . . Especially after the way we'd parted. He walked to the edge of the stage and leaned down to kiss Flo on the lips. He waved to the crowd, then winked at me.

"Ladies, I hope you brought your dancing shoes. The band is with me, and we'll run through our set. Are you ready?"

"Yes!" There were cheers and squeals, and Lacy actually cartwheeled around the room like a kitty on a catnip high.

"Okay, then. Flo, get up here. Sit next to me for this first number. I seem to remember this song is one of your favorites." Ray walked to the edge of the stage and held out his hand. My sophisticated friend blushed as she let him help her to the piano bench. He settled her next to him, then sang a ballad she'd asked for the night she'd announced her first marriage to Richard. There wasn't a dry eye in the place.

"Oh, wow. You're an idiot to let that one get away. Tell me we're dumping the Scot and going for him."

I sighed. Alesa didn't get it. If you had a soul mate, you held on to him. It didn't always make sense. It just *was*. But gestures like this were why Ray would always be dear to me.

He and the band rocked the house. We all danced, the waiters dragged into partnering on some of the slow ones. And wasn't that a treat with their skimpy costumes? I longed for Rafe to come out of hiding and dance with me, but he was too smart for that. The less face time he and Ray had before the club opening, the better.

Ray's set was almost finished when Aggie spoke up.

"Hey, Candy Caine, what about that duet you sang at the Grammys? Aren't you going to sing that for us?" There were encouraging cheers and whistles.

"Sorry, Aggie, but Sienna Star's not here tonight. Glory didn't invite her." Ray grinned at me. "Wonder why?"

I grinned back. "I like Sienna, but decided she really didn't know Flo and her special friends well enough." Translation: The mortal would have ended up on the buffet.

"Well, how about you let me take Sienna's place? Willing to give it a try?" Aggie held out her hand.

Ray laughed and glanced back at his band, all mortal and without a clue that they were surrounded by paranormals. "Why the hell not? You're dressed as a Siren, right? Let's see if you've got the pipes of one."

"Prepare to be amazed, sweet cheeks." Aggie leaped onto the stage, then perched on the closed grand piano. She made quite a picture in her mini and tiny top with that awesome hair. The waiters quit serving just to watch. When the song started, not a male in the house could have been kept away. Even Rafe hovered in the wings. Much to my relief, he'd changed into jeans to keep his identity a secret.

The duet was a love song of course. Aggie's voice was hypnotic, and the band didn't play, just let Ray do the acoustic thing with the piano as he and Aggie sang together. It was a showstopper and we froze until the last golden notes hit the air.

Aggie and Ray smiled at each other, then Aggie looked out at the crowd. Clearly she could have her pick of any man and several of the women there.

"Hey, Tarzan!" She ran her finger down the middle of her outfit. "How'd you like to swim in my . . . lake?"

A jungle yell, then Trey leaped on the stage, threw Aggie over his shoulder and carried her laughing out of the club. That seemed a fitting end to the party. Everyone clapped and pronounced the event a roaring success. I was exhausted and exhilarated. I jumped on the stage to thank Ray as he accepted a final kiss on the cheek from Flo.

"Thanks for this, Ray." I sat next to him on the piano bench after waving good-bye to my euphoric friend.

"No problem. We needed to run through the set before the opening. Actually found a few things that need adjusting that the crew can fix today while I'm asleep. I told the guys to hurry out of here, but I have a feeling a few of them are going to get a tumble with a vamp woman tonight. Don't think they'll mind or even remember it." Ray bumped shoulders with me. "Hot costume. I like."

I looked down. Yeah, I bet he liked. I'd burst out of the top. Too much dancing. I shoved down one of my boobs.

"Thanks. Flo was thrilled that you did this, but I guess you could tell."

"She loved the whole party. Saw your shifter doing his thing from the wings before we played. That was quite a show." Ray played a bit from the song "The Stripper."

"Shhh. No one knows who the mystery man was."

"So I have something on him now." Ray grinned. "Excellent. Guy danced like a pro."

"He's been around hundreds of years. Maybe he's done it before." I yawned. "Dawn's coming. I just wanted to say thanks."

"I didn't do this for you. I told you, I've moved on." Ray played some drama music, and it sounded ominous as hell. "I did it for Flo and access to the club tonight. That's it."

"Fine. I get it. But you're a good guy, don't try to deny it. 'Night." I stood and started to walk away but was jerked to a stop by his hand on my skirt.

"Be careful with the shifter. Nadia's dropped some hints. He's got a dark side." Ray lifted my skirt, looked under it and grinned. "Damn, girl. Forget something?"

"We're done, remember?"

"Doesn't mean I can't appreciate a fine ass when I see one." He winked, then got serious again. "Remember what I said. You and me? I get it, not happening. But that doesn't mean I want to see you hurt. Just keep your eyes open is all I'm saying."

"Thanks." I jerked my skirt out of his hands. "I don't want to see you hurt either. Nadia's been around a long time. Keep your eyes open too."

Ray laughed. "Babe, I can handle women, even vamp ones. But I'll be around, and you can see for yourself. Chip's studio here is where I'll be recording my new album. My throat's better in Austin for some reason. Don't know why but something in L.A. messes with my voice."

I started to reach for him, worried that he'd had problems, but stopped myself. "Okay, then. See you around. And don't worry about me. I can take care of myself. Just tell Nadia to stay out of my business."

"I heard that." Nadia strolled up from the wings. "No problem, Glory. Ray and I just thought you should know a few things, but you're a big girl." She looked me up and down. "A very big girl. We'll butt out of your business."

"Thanks a lot." I started to stomp off but made myself take a moment. "And thanks for the use of the club, Nadia."

"You'll be getting a bill. Or at least your friend Florence will. Rafael may want to do you favors, but I'm strictly business and don't you forget it." Nadia had her hand on Ray's shoulder. She slid it up to touch his jugular in an intimate gesture I couldn't possibly miss.

"Right. Good night." I started to stalk off the stage, then stopped and turned. Nadia had crawled into Ray's lap and had her tongue down his throat. "Oh, Ray."

He came up for air. "Yeah?"

"I'm glad you're feeling better, and remember, I'll always be your friend." I was rewarded by Nadia's frown. "'Night." I smiled and sashayed over to the bar where I picked up one more glass of Blott-O and drained it.

"Woo-hoo! Way to shove it in that bitch's face!" Alesa crowed.

I looked around for Rafe, anxious to talk to him about that dance and Nadia's insinuations. Was it his demon side that bothered her? Hell, I could handle that. I looked back to where she had her hands all over Ray again. I felt a hitch in my heart. Not right. He was a free agent, but that didn't mean I didn't have the urge to fry her where she sat. Too bad it would torch Ray too.

"Yeah, let's test those powers. You could wipe out this whole place with a look, hot stuff."

Oh, no. Not going there. Alesa wanted it too badly. And

wasn't that something to think about when I wasn't drunk on my butt? I hit the door, and the cool night air sobered me a bit. Dawn was still over an hour away, but I was tired.

"Buy you a drink, pretty lady?"

I smiled and faced the man lounging next to the door. "I think I've had more than enough. But you can carry me home." I glanced down. "My feet hurt. New shoes."

Jerry stepped out of the shadows and pulled me up into his arms. "I would have come inside, but I think I'm over-dressed."

"You're right. You'd have been a big hit in your kilt though." He had on jeans and a dark shirt. His hair was windblown, like maybe he'd come straight here from Flor-ida. "I'm glad to see you." I pulled his head down to kiss him. Oh, yes, this was my man. He tasted right, fit perfectly against me. But we were in front of Rafe's club, and he could come out any moment. I pushed back. "You bring your car?"

"It's right down the street." Jerry ran a finger along the edge of my bodice. "What's with the costume?"

"I'm supposed to be a seductress."

"It's working." He held me tighter.

"Let's go to your place."

"Yours is closer." Jerry started walking down the sidewalk.

"Rafe might come in. He lives there too, you know. Let's go to yours." I saw Jerry's Mercedes and nodded toward it. "We need privacy if I'm going to show you my cancan. I'm a dance-hall girl, you know." I ran a fingertip around his ear. "We're notorious for our . . . dancing."

"I'd like to see you . . . dance." He grinned and stopped next to the car. After he unlocked it, he settled me inside. "Not much time tonight, but we'll have more when we wake in the evening, won't we?" He kissed me, then slammed the door, getting us going in record time.

My stomach knotted. When we woke, I was going to have to tell him about Rafe. I listened to Jerry's report on his Florida trip while he sped through the deserted streets. He was happy, glad to be back and eager to be with me.

I felt like the lowest kind of slut, unworthy of his trust. He had no clue what I'd been up to while he'd been gone. And did I have any doubt he'd been faithful in Florida? Not one bit. I knew Jerry. He assumed we were together and that meant we were exclusive. Oh, God, but I'd ruined everything. For once I could see no way to fix the mess I'd gotten myself into.

Twenty-two

"Okay. Let's see this cancan." Jerry lounged on his king-size bed, stripped down to his briefs.

I savored the sight of his rough-hewn body. I'd explored every inch of it at one time or another yet never tired of the journey. He was so unabashedly male.

"Forget the dance." I flipped my skirt at him. "Come here, lover."

His eyes darkened, and he sat up to pull me between his legs. "I like it when you call me that. Now let me see what's under that skirt." He drew it up, just as Rafe had. No, no, no. Had to get that name out of my head.

"What's this? You're a bold lass." He took the garter between his teeth, sliding his hand under my leg to pull it up next to his hard thigh. He worked the garter down, his warm lips grazing my skin.

"I like it when you call me that." I combed my fingers through his thick hair, terrified he'd wonder . . . It didn't take long. He made it to my knee before he released the black elastic with a snap.

"You wore this to Valdez's club tonight." He gazed into my eyes, probing. "Why?"

"A seductress wouldn't wear panties, now would she? And I hoped you'd make it back before dawn." I shamelessly reached between us to slide my hand inside his briefs. "I was right, wasn't I?" Distraction. Of course it worked. I hadn't lived four hundred years for nothing, and I was fighting for my future. I wanted Jerry to have a wonderful night before I gave him my confession.

"You go, girl. Whatever it takes. This man is yummy." Oh, God, was I going to have Alesa in this bed too? I couldn't stand it. I ordered her to close her eyes and shut the hell up. *"In your dreams, sunshine."* Her laughter mocked me.

"Gloriana," Jerry groaned, then he ripped off the hose before flinging me onto the bed.

I looked up at him and realized I couldn't do it. Couldn't make love and pretend nothing had happened while he'd been gone. I put my hand on his chest when he tried to come down on top of me.

"No. We need to talk."

"Now? When dawn is so close?" Jerry smiled and palmed my breast. "I've missed you."

Oh, God. I hated to do this. Hated to ruin what we had, and this would do it too.

Jerry pulled me into his arms and nuzzled my neck. "I brought us something from L.A. to share later. Look on the nightstand."

I recognized the bottles instantly. "Ian's daylight drug." The Campbell enemy made the potion that allowed vampires to stay awake for a little while past dawn. My heart stalled. "Oh, Jerry, I'd love to see a sunrise with you."

"Had the Devil's own time getting it, but I've always wanted to make love to you as the sun came up." Jerry kissed me. "Stop now, no tears. We'll do it tomorrow night."

Would we? I knew that after I told him about Rafe, making love would be the last thing on Jerry's mind. I managed a smile.

"I'd love that. But we can't skip the club opening."

"You sure? Spending an evening watching Israel Caine isn't my idea of fun."

"He came to the club tonight and sang for Flo. It was so sweet." I eased out of Jerry's arms.

"Sweet? Doubt that." Jerry frowned. "Probably trying to score points with you. Did he?"

"I'm not on his radar, Jerry. Ray's into Nadia now. He just did it for Flo, and so he could practice his set. We have to go tomorrow night. Flo and CiCi are looking forward to it. Think of it as a wedding party." I pushed him away and sat up. "I'm serious. We need to talk."

"On the bed." Jerry grinned. "Whatever you say, *lover*."

I stood and stepped back. "This is serious, Jerry."

"All right, then. Talk." He still smiled, obviously thinking I was playing.

"You knew that Rafe is part demon and didn't tell me." I lifted my chin. "Didn't it occur to you I should have been clued in about that when you made him my bodyguard?"

"What the hell?" Jerry jumped up. "Did he use his powers around you?" He put his hands on my shoulders. "Why can't I hear your thoughts? Damn it, quit blocking me."

"I'm not blocking you, Jerry. No one can hear my thoughts now." I sighed. "Sit and listen."

"What the hell's going on, Gloriana?" Jerry touched my cheek, his concern so real, so complete, I wanted to throw myself into his arms and sob.

"I had a couple of visits in the shop from a she-demon who claimed to be married to Rafe."

"*Claimed? I* am *married to that cheating asshole. The Mayor's annulment is a nonstarter. It's till death do us part, sweet cheeks.*"

"Shit." Jerry put his arms around me. "How bad was it?"

"She attacked me. I called in Richard, and he did some things to try to get rid of her. He thought he'd obliterated the bitch. But instead, she slithered inside me." I took a watery breath.

"*Bitch? Take this, bloodsucker.*" Alesa hit me so hard I

collapsed, a wave of nausea and heat sucking the life right out of me. Anything she'd done before seemed like a love tap.

"Gloriana? What's the matter? Love?" Jerry laid me on the bed. He patted my cheeks, then bit his wrist and held it to my lips. A drink from him and I finally came back from wherever I'd been.

"When Alesa gets mad, she hits me with heat. That was worse than usual." I sat up with Jerry's help, but the room spun.

"Watch your mouth, that's all I'm sayin'." Alesa huffed and puffed, so maybe a serious hit took something out of her too.

"Damn it. You mean she's still inside you?" Jerry paced the rug next to the bed after I nodded. "Can't Richard do something about this?"

"I've asked him about it. He's researching. Maybe he'll know something tomorrow night." I sighed. "She talks inside my head, Jerry. It's a running commentary."

"You can't be serious." Jerry stopped in his tracks.

"Oh, yes. She's driving me crazy."

Jerry pulled me to my feet to hold me. "I'm sorry."

"I like this guy. He's hot. So quit talking and get with it." Alesa just had to remind me she was on board.

If I bitch slapped myself, would she feel it? I almost tried it.

"Gloriana, this is intolerable. I never should have hired a demon to guard you." Jerry stroked my hair, his arms strong around me.

"You had no way of knowing this could happen." I sighed and pushed back to sit on the bed again. "But maybe this is a sign. You should let him off the hook. Rafe told me all about it."

Jerry frowned at me. "What is this? Best buds sharing secrets? That's why he still owes me, Gloriana. Valdez's first loyalty should have been to me. A demon bride. Damn it, I guess it's a miracle he kept you safe for five years."

"He'd die for me, Jerry. You know that. He's proved it more than once. Give him a break." I reached for his hand.

"This is between Valdez and me, Gloriana. I'm worried about this demon. You say Richard will be at the club tomorrow night? I want his take on the situation. We'll get rid of this demon for you. No matter what it takes." Jerry ran a hand through his hair, his sure sign of agitation.

It was now or never, and never wasn't really an option. "I have something else to tell you."

"What?" Jerry sat beside me. "Something about the demon?"

"No, it's . . . well, maybe it's connected to the demon." I took a breath and tried to unclench my fists. Couldn't do it. Oh, God, but I hated to hurt Jerry. "While you were gone, I, well, Rafe and I hooked up."

Jerry moved fast, like only an ancient vampire could. He suddenly stood across the room, his hands fisted, his back to me. His nearly naked body trembled with rage.

"Hooked up." He said it so quietly only vamp hearing could have picked it up. "That's modern slang. It means . . ."

"We slept together."

He turned in a blur and pinned me with blazing eyes. I squirmed and wanted to disappear.

"Tell it like it is, Gloriana. Vampires don't 'sleep together.' Sleep is death to us. Vampires fuck. You fucked Rafe. He fucked you. Is that right?" His voice was cold, hard.

"Yes." I picked at the bedspread. Tears filled my eyes and spilled down my cheeks. "I'm so sorry, Jerry."

"Are you?" He stared at me like he was trying to figure me out, this woman he couldn't read and no longer knew. I shuddered with a chill and for once wished Alesa would throw me some heat. "Why?"

"Because I love *you*. It was a mistake. Rafe is my friend. I was a fool, thinking what I felt for him was more than friendship. It wasn't."

"How nice that you found that out by screwing him first." Jerry's laugh killed me. "How was it with the shifter? Did he do it doggie-style?" He streaked across the room and lifted me by my shoulders. "Did he? Was this the first time? Or did he shift into human form when he was with you before for five long years. Your dear friend. How close were you, Gloriana?"

"I swear, Jeremiah, it wasn't until after Alesa got inside me that I gave in to the urge—" I shut up. Too late.

"So the urge was there, but then the Devil made you do it. What a convenient excuse. And then I left town so you didn't have to sneak around." Jerry released me, and I fell back to the bed. "Obviously you didn't bother since I'm sure Richard knows and Flo, of course. Who else?" Jerry's dark eyes bored into me. "Christ, is every vampire in Austin laughing at me because my woman lifted her skirts for a damned dog?"

"Rafe's not—"

"You will not defend him to me, Gloriana!" Jerry roared, yes, roared until plates in the downstairs china cabinet rattled.

"Please, calm down. I love you, Jeremiah, only you. I will never be with Rafe again. I told him that. That it was a mistake." I wanted to touch him, to melt some of the steel out of his jaw with a kiss. But the blaze in his eyes and stiff posture warned me away. He didn't say another word, his face hard. Just stalked into his closet and grabbed black trousers, stepping into them and zipping them up. Next came a white shirt that he buttoned while he slipped into black loafers.

"Go home, Gloriana. You can find your way. Go to your lover. He is still living with you, isn't he?" Jerry's gaze scraped over me, brutal as a fist, as he waited for my nod. "How . . . convenient." He picked up his wallet and cell phone and strode out of the room. Then I heard the back door slam. A plate shattered in the dining room. Too many vibrations.

I sat there for a minute or maybe five. I didn't bother to check a clock. I was numb. Well, not exactly. Numb would have been way better. This ache radiated from my chest. Like I'd been body-slammed into a concrete wall.

What had I expected? I'd cheated and, even worse, betrayed him with a shape-shifter he'd trusted. Jerry's pride was hurt, and I'd acted like the lowborn slut his mother had always called me. Mag Campbell would love this.

I jumped up, suddenly scared that Jerry had left here with violence in mind. He could be hurt, or worse, going up against a man with demon skills. I tried to call Rafe to warn him but got voice mail. I left a two-word message. "Jerry knows." It was enough. Surely Rafe knew I'd never forgive him if he killed Jerry. Then I ran to the closet. Broadsword still there. Stupid, of course it was. I think I would have noticed if Jerry had gone charging out of here with it.

He had two. I hurried down the stairs and sighed with relief to see his spare hanging over the mantel, where it belonged. Okay, he was using his fists and fangs, not his usual weapon of choice. Then again, maybe he wasn't going after Rafe at all. Maybe he'd decided I wasn't worth it.

I didn't know how to take that. Jerry's disdain was what I deserved. But to never be with him again . . . Worse. To lose his love and respect. I fell to the floor in front of the fireplace and gave in to the sobs that had been building inside me.

"He'll come back. He was hot for you before, he'll be hot for you again. I'll give you pointers." Alesa's voice hit my last nerve.

"Shut up, you stupid bitch. Don't even pretend to understand an honorable man." I slammed my head against the floor. "I've lost the best thing I had in my life." Jerry. God, I hated what I'd done. Didn't see any way he'd ever forgive me. Alesa stayed silent, rightly figuring I'd reached my limit with her.

I shuddered and wiped my eyes on my petticoat. I had to get going, and indulging in tears wasn't getting me anything but swollen eyes. I let myself out of Jerry's house, leaving my key on the kitchen counter. It was the right thing to do, but it started the waterworks again. So, as I shifted and flew home to change, it was a crying mockingbird that flew through the night toward Sixth Street.

N-V was packed, with a long line of ticket holders eager to hear Israel Caine at the door. Not that I had to wait in a line.

I whammied my way to the front and was ushered inside, a special guest of the owners. Nadia greeted me, radiant in a red mini. She was actually friendly, obviously certain I was no competition, and claimed Rafe was busy in the back. Just as well. I didn't have a clue what to say to him except to ask him to hide from Jerry, and I doubted he'd do that.

I settled into my chair at our reserved table. Flo and Richard were there, along with CiCi, Freddy and Derek. Damian arrived with Diana on his arm, causing all of us to wonder if that old affair might be heating up again. The empty chair next to me caused comment, which I waved away with a vague mention of Jerry's business problems.

"Richard, do you have a minute?" I smiled at him and nodded toward the hall.

He glanced around the table. "Darling, Gloriana and I will be right back. Need anything?" He kissed Flo on the cheek.

"No, take care of my friend. Tell her about your conversation with Jeremiah earlier." Flo smiled at me, but I could tell she was worried.

"We'll only be a few minutes." I touched Flo's shoulder. She looked gorgeous as usual in a bright blue designer dress with a fabulous diamond pin holding up one shoulder. Her dark hair was pulled back, and she glowed with happiness, except when she looked at me. "I'll be okay. You're the bride. Enjoy this week. Promise not to let my messes worry you."

"We will fix your messes, I hope. Last night's party was the best." She stood and hugged me, then shooed Richard away. "Go, take care of my BFF."

"On it." Richard smiled and took my elbow. He found a storage room, and we stepped inside, then shut the door.

"Can you help me get rid of this demon, Richard?"

"*Oh, please. Like this pious asshole can help you. Remember who got us together in the first place?*" Alesa turned up the thermostat, and I grabbed a pamphlet to fan myself.

"I brought my things. When the show is over, we can go to your place and try an exorcism." Richard put his hand on my shoulder, then snatched it away. "God, Glory, you're burning up."

"You don't have to tell me that. Alesa shoots me with hellfire on a regular basis." I wished for ice and looked around. A vent was overhead, and I stood under it. Thank God Rafe had the air-conditioning going.

"I have to warn you, Gloriana, this demon is stronger than any I've dealt with before. The very fact that she was able to get inside you after what I did in the shop proves that." Richard took the paper I handed him and began to fan me too. "Obviously you're desperate."

"Damn right." I sighed. "Just do your best, Richard."

"Hah. Let him try. I'm not afraid of his puny holy water routine." Alesa cackled, and the hairs on my arms stood up. *"By the time I get through with you, Glory St. Clair, you'll be Lucifer's sock puppet. Just wait and see."*

"Flo said . . . You talked to Jerry?" I realized Richard wasn't meeting my gaze. "I told him about Rafe. He lost it."

"I know. He came by the house. I tried to calm him down. Put the blame on this demon. It seemed as good a reason as any for you and Rafe." Richard's smile was wry. "My bride told him the same thing. Flo will do anything to make you happy, Gloriana, and thinks you want to be with Blade."

"She's right. Flo's the best." I sniffed but refused to cry again. I usually healed fast, but too much drinking and demon were taking a toll, and I knew I looked like hell. I'd pulled out a low-cut red dress to distract but had a feeling my fake smile wasn't fooling anyone.

"I hated hurting Jerry, but what's done is done. I just hope Jerry can look past it and we can figure out a way to move on." I sighed. "Thanks for trying, Richard. I know he's your friend, and I don't want you caught in the middle."

"Oh, that won't happen. Flo and I are leaving on our honeymoon right after the wedding. We hope you two will resolve things before we get back." Richard tried to touch my shoulder again but shook his head. "The heat. Still can't believe it."

"Believe it." I headed back to our table. Jerry was there, looking so good and so completely unconcerned that I'd arrived that my heart broke. He was laughing with CiCi and the rest of the crew, then signaled the waiter for another round before he stood to hold out my chair, always the gentleman. As soon as I was seated, he turned back to Damian.

"Bachelor party tomorrow night at my house to give Richard a proper send-off." He smiled at Freddy and Derek. "You two'll be there, right?"

"Wouldn't miss it." Freddy glanced at me. "Glory, can you send over that male stripper you had here? Mother won't quit raving about him. The rest of the guys won't appreciate him, but Derek and I'd like a peek."

"Nope, that was a onetime deal." I grinned at them. "Flo, you allowing Richard to have a female stripper at his party?"

"Allowing?" Jerry finally looked at me. "Surely Richard doesn't ask permission to do as he pleases. Do you, Richard?"

"No, Florence is free to pursue her interests, and I'm free to—" Richard grunted. "Well, maybe not." He laughed. "I have a very expensive shoe pointing . . . Well, gentlemen, since I hope to enjoy my honeymoon, we're changing the subject."

Everyone laughed, and the waiter arrived with refills of the Blott-O Nadia had available for vampires who came to the club.

By the time the show started, the place was packed, standing room only. We settled back to watch the show, a great Israel Caine performance. Ray coaxed Sienna Star from another balcony table to sing their famous duet, and they brought down the house. When the lights finally went up, I turned to say something to Jerry, but he was gone. He'd shown up just long enough to greet old friends, and that was all. Damn.

We said good-bye to the rest, then Flo, Richard and I headed to my apartment. To my surprise, CiCi insisted on coming along.

"I have some things to try if Richard's exorcism doesn't

work. I hope you don't mind." CiCi pulled a tote bag from her car, parked at the curb near my shop.

"No, not at all. I just hope I don't need anything else." I turned to Richard, who had his own bag of tricks with him.

"Relax, *mia amica*. Ricardo has done this before." Flo slipped off her shoes and settled on my living room couch.

"Yes, but exorcisms are tricky. No guarantees. And I'm no longer a priest, you know. I can bring you one, if you wish." Richard took my hand.

"No, we'd have to whammy a real priest, and he'd be freaked by the whole vampire thing anyway." I squeezed his hand. "I think you're my best shot, Richard. Where do you want me?"

He pointed toward the bedroom. "In there. Florence, you two wait out here. I don't need an audience."

"Fine." CiCi opened my laptop. "Do you mind if I do a little research, Glory?"

"Help yourself." I followed Richard into my bedroom. I admit I was scared. What would Alesa do during this? She'd hit me pretty hard just for calling her a bitch.

"That's right, honey. So get ready. Priest Boy's going down." Alesa sounded gleeful.

"Richard." I grabbed his arm. "Alesa's gearing up. Please promise you'll stop if it looks like my head's going to explode or spin like a top."

"Of course. There's no point in exorcising the demon if I kill you doing it." Richard patted my hand. "Now you feel cool. That's a good sign."

"Or really bad." I looked toward Heaven. "Oh, Lord, give me strength." I crossed myself even though I'd never been Catholic.

"Take off your shoes and lie on the bed. Close your eyes and let me do my thing. No matter what, try to lie still and not fight me." Richard sounded so serious my stomach flipped.

My eyes snapped open. "Wait. Don't hurt yourself. Flo would never forgive me. Promise. If it looks like Alesa is trying to jump into you, stop. I'll keep her if I have to."

I heard a trill of hysterical laughter that shredded my nerves. *"Are you kidding me? Inhabit that uptight prick? I'd as soon live inside your beat-up dresser, numbnut."*

"Close your eyes. Here goes." Richard began reciting prayers and sprinkling me with what I figured was holy water. I hissed as heat seared me and the water sizzled. Great. I'd turned into a damned griddle. Sweat ran down my sides, and I cursed myself for not changing out of that cute red dress. Forget dresses. When my head blew and my brains hit the ceiling, what I wore wouldn't matter. My arms twitched and my feet drummed the mattress, but I knew Alesa was still on board.

Richard's voice got louder and more desperate. I was so drenched now that I appreciated my waterproof mattress pad. He touched my shoulder and my forehead, then jerked his hands away with a yell. I figured Alesa had given him a jolt of electricity. Running feet and the door crashed open.

"Stop!" Flo's voice. *"Mio amante!* Look at your hands."

My eyes popped open, and I sat up. Flo cradled Richard's blackened and charred hands.

"Richard, no! We're stopping this." I fell back.

"It didn't work, did it?" Richard croaked.

"Hell, no, it didn't work. How'd you like that demo, Glory? You could do that. Scorch anyone who touched you. Or flame them with a look. Talk about power. Major buzz, baby."

"She's still here, and she's gloating. Give it up, Richard." I sighed. "I guess I'm stuck with her forever."

"No, we're not giving up." CiCi held some printed pages. "Flo, give your husband a drink, heal him, and then send him home. Time for plan B. Glory, are you game?"

I sighed. "What can it hurt? Right now I'm Alesa's bitch. Couldn't get much worse." Or at least I hoped not.

Twenty-three

I jumped in the shower while Flo gave Richard some of her juice, then sent him protesting on his way. She and CiCi decided to start with a clean slate. CiCi changed the sheets while I was in the bathroom. I came out in my robe ready for whatever.

"Before we start, I want to be clear. Don't risk yourself, CiCi. I won't let you or Flo sacrifice—"

CiCi held up her hand. "Florence and I are perfectly safe." She pulled out two beautiful jeweled rosaries with large crosses. "Blessed by a saint and two Holy Fathers. There's also a small piece of the ankle bone of a sainted nun hidden in a compartment in the back of each cross." She pressed on one to reveal a tiny opening in the gold. "See?"

"Wow. But still . . ."

"I'm not finished. Florence sleeps with Richard, who this demon hates, and I am from a long line of priests, popes and cardinals." She stepped close to me and poked me in the chest. "Listen to me, demon. You dare to jump into me, and I'll run straight to the Vatican. How would you like that?"

"Gaaa! Get this pious bitch away from me. She's giving me the hives."

I smiled. "Alesa got the message. We're clear."

"Fine. Now we use logic. We make the host intolerable to the demon. Glory, Alesa's from hell. What would she absolutely hate?" CiCi had a notepad, hell's secretary.

"Let me think." I sat on the bed.

"Swell. When she's done, she can write Exorcisms for Dummies." Alesa was all snark.

I smiled at CiCi. Desperate times and all that. Maybe the very fact that Alesa was making fun meant she was afraid. "She's from down below." I nodded to CiCi. "So I say we go high. What do you say, Alesa?"

"Heights?" A few octaves higher than usual. *"No problem for me. No, sirree."* We were definitely onto something.

I nodded at CiCi and mouthed "Write it down."

"Hey, Your Hellness. You're so crazy about heat. How do you feel about cold?"

"Oh, no, not the cold. Even Lucifer can't get me to Siberia or the poles. Not even with insulated underwear and no matter how many souls I could snatch there. I'm not freezing my ass off." Alesa poked me until I doubled over. *"I mean it, vampire. You pull something with cold, and you'll regret it. I swear that on Lucifer's crown."*

"Oooo. I'm scared. Seems cold is freaking her out." I hugged my pillow. "Well, CiCi, what do you think?"

"I think we go to the roof first." CiCi grinned. "You able to get dressed?"

"Definitely." I sucked it up and jumped into jeans and a T-shirt. How high could I fly? Would it be enough to make Alesa jump out? Where would she go? Did I care? Bottom line, could she if she tried? Oh, no, I had to believe . . . Anyway, Flo was all for going with me, and we shifted into birds.

We flew straight up until we hit clouds. Alesa screeched and singed my feathers. Flo finally made me head down when I started smoking. We landed on the tallest building in Austin.

"What do you think, Glory?" Flo was a pretty blue bird while my mockingbird had pitiful blackened wing tips.

"She's still here so look out below!" We jumped off the ledge, dive-bombing the sidewalk. I heard some nasty language inside my head, but all that got me was a roaring headache and flop sweat before we pulled up at the last minute.

"Glory, that's one stubborn demon you have there." CiCi met us as we shifted back in the alley near Rafe's club, which had closed for the night. "You look like hell. Can you keep going?"

"I have to. What's next?" I leaned against the brick wall, my head pounding, my clothes soaked.

"You'll see." CiCi put her finger over her lips. "Rafe is letting us in. Here he is."

"What's going on, ladies?" Rafe frowned at me. "You're wet." He looked up at the cloudless night sky. "Get caught in a sprinkler system or a car wash? Or did you get run over by one of those street-cleaning trucks?" He took my arm and helped me inside. "Seriously, you look terrible, Glory."

I was grateful for his support. "Alesa's been busting my chops. We're working on our own exorcism since Richard's didn't do the trick." Rafe didn't seem to mind that I was getting him wet as I sagged against him. "Opening seemed to go well."

"It was great. Nadia's pleased. We're well on our way." Rafe grinned. "So what's this about my walk-in cooler? If this hadn't been a restaurant once, we wouldn't even have one."

"The demon hates the cold, Rafael. We're going to freeze her out, eh, Glory?" Flo tugged me toward the kitchen when Alesa balked and made my legs go limp.

I would have hit the floor if Rafe hadn't grabbed me and picked me up.

"I hope this is worth it. In wet clothes?" I clung to Rafe as we got to the cooler door.

"You can change into my extra shirt." Rafe winked at Flo. "Not very warm though. White satin."

CiCi gasped. "You were the one! The dancer."

"Don't tell anyone, CiCi. I did it for Flo." Rafe looked from CiCi to Flo. "What did you think, ladies? How'd I do?"

"Are you kidding?" CiCi bumped her hip against his. "You get lonely, you know where I live."

"CiCi! Remember why we're here? Demon on board." I wanted to scratch her eyes out but knew I had no right to be jealous. Flo murmured something to Rafe in Italian, which he answered as he kissed her cheek. I noticed he avoided touching those crosses the ladies wore. My semidemon friend. I didn't have time to waste worrying about Rafe just now, but I bet he'd had many issues to deal with in his long life.

"Alesa's revving up again." My wet clothes started to steam, and she kept stabbing me viciously.

"Damn straight. You go into that cooler, and I'll give you hell with a side order of fried Glory." She stabbed me again, right between the eyes, then turned up the heat. I gasped.

"Glory?" Rafe winced, obviously feeling my fire as he held me.

"Alesa really doesn't want to go in there. Hurry inside. Now." I couldn't open my eyes against the pain. "And put me down before you get hurt."

"I can deal. Let's go." Rafe carried me. Flo and CiCi followed, slamming the door shut.

The chill hit me hard, and my teeth started chattering. Ridiculous. Vampires usually handled temps better than this. Damned demon influence.

"Let's sing church songs. She should hate that." CiCi broke into a tune from the Moonlight Church. Rafe must know it from sitting outside waiting for me, but I didn't hear him join in. The demon in him? I finally managed to slide to my feet but held on to his hand. His grip was tight. So this was hard for him too. My wet clothes crackled as I turned into an ice sculpture. No more inner heat. I guess the cold was getting to Alesa.

"This is crazy. Glory's lips are turning blue." Rafe pulled off his shirt and wrapped it around me. "Come on. Out of here."

"J-j-just a l-l-little l-l-longer." I shuddered and icicles broke off the ends of my wet hair.

"Glory's gone from blue to purple. She's had enough." Rafe looked uncomfortable too and not just because I wore his shirt. Flo sang "Jesus Loves Me" at the top of her lungs.

"Y-y-yes, out. N-n-now." I collapsed in a heap.

Rafe picked me up and carried me out. He pulled a table-cloth off a table and wrapped it around me, then held me tight. Flo and CiCi each grabbed their own tablecloth.

"Is she still in there?" Flo put her hand on my arm. "You feel cold. Isn't that a good sign?"

"Give me a minute, and I'll fry your friend's hand if she touches you again." Alesa sounded hoarse.

"She's here and she's mad." I reluctantly let go of Rafe, warming up fast. "Too bad I can't parachute over the North Pole singing the Lord's Prayer."

Flo and CiCi nodded solemnly.

"We could charter a plane," Flo said.

CiCi patted my shoulder. "Good idea. My treat."

I just shook my head and looked at Rafe. "Somehow I don't think we can blast this thing out until she's ready to go." I handed Rafe back his shirt. "Congratulations on the opening. It was awesome."

"Thanks. Sorry you're stuck." He glanced at my friends. "I'll be home before dawn. Maybe we can talk." He slid his hand down my arm in a comforting gesture.

"Now he can touch us anytime." Alesa sounded stronger.

"Talk. Yes, I'd like that." I wondered if Rafe had ever tried to obliterate his demon side. I didn't dare mention it in front of Flo and CiCi.

Back at the apartment my friends had one more thing they wanted to try.

"This is called 'Soul Walking.'" CiCi opened her tote bag. "Florence, did you bring what I asked you to?"

"Not exactly." Flo looked sheepish. "I just couldn't risk my best pair of shoes. What if they got stained? Have you seen the way Glory sweats? We're talking vintage Chanel, CiCi."

"What kind of friend are you?" CiCi pulled out a pair of

lilac satin pumps so exquisite my eyes watered. They had to be several hundred years old with genuine diamond buckles on the toes. "This must be done right. What did you bring, cheapskate?"

"You call me cheap? Look at those things you dragged in here. I happen to know the buckles are paste. Didn't you sell the diamonds during the terror?" Flo stood toe-to-toe with CiCi.

"I replaced them with diamonds again during Victoria's reign, smart ass."

"Smart ass? I brought some beautiful pumps that are irreplaceable. They were handmade in Italia by a master craftsman who's been dead for over a hundred years. To get these shoes I had to sleep with him, and he with only one eye and a hunch back." Flo's face was pink.

"Ladies, please. What's the plan? Is this an exorcism or a costume ball?" I bit my lip. If I laughed, I'd be hit with a tote bag. Not a shoe—there was the danger of staining.

"Well, yes, we had a plan. We knew you probably wouldn't go for the cleansing ritual." CiCi pulled out an ominous length of tubing and a rubber bag. "This was to be filled with more holy water, and the tube goes you know where."

"No, oh, hell no." I backed away. "Let's stick to the shoes. How does that one go? And don't say you know where."

"It's the 'Soul Walk,' as I said." CiCi sat down to slip on her shoes. They really were beautiful. "Flo, put on yours. Glory, you lie on the floor, facedown, and we walk on you and we chant, of course." She handed Flo several sheets of paper. "Start with the one highlighted in yellow, Florence."

"Wait a minute. You're going to walk on my back with those pointy heels?" I eyed them. CiCi's might be old, but they'd have made a decent secret weapon in King Louis's court. And Flo's? Her one-eyed cobbler had a thing for metal because her heels were sheathed in copper and would leave cuts wherever they landed. Ouch!

"They're not so bad. I could have brought some of my

new shoes, with the thin high heels. I did you a favor. I think if we don't hurt this demon, what will be the point?" Flo looked at CiCi, and they both laughed. "Oh, I made a little joke."

"A very little joke. I get to lie here with the pedestrian parade on my back. Where'd you get this idea?"

"The Internet. It's a fount of information. Shirley Mac-Laine did a soul trek through Spain. It totally focused her and brought her peace, closer to God. A demon will hate it, right?" CiCi looked so hopeful I didn't have the heart to tell her what I really thought, which was that she needed to check into Dr. Simon's hospital to have her head examined.

"Your friends are a hoot but great shoes. I can't believe you're going to let them do this." Alesa wasn't encouraging it, so maybe there was hope.

"I think you have sole and soul mixed up, but try it. Chant away, just tread carefully. I've had a rough night." I moved the coffee table out of way and lay facedown on the area rug in front of the couch.

"Okay, here goes. Close your eyes, Glory. Florence, on three." CiCi counted down. "Demon, demon, go away. The fires of hell are where you play. Glory says you cannot stay. Demon, demon, go away." CiCi chanted this three times as she trod over my body, her sharp heels doing a number on my back and thighs. I groaned while Alesa laughed hysterically. So much for that.

Then it was Flo's turn. "Demon, demon, servant of hell. My soul doesn't want you or wish you well. Go back, go back, you I do expel. In my body you cannot dwell." Flo really put some oomph into it, forgetting that her friend lay under her as she stomped in each word. I gritted my teeth and took it because I liked that chant.

"Say it again, Flo. Alesa's quiet and no heat. CiCi, jump on board." I could smell my own blood and agony would be an improvement, but if this got rid of Alesa, it was so worth it.

We chanted, louder and stronger as CiCi and Flo pounded

me into the rug. By the time the door into the apartment burst open, we'd worked ourselves into a frenzy of beat the hell out of Glory, er, her demon.

"Stop!" Rafe shouted from the doorway.

CiCi and Flo froze. CiCi had one foot planted on each thigh. Flo stood on my shoulders. I drifted somewhere between hell and unconsciousness. Alesa was silent, and I prayed that meant she'd left. Since neither of my friends had screamed or stopped chanting, I figured they hadn't been invaded. If Alesa had run to that dresser in my bedroom, she could have it. I'd get Rafe to haul it to the Dumpster and burn it as soon as I could speak again.

"What are you doing? Look at her."

Flo and CiCi cried out. "No! Glory, we didn't mean—"

"Go. I'll take care of her. Dawn's coming, and you both need to get home." Rafe must have looked pretty scary because they just grabbed their things and left without another word.

"Glory, baby." Rafe scooped me into his arms and carried me into the bathroom. He carefully peeled off my shredded clothes and gently cleaned my wounds. I was too hurt to be embarrassed. "Drink. So you can heal."

I didn't argue, just sank my fangs into his wrist. I needed it. When I figured I'd had enough, I released him. At some point, he laid me on the bed and dressed me in a nightgown.

"What did I walk in on?" Rafe touched my cheek, the only part of me not sore.

"Another version of an exorcism. I think it worked, Rafe. I think she's gone." I managed a smile. "Totally worth it."

"You're going to pay for that dumb stunt, bitch." Alesa blasted me with so much heat and pain that I leaned over and threw up on Rafe's shoes.

The next two nights I gave in to the inevitable and just did my routine. Rafe and I talked, but he admitted that his demon thing was in his blood so there was no exorcism that could possibly work on him. No one in his family had ever even tried. And I had to give it up. At least for now.

Alesa wasn't making it easy. After the first night in the shop with her hell-bent on insulting every customer I came in contact with, Lacy and Erin begged me to just stay in the back room and work on paperwork. To say I had a ticked-off demon inside was an understatement.

Flo and CiCi both came by to apologize for going overboard. I wanted to pretend for their sakes that they'd cured me, but Alesa wouldn't have it, blasting me with enough heat that their attempted hugs scorched them. Damn, I hated that demon bitch.

At least Flo had decided she could skip one bridal tradition, and I didn't have to endure a rehearsal and rehearsal dinner on Friday night. Instead, she just e-mailed everyone some general instructions. It was a relief not to have to see Jerry. I figured he needed a cooling-off period. But by the time Saturday night came around, I was pretty depressed.

Simon called just as I was ready to close the shop at midnight. Flo and Richard's wedding was at three, just hours away, and I was headed to Damian's to change into my bridesmaid dress as soon as I locked up.

"Good evening, Gloriana. How do you like your new car?" Simon sounded smug. I decided to tolerate it.

"I love it. Is Westwood suffering as promised?"

"Oh, I'm teaching him his place, never doubt it." Simon chuckled. "He got his finances straightened out. It's amazing what billions can buy."

"Yeah, well. I wouldn't know about that." I sat on a stool and looked around the back room. My inventory was low, which was a good thing. We'd been busy with the music festival crowd in town. I needed to shop but couldn't work up much enthusiasm. My laptop was open, and I'd made a few halfhearted bids on an online site. All I could think about was Jerry and that he hadn't called or picked up when I'd called him. Hadn't responded to my desperate voice mails either. I couldn't blame him, but that didn't mean I wasn't frantic for some kind of sign that he was willing to give me another chance.

"Gloriana, are you still there?"

"Oh, sure. Drives like a dream." I think Simon had asked about the car while I'd been off on Planet Angst.

"Did you look in the glove box?" Simon sounded amused.

"No, why? Did you hide a tarantula in there or something? To remind me of my place?" I wouldn't put it past him. Simon always wanted the upper hand, and I'd been pretty bold with him.

"On the contrary. I'm courting you. To get you to join my band of merry men." Simon laughed, his creepy straight-from-the-dungeon chuckle. "Get the Robin Hood reference?"

"I'd have to be stupid to miss it. Oh, yeah, rob from the rich and give to poor little old me. Thanks a bunch." I opened the door to the alley to stare at my pretty car. Maybe a smart woman would send it back. Courting me? I choked back a gag.

"Loosen up, Glory. This guy just got a billionaire to give him his stash. Brilliant." Alesa sighed. *"I think I'm in love."*

Okay, now I really had to wonder if the car was jinxed. I walked out and hit the remote to unlock it.

"I'm going out to check the glove compartment. What am I going to find exactly?" I popped it open and saw the owner's manual and a few papers that included my title and a year's worth of paid insurance. Wow. Unexpected bonus. I hadn't called my agent yet, dreading how the premiums would jump.

"Look inside the leather case for the owner's manual." Simon was clearly excited. "It's a little gift. Besides the insurance. Did you notice that?"

"Yes, thanks." I snapped open the case. There, nestled next to the book with the famous logo, was a plastic gas card. "I see a credit card. Are you kidding me? You're giving me gas?"

"Yes, indeed. Use it. Premium. As much as you need. The bills come to me. You'll never have to buy gas again, Gloriana." Simon said this firmly, and my eyes teared up. Oh, man, I could see how people were seduced to give up their souls. The Devil couldn't have done a better job.

Alesa happy danced on my kidneys. *"I love this guy. He actually has you thinking about it. I'm in the presence of a master. Well, not in his presence, but you know what I mean."*

I wanted her to shut the hell up so I could think. Wait, not thinking. I wasn't going to become an EV, end of story. Use the gas card? Why not? It was Westwood's money paying for it, and he owed me after all the vampires he'd killed.

"Thanks, Simon. As for your courting thing? Forget it. I'll never, repeat, never be interested in anything you've got going out there. Leave me the hell alone. We're done. Get it? Done." I snapped the phone shut.

"Dumb ass. He could do you a lot of good." Alesa jabbed me between the eyes.

"Shut up. I'm going to a wedding. If I want your opinion on anything, I'll ask for it." I grabbed my purse out of the back room, locked the door and got into the car. Insurance and a gas card. That bastard. He really knew the way to a woman's heart.

I headed for Damian's. What Simon didn't know was that my heart had been ripped apart this week and only Jerry could put it back together. We'd be standing at the altar on either side of the bride and groom in a little while. I hoped seeing Flo and Richard so in love and the vision of me in my beautiful bridesmaid dress would soften Jerry toward me. It was worth a shot.

Twenty-four

"I'm so sorry, Glory. I don't know what happened." Flo fluttered around me. "I gave the operator your measurements."

I froze. "How did you know my measurements?" I sure never let her within a foot of me with a tape.

"I guessed." Flo moved out of range. Wise woman.

"I think you got confused with meters and feet, chickie." Aggie looked perfect in her purple bridesmaid dress that fit like a dream.

"Feet?" I shrieked, then fought for control. Alesa loved it, though I don't think she'd be quite so thrilled if she could have seen us. I had on a purple tent. It was supposed to be an elegant off the shoulder gown with a fitted bodice. My bodice didn't fit anywhere, and a family of five could have hidden under the skirt. I wanted to cry.

"Pins. We need pins. A tuck here and there, and it will be perfect." CiCi had come into the upstairs bedroom where we were getting dressed. Lacy rushed out in search.

"Give it up, CiCi. The only thing that can fix this nightmare is a stick of dynamite." I plopped on the bed.

"You'll wrinkle it." Flo hadn't put on her dress yet.

I jumped up even though I wanted nothing more than to

let Alesa take over and scream curses. Nope, my best bud was getting married. My demon jabbed and stabbed, but I swallowed my bile.

"Sorry." There went my dreams of a big reconciliation scene with Jerry. I was an enormous eggplant while the rest of the five bridesmaids were visions of loveliness. He'd take one look at me coming down the aisle and think celibacy beat the hell out of sex with a giant vegetable.

"Let CiCi pin it. I'm so so sorry." Flo grabbed my hand. "I didn't want it to be too tight, and I guess I went overboard. I need you to be by my side down there." Her eyes filled with tears.

"Don't you dare cry and ruin your makeup." I hugged her. "I'm sure CiCi will be able to fix it. Go, make yourself more beautiful. Richard will be stunned and realize he's the luckiest man on the planet." Especially when he saw her next to the purple monster acting as maid of honor. I patted her shoulder, then shoved her toward the bedroom where I knew her wedding dress waited.

"But this is a *disastro*!" Flo brushed at the fabric.

"Don't worry. We'll figure something out. And my shoes fit. Love them." Flo had given us each gorgeous designer shoes to match our dresses.

When Flo was out of sight, I turned to CiCi. "Well? Any hope?"

"I'll cut and pin." She pulled scissors out of her bag. "But don't go wild on the dance floor. This is a temporary fix."

"Fine. I just need to look presentable coming down the aisle." I sighed when Lacy hurried back in.

"Sorry. Bachelor's house. The only pins I could find were corsage pins from the florist." She handed CiCi a box.

"They'll have to do." CiCi used my strapless bra as a base. But she was right, the pearl-tipped straight pins were definitely temporary. Sudden moves caused jabs that made even Alesa gasp.

The music started and we assembled at the top of the stairs. Flo stood behind me, Damian at her side to give her away. My best friend glowed with happiness. Her designer gown had cost a mint and looked worth every penny.

Richard waited at the bottom of the stairs, and he had eyes only for his bride. The actual ceremony was to take place outside, and we proceeded out there to the music of a string quartet. Jerry, looking much too handsome in a black tux, white shirt and bow tie, was lined up with the other grooms-men in front of an altar covered in white roses and green leaves. Another ex-priest, a friend of Richard's, waited to seal the deal though this ceremony was a renewal of vows. My friends had done the real thing in the catacombs under the Vatican.

When we came to a stop, Ray's voice filled the night with a beautiful song about eternal love. I looked over and saw him at a piano. He didn't glance at me, only at the happy couple. Eternal love. I studied Jerry, praying he'd feel compelled to look my way and remember what we had. But he stared into the assembled crowd sitting in chairs facing the makeshift altar. Who was he watching?

I searched the onlookers and saw many familiar faces, friends I'd known for years. Then I spotted a woman sitting next to Jerry's daughter. Oh, no, he didn't.

"Glory, your heartbeat just doubled, and you're generating your own heat. Ooo, hate. That beats the hell out of this lovefest. What's up?" Alesa would have to wait. The ceremony had started.

I took Flo's bouquet, gripping it so hard I crushed a delicate orchid. Aggie gasped and jerked it out of my hand. Luckily Flo didn't notice as she said her vows. The endless ceremony droned on until they paused for Ray to sing another sweet love song. Sappy, sentimental tripe.

"Oookay, Glory. Something's up. You usually like rocker boy's stuff. What's the deal? Who you got the hate on for? I get it's a woman. Cat fight. Oh, yeah. Destroying this wedding would make my night." Alesa gave me a tiny heat flash to get me to answer. Nothing doing. We all knelt for the final prayer and blessing. A pin popped under my arm. Ventilation. Thank

you, God. Alesa growled and heated me some more. She didn't like prayers or the "G" word.

Time to walk back down the aisle. Aggie handed off the bouquet, and I thrust it at Flo. She didn't notice that it was a little worse for wear. She just gazed at Richard. I gave Jerry a look that should have blown him right out of his black socks. He smirked and offered his arm. I took it, and we strode down the aisle after the bride and groom. I felt another pin go. Fine. I was burning up, and the breeze under my arms was welcome.

"I can't believe you brought her to this wedding," I hissed at Jerry as soon as we left the aisle.

"What makes you think—"

"Save it, Jerry." I felt my face flush and the room blurred. Oh, no. Hang on to your mad, Glory. For God's sake, don't cry. Needless to say, Alesa was horrified at the thought. I blinked rapidly and held on to Jerry's arm. "Damn it, Jerry, that was so . . . mean." I rounded on him as we reached the living room.

"I'm a warrior, Gloriana. When I'm hit, I use what weapons I have at hand to hit back." He glanced at Mara, who'd come to stand in the doorway, and smiled. "Good to know I landed a blow." He lifted my hand off his arm and strode over to Richard, slapping his back and offering congratulations like he hadn't a care in the world.

"What's going on with you two?" Flo grabbed my arm. "Glory?"

"The photographer's calling for us, Flo." Aggie, who'd obviously seen and heard the whole thing, gave me a shut-up look. "Picture time? Don't we have to go get photos made at the altar?"

"Yes, yes, she's right." I wasn't about to unload my drama on the bride, so I helped hustle Flo and Richard back toward the altar. I looked down and saw some pins on the floor behind me. Great. I would be down to my underwear before Flo cut the cake. A waiter came by with pink champagne. I took a flute and sniffed. Wow. Joy juice of the vampire kind, and did I need it. The joy, that is. I downed it and grabbed a refill, then moved to my place in line for the photographer, a shifter who'd been hired for the occasion.

"Just a minute." Aggie reached over and tucked some of my top into my bra. "You're coming apart," she whispered in my ear.

I glanced at Jerry, who was ignoring me. "You are so right."

Aggie gave me an inquiring look, but we were soon in the middle of a whirlwind as the poses began. By the time we were finally cut loose for the reception, I'd gone from hurt to furious to homicidal to numb. Alesa was doing backflips with glee. Nothing like a meltdown to keep a demon happy.

A band had set up and music started. The leader announced that Mr. and Mrs. Mainwaring were going to have their first dance. Everyone clapped as Flo and Richard took the floor.

"How sweet."

I turned slowly, knowing exactly who hadn't waited a minute to rub my nose in the fact that Jerry had brought her here.

"Mara. Did Flo invite you?" I knew my friend certainly hadn't. Flo would never invite the mother of Jerry's child here. My friend knew I hated Mara because she'd never made her pursuit of Jerry a secret.

"No, Jeremiah asked me to come as his date and to see our daughter, of course." Mara smiled at Jerry, who was hurrying toward us. What? Did he think I was going to get violent? He should have thought of that before he'd brought the bitch here.

"How . . . interesting. Did you wonder why the last-minute invitation?" I looked up as Jerry stepped between us.

Jerry threw his arm around Mara. "Mara is an old and dear friend, Gloriana. Naturally I'd want to reconnect with the mother of my child." He smiled down at Mara, and she leaned into him, clearly willing to do whatever it took to latch on to him permanently.

Aggie grabbed my arm while I still reeled from Blade's sucker punch. "Come on, you two. The wedding party is supposed to be on the floor." She shoved me at Jerry. "Blade, the best man has to dance with the maid of honor." She was pressed against the tall English vampire Richard had imported as one of his groomsmen.

Jerry kissed Mara's pale cheek. "I'll be right back." Then he swept me into his arms.

I couldn't believe I let him get away with it, then noticed Flo and Richard beaming at us. I forced a smile for their sakes. "Thank God this is a slow one. Even you can handle that."

Jerry looked down at me, not bothering to smile. "Cheap shot. Just shut up and dance."

"You'd like that, wouldn't you?" I smiled as he swore and pulled a pin from his palm.

"What the hell is this? Your dress is a damned mine field."

"So it is." I intended to dance in silence but couldn't stand it. "Mara, Jerry? Seriously?"

"Why not?" He glanced back to where she stood next to Lily. "We have a history, a daughter together, and she was more than happy to come."

"I'm sure." I stared at his snowy shirt front with the gold and onyx studs I'd given him one Christmas. I'd saved for them for months. I felt a lump in my throat and more tears behind my eyes. Would this music ever end?

"You shouldn't be surprised, Gloriana. Clearly we are taking a break. I was just the last to know." Jerry stepped back. Music over. He strode away, his shoulders broad, his stride still that of a warrior.

I couldn't have a crying jag here in the middle of Flo's wedding reception. I grabbed a glass of champagne, looked around and focused on the enormous wedding cake. The vamps wouldn't be eating it, but Flo had insisted on the tradition, and the shifters would make short work of it.

The band started a tango, Damian's favorite, and he and

Diana swept onto the floor to the applause of the guests. Show-offs. Several other couples had also taken up the challenge.

"Dance?"

I looked up from my study of the bottom of my empty glass to meet Rafe's eyes. "Are you kidding? Why would you even ask me after the way we left things?"

"I see an opportunity here. Blade's obviously moving on. Seems like that clears the way for you to do the same." Rafe nodded toward where Mara stood close to Jerry, her hands on his chest.

I couldn't deny I was tempted. The music was sensual and throbbed with desires barely leashed. I loved to dance and knew Rafe was a man with some moves, but . . . "I can't." I smiled to take the sting out of my refusal. "Not playing those games."

"Coward." Rafe swung me into his arms until we were pressed together hip to hip, breast to hard chest. He grinned. "Blade is patting his pockets like he's checking for a dagger to throw. At the very least we could make him jealous. I don't mind being used as long as I get to hold you like this."

Oh, his body felt good against mine. And I'd never forget how we'd been together. Neither would Alesa. She was trying to glue me to Rafe. Nope, not happening. I wasn't about to make a scene, but I also wasn't going to join the couples doing Latin dirty dancing in the center of the floor.

"Give it up, Rafe. I won't use you, and I'm in a dress that's a few pins away from self-destructing."

He looked down and grinned. "I'll say." He tucked a piece of fabric into my bra with a familiarity that was probably being duly noted across the room. "What happened?"

"Don't ask." I sighed and gently shoved him away. "Quit acting loverlike and hit the buffet. I hear it's awesome."

Rafe stepped back, releasing everything but my hand. "Might as well. It's clear I'm wasting my time tonight. But, just so you know, I meant it when I said I'm not giving up. No pressure. But I'm here for you, Glory. Whatever you need, whenever you need it." Then he turned and strode away into the crowd.

"Are you kidding me? Go after him. A dance with him would be as hot as the seventh level of hell." Alesa growled. *"I swear I'm getting out my pitchfork again."* She popped me with some heat.

"Gloriana, look at you. Pull yourself together." CiCi grabbed my arm before Alesa could push me after him. "Seriously. Your bra is showing. Let me try to pin this back in order." She dragged me into the powder room and did what she could.

"I know, but I'm having a hard time caring. Did you see who Jerry brought to the wedding, CiCi?"

"Mara." CiCi frowned. "I have never liked that woman."

"She's taking dead aim at Jerry."

"Let her. He watched you talk to the shifter. He was clearly jealous. You were smart to rub his nose in that relationship."

"I wasn't. I wouldn't." I hadn't been using Rafe.

"Hell Boy can take it. Get over it and go after him and dance this time." Alesa wasn't worried about a thing. I think the champagne had taken her edge off.

"Come on, Glory. They're cutting the cake." CiCi pulled me toward the crowd again.

"Interesting dress. How's my little devil tonight?" Greg Kaplan held out two glasses of champagne.

I took one. "Don't know what you mean."

"Oh, come on. I heard you've got a demon thing going on. No wonder you're shooting the red eye and standing up to Simon." Greg sipped his champagne. "I've already texted my fearless leader about it. He's thrilled."

"What? You're nuts. No demon thing here." I drained my glass and felt a nice buzz. "Who let you in, anyway?"

"EVs are catering. The champagne is one of our newest items. Rocks, doesn't it?" Greg polished his off and signaled a waiter for more. "Join our crew, and you'll have unlimited access to these kinds of goodies."

"Never. Who told you about this fictional demon?" I

accepted yet another glass. Why not? It was a celebration of love. Flo had just cut the cake and smashed a bite into Richard's lips. Another precious moment for the photographer. Gag me. I couldn't believe this was me, not Alesa, being so cynical and uncaring. Then I saw Jerry laugh at something Mara said as they drank champagne together. Cozy. Nothing Alesa could do to me hurt like the pain of seeing the man I loved with another woman. I couldn't stand to watch and focused on Greg.

"Let's see. Aggie found out from Flo, who apparently did her best to stomp the bejesus out of the demon, which has taken up residence in her BFF." Greg winked. "Still denying it?"

"Leave me alone, Greg. Flo and Richard are about to take off. They're calling all singles to catch the bouquet or garter. You still single?" I cast an eye over the eager women gathered near Flo. Mara was there, of course. And Aggie. Even Nadia, who'd danced with Ray and made no secret of her claim on him. A few men had been dragged by Damian for the garter toss, Blade among them. Ray just leaned against the piano and drank some of Damian's blood with a kick. That worried me.

"Eternally. Never could see any reason to tie myself down."

"Me either." I polished off my drink. "Guess I'd better go over there and be a good sport for Flo."

"Yeah, maid of honor." Greg winked. "Remember. Simon wants you, and he always gets what he wants. He could even help you with your demon problem. Hook you up to the energy pump and give our goddess a new plaything."

Now that actually made me stop and think for a nanosecond. Alesa stayed quiet. Which made me think for another nanosecond.

"Forget it, Greg. Nothing could get me to hook up with anything or anyone"—I looked him up and down—"connected to the EVs. Tell Simon to give it up."

"No way. He kills the messenger." Greg steered me toward the gathering ladies. "Don't sell Simon short. Next time you're in your car, check the trunk. You won't be sorry."

Another gift? That bastard. He couldn't buy me. I wasn't going over to the dark side. Alesa torched me just then to show she wasn't happy with my goody-two-shoes attitude.

"Glory, your face is red. Are you all right?" Blade's daughter, Lily, took my arm.

"Fine, thanks. Just a little overheated." I patted her hand. Lily really didn't deserve her mother.

"Still shagging the bodyguard, Gloriana?" Mara, smiling of course, appeared next to her daughter. "Thank you. You finally got Jeremiah to see you for the slut you are."

"Go stake yourself, Mara." I faced Flo, who was waving her bouquet and trying to catch my eye. My poor friend had no clue of the meltdown I was trying desperately to avoid. "Just because Jerry and I are done doesn't mean he'll be satisfied with you." I smiled at Lily. "Sorry, sweetie, but your mother and I have issues."

Lily frowned at her mother. "No problem. Mother and I have issues too. Don't give up on Dad, Glory. You can work things out."

"Gloriana, what is this?" Mara plucked out a pin. "And this?" Before I could stop her, she'd managed to pull out half a dozen critical pins. "What did they have to do, put two dresses together to get one big enough to fit you?" She laughed.

I growled and slapped a hand across my chest to keep up the fabric. Alesa offered a few choice suggestions along the lines of "kill the bitch." Tempting.

"Ladies, get ready to catch the bouquet," the band leader announced, and there was a flourish and drums.

Flo had a good right arm, and the flowers sailed straight at me. I didn't want them but couldn't let them hit the ground. I reached up when Mara made a leap and snatched that bouquet out of midair. She landed next to me, the flowers clutched in her hand.

"Well, looks like we have the next bride." The band broke into "The Wedding March."

"Anything's possible," Mara said. She patted her small evening bag. "Guess what I found next to Jeremiah's bed. A drug from Los Angeles that will allow us to see the sunrise together. I think I'll persuade Jeremiah to share it with me tonight after the wedding. It will be so romantic."

I couldn't speak. What had she been doing in Jerry's bedroom? And how would she even know about the drug unless Jerry had told her?

"Glory?" Lily steered me away from her mother. "Don't listen to her. She'll say anything to get together with Dad again."

"Yes, well. I get it." Oh, did I get it. But maybe Jerry's mother had told Mara about the drug. And maybe Mara had sneaked into the bedroom. And maybe I was making excuses for Jerry. He might be perfectly happy to have a romantic evening with another woman. My head swam, and I held on to Lily.

"Sit, Glory, you don't look good." Lily helped me into a chair.

"I'm, I'm fine. Too much champagne I guess." I saw Mara make a beeline for Blade and thrust the bouquet under his nose. He threw his arm around her and leaned close to listen, then laughed. Oh, but I hated her. And him. Yes, I'd hurt him, but to zoom into her arms . . . What was he thinking? Hah. What was he thinking *with*?

"Let her have him. Hell Boy is still ours." Alesa hiccuped. A drunk demon. Wasn't that a scary thought?

"Time for the happy couple to leave on their honeymoon. You'll find bags of confetti on the tables. Let's send them off in a blizzard."

Flo ran up and gave me a hug. "Take care of yourself, Glory. Don't let that bitch worry you."

"Which bitch? That one or the one inside me?" I glanced at Mara, then down where I'd shoved fabric into my bra again.

"Any of them. I'll help you when we get back. We'll figure things out. I love you." Flo ran back to Richard, and we showered them with confetti in the shape of tiny bats. A cliché, but Flo couldn't talk Aggie and me into cutting out thousands of tiny fangs.

I sighed and looked around. The party was still going strong, and everyone seemed to be having a good time. Everyone except me, that is. The band started to play a song I recognized, a romantic ballad I'd considered my song with Jerry. We'd had lots of those over the centuries, this was one of them. It was the slow kind, an excuse to make love on the dance floor, and we'd danced to it not long ago.

The lights dimmed, then I saw Mara leading Jerry to the dance floor. No. She was stealing my life. Every bit of it. My man. My sunrise. Even my damned dance.

She glanced back at me over her shoulder, her smile so superior and so triumphant, I felt my own hellfire rise inside me. People around me gasped, and I knew my eyes had gone red. Jerry's horrified glare brought me down to earth, and I spun on my heel before I could let the fire fly.

I had to get out of there. My dress was losing the battle, and I finally ripped it off in the parking lot. Not smart. My purse was upstairs, along with the clothes I'd worn to Damian's.

"Shit." Rafe appeared out of the darkness, took off his coat and wrapped it around me. "What now, Glory?"

"I should have flamed her. Roasted her where she stood." I sighed and leaned against my car.

"Would have been a fine ending to the wedding, but I already warned you about the consequences of that so I'm glad you restrained yourself." He put his hands on my shoulders. "You need me to go grab some things from upstairs?" He tugged at the lapels of that jacket. "Or do you want a ride home?"

"Always taking care of me, aren't you?" I pushed away from the car. "Thanks, Rafe. I mean it. But you're off the clock now, and there's an upstairs window open. I'll take it from here." I handed him his coat. I didn't wait to see his reaction, just shifted into a bird and, with a flutter of wings, headed up to get my things. It felt good. No man rescuing me, just Glory taking care of herself. That sense of purpose and fine feeling lasted until I managed to sneak out of the house again and out to my car. I drove out of the lot in a shower of gravel.

The tears I'd been holding back hit me about a block away, and I had to pull over because I couldn't see to drive. I leaned against the steering wheel and let it all out—the pain, the humiliation and the fury. Yes, I was mad at Jerry, but at myself too. What was up with this sleazy behavior? Sure, I'd been attracted to Rafe, but it wasn't like me to jump into bed with a man unless Jerry and I were on a break. Alesa. This was all Alesa's fault.

I hit my chest. "You damned bitch. You turned me into an amoral hell-bound cheater. I could have had an affair with Rafe if I'd just waited for Jerry to get back in town. Then I could have calmly sat down with him and told him I thought we needed to take a break. We've done it before."

"Oh, yeah?" Alesa cackled. "The man who just waved his little skinny bitch in your face tonight would have calmly accepted that you wanted a break? So you could bang your shifter room-mate?" Now Alesa was hitting high C with her laughter. "Honey, do you really know this man?"

Okay, maybe the demon had a point. But sneaking around and doing the wild thing behind Jerry's back wasn't my style. If I was ever going to have a relationship with Jerry again, I was going to have to make that clear to him. I was the Glory he'd known for years. The Glory he usually could trust. So what had changed? Oh, yeah. Demon on board.

"That's right, honey. And you've had a hell of a ride, haven't you? Don't go telling me you're sorry for it. Rafe is a fine man, a great lover and has that demon thing going on." Alesa sighed. "If you don't keep him on a string, you're even dumber than you look, Blondie."

I finally pulled myself together and put the car in gear. I

had serious work to do, not the least of which was to get rid
of this damned demon once and for all. But how?

I spent the next forty-eight hours holed up in my apartment
consoling myself with EV snacks left over from the bachelorette party and the case of Nadia's premium synthetic she'd
left as a thank-you. I didn't bother to get out of the granny
gown I'd put on for comfort or even brush my hair. There
was a Lifetime movie marathon on TV, and the three-hanky
sob stories suited my mood.

When the knock came on the door, I tried to ignore it,
but Flo's voice shocked me off the couch. I flung open the
door.

"What are you doing here? I thought you two were going
to be gone for a couple of weeks. On your honeymoon." I
stepped back as Flo pushed inside, followed by Richard.

"I couldn't leave you in this mess, *mia amica*. So I said
to Ricardo that we must go to New Orleans, to a woman I
know. She will tell us how to send this demon screaming
back to hell, eh?" Flo grabbed me and hugged me, then
wrinkled her nose. "You are a mess. Go, clean up, get dressed.
You are about to have company."

I held on to Flo's arm. "But what about this woman? Did
she have the answer? Are we going to be able to get rid of
Alesa?"

*"In your dreams, vampire. In mine too. You think I like watch-
ing you pine away here like a lost little girl? Gag me. And you let
Rafe just stroll off to work without so much as a good-bye kiss.
Stupid."* Alesa gave me a poke and some heat.

"I'm sure of it. We're going to use the power of love." Flo
began pulling things out of a tote bag Richard handed her.
"Go take a shower. Make yourself pretty. Everyone I could
find who loves you will be here in fifteen minutes." Flo nodded toward the bathroom.

Everyone who loved me. That was a pretty short list. Was
CiCi going to help again? Had Flo called Rafe to come back

from the club? I'd asked Rafe to look for a new place to live, so he wasn't exactly feeling the love right now. But he still seemed to care for me. He'd even gone down to check my trunk for Simon's latest surprise. He'd brought up three pairs of designer shoes that had made my eyes water. Oh, the EV king was diabolical. I'd built a shrine to those shoes on my dresser.

Another exorcism. I knew this was probably one more wasted effort, but who could resist Flo when she was in top form? And I was desperate anyway. I allowed myself the tiniest glimmer of hope as I rushed through making myself presentable, slapping on makeup and pulling on a sweater in Blade's favorite blue. Talk about hope. Would he show up? Knowing Flo, she'd called him, asked him to help poor pitiful Glory. Would four hundred years of history be enough to persuade him to help rid me of this demon?

Poor pitiful Glory would be pathetically grateful if he did agree to help. It would mean I hadn't killed every bit of the love we'd once had. The power of love. One of the movies I'd watched had proved it could do everything from cure disease to end wars. Maybe shoving out a demon wasn't such a stretch.

"Sentimental crap. Get a grip, Glory. In hell, we know it's lust that counts. Love is a useful tool that Heaven has sold for millennia. Saps fall for it, live and die for it. But it's all a fairy tale." Alesa laughed like a hyena. *"Tell Flo to bring it on. This is going to be the biggest joke yet."*

I dragged myself out to the living room, which had been transformed while I'd been dressing. Red candles were everywhere, perfuming the air with the scent of roses. A tablecloth with a giant gold cupid covered the couch. Flo had draped a gold shawl with red hearts on it over her shoulders, and CiCi wore one too as she hugged me. Rafe arrived.

"Glad to see you out of that blanket you call a gown." He sniffed. "Showered too. One more day and I was going to hose you down myself."

I socked him on the arm. "I'm allowed a little wallowing, aren't I? My heart is broken."

Alesa gagged. *"No more TV for you unless it's a brutal action flick or porn."*

There was a knock on the door, and I saw Rafe stiffen. One whiff and I knew why. I hurried to throw open the door.

"Jerry." I smiled and stepped aside to let him in. "I can't believe—"

"Florence told me we have a chance to rid you of this demon. I can't let you live like this." He exchanged frosty looks with Rafe. "So here I am."

Flo clapped her hands. "Yes, it is wonderful, isn't it, Glory? So many people love you. Viola said that for this to work, we must use all the love we can bring together. Friends, lovers." She ignored Jerry's growl and Rafe's move that had Richard suddenly standing between the two men. She covered my shoulders in a shawl like her own.

"I wish I could have found more of your friends, but I didn't think you wanted to close your shop. Lacy is working, and Erin didn't answer her phone." Flo shook her head. "Damian should be here. I know he loves you like a brother, but he has disappeared again. Council business, I think." She settled a gaudy heart pendant over my head.

"Gee, Flo, this isn't your usual fashion statement." I couldn't help noticing her own diamond and ruby heart pendant and matching earrings.

"Viola sold it to me. It has a secret compartment with special herbs inside. Ricardo, bring in the bags from the kitchen." She leaned closer. "My husband doesn't know, but she did a ceremony. Powerful stuff to a goddess. Put it next to your own heart."

"Florence, are you sure about this?" Richard was back and handed Flo two bags of Cheetos.

"What are you doing, Flo?" I gasped as she ripped open the bags and started flinging Cheetos into the air.

"You love these things. Am I right?" Flo scattered cheese

puffs on the floor around me. "We have the people, the things, and we will have the music. Before we are done, that demon bitch will think she is one inch away from the heavenly gates. She will run straight down to hell to get away from such a lovefest." Flo beamed at me.

"Anyone ever tell you your bud there is nuttier than the snack aisle at Wally World?" Alesa snickered. *"Nice shoes, though."*

I looked down. Sure enough, Flo's red pumps had hearts on them.

"Freddy and Derek would be here, but they'd already left for Houston. A little road trip." CiCi squeezed my hand. "But you know they love you, don't you?"

"Sure, CiCi, thanks for coming." I smiled at Flo and Richard. "You two are amazing, breaking up your honeymoon for me."

"Ricardo would not go with me to see Viola." Flo sniffed. "He doesn't approve of her."

"Voodoo." Richard held a Bible. "I'll go along with this because of the love angle, but if Flo brings out a doll with stick pins, I'm out of it."

"Ricardo, you are stereotyping. Shame on you." Flo pulled a CD from the tote and stuck it in the player. "Now we need to surround Glory with love. Rafael, you will hold one of her hands."

Rafe had been ominously quiet since Jerry had come into the room. Now he grabbed my hand, his stare warning Jerry not to try to interfere.

"Of course I love Glory, she knows that." He plucked one of the Cheetos out of my hair with his other hand. "I would do anything to keep her from getting hurt. Anything." His eyes swept over Jerry, eyes hard with the promise of dire consequences if Jerry did anything else to cause me pain.

"Perfetto." Flo beamed and pulled a silent Jerry to my other side. "And you, Jeremiah, will hold her other hand. You did tell me that you still love our Glory. Am I right?" Her eyes darted from me to Jerry, and she licked her lips. Flo? Nervous?

"I think Gloriana knows that I have always loved her. Some centuries more than others." Jerry gripped my hand and looked down at me.

My eyes filled with tears. "Jerry."

"I'll do whatever necessary to keep her safe from the fires of hell and their spawn." He gave Rafe the force of his gaze now, then looked at Flo. "Let's get this done."

"Fine. Ricardo, you put your hand on Glory's shoulder, just there, and use the Bible, it cannot hurt." Flo bustled around, placing CiCi and deciding where she would stand. Then she picked up the remote so she could turn on the CD player.

"This is so lame it isn't funny." Alesa cackled. *"'I am your lady'? Yeah, right. Which man is it, Glory? You've got two to choose from. Of course you know I'd keep both."*

I wasn't listening to her. I was letting the music and the warmth from the bodies around me heal my wounded soul. Celine Dion's pure voice soared, and I looked at Flo. How had I ever found such a loyal friend? Her eyes were damp. And her husband beside her? He murmured prayers for me, crossing himself as he prayed. They believed in my goodness even when I wasn't so sure I had any decency left in me.

I turned to Rafe. He stared at me, willing me to look at him. I sent him a mental message that I did love him, as a friend that I would always treasure. He got it. He realized he could either have me as a friend or distance himself. But the lover thing wasn't going to work for us. I saw a flash of his pain before he quickly hid it behind a firm jaw and a solemn expression. I wondered if he believed me. So far he'd been in denial, sure he could still win me away from Jerry.

Jerry. I sighed and turned to him. As if he sensed my gaze, he stared down at me. So much between us. He was easy to read after all our years together. I asked him in my mind if he was with Mara now. He let me know he'd sent her on her way, sorry that he'd used her to hurt me. I could almost pity Mara. Almost. I sent Jerry yet another apology, yet another groveling message asking for another chance. Silence.

It didn't take words to know that Jerry wasn't ready to forgive me yet, that the pain was too fresh and the wound to his pride too deep. The miracle was that he still seemed to love me, even when I wasn't very lovable. He'd proved it by coming here and clasping my hand in his.

The music was reaching a crescendo. "I am your lady and you are my man." I let the truth of that message show in my eyes as I kept staring at Jerry. The power of love. Hands on me were warm with it as love poured into me. The heart amulet heated against my breast, and Alesa screamed.

"Lucifer, save me! I can't stand this!" She sobbed, and I felt her writhe inside me. I gasped at the pain, and the amulet got hotter. I tightened my hold on Jerry and Rafe, and the others gripped my shoulders as if sensing that something was finally happening. It was all I could do to stand as Alesa kicked and clawed, vile curses making my ears ring and my head pound.

Clear notes shimmered in the air as Celine came to her soaring conclusion. I shivered as I felt a chill, so welcome after weeks of hellish heat.

Alesa wailed and sobbed. *"Lucifer, by all the fires of the damned, if you ever cared for me, get me the hell out of here!"*

And suddenly, with a rippling tear that almost knocked me to my knees, I was free. I knew it. I felt empty, wonderfully, totally empty. Nobody home but Glory. The last notes faded away. Flo hit the off button on the remote, and everyone stared at me.

"Gloriana?" Jerry drew me toward him. "Are you all right?"

I couldn't speak for a moment, gasping as I leaned against him. Finally I looked up and touched the now cool amulet between my breasts.

"She's gone, Jerry. We finally did it. We drove Alesa out with the power of love." I laughed and hugged him, then Flo grabbed me.

"You did it, Flo. You are a genius, a hero!" I hugged her, and we both shed a few tears. There was laughter and more hugs all around before I collapsed on the couch, suddenly completely drained.

"Glory, you need to rest. Obviously this was hard on you." Flo shooed CiCi toward the door, dragging Richard with her. "We have left a mess, I'm afraid, my friend."

"No problem, I'll clean it later. Totally worth it." I smiled at Flo and threw her a kiss. There were crushed Cheetos everywhere, and the place reeked of roses and smoke since Flo had blown out the candles. I could deal with that. I was so relieved to be rid of Alesa, I felt giddy if weak in the knees.

"I still say it wouldn't have worked without the Bible and the prayers."

"I'm sure you're right, Richard." I sighed and leaned back. "God's love is powerful too. Am I right, Flo?" I sent her a mental message to be smart.

"Yes, indeed." Flo kissed Richard's cheek. "We're going to our real honeymoon now. See you in a few weeks." She glanced at Rafe, who'd stepped over to the couch and put his hand on my shoulder. "Rafael, you coming?"

"Yes. I'll be at the club if you need me, Glory."

"Right. Thanks, Rafe." I smiled at him and squeezed his hand.

Rafe gave Blade a warning look, then followed them out the door.

"Are you leaving too?" I saw Jerry lean next to that door as if he was thinking about it. "I wish you would stay. As a friend. I still feel a little shaky. What if she comes back?"

He shut the door and walked over to sit beside me on the couch. "What did she say when she left?"

"She called on Lucifer to get her the hell out of me." I smiled. "Flo was right. The lovefest was too much for her."

"Guess we'd better make sure you keep that love alive, then." Jerry picked up my hand. "This is hard for me, Gloriana."

"God, Jerry, I know. I am so, so sorry. And grateful that you came tonight. I know you probably didn't want to."

"I couldn't stay away. I'd never see you hurt, no matter how you hurt me." He squeezed my hand.

"Could have fooled me. Mara at the wedding?" I got up and walked over to my DVD player.

"A flesh wound only. Now if I'd shagged her . . ." He watched me sift through my movies.

"You didn't?" I held up a DVD.

"No."

"Wouldn't have blamed you if you did." I sighed. "I know that what I did was wrong. I admit I love Rafe, as a friend. And that I've been attracted to him."

I saw Jerry frown, his body stiffen.

"Just listen, please. I have to say this."

"I'm listening. Can't say I like what I'm hearing."

"I'm trying to clear the air. Tell the truth." I faced him, my hands behind my back. "I've been attracted to Rafe, but I know you and I have a relationship, an exclusive relationship. Then this demon got inside me, and somehow I lost control." I held up my hand when Jerry started to speak. "No, I'm not going to say the Devil made me do it. I'm the one who decided to sneak around and, as Mara said, 'shag the bodyguard.'" I winced when I saw Jerry's expression harden. "But, Jerry, I can't believe that was normal Glory behavior. Sure, Rafe is hot. And sure, Rafe made moves, but I usually have some resistance. And the ability to remain true to the man I love."

I shifted from one foot to the other. "That demon inside me did something to me, always whispering in my ear, urging me on. And I was on fire for any guy I saw. Honestly?" I looked Jerry up and down. "I wish you'd been here so you could have had the benefit of those hormonal surges or whatever the hell they were."

"Shit, Glory, I don't think I can listen to much more of this." Jerry leaned forward, his elbows on his knees.

"There isn't much more." I cleared my throat. "I know it's going to take a while for you to get over this. To forget what I did. To forgive what I did. But while you're working through it, can we declare a truce?"

Jerry stared at me for a long few minutes, his dark eyes

giving away none of his thoughts. I held my breath, wondering whether he was going to walk out the door and out of my life or give us another chance. Finally, finally, he leaned back and stretched out his long legs, propping his boots on my coffee table.

"A truce, you say. Depends. What movie are you holding there? Not one of those English things with country houses and men forever taking tea, is it?"

"*Braveheart*."

"Ah, well. Truce it is, then." Jerry smiled and patted the seat next to him. "Will there be benefits with this truce?"

"Guess we'll have to work out the terms, won't we?" I put in the film and settled beside him.

"Guess we will, lass. Guess we will."

I handed him the remote. I knew my guy.

Read on for a special preview of
Gerry Bartlett's next novel

Real Vampires Don't
Wear Size Six

Available August 2011 from Berkley Books!

"The vampire council is all for running you out of town, Glory." Damian frowned at me, for once not bothering to put on his sexy vibe.

"No! Austin is my home now. I have friends, my business." Could I be at any more of a disadvantage? I'd just stepped out of the shower when I'd heard that knock on the door. I'd hoped it was Blade, my boyfriend who'd been sulking since we'd almost broken up recently. So I'd thrown on a robe and dashed to the door. Now I tightened the sash on my admittedly ratty robe and jerked off my shower cap.

"That business was part of the problem, Glory. Vintage Vamp's Emporium. You know we like for vampires to stay under the radar here, and then you name your little store something like that." Damian Sabatini always made moves on a woman, even one without makeup and with bed head. The fact that he looked serious and was pacing around me like I was a piece of furniture worried me.

"Vamps are roaring-twenties hotties, you know that. What's up with these council members? Where's their sense of humor?" I grabbed Damian's sleeve. "Help me out here, Damian."

"I know what vamps are. I got lucky with quite a few, back in the day." Damian smiled and suddenly seemed to realize I was naked under my robe. "And I did go to bat for you. Explained that my sister had painted that mural of a vampire on your wall as a joke."

"Flo *did*." His sister, Florence da Vinci, was my best friend. She had spent a long lifetime admiring artists up close and personally. Her mural had caused a burst of publicity that had brought me business but also some vampire rumors.

Damian's eyes were gleaming in a way that reminded me his nickname was Casanova. Okay, I could use that. I locked the door and gestured to the couch. "Sit, talk to me. Tell me what I can do to fix this. You want a bottle of something?" I drink synthetic blood. I happened to have several different brands on hand for a change.

"No, thanks." Damian patted the seat next to him. "You flashed red eyes at Florence's wedding. Several council members saw them. We all know what that means, and it's what really got the 'get rid of Glory' thing moving. We don't tolerate demons in Austin."

"Yes, well, I was possessed. Past tense. And my temper got the best of me that night." I collapsed next to Damian. He *was* a friend. We'd figured out a long time ago that we weren't going to have a love connection. Or at least *I'd* figured that out. I plucked his hand off my knee where my robe had parted and smiled. "As I was saying, I *had* a demon on board, but she's gone now. My friends arranged an intervention, and Alesa went screaming back to hell. I'm all better now. Good as gold."

"I'm happy for you. But I'm not sure everyone on the council will be reassured. The best way to prove your goodness to the members would be an act of contrition. Do a favor, perhaps." Damian leaned back, and I realized he was trying to scope out my cleavage. They didn't call him Casanova for nothing.

There was a thump in the hall, and I jumped up. "What was that? Is there someone out there?" I looked for a weapon and came up with my hot pink umbrella. Lame, but better than nothing. At least it had a point on it.

"Relax. I have other tenants in this building, don't I?" Damian put his hand on my shoulder and took the umbrella, leaning it against the wall. "You're still on edge, I think. That brush with the demon obviously upset you."

"Of course it did! I was on the fast track to hell." I sighed and plopped into the chair across from the couch. "How am I supposed to make the council happy? I *am* demon free. Ask your sister. Flo and Richard came back from their honeymoon for just one night. They're the ones who did the ceremony that got that demon out of me."

"That's good. That you have reliable witnesses." Damian sat and leaned forward to stare at me.

"Blade was here too. And Valdez." I sighed. It had been quite a night. Everyone who I loved. Who loved me. Jeremy Blade, Jerry, was the boyfriend and my sire, the vampire who'd turned me. Rafael Valdez was the shape-shifter who'd been my bodyguard until recently. I loved him too, and we'd gotten close, too close for it not to hurt my relationship with Blade.

"Glory, is Valdez still living here with you?" Damian looked around, like maybe Rafe would pop out of the back bedroom.

"Quit reading my mind. And, no, he has his own place now." I'd asked him to move out in hopes that would prove to Jerry that I was serious about making our relationship work again.

"Then you have an extra bedroom and are living here all alone." Damian stood, and I jumped up.

"Yes, but I don't know what that has to do with you. You have a castle on a hill, for crying out loud." I freaked for a moment. I'd never been afraid of Damian, but he was an ancient vampire and could overpower me without breaking a sweat. Of course he was a lover, usually, not a fighter. He looked at me and smiled. Oops, should have blocked my thoughts. He was still reading them and liked what he'd heard.

"Relax, Glory. I have a proposition for you, but it's to help you get in good with the council. Nothing to do with love-making. Though if you want to pursue that thought . . . " He was close in a heartbeat and had his hand on my shoulder. "You smell fresh from your shower and full of that Bulgarian synthetic." He smiled and showed fang. "Did you know it's made with real blood?"

"No. Make that a double no." I straight-armed him, my hand on his broad chest. "What's the proposition, Damian? The one not headed to my bedroom."

"Ah, Glory. Someday." He backed off and lounged on the couch so casually that I was convinced he'd never meant me to take the pass seriously. "I have a young vampire, a fledgling. She was turned by a vamp who has been disciplined and is no longer with us." Damian's face grew hard, and I was reminded that he could be a fighter when he wanted to be. "Anyway, she's stuck now and not happy about it. I need to find a mentor for her, and you've proved you can handle that job. Like you did for Israel Caine."

Another new vampire. I sat back in my chair. Yes, I'd mentored Ray, Israel Caine. But he'd been a rock star, my crush and still held a place in my heart. To take on some poor girl who'd been turned against her will . . . Well, it would sure prove to the council that Glory was a good person, willing to sacrifice. Because new vamps could be a pain in the butt. I sure didn't want to leave Austin though.

I had a thriving business where I sold antiques and vintage clothing. And I had friends who'd turned into the kind of extended family I'd always craved. Of course Jerry was here too. I had to stay here to work on getting our relationship back on track.

"I'll do it. When do I meet her?"

Damian grinned. "I knew you wouldn't fail me. She's right outside. I'm sure she was the source of that noise you heard." He got up, unlocked my door and opened it. "Come in, Penny."

I took one look at the girl who strode into my apartment with a scowl on her face and knew I had my work cut out for me. My sad-sack robe and wild hair were an aberration for me. I pride myself on never facing the public looking less than my best.

"Glory, meet Penny Patterson."

"Hello, Penny."

Penny just glared at me. Bad makeup, which is worse than no makeup at all. Hair that needed a decent cut and, please, a wash. Then there were the clothes. Penny and I have some of the same figure issues. Demon thing aside, had Damian brought her here to me because she carried too many pounds for her five-foot-tall frame? I sent him a glaring mental message, but he put out his hands and put on an innocent face, the picture of denial. Anyway, Penny was a little round, okay, a lot round, and she'd done the unthinkable—she'd worn horizontal stripes.

This girl needed me. And not just because she was now a vampire. She needed a wardrobe intervention and a makeover, stat. I turned to say something to Damian, but the man had slipped out while my back was turned and quietly closed the door.

"Well, Penny, looks like you're stuck with me." I smiled and gestured at her bulging backpack. "Is that all your stuff? Want me to show you to your bedroom?"

"Forget that." Penny stepped close to me, a rookie mistake, and grabbed the lapels of my robe. "There's only one thing I want from you."

"Whoa, girlfriend." I jerked her hands off my robe. "Rule number one. Back off the intensity." I tried to read her mind. What the hell? How had this fledgling already learned to block her thoughts?

She smiled, a creepy smile, and looked me over. "You'll learn that I'm a quick study. I'm nineteen, and I've already got three degrees from UT."

"Three college degrees? At nineteen?" I knew UT was the University of Texas. I was turned vampire in 1604. Back when I'd been school age, I'd been lucky to learn basic letters. I'd had to teach myself what I knew today.

"Yeah. I'm a geek and a freak. Big whoop." The smile had changed from creepy to a sad little twist.

I realized that this girl could be pretty if she'd let me guide her. She had nice auburn hair and skin that would be golden if she didn't mask it with pale makeup. She sure didn't need the black lipstick she'd decided went with being a vampire.

"Hey, being a brain *is* a big whoop. And your new vamp status isn't all bad. Trust me on that." I sat on the couch. "Now what is it you want from me? I'm going to be your mentor. I'll do what I can to help you adjust to your new life." I smiled and gestured at the chair across from me.

Penny sat, then leaned forward. Her eyes were a golden brown, and they did have an intelligence that saw too much. I put up a block. If Penny had already figured out how to block her thoughts, she was probably already reading others' too.

"There's just one thing that will make me happy right now, Glory. Damian said that's your name, right?"

"Yes, it's Gloriana St. Clair. I'm a four-hundred-plus-year-old vampire, Penny. I've had a few centuries to learn the ropes. So if there's something you need, something you want to learn, I'm your gal." I smiled, feeling all motherly, even though to look at me, I'm only twenty-three or thereabouts to Penny's nineteen. Mortals would think we were sisters. Maybe I'd even introduce her as my sister from out of town. Yes, that would work. I realized Penny was waiting for me to focus on her, to give her my full attention. I finally did.

"Okay, Penny, what do you need?"

"Help me kill my sister."